DANCERS IN THE DARK

ALSO BY DANIEL B. DODSON

LOOKING FOR ZOE

THE MAN WHO RAN AWAY

THE DANCE OF LOVE

SCALA DEI

ON A DARKLING PLAIN

MALCOLM LOWRY (A LITERARY STUDY)

DANIEL B. DODSON

Dancers in the Dark

A NOVEL

DODD, MEAD & COMPANY · NEW YORK

Library of Congress Cataloging in Publication Data
Dodson, Daniel Boone.
  Dancers in the dark.

  I. Title.
PS3554.034D3   1983   813'.54   83-9071
ISBN 0-396-08148-7

DANCERS IN THE DARK

I NEVER KNEW whether the colonel who bellowed over the intercom, "Who *was* that son of a bitch?" ever learned that encased in the cockpit of the P-38 that had just buzzed the field—inverted—was the heir to thirty million dollars. I was on tower duty, and I knew. But nobody on the field or in the tower had the wit to read the serial number on the fuselage.

The colonel was trying to control his wrath, but his voice was trembling with the promise of exorbitant punishment. *"Tower,"* he said, "I *asked* you who just buzzed the field."

The master sergeant in command, after me that is, looked at me and performed a gracious gesture of invitation toward the intercom, but I deferred the privilege to him, watching the P-38 nose up about a mile away.

"We weren't able to read the serial numbers, sir," the sergeant said. "He was in inverted flight."

"Did it occur to you that it is also possible to invert the head, sergeant?"

"Not at the moment, sir."

"Well, call Lashkam Field and see who they have in the air."

"Yes, sir," the sergeant said, looking at me with the controlled scorn that only a master sergeant can nourish for a second lieutenant. Gesturing the corporal to the telephone, he returned to the transmitter to try to restore some order in the exploded traffic pattern of student pilots.

If he was wise, the tower officer didn't interfere with the methodical procedure of takeoffs and landings regulated by the noncoms in the tower. The officer was there only to take the rap if something serious happened. It was an assignment that relieved us from a day of flying once every two months or so, and for me it meant four hours of sitting in a ragged chair on stilts reading a book one hundred feet above the field. I don't remember what book I was reading, but it must have had some slow passages because I had looked out over the field to the west in time to see the P-38 approaching at about a thousand feet, coming fast, perhaps three hundred miles an hour, fast for those days, and slowly beginning to roll over and descend toward the field. My God, I remember thinking, he's going to kill himself and take the base with him.

I

To execute this maneuver in the propeller-driven planes we flew in World War II you needed enormous speed, extraordinary skill, and nerves of granite since the engines of those beautiful old airplanes— and the P-38 was the most beautiful—had a confirmed habit of cutting out when inverted. And, in fact, as it came across the field at perhaps twenty-five feet both motors were coughing ominously. But the airspeed he had built up carried him across and beyond over some barracks and a forest where he began to climb, still inverted.

1

WE WERE AN EXOTIC, scarcely military assortment of men collected on Elmore Field, an Army Air Corps training field in Alabama, assembled on the basis of what were alleged to be two competencies: our ability to fly airplanes, and our speaking knowledge of French. We came from training fields across the entire country, from California to Florida, and among us were Canadians (we called them Canucks) who spoke a flat, ugly French, gentle Louisianians with a Creole accent, and others, like me, who had had French governesses as children, or had spent some *Wanderjahre* in France. We had been gathered by a decision on the part of the American government to import French air force officers and cadets who had escaped from France or North Africa for flight training in the States.

The Training Command consisted of flying officers who had been selected, on what basis no one ever knew, to teach others to fly. We were held in slightly scornful suspicion by members of those squadrons that had been hastily assembled and sent to England, North Africa, or the Pacific where a war was going on, but it was part of the discreet legend of the Training Command that everyone professed an urgent desire to go overseas into combat. Some professed it less than others.

The further refinement that resulted in the assemblage of what was known (not by us, but by the American squadrons on the field) as the "Frog Squadron" was some remote claim in your personnel file to a knowledge of French. In some cases this amounted to a faltering ability to pronounce "oui" and "non" recognizably to some high school teacher in uniform.

I had arrived early since I was instructing in a swamp in Missouri close by and I had already considered a number of violent stratagems for escape. At the new base I had just settled my bags in the BOQ when a French captain with thick glasses and a rather mottled face saluted smartly and informed me that we would collaborate on a French-English dictionary of aeronautical terms. In fact it had occurred to me on the way to Elmore Field that I didn't even know the French word for propeller.

We worked for a week while other instructors began to arrive and the first contingent of French officers came in. Our pamphlet received no literary prizes, and I later learned it was filled with some wild inaccuracies, but it served as an agreement on language, though the flying French thought it was the funniest thing they had read since Rabelais. Part of this, I'm convinced, was owing to the eccentricities of my collaborator, who was a university professor from Paris with a reserve commission. I later learned he was having an affair with a corporal in the ground crew.

I had just been assigned my first class of five officers, two commandants (majors), two captains, and one lieutenant, all of whom, except the lieutenant, outranked me, but they leapt to their feet when I entered and saluted with a flourish that left me limp. We spent that first afternoon examining the airplane, an AT-6, considered very hot, while I described its performance data and peculiarities. It was known to have a lamentable habit of ground-looping on landing, usually tearing off a wing. The session was hard work, trying to answer their questions in my lapsed French, and when I finished I took a shower and hurried toward the Officers' Club for a drink.

On the company street, followed by a siren and then an MP in a jeep, a long, black Continental, a streamlined, twelve-cylindered abnormality produced in rare quantities by the Ford Motor Company in years just before the war, came to a reluctant halt from a speed far in excess of the post limit, and the jeep slid up behind. The MP approached the driver's window, saluted, and began his lecture. About fifty feet away, I was halfway from this encounter when the MP saluted again and returned to his jeep. I was deciding that it must be a general or high-ranking civilian when the jeep left, the door of the Continental opened, and a uniformed figure stepped out and called, "Hey, *Matt.*"

The sun was in my eyes, but I recognized the voice. "Teddy? Well, I'll be damned." I almost ran the last twenty feet. People develop a habit of running for Teddy. He was leaning against the throbbing black monster when I arrived and stuck out my hand. Then I remembered. He didn't like to shake hands, perhaps because he was left-handed, but he did, in that diffident, curiously unresponsive way, not more than a touch. It was obvious though, as obvious as anything about Teddy could be, that he was glad to see me. He smiled in the Arnheim manner. His mouth, that rather small, slightly crooked slit, smiled. But Teddy's eyes and his mouth always said different things. His eyes were blue-gray, set rather closely together, always attentive, always analyzing. But you were aware of his nose first, large, thin, and slightly hooked, and only after passing over the nose were you able to concentrate on the eyes. Most people found them disconcerting. I was never able to decide just what they were expressing, but it always seemed to me to disagree with the message of the mouth. The mouth was civilized, social. The eyes weren't.

Teddy Arnheim was not a large man, five feet nine perhaps, and slender, wiry, but surprisingly strong and agile. His hair was wavy, dark blond, far longer than military etiquette permitted, and it clustered at the sides of his head in unruly swathes, presumably to disguise his protuberant ears.

I noticed immediately that he was a first lieutenant, while I was still a second, but about all that identified this meteoric rise in rank was a silver bar dangling precariously from a rumpled, dirty collar. He was just as slovenly as ever.

We hadn't seen one another in two years, and for several minutes standing by the hot, rumbling Continental we exchanged recent histories. "Climb in," he said finally in that very deep, slightly cracked voice. "I'm looking for my quarters."

"What's the number?"

"Q-8."

"Not far from me. Turn left here."

"Do you have a roommate?"

"Not yet. He's due in tomorrow, I think. I'm right here."

He halted the monster suddenly. "This looks pretty good. Maybe I'll come in with you. If you don't mind."

"No, I'd be delighted, but the other patriot has been assigned."

"Well," he said, opening the door, "we can take care of that tomorrow."

I helped him carry his gear in, two B-4 bags, a small, battered, brown satchel, and a laundry bag that when emptied in the middle of the floor turned out to be filled with a mountain of filthy clothes.

"I've been on the road a while," he said. It was an objective assessment, not an explanation. He never explained.

"From where?"

"New York."

"How did you manage that?"

"I told them my mother was dying." He had begun removing the disreputable uniform and dropping it piece by rumpled piece onto the soiled pile until he was naked.

"I'm terribly sorry to hear . . ."

"No, Howard, you don't understand. She died a long time ago," he said, pulling a toilet kit out of one of the B-4 bags. "Do you have any soap?"

"In the bathroom. But what do you . . . ?" But he had disappeared.

While the water ran and a bass voice hummed a current song so badly that I didn't recognize it at first I considered what he had said. His mother had *not* been dead for a long time, and probably even in the swamps of Missouri I would have heard that she *had* died.

When he came out of the bathroom with a towel draped over his shoulders I said, "You meant, I suppose, that your mother was still alive physically, but dead . . ."

With water running off his slender, almost emaciated, naked body he turned to look at me, his mouth smiling. "That's what I meant, Howard." After the first moments he was reverting to St. Paul's and Princeton where, in our day, it had been considered bad form to address a fellow student by his first name.

With a naked foot he was separating clothes in one of the B-4 bags. "Do you have a clean shirt?"

I pointed to the closet. "But they won't fit."

"Doesn't matter," he said, pulling one of my summer khakis off a hanger. "My mother died twenty-four years ago after her third and only surviving child was born. Since then she's been dead. It's not too bad," he said, pulling the overlarge shirt onto his still damp body. "How's the Club?"

"All right. Big drinks."

"Well, let's go and get some of them."

"You need a tie here."

"Oh, shit. Do you have one?"

I pointed to the closet.

As he tied the knot I noticed that the small hands still trembled slightly, betraying an inner tension that was otherwise totally disguised by the casual rhythm of his body, a deliberate discipline. Even when he was a boy his hands had trembled.

Teddy never walked more than five hundred feet. In the monster we caromed an eighth of a mile to the Club and installed ourselves with heavy intentions at the bar. I have no memory of how many martinis we drank before we staggered, or rather I staggered, to the dining room. Teddy never staggered.

We must have eaten something, but I had no recollection of it the next morning. When we returned to our quarters I stripped and fell onto my cot in sodden squalor.

In the middle of the hot night I had to piss. Teddy was naked on the other cot, no sheets, and the laundry bag for a pillow. He was snoring in great ragged sobs.

After relieving myself I remembered to set the alarm for seven, and fell back on my cot.

Flying the next day with my French officers, one after the other, was a near disaster.

2

MY GOD, how we drank at that field! I wonder why.

Contrary to all regulations forbidding the use of alcohol twenty-four hours before flying, we drank as though an alcoholic drought had been predicted. Not only at the Club.

Buying liquor in the bottle wasn't a simple matter in America during the rigors of that war. Usually, for reasons that no one was able to explain satisfactorily (though it probably had something to do with arms payments), for each bottle of bourbon or gin—there wasn't much scotch—you bought, you also had to buy two bottles of some mysterious white wine with a South American label of origin. Teddy would leave the post in the monster and return an hour later with two bottles of white wine and four pints of bourbon. Within a week one corner of our quarters was made inaccessible by an accumulation of white wine.

Owing, I believe, to the power of a local Coca Cola franchise, that native American vintage was available in a machine every fifty feet: on the flight line, the company streets, the barracks and the BOQ. Since ice was scarce and the tap water tasted vaguely paludian, one of the prevailing sins in that land of cola was bourbon and Coke. It tasted like a failed perfume, but it was cold. And the climate was suffocating.

Teddy was in no particular hurry to report. The next day we slipped into another heavy evening, and the following morning I was with him when he appeared before the commander of the Frog Squadron, a captain who had automatically been appointed the leader of our assorted group. He sweated constantly, and his large round face seemed to implore pity. When he issued a command, his big blue eyes would stare at the recipient in terrified expectation of disagreement. His name was Duke.

Headquarters of the Frog Squadron was a corner of the briefing room where a desk had been placed to form a triangle with two walls. Before this desk Teddy drew himself partly out of his habitual slouch and said, "Arnheim." His salute was more like a wave to a departing friend than a military gesture. Duke looked up, trying to disguise his terror, and returned the salute that he could not have seen since Teddy's arm was now dangling loosely at the side of his flight coveralls. He then reached across the desk, stabbing his heavy belly on the pen poised in its holder, to offer his hand. Teddy hesitated, took it reluctantly, and let it drop.

"Good to have you aboard, Arnheim."

Teddy said nothing. And I had to agree with him.

Badly concealed on the desk was a personnel file, and I was close enough to recognize Teddy's photograph pasted to the upper right-hand corner. Later I wished that I had had a chance to study it carefully to discover if by some cryptic method the information was passed along that it concerned the heir to Arnheim Industries. Was it a coded message that preceded Teddy in his military career, or simply the man himself who alerted his fellow officers, as well as his superiors, that here was something rich and strange? Since I had known him for years I was habituated: I could not distinguish between the wealth and the personality. They were a unity to me. At times I tried to imagine the man without the wealth: a salesman, mechanic, or small retailer. I couldn't conceive of it.

Still on his feet Duke said, "I'll have the sergeant get your class list."

"I have it," Teddy said.

"Oh, all right. Good. Well, if there's anything you need just ask for it."

"I will," Teddy said.

It wasn't insolence. Just an elimination of the unnecessary. Duke was obviously high on the list of the unnecessary.

A light fog had settled over the field during the night. We loved fog. Though, like children, we knew we would have to make the time up later, fog delighted us since it relieved us from flying for an hour or so until it burned off.

I had had in mind acting as a temporary host, introducing Teddy to his squadron mates, but it didn't interest him. He was civil but perfunctory, shaking hands when necessary but passing on as soon as the introduction was over. Eventually I located his students waiting in a small cluster, four officers and a cadet, and I prepared to repeat the introduction. But that was unnecessary too. As soon as he had relieved them by returning their rigid salutes with another wave toward his temple he began speaking in a lazy rhythm of totally unaccented French, a deliberate flow of guttural vibrations that surprisingly made rudimentary sense. *"Je suis Teddy Arnheim,"* he began, and the faces of his five students, almost imperceptibly, commenced to relax.

I was astonished. I had never heard him speak French, and even though he was there in the Frog Squadron, if I had been asked if Teddy Arnheim spoke French, I would certainly have blurted out, "My *God*, no!" But before I left, his students were smiling. Fifteen minutes later I glanced over from my group, and Teddy's Frenchmen were trying to restrain themselves from convulsions of hilarity. And they were laughing *with* him. His mouth was curved in the Arnheim smile.

Before the first week was out Teddy knew things about the city, ten miles from the field, that I had not uncovered in the month I had been there, though I had gone in a few times to explore its reputed antebellum charms. My transportation was an aging Ford convertible with a very fragile canvas top that leaked badly and that I couldn't replace under wartime restrictions. I had drinks in the bar of the respectable hotel in town a couple of times, for obvious reasons, and the obvious reasons were there, one a large and generous blonde.

After Teddy arrived we went together at least once a week, not to the respectable hotel, but to a small bar known as Le Cave. I don't know if that was its original name, or if it had been rechristened in deference to our allies at the field, though it was off limits to them. Apparently no one had told the proprietor that *cave*, by its very configuration, was feminine: *la cave*. On entering it seemed to be the kind of *boite* the name implied, small, dark, and cavernous, filled with smoke and sound. Twice an evening there was a floor show, vaguely indecent, but no real strips. Snakes and that sort of thing. We had a couple of drinks at the bar, each paying for a round. The bartender already knew Teddy. I was about to suggest that this wasn't answering any of our problems when he herded me silently, without contact, down a narrow hall to a heavy red curtain that looked promising. But when he lifted it my libidinous expectations were disappointed. A large room, also filled with smoke, and tables of blackjack, poker, craps, backgammon, and a roulette wheel. Gambling was not legal in the state of Alabama, but our entrance created no alarm; in fact nobody noticed us.

Teddy moved through the various games to a dark corner where four poker players sat at a table with a fifth chair empty as though reserved for the Messiah. When he sat down he was recognized by discreet shuffling of chairs, but nothing else. I was not invited to join the game, and without being told, I soon knew why. It was a *serious* game. No limit.

I recognized two of the players. One was a dentist, a captain from the base, who had sadistically drilled a hole in my jaw two weeks earlier, and another, a flight-line master sergeant, in civvies—against wartime regulations for noncoms—but he couldn't have been in the game in uniform. The other two were locals, I gathered, one young and the other middle-aged.

I watched for a while, sipping a drink that had come to me without my order at the same time one came to Teddy. He drank less than half of it, and he played astutely irregular poker. I was behind him and saw every card he received and played. Draw and stud. Nothing wild admitted.

He lost a few times on weak threes-of-kind, and a strong pair, perhaps a hundred dollars. But on a nine-high straight he started casually and raised two hundred dollars on the third round. And won. His deal, jacks or better, turned into a quiet battle between him and the master sergeant. They never looked at one another, but on the second round the sergeant raised a hundred dollars, and Teddy, who had not drawn, raised a thousand dollars from a bulky wad he extracted from a side pocket.

The master sergeant studied his cards for a moment, and turned them face down. Teddy reached for the pot, four or five hundred dollars above his thousand.

"Sir," the master sergeant said, "may I see your openers?"

"Sure," Teddy said, and displayed the two pair with an agitated thumb over the other card, holding it face down. Only Teddy and I knew that it was a six. The two pair were nines and fours.

He played very good, very hard poker, his face a mask, a Chesterfield dangling from his lips, but his winnings, which became enormous, resulted from the bludgeoning of that huge roll of bills he always carried with him. He would play poker for a while, and then, as though bored, would start buying the pot, raising a thousand, three thousand, or even, in a later game I witnessed, five thousand dollars, and apparently no one was able, or had the courage, to pay for a look at his cards.

I couldn't understand why those four—the players didn't change much—continued to play with him, or at least didn't insist on table stakes. Master sergeants always seem to have mysterious sources of income, and dentists, at least in civilian life, can always recover from a failed full house on someone's molars. The civilians may have owned half of the city so far as I knew, but Teddy eventually always smashed the game with a mallet of gold. If I had been Teddy I would not have flown an airplane the master sergeant had touched, and I would have carried an excruciating tooth into town for private therapy.

Finally I grew tired of watching him hammer the game to fragments and went out to the bar for another drink. A contortionist, an eighteen- or nineteen-year-old girl in, for those days, a radically abbreviated bra and panties, was writhing and twisting her body into square knots and bowlines under the light of a spot. It was a curiously innocent display of cryptic sexuality, and the room was thick with concupiscence. But she untied herself suddenly and leapt to her feet, the lights came on, and amid sullen applause she ran to a corner where a Cro-Magnon woman threw a robe around her glistening young body and jerked her through a door.

It was her mother, the bartender told me, and she carried a knife.

I had two more drinks while I waited for Teddy, and I decided I would not come to town with him again without my own car. I resented the developing status of dependence, and it became clear to me with my second drink that insidiously I was being fashioned into a kind of companion-valet. Small patterns came to mind suddenly: if we ran out of those evil Cokes for the bourbon, I was the one who

walked the fifty feet down the porch of the BOQ to the machine; if
before the civilian cleaning force arrived at our quarters and Teddy's
dirty shorts, shirts, or socks littered the floor—and they usually
did—I picked them up and stuffed them into his laundry bag; it was
my toothpaste, soap, and shaving cream we used; when the Continental developed a very flat tire and Teddy couldn't find anyone in the
parking lot to change it, since he claimed he had no competence in the
art, I changed it, though he watched me, a Chesterfield dangling from
his lips.

It hadn't always been like that.

3

I'M FROM NEW YORK CITY. I'm in the Social Register. My ancestors
were good burghers who served Peter Stuyvesant in expelling those
avaricious Spaniards from New York in 1649. One of my ancestors
was later governor of the state of New York. I went to St. Paul's,
Princeton, and Harvard Law School, but when my father died I was
called back from Cambridge and took my law degree from Columbia.
A month or so later I volunteered for the Army Air Corps.

Teddy's ancestors, or his father, came from some obscure village
in Eastern Germany. I think his father was a peddler to begin with,
but then with a fierce, brute determination he became what he was at
the moment, president and sole owner of Arnheim Industries, one of
the most successful, relatively small companies in the country, with a
platinum grip on rare metals.

I knew Teddy at St. Paul's, but we weren't intimate. Our back-
grounds were different, or rather his was different from the back-
grounds of ninety percent of the other students at St. Paul's. He was a
year ahead of me. The same at Princeton. But during our adolescence
I was occasionally invited to the Arnheim estate, Collincourt.

At Princeton I was invited to join the Ivy Club. Teddy wasn't. He
didn't belong to any club. He lived alone in rooms just off Nassau
Street where I visited him several times. He was not what was known
as a good student. He majored in economics, but he was either bored
by the classes, too lazy to work, or more interested in other matters,
specifically, in the relatively limited availability of his kind of girl in
town.

For Teddy was lecherous. It's the only word that can describe his insatiable libido. He screwed barmaids, waitresses, salesgirls, hairdressers, secretaries, and pedicurists in a bewildering succession of yearning young female bodies. I didn't understand his success at first because he was not by the usual standards an attractive, a "handsome" young man. His teeth were yellow from constant relays of Chesterfields, and uneven (much later they were all capped), and the large, irregular nose produced an acentric effect to his face. And he wasn't remotely athletic. I am, or was, and I'm a good deal larger than Teddy. In an old wallet somewhere, I must still have a yellow clipping from the *New York Post* containing the sentence, "It's unusual to talk to a politician with the face of a poet." From an interview when I was running, unsuccessfully, for the state legislature.

I'm not sure I ever understood. There was the money, of course, but even though he was probably the richest heir at the university, he didn't flourish it in vulgar ostentation. His rooms were always untidy but expensively furnished, and there was the Packard convertible. But he dressed carelessly, in the first thing he laid his hands on in the morning. Slowly, however, I began to recognize a sly sort of charm that presumably seized the hearts of the pedicurists.

He was treated with slightly awed but tentative respect by the other students, and he made no attempt to form close friendships, except with me, and our relationship dated back a good many years. I'm not even sure he was trying to develop a friendship, but we were in a couple of classes together, drank coffee together a few times, and eventually, very casually, he implied there would be a drink available if I cared to stop by his rooms one afternoon.

The first day was sharp and windy, early in November. Most of the leaves had disappeared, and the sun, low in the west, illuminated the white facades of Princeton architecture with terrible brilliance. Just off Nassau Street I found his name above a button in a very simple but solid-looking, two-story house. He had a private entrance to the second floor, and when I knocked, that deep, guttural voice said, "Come in." He was sitting on the floor before a fire, an empty glass at his side, a book folded over a thumb, barefooted.

"Hi," he said without rising. It was a large room with windows along one entire side, and there was a study, bedroom, bathroom, and kitchen. It was comfortable and, in the cold, windy afternoon, very pleasant.

I noticed the title of the book: Veblen's *Theory of the Leisure Class*, an assignment in Winters's course called "The Sociology of Economics," which I found rather bewildering.

"It has an interesting plot, doesn't it?" I said, indicating the book.

"Yeah, it sure has. But I think he understands the importance of waste."

"I couldn't decide whether he approved or disapproved."

"Approved," he said. "There's booze in the kitchen there." I started in that direction, and he added, "While you're up, get me a Grant, will you?" He extended his empty glass.

The kitchen was a disaster, ice melting in trays, scraps of meat on a platter, and a soiled head of lettuce on the floor. I wondered who hadn't cleaned up after him.

When I returned with the two glasses he was still on the floor before the fireplace, leaning forward slightly to pick at his naked toes with one hand, a habit he never relinquished. "Thanks," he said, as I handed him his glass and sat in one of the chairs by the fireplace. "Did you know Polly Kraft?"

"Not very well. I knew her sister better."

"She was killed day before yesterday."

"*What?*"

"Yeah. My Old Lady called this morning. Killed. Crashed into a revetment on Route Seventeen on her way to Tuxedo."

"My *God*," I said, genuinely shocked. *"How?"*

"I don't know. My Old Lady just said she was killed."

"That's *terrible*. She was a lovely girl. It will destroy her parents. They adored her."

"Yeah, she was a nice kid. A good lay."

He shocked me again. I would have sworn that Polly Kraft was a virgin, and I considered it ungentlemanly to discuss the objects of sexual conquests. But even more, the inappropriateness of the admission at the moment seemed to me to be inexcusable. I thought of leaving. What a prig I was.

Teddy turned from his toes and looked up at me. It was the first time I had seen the violent contrast of the Arnheim smile clearly, and there was something approaching pain, very uncharacteristic. "You think I'm a shit, don't you?"

"I think you could have kept that information to yourself."

"I've never told anyone else. Only you. And, Howard, those are two big things in life. Screwing and dying." He looked back at the fire. "They go together somehow."

I protested, but a conversation on the subject didn't interest him, and we went on to other matters, a little awkwardly at first since I still hadn't entirely recovered. Winters's course came up.

"I don't think he understands his subject," Teddy said. We, or at least I, were on the second drink. I don't know how many he had had before I arrived. I never knew unless I counted.

"Why?"

"All the ideas come from the books he assigns, but they come out in chunks, one book after another. And usually the chunks don't agree with each other."

"Isn't that the ideal of objectivity?"

"But why bother with the lectures? Just read the books."

"He, on the other hand, has a high opinion of you."

"Winters?"

"Yes. I had a conference with him last week, and . . . I don't know how the subject came up, but he said something like, 'Too bad young Arnheim is so wealthy. He has a good head.' "

Teddy was staring at the fire again. "Meaning that inherited money keeps the head from working?"

"That's my guess at what he meant."

Teddy continued staring at the fire for a moment before he said, "He's wrong." And that's all he said. We went on to other subjects.

It was dark long before I left and I was late for dinner, a breach of etiquette considered evidence of ill-breeding at the Ivy Club.

I think I could count the number of times Teddy used a word with more than two syllables. His speech was laconic, controlled, and brief, but I began to realize it always centered in on the subject at hand without any rhetorical flourishes or attempts to persuade his listener. And he tired of subjects easily. When an issue had been analyzed and discussed, however briefly, he was prepared to move on to something else. He was not a great conversationalist. I'm not suggesting he didn't listen: he did, acutely, though he didn't give that impression. But when the speaker lost control of his subject, Teddy would tune him out.

I saw him irregularly after that, two or three times a month, and I began to suspect that Winters was right. At age twenty-one Teddy, I think, knew what he was doing. I realize now that I didn't. I don't think many men know what they're doing at age twenty-one, or even at twenty-five. In retrospect I can see what I was doing: not much. I hadn't even firmly decided on a major, and I had no idea what I would do when I left Princeton. My father was a successful lawyer, and a political power without political ambition. We lived, I realize now, elegantly: servants, a town house, another house in Southampton, a chauffeur, and so on. It was possible in those days with a small fraction of what Arnheim Industries represented. Apparently without any conscious consideration of the matter, I assumed it would go on like that.

I can't say precisely when the idea came to me, sometime early in the second semester, and as well as I can remember, it was not prompted by hints or allusions on Teddy's part.

Or perhaps it was, subliminal hints.

I was very innocent.

If you were going to be invited to join a club it usually happened in your sophomore year, and Teddy was already a junior. The procedure was very Old World: two or three members of a club would call on expectant sophomores during "Bicker Week," and a conversation would take place that had nothing to do with joining a club. Thereafter the president of the club and other prestigious officers would make the decision by means of some obscure, totally undemocratic procedure that was never clear to me. I had a very vivid picture of what may have happened if members had called on Teddy in his rooms.

However, I concluded that someone of his stature should be a member of the Ivy Club, and I insisted on a meeting that inaugurated a radical departure from everything the club had adhered to during its long history. I rose and made my nomination to the president, and a long, crepitating silence followed. Then, behind me, a chair was thrust back violently, and a voice began to speak, shrilly, emotionally. I didn't have to look back since I knew the voice very well.

Clyde Morrison was over six feet, slender, with rather hunched shoulders, a sharp jawline that he tightened whenever he knew he was under observation, piercing, rather maniacal eyes, and straight black hair combed severely in a part. I had known him since about the age of six. I detested him even then. His father was an investment banker who, it was said, controlled forces that could plunge the country into depressions, wars, revolutions, or in an unlikely seizure of benevolence, prosperity. Clyde was unpredictably volatile and would strike out at anyone who he imagined had injured him. As children we had cuffed one another regularly. When he was drunk Clyde insulted waiters, and used words like "spic," "guinea," and "kike." He considered himself an orator.

If successful oratory consists of a long, emotional flow of words, he qualified. Unusually polite at the beginning, he referred to the nomination as misguided, but then commenced to warm up to his subject, characterizing the nominee as a man of dubious morals who frequented questionable dives and seduced girls from the "lower orders." (Clyde was jealous. Although physically he was much more impressive than Teddy, he was notoriously unsuccessful with women, who, after one evening, were terrified of him.) He became more and more abusive, not directly of me, but of that vulgar son of the nouveau riche who believed that everything was for sale. The nomination was an affront to the club, and the member should withdraw it.

I was becoming angry. I refused to withdraw the nomination, and I sensed I would receive some support.

Clyde began again, shouting and rattling his chair in insane violence. The president, a decent fellow, cocaptain of the football team, warned him to moderate his voice.

"I will moderate my voice, but if that kike is elected, I'll resign! No kike has ever been a member of the Ivy Club!"

I was on my feet again. "I object to that language. The nominee is one-quarter Jewish by his paternal grandfather." As I recall, I said it without the slightest embarrassment. What a decent little WASP I was, measuring out blood by the quarter. "The member's language reminds me of what we hear coming out of Nazi Germany."

"Well, we could use a few Nazis in this country!" Clyde screamed and slammed out of the room.

I didn't get Teddy into the Ivy Club. *Clyde* did.

I don't believe Teddy ever heard of the incident. Certainly I never told him, and when he moved in even members who had been against him found him benign, though perhaps not very warm, in spite of the regrettable accident of his ancestry. Clyde, who, of course, did not resign, seemed to forget his hostility; he made public demonstrations of his altruism by slapping Teddy on the back in a vigorous expression of fraternity. Teddy regarded him with slate eyes while his mouth twisted into something that might have been taken for a smile.

Before he moved in, however, he asked me to his rooms again one day in February. From the sequence of events it was perfectly obvious that I had been responsible for nominating him, but he never referred to it, and certainly never offered thanks. Perhaps there was a shade more warmth in his attitude toward me; his smile when I came in the room was slightly more relaxed. We talked lazily about classes and other undergraduate matters. He was picking his toes again. "Howard," he said casually, "do you know a good doctor?"

"Certainly. Thompson in the clinic is . . ."

"I mean New York."

"Well . . . yes, but there are some good GPs in Princeton. What's the matter?"

"Princeton's too small. Do you know one in New York?"

"Of course. But you must have a family doctor."

"I can't go to the family doctor. The Old Man would hear."

"What's the matter with you?"

"I've caught an old clap."

"*What?*" In my hurry to get rid of my glass I splashed whiskey over my trousers.

"A clap. Some girl was clapped up."

"My God!" I knew about venereal diseases, of course—social diseases we called them—but so far as I knew I had never talked to anyone who was suffering from such an unspeakable affliction. Unconsciously I had started wiping my hands with my handkerchief. My God! I had introduced a leper into the Ivy Club.

Teddy turned to look at me, the cracked smile almost tender. "It's not that contagious, Howard."

"Oh . . . I wasn't . . ." But I was. Everything in the room impressed me as dirty and threatening, and I wanted to leave. I gave him the name of a doctor my family knew. "Don't use your real name!"

"Don't worry, Howard."

I left as soon as I was able without offending him, and it was the last time I visited his rooms. He was absent from classes for two days, and the next time I saw him, he winked at me to indicate, I suppose, that the medical mission had been successful, but it took me a long time to forget that Teddy Arnheim was susceptible to the disorders of the unwashed masses.

I don't think the experience changed his venereal habits much: he still took the pedicurists to dinner and presumably ravished them somewhere, probably in his rooms.

Three years later he was still ravishing them in the town near the base, but that was before the "better" southern families discovered what a jewel the war had served up for their daughters.

4

SMALL INADVERTENCIES alter our lives in ways that are impossible to understand at the moment. If we realized how important every chance encounter of idle decision was we would probably never act spontaneously. Turning left instead of right in a corridor can lead to incalculable disaster. Accepting an invitation we really preferred to refuse can introduce us to Helen of Troy and a fortune. The wind of circumstance blows on us even in the quietest moments, but we never feel its breath.

It took the base commander and his adjutants three months to discover that Duke was an imbecile, and the same length of time to realize that Teddy had qualities of leadership that I had never suspected. He was appointed squadron commander, and a week later he was promoted to captain.

This rise in the military hierarchy changed his habits very little. We still drank bourbon and Coke, Teddy continued to smash poker games at Le Cave, and to pursue the pedicurists. He was just as slovenly in dress and totally unmilitary in his bearing. The French adored him. When a few wisps of morning fog relieved us from flying, his students gathered around his desk eagerly while he entertained them in his flat, American French, with what anecdotes I never discovered.

The Frog Squadron was still growing, and shortly after Teddy took command another second lieutenant reported in from California. I was sitting on the corner of Teddy's desk talking about a problem student when Henderson approached, saluted, and gave his name in the approved military formula that Teddy never bothered with. Teddy waved casually and invited him to sit down. I wandered off, but later I introduced myself. He seemed civilized, friendly enough, and after a few minutes I decided we had some interests in common.

He had graduated from college in the West just before volunteering, a year after me. He was about my height, physically a little flabby, I thought, and the expression around his eyes suggested that bourbon and Coke, or some western equivalent, was not unknown in California. He had a great mop of curly brown hair that extended down over his collar and around his ears, in a different style just as unmilitary as Teddy's. I couldn't define exactly the impression he gave of somehow being soft, not feminine and certainly not homosexual, but untested, slack. But we had some intellectual interests in common, and after the first week or two we would pass a few minutes talking during breaks. He had majored in literature, and occasionally he spoke passionately about his favorite authors—Faulkner, Scott Fitzgerald, Shakespeare, and others I didn't know.

One hot September afternoon after we had finished flying for the day we left the flight line together, and I invited him to our quarters for a drink.

He glanced at his watch. "Okay, thanks."

In our coveralls we walked along the company street, passing a formation of French cadets, returning the salute offered stiffly by the noncom in charge. "You don't live on the base?" I asked.

"No. In town."

"You're married."

"Yes. We have a couple of rooms in an old house, but it's a disaster. Roaches like dogs, and mosquitoes like vultures. We're looking for a place outside of town. My wife is looking today as a matter of fact. She's supposed to pick me up at six."

"How long have you been married?"

"Only a couple of months, but we went to college together."

Teddy was still on the flight line when we reached the BOQ, which, as usual, was in a wildly disreputable state. I think the cleaning squad had given us up. I kicked some of Teddy's things into a corner. "Sorry about the mess."

"Oh, it doesn't bother me," he said, looking around. "You have a roommate?"

"Teddy."

"Who?"

"Teddy Arnheim."

"Oh, the C.O." The chaos of the room seemed to become more interesting to him. "He's a friend?"

"We went to college together. Have you been initiated into the standard drink?"

"Southern Comfort?"

"No. Bourbon and Coke."

He tried to suppress a legitimate shudder. "That's . . . fine."

I went down the porch for the Cokes and when I returned he was examining my few books. "You're a lawyer, I think you said."

"I was. I've never had a chance to practice." I opened the Cokes, poured the bourbon, and handed him a glass.

"Salut." He drank and shuddered.

"You don't have to pretend you like it, but it's cold and it gets the bourbon into you."

"No, it's all right."

"You speak French well. Where did you learn?" We took the only two chairs that weren't piled with soiled clothes.

"Junior year abroad, in Paris."

That took us to Paris, which I knew pretty well, and we discovered we had been there at the same time one summer and were only a couple of streets away on the Left Bank, and we had eaten in the same modest restaurant several times. Henderson (his first name was Michael) was enthusiastic about France and described his attempts to join the OSS to work behind the lines, but his accent wasn't that good. I had just poured a second drink when Teddy wandered in. Henderson put his drink down and rose from his chair.

"Hi," Teddy said.

"Sir," Henderson replied with strict military courtesy. Teddy looked at him a moment and his mouth smiled. "Teddy," he said.

"Sir?"

"My name is Teddy."

"Oh, thanks. Mike."

"Yeah," Teddy said. "Howard, are there any more Cokes?"

"On the table."

He opened the bottle and searched around for a glass. "Where the hell are all the glasses?"

"You'll have to use the one in the bathroom that has your filthy toothbrush in it. Tell me, Teddy," I called out, "when was the last time you bought a new toothbrush."

"I think it was in 1933," he said from the bathroom. "But I like yours. It's nice and stiff."

I saw the reaction in Henderson's eyes.

"Where's the bourbon?" Teddy said reentering.

"On the table, for God's sake."

"Oh, yeah." He poured an immense drink, added a little Coke, and tilted the glass. "If you don't put too much Coke in, it almost tastes like a drink," he said to Henderson, who was still standing. "Why don't you sit down?"

"Oh, thank you."

Teddy wandered over to one of the chairs piled with his dirty clothes. "Howard," he said, dumping the chair, "I wish you'd take better care of your shit. The place is a goddamned mess." He sat down and began removing his boots.

"Yes, sir, oh my captain."

Teddy looked up at Henderson, took a drink, and said, "He's only half civilized. We tried to make a gentleman of him at Princeton, but they didn't have good manners at the Howard homestead."

Henderson had caught on, and he was smiling when Teddy leaned over to pick at his toes. His expression changed again briefly.

"That madman of yours, Harchinchu, almost killed me this afternoon, Howard."

"I thought I showed him how to do it better."

"I think he closes his eyes when he lands the airplane."

"I told you he should be washed out."

"Oh, I think we can pull him through. He was probably a pretty good pilot before you got hold of him. I'll check him again next week."

"You're crazy. I don't care if he kills himself, but I'm not going to fly with him on my wing again."

"You spent time in France?" he said to Henderson.

"Yes, s. . . . Yes."

"You speak good French."

"Thank you."

"Howard thinks he speaks good French, but one of his students told me he thought he was speaking German." He smiled at me and continued to pick at his toes.

"How did you communicate with him?" I asked. "In sign language?"

Teddy leaned back and took a large portion of his drink, sticking his naked feet out onto the floor tiles. "You want to go to Le Cave tonight, Howard?"

"No," I said. "It doesn't amuse me any more to watch you fleece enlisted men."

"Have you been to Le Cave?" he asked Henderson.

"No. I haven't seen much of the town."

"Mike's married," I said. "He doesn't consort with gamblers and drunks."

"You were married just before you came," Teddy said.

I was learning more about Teddy's unsuspected abilities. He seemed to have committed all the personnel files to memory.

"Yes, in California."

Teddy got to his feet and shuffled toward the table. "Remind me to get married, Howard, so I don't have to consort with uncivilized roommates. Is this all the bourbon that's left?"

"Yes. You drank almost a pint after dinner last night."

"Shit. It's your turn to get more. And try to get a quart this time."

"You know damned well they don't sell it in quarts."

"They will if you add ten dollars."

"*You* add ten dollars."

"Okay." He picked up the almost empty pint and padded over to Henderson to fill his glass.

"No, thanks. I have to go. I'm supposed to meet my wife at the gate."

"She can come through if you have a post sticker on the car."

"I didn't know that."

"Yeah." He poured the rest of the pint in his glass. "Give me her name tomorrow and I'll have an I.D. card made out for her."

"Oh, thank you," Henderson said, rising. "And thanks for the drinks. I've . . ."

"Wait a minute," I said. "Since I have to go into town to furnish more booze for this infamous blackguard I'll drive you to the gate." I held out a hand to Teddy. "Give, you infamous blackguard. It's your turn to pay."

"Is it? I don't think I can really afford it, but . . ." He wandered over to a corner where he picked up the small brown satchel and carried it to the table. Opening it, he came out with a handful of greenbacks that trembled slightly. "Here," he said, thrusting at me.

"Just give me twenty dollars, Arnheim."

"Take it. My hands are full."

I extracted two tens and he stuffed the rest back into the satchel. "Let's go," I said to Henderson.

As I backed the Ford out of the parking area Henderson said, "Does he leave all that money lying around in the room?"

"Yes. Forty-five thousand dollars at last count. Poker winnings."

"Wow! But isn't it rather dangerous?"

"It's my conviction that it is, but he doesn't share my conviction." I turned down the street toward the post gate.

"Why doesn't he put it in a bank?"

"Because, according to him, the Old Man would hear about it, and know he's been gambling. The Old Man doesn't believe in gambling, at least with cards."

"Who's the Old Man?"

"Theodore Arnheim the First."

"Is he somebody important?"

"You've never heard of him?"

"No."

"He owns a company that's worth around thirty million dollars."

"Oh, I understand."

We returned the salute of the guard at the gate and passed through. "There she is," Michael said. "I hope she hasn't been waiting long."

An enormous, auburn La Salle sedan was parked at the side of the road.

"That's quite an automobile," I commented.

He had reached for the door handle. "The only thing I could find. I paid three hundred dollars for it in Bakersfield and we drove it across the country. Matt, thanks for the drink. If we find a place we'll have you over." He left the Ford and started across the road.

The young woman at the wheel of the La Salle turned, recognized him and smiled. I could see her only down to her shoulders, but in that moment I decided Henderson was a lucky man. Her hair was light brown with blond highlights, perfectly straight, worn in a puffed pompadour and gathered in a chignon high on the back of her head. She had a soft, oval face with eyes that were close to almond-shaped. And her smile in a radiant welcome injured me into the awareness that I was missing something in life.

I threw the Ford into gear and started on my way into town to find the blackguard a quart of bourbon.

5

I CONSIDER MYSELF knowledgeable about society since I was shuffled into it at an early age by my mother, but I'm not really certain how the word got around that Teddy Arnheim was on the base. Probably through some southern officers from the area who were instructing in the Frog, or one of the other squadrons. Invitations to dinner, dinner dances, and soirées began to arrive for Teddy, and at first he simply ignored them, without even bothering to RSVP. But tactics were altered subtly then, and, as if sensing my credentials (someone may have checked the N.Y. Social Register), invitations began to arrive for both of us, and my training would not permit me to disregard them. I decided to accept one. It was for dinner, and the hostess bore a revered name in that part of the South.

Sipping bourbon and Coke, Teddy watched me dressing. "You're really going to go?"

"Certainly. I'm not a vulgarian."

He picked up the invitation and studied it casually. "Do you think they have a Confederate flag on the pole?"

"Probably."

"You know what those cunts will be like, don't you?"

"I have a pretty good idea. I want to see if I'm right."

He dropped the invitation, finished his drink, and stood wearily. "Oh, shit," he said, and shuffled off to the shower.

I expected it to be pleasant. It was much more than that. It was elegant. A fine old house decorated with taste, excellent liquor, a delicious dinner, and the host and hostess were charming, gracious, and cultured. Teddy and I were folded into generous arms of hospitality as though we had been on the right side at Vicksburg. There were other officers present, but we were the only northerners.

We were urged to make repeated visits to the bar where a very dignified black man in formal serving dress produced anything the most exotic taste could have desired. We were sixteen at table, under a sparkling, antebellum chandelier, served on gleaming linen by six black serfs and a sommelier who poured a Bordeaux that I had heard of but never drunk.

On one issue Teddy's instincts were infallible. There were two daughters in the family and a seraglio of other young women who, with the cognac and coffee, circled Teddy, listening to his witticisms, and after he had drunk enough to fell the average man, Teddy could be very witty. They squealed in shrieks of laughter, pressing kerchiefs to their rosy lips and turning to one another to implore relief from such exquisite torture. I knew them. I had seen their northern sisters. In those days all young ladies from certain social levels were indoctrinated in schools of charm from about age six. But with perhaps one exception, and she was engaged, these young southern girls seemed to have been programmed in an anachronistic art of social seduction. They laughed at small opportunity, gestured in practiced grace, and spoke volubly, in high caressing voices, of inanities. Invariably their names were double, as though their parents, trying to satisfy two impulses, had finally surrendered to a hyphen: Marie-Louise, Anne-Clotilde, Florence-Jane. I always felt I was addressing two young women.

Long after midnight we rolled away in the monster, Teddy silent, morose, driving like a trainee for suicide. I tried to rouse him from his dangerous stupor, but all I received were grunts. He didn't speak an intelligible word until we arrived at the BOQ where he began removing his uniform item by item, dropping them on the floor where he stood.

"Did you see what those cunts were like, Howard?"

"Yes, I saw."

"Do you think any of them has ever been laid?"

"I doubt it. I think they're from the old school, and it's very old in the South."

Naked, he hunted vaguely through the debris on the table until he found half a pint of bourbon. He carried it to his bed, sat down, and took a gulp from the bottle. "Do you remember Polly Kraft?"

"Yes, certainly," I said, yawning.

"She could have been like those cunts, but she wasn't."

I lay on my bed. "I don't think I'm up to comparative sociology at the moment."

I was almost asleep when I heard him say, "Polly Kraft was the only woman I ever wanted to marry, but the Old Man vetoed it." A moment's silence, and he added, "So she killed herself. Because she was pregnant."

I sat up in bed. *"What* did you say?"

"She was pregnant."

"By . . . by *whom?"*

He took another gulp of bourbon, placed the bottle on the floor, and lay down. "By me," he said turning his face to the wall.

That was the way Teddy came to me: in bits and apparently unrelated fragments that I had to reassemble in order to deduce something approaching coherence from them. I remembered the incident from years earlier in his rooms at Princeton. In his grief all he could say was, "She was a good lay."

We must have been a success in our first venture into southern society since we received more invitations than we could possibly accept, and inevitably I assumed the responsibility of responding to the excess. "Captain Arnheim regrets . . ." "Lieutenant Howard regrets . . ." I was a first lieutenant by then, obviously owing to Teddy's efforts, though he denied any knowledge of it.

In spite of Teddy's reluctance we did accept a good many to other hospitable homes, to the country club, and to the officer's club at a nearby naval station, where one of the sons of an old local family was an admiral. And eventually two of the young women seemed to have negotiated a truce among the other aspirants to our attention, emerging as our "dates." We were invited as a unit of four, and since with the rainy season setting in my Ford did not provide protection for crinoline and satin, we usually *did* travel as an implausible foursome in the monster. And tacitly we were expected to initiate some courtesy in return. We did. We took them to dinner a couple of times, not to dances, since Teddy could not, or refused to, dance.

The ultimate intimacy on these occasions, for both of us—we compared notes—was a chaste, tightly compressed, good-night kiss before the door of each, in the case of my date awarded with much giggling. Inevitably when Teddy had delivered his charge back to her father's custody and returned to the monster where I was waiting, he would drop in the driver's seat, place his hands heavily on the wheel, and groan in anguish, "Oh, shit." Once when the four of us were back in the monster after dinner at a restaurant where Teddy had been bored into a stupor, he eased himself into the seat, dropped his hands on the wheel, and in an expression of utterly annihilating boredom,] relieved himself prematurely. "Oh, shit," he groaned.

Two sharp gasps, almost in unison, and total silence on the way home.

They got over it, of course.

It was sometime in October while Teddy and I were limply conducting our social life that Mike Henderson taxied his airplane onto the line next to mine, a student in the rear cockpit for instrument training. He waved to me, and as soon as he climbed out and unstrapped his parachute, he came over. "Matt, we found a place, out in the country. Can you come to dinner on Sunday?"

Surprisingly I had nothing scheduled for Sunday. "I'd like to."

"Good. I'll see you inside for directions."

Postflight critiques took quite a lot of our time, involving oral and manual dexterity, explaining and describing the position of the airplane with a hand that climbed, turned, dived, and rolled in an imperfect ballet. I finished with my student while Mike was patiently explaining the maneuvers necessary to cross the nul, the zone of silence in beam-flying, our primitive method of navigating an airplane in clouds or fog. Watching him, I decided again that he was congenial. He came from a different culture, the West, but he was intelligent and friendly; yet somehow I felt there was a certain vitality or awareness lacking. He, too, I decided, didn't know what he was doing.

He came over to me. "I don't think he understands it yet, but if he's lucky he'll never run into a cloud. Here's how to fly the beam to our place. Turn right at the southern gate and go straight to Weshenka, then . . ." And he explained that it was on an artificial lake, Lake Mason. "Fifteen miles. We'll expect you around five."

"Good. I'll be there."

We both started to leave, but at that moment Teddy came in from the flight line lugging his parachute, talking to a student pilot he had just checked. When I remember that moment I am unable to decide what impulse moved me. The parachute seemed too heavy for that slender body, there was a weariness about the eyes, and his cheek was dusted with the powder of the field, slightly furrowed with sweat. I put my hand on Mike's shoulder. "Would you like to have Teddy, too?" I immediately wanted to retract. No one from my background would have been so boorish as to invite another guest unless it was a wife or "date."

But Mike looked over at Teddy. "Oh, certainly," he said with enthusiasm, "if you think he'd come. Would you ask him?"

The breath of circumstance was blowing, and I didn't even feel its caress.

During the week I decided I'd retract, not mention it to Teddy, and make an excuse to Mike, and I think it would have gone that way if on Friday evening Teddy, in finishing the last pint of bourbon, hadn't said casually, "I heard of a moonshiner down south a few miles who sells it by the gallon. Maybe we ought to try a run Sunday."

Impulsively overriding my decision, I said, "Oh, I forgot to tell you Henderson asked us to dinner Sunday. They found a place on a lake down near Weshenka."

He looked at me, a mute question in his eyes, but he asked a different question. "They asked both of us?"

"Yes."

He continued to look at me for a moment, then he said, "Okay," and turned away.

Some of the prodigious heat of summer had given way to a brisk, shining afternoon when we found Lake Mason, and turning right on Henderson's directions, located the dirt road that ran through cotton fields above the water on our right. It was not yet a resort area, but a few modest summer places had been built above the lake, and we found the one that fit Henderson's description, with the monstrous La Salle in the half-circle of the driveway. It was a log cabin settled among pine trees that ran down to the shoreline, and though it was not luxurious it had summer charm. I wondered what it would be like in the winter.

I was about to knock when Mike appeared, climbing up from the side of the cabin on our right.

"Hi," he said. "Did you have any problems finding it?"

"No. We crossed the zone of silence right here."

"Come down this way. We don't use the upstairs much except to sleep." He led us down a path by the side, past a woodpile. "The pioneering spirit," he said, indicating an axe.

The back of the cabin was on a lower level, built into the hillside, including a terrace where a table was set with rather battered china and glasses which seemed only recently to have been scoured of their jelly labels. A screened interior with an entrance to the lower level abutted the terrace, and inside I saw the filtered figure of his wife moving about in what I assumed was the kitchen.

The setting was superb. The lake, twenty feet below us, was sun-splashed in October light, over a mile across, and on the other side stood glaucous pine forests garnished by a few brilliant maples in red. There was not a sound.

"How long is it?" Teddy spoke for the first time.

"About ten miles. The dam is down there a couple of miles."

"Does it have any fish?"

I was not aware that Teddy had the remotest interest in fishing.

"Some bass," Mike said, "and according to legend, some hundred-and-fifty-pound catfish on the bottom."

"This is for you." I handed Mike the bag I had carried down, containing two pints of bourbon and six bottles of South America's best.

"Oh, thanks. I'll make drinks. What would . . . ?"

The screen door opened on the side of the porch, and Mike's wife appeared.

"Oh, Chris, this is Matt Howard and Teddy Arnheim."

She came to me and offered her hand, European style. "I'm glad you could come," she said simply. She turned to Teddy, who was still looking out over the lake, his back to us. She waited.

"Teddy," I said, and he turned.

"I'm glad you could come, too," she said, offering her hand again.

He looked at her for a moment, startled, and then took her hand, his eyes blank, the habitual constancy of surveillance gone for the first time that I could remember. He was mute.

It wasn't difficult to understand. I felt it, too, strongly. His eyes had turned from the splendor of the distant forest, the radiance of the lake to radiance of another kind. She was not fashioned after the contemporary pinup that was running strongly toward Betty Grable at the time, but there was such a winning girl-grace in her presence, such consistency of tone and form that she became the essential adornment of the terrace in the forest of pines. Her eyes, as I had seen them only briefly before the post gate, were markedly almond-shaped, at first impression one might have been tempted to guess Eurasian, but set in an oval face that could have been high English. Her hair, slightly more blond in the later afternoon light, was in pompadour again, with the chignon. She was wearing a white shirt, open at the throat, and a light blue skirt. Her body was slender, long-legged, but full-breasted. She had been in the sun. Her arms, bare calves, and her face were golden brown. There was something coltish about the way she moved to the table suddenly to rearrange a bouquet of wild daisies. A wide silver bracelet was on her left arm, and a silver ring on her ring finger. No other jewelry and no make up. Teddy was staring at her. So was I.

"Well," Mike said, "what would you like? We have a bottle of scotch and your bourbon."

"I'll have scotch," I said.

"Teddy?" The first name was still difficult for him.

"Uh . . . bourbon and branch." The mouth smiled.

"Chris?"

"Nothing yet, Michael."

He entered the cabin, and in a conspiracy of silence we watched her arrange her flowers and study the table for a moment, frowning. Then she turned to us. "I don't know what our landlord does out here, but I don't think he entertains. There were four plates, five knives, and three forks. And the jelly glasses." She came back to us. "Do you think we're crazy to move into a log cabin?"

"Yes," Teddy said quickly, "but I like crazy people."

I was trying to place her accent, predominantly Manhattan, but with undertones of New England, perhaps Maine. Her voice was low and resonant.

"We wonder what winter will be like," she said looking out over the lake.

"Do you have any heat?" I asked.

"A fireplace upstairs and downstairs, and a wood stove, but fortunately Michael enjoys sawing and splitting. But I think we'll probably be huddling around the stove for several months," she said, smiling. "Excuse me. I have to go back to my wood stove."

She left us, and Teddy watched her disappear, his face curiously empty of expression.

"Nice people," I said.

He didn't answer.

Michael returned carrying a tray with bottles, more jelly glasses, and ice. "Our one luxury is electricity, and therefore ice." He poured the drinks, a stiff scotch, I noticed, for himself. "Would you like to go down to the water?"

We followed him down a short trail to the edge of the lake, carrying our drinks. In two years I had not seen anything so beautiful, so enchanted. A decaying rowboat was tied to an even more decayed wooden pier, but the lowering sun painted the undisturbed surface of the water with lustrous gold, and in that fallow swathe a fish jumped hard.

"Have you caught any?" Teddy asked.

"A couple of small bass, but I don't have the patience to be a good fisherman."

"Do you swim?" I asked.

"Every day I'm home. I was in this afternoon. It's still quite warm. Do you want to go in?"

"I don't have a suit."

"You don't need one. All the summer people have left."

I glanced up at the cabin.

"Chris won't even see you, and if she does it won't bother her."

I took a big swallow from my glass and set it down. "I think I will." I began removing my uniform.

"Teddy?" Mike asked.

"I can't swim."

Either it struck Mike as unusual or he thought it was Teddy's unaccented humor. "Really?"

"I never learned."

Naked, I started down toward the water.

"If you go out on the pier you can dive, but be careful. It's not very solid."

I went out and dived into the dark warmth of the lake, intoxicated by pleasure and the sense of release that open water provides. I detest swimming pools, and that's all I had had available for two years, and very few of those. I swam out several hundred feet and rolled over to float. Below the light of the sun now the lake had become an immense dark world of utter silence. Looking back, I saw the cabin suddenly flooded in golden light, and on the terrace two motionless figures like distant statuary on a mythic shore, frozen artifacts, Chris, her skirt and shirt aflame in the last rays of the sun, and I thought, Michael at her side. Then light left the cabin.

But when I reached the shore Michael was there, seated in the boat, barefooted, his trousers rolled to his knees, working at something. "How was it?"

"Unforgettable."

"There's a towel there on the bush."

"Thank you." I staggered up a muddy bank and began to dry myself. "What are you working at?"

"The old scow takes on water faster than you can bail, but I can't find the leak."

I started dressing. "What happened to Teddy? He didn't try to walk on the water, did he?"

Mike laughed. "He went up a while ago to get a drink." He glanced at his watch. "We'd better go, too. Dinner's almost ready."

We ate the stew Chris had prepared in candlelight on the terrace, and it was a very good, thick beef stew. She laughed in deprecation at our compliments. "At least I *hope* it's beef. It looked like it, but the butcher in Weshenka is a sly one, and I don't think he believes in Yankees."

"We meant to do steaks on the grill," Michael said, "but we ran out of red points."

"I have some red points you can have," Teddy said.

"Oh," Chris objected, "we couldn't accept them."

"Please do," Teddy said with a gallantry I had never heard. "The Army Air Corps feeds me. I don't need them. I'll give them to Michael next week."

"If you do, you will force us to invite you to dinner again," Chris said, smiling.

"Then I will certainly give them to Michael next week."

Somehow they had found three bottles of red wine, and Chris accepted several glasses, though in the candlelight the only change I could see was a slight flush in her tanned cheeks, and perhaps a certain whimsy in her conversation. It made her even more charming. I didn't know how much he had drunk before dinner, but Michael, on the other hand, seemed to have slipped past that undetectable and unpredictable point where alcohol changes the personality: he wasn't offensive, just slightly sodden, withdrawn, captured by a mood.

When we had finished we all carried dishes to the kitchen where Chris had two huge pots of water on the wood stove. She began washing a mountainous stack of plates and pots while the three of us withdrew to the adjoining dining area, a cavelike extension of the kitchen with a long table and benches. Michael produced a bottle of brandy. It wasn't very good brandy, and I didn't go for a second round, though Michael drank several, becoming more remote and less intelligible. Teddy remained as always, quietly aware, listening, but adding very little to a not very brilliant conversation. After two shots of brandy he left to find the toilet just off the screened area, but when he reappeared he stayed in the kitchen with Chris, only about twenty feet away, taking on a task which I'm reasonably certain he had never performed in his life before: drying dishes. I heard Chris object, and Teddy's rumbling bass reply. Michael was oblivious, engaged in a long and not very coherent discussion of a writer I had never heard of.

It was after midnight when we left, with an invitation from Michael to return whenever we felt the urge.

"You drive," Teddy said.

I took the monster down the dirt road to the highway while Teddy sat silently looking at the waning moon.

"I like them," I said finally. "Didn't you?"

"He can't drink."

"Well, he didn't pass out, and not everyone has a cast-iron stomach."

There was no allusion to Chris, but when we were near the field I remembered. "I didn't know you had any red points."

"I don't, but I know where I can get some."

He must have found quite a wad. I never knew how much he paid for them, but I saw him slip Michael a thick envelope the following week.

He was providing meat for the cabin on the Lake.

6

THE FRENCH must have decided they had stumbled onto an amiable assortment of drunken derelicts. The first two classes consisted largely of officers who were, of course, made members of the Officers' Club, and as they sipped a single vermouth or glass of wine at the bar before dinner, they watched with quiet astonishment while the

Americans poured down martini after martini. Some of the French came from old and very traditional families, and I think they found the absence of tradition in us, that vacancy lying very close under the surface of the imposed military discipline, disturbing. Some of them were also highly educated, and the catastrophe of the war and defeat of France had left them stunned. One of my students, Delaporte, was, like me, a lawyer who had never practiced law. He had escaped from France directly after finishing law school. We talked more about the differences between French and American law than we did about flying.

But the enlisted men were a jolly group who found America a dreamland, and Teddy a kind of clown-god. The first time he was called upon to make an inspection of the enlisted men's barracks, he asked me to go along, and we prepared ourselves for the ordeal with a couple of bourbon and Cokes. When we passed through the door of the barracks, the first man to see us bellowed such a thunderous *"Fixe!"* (*"Attention"*) that I thought he had seen something dangerous that we hadn't seen. To a man they went into a rigid brace wherever they happened to be in the room, and we began shuffling around and between them while Teddy looked them over, muttering compliments on the sheen of shoes or the press of a shirt. Their rigidity was fervent, painful.

"Howard," he muttered to me after a few minutes, "do you know how to say 'at ease' in French?"

"No. Why don't you try *'à l'aise'*?"

He did, and it didn't work. Not a muscle relaxed in the entire room.

"Think of something else."

"Try *'soyez tranquil.'*"

It didn't work either, but by now gasps of what sounded like imperfectly suppressed seizures of agony had begun to erupt from various parts of the room.

"We could just go out and leave them," I suggested.

"No, I think they'd stay like that, and by morning they couldn't be untied." Walking to an area where he was visible from every part of the barrack he assumed a posture of such abject indolence that he remained scarcely vertical. It produced nothing but an increase in painful attempts at control. Their faces were becoming red, and tears ran down their trembling cheeks.

"This is getting serious," Teddy said, but another inspiration seized him. Reclining on a nearby cot, he folded his hand under his cheeks and closed his eyes.

Men trembled in spasms of anguish. Their breathing was an agonized whistle.

"For God's *sake*," Teddy said, rising, "think of every synonym for 'ease' you can, or we'll have a hospital full of ruptured spleens."

"Well, you were sleeping, relaxing, reposing. Try *'repos'* or better, try *'à repos.'* "

"*À repos!*" he bellowed in a monstrous growl.

The effect was alarming, a human jackpot. They came out of the brace, but they began to howl, to cry, to fall into one another's arms, to roll on the floor.

We sneaked out the back door.

The first class of French students was ending its training in mid-October, to the vast relief of the commanding officer of the base, who had expected disaster when these volatile foreigners had been assigned to his care. There had been no serious accident, and our French pilots had performed extremely well, better than the average American class who passed through advanced training to receive their wings. Of course they were an exceptional group, and we had formed friendships that, with the usual good intentions, we promised to sustain after the war. And Teddy had become an object of something approaching hero worship for them. To me this charisma was always difficult to understand: at Princeton, in the Ivy Club, he had been tolerated as a necessary eccentricity, but he had formed no intimacies except with me, if our relationship could be called intimate. In the Frog Squadron he was revered.

It was perhaps in response to that, or the birth of some other uncharacteristic social impulse, that led him to the decision to have a party in celebration of the French achievement. Or even something more complex that I didn't understand then.

He brought the subject up casually one evening just before we went to bed.

"Sounds like a good idea. At the Club?"

"I thought we ought to have some of the noncoms, too, so the Club's out."

"You'd better check with one of the officers. They might not come if there are noncoms."

"I already have. They'll come if it's off the base."

"Hire a hall?"

"That would be shitty."

"Well, ask one of our aristocratic friends to lend us their house for the evening," I said, pulling the blanket up to my chin. The nights had become cooler.

I was almost asleep when he said, "Howard?"

"Yes?"

"How about the Hendersons' place on the lake?"

"A good place, but maybe the Hendersons should be consulted."

"Yeah. Ask Michael tomorrow."

"Why me?"

"I think it would be better. If it came from me it might sound like something military."

I thought about it for a while, not liking it, but it had the logical structure characteristic of Teddy's reasoning. "All right. I'll ask him tomorrow, but it's putting quite a load on Chris."

"I'll take care of that."

The next morning when I mentioned it to Michael he hesitated a moment, but then said, "Yes, it's a good idea. I'll have to ask Chris, of course."

"Of course."

When he had had time to ask Chris he reported that they agreed, but I seemed to detect less enthusiasm. However, Teddy did take care of the arrangements. On the morning of the Saturday we had decided on, a van arrived at the cabin on the lake with glasses, ice, a good many pints of bourbon, some scotch, enough wine to supply a regiment of thirsty French soldiers, along with a variety of food, including a large baked ham. I have no idea how Teddy managed to provide such a banquet, but a lot of poker winnings must have been exchanged for red points.

We arrived around five, and the cabin was splendid in wild flowers, food, and drink. Chris welcomed us again with that charming directness and spontaneity that spread a kind of sorcery over the cabin, though her eyes suggested tension, a certain anxiety that I attributed to her role as hostess to about twenty men. Her hair was done up on the top of her head, and she was wearing a gorgeous blue mandarin coat embroidered in red and gold, and slit on the sides above her knees. She was stunning.

To begin with Teddy was curiously shy as he looked around at the preparations. "Is everything all right?" he asked finally.

"Yes, perfect. I don't know where you got all that food, but I won't ask."

"Is there anything I can do?"

"No, I don't think so. Unless . . . Michael, did you split enough wood? It's going to be cool this evening."

Michael and I were arranging bottles. "I think so," he said, without looking up.

Chris went to the corner of the cabin. "Oh, we'll need more than that. Teddy, if you could split a little more. The axe is over there." She went back into the kitchen.

I saw him study the woodpile, remove his tunic, and disappear. Shortly afterward a dull detonation occurred and a small log was catapulted around the corner.

"My God!" Chris screamed and ran out of the kitchen. "Stop it! You'll kill yourself." A window in the kitchen gave out onto the woodpile, I discovered later. "Don't you know how to split wood?"

We couldn't hear the answer, but Chris disappeared and returned clutching the axe, followed by Teddy. "No!" she said firmly. "Do something else. Come in and help me in the kitchen."

He followed docilely without a glance at us.

The party was a stupendous success. Some of the officers had bought third- or fourth-hand cars, and they arrived, eighteen officers and two noncoms, in a caravan of antiquated Dodges, Fords, and Plymouths. They were enchanted by the hospitality of the log cabin, delighted with Chris, and thirsty. They drank strange elixirs, and returned for more. Late in the evening they formed a circle around Chris and sang some song I had never heard and didn't entirely understand. She was embarrassed and blushed, but she handled it with that quiet dignity that was part of her charm. Some of our guests had been stranded in North Africa for long periods where they had learned Arab chants which they performed for us with ferocity. They drank, they ate, and they drank again. Even the most sedate, including Delaporte, discovered the radiant charms of bourbon and branch. One contingent descended to the lake, where a lieutenant fell in and had to be fished out, a sodden, muddy apparition, giggling explanations in an Auvergne dialect. They presented Teddy with a scroll signed by all, extolling his virtues as man and C.O. And finally, after

a long and tortuous selection of the most competent drivers, involving a test of walking a straight line in the moonlight, they left.

The four of us returned to the cabin to clean up and sit by the fire
where Michael, who had got very drunk, fell asleep. Eventually I
suggested to Teddy that it was time to leave.

"Oh, don't go," Chris said impetuously, "I made up the two beds
in the room off the kitchen just in case."

It was late, and we agreed.

Above we heard Chris wake Michael, and their footsteps were just
over our heads when they entered the bedroom. Then bedsprings
squeaked, and I heard Teddy turn over and groan.

7

PROBABLY I should have been stronger, more assertive, more astute,
or at least I should not have cooperated in such a mindless fashion.

For most people Teddy was an enigma, and after knowing him for
years, I still found him difficult to decipher. He was far from garrulous under any circumstance, and even when he talked about apparently insignificant matters, I had the sense that they signified
something else, or that he had gone through several stages in reasoning and was now talking about a decision that had come at the end of a
complicated process.

For example, he now began to refer to the Old Man rather often, a
subject he had always been singularly reticent about. That his father
was a tyrant, capable of brutality, was scarcely news to anyone who
knew anything about Arnheim Industries. The symbol that was popu-
larly associated with the president's office was the guillotine. Those
unfortunates who were called into the presence, it was said, gave the
impression that, indeed, they were riding a tumbril.

I had met his father and mother casually over the years, not really
in a social context, since they occupied no social class, certainly not
mine. His mother was the closest thing to a Hausfrau I had ever met,
simple, good-hearted, ample, when not in her husband's presence. In
his presence she was silent. She ceased to exist. His father was rather
small, gnarled, and totally humorless. He was almost bald, with a
blunt, high forehead, and eyes that seemed to me to be reflecting evil
intentions. He had never lost his German accent, and he used it to

Prussian effect. Teddy's relations with his father, so far as I had been able to make out, had been a long, obdurate, and bitter struggle. He admitted that on several occasions he had threatened to bolt, to move out into the world, leaving Arnheim Industries without an heir, but implicit in that admission was a clear intention to remain and to take over upon his father's death, almost as an act of revenge.

With an Alabama winter coming on, the cabin on the lake became even more attractive to us, and we began spending almost every Sunday with the Hendersons. We always brought supplies, and ineptly we helped in various tasks around the house. Teddy learned to split wood, and it apparently gave him enormous pleasure. He split mountains of pine and maple and carried it to the upper fireplace where we would have drinks before dinner. Dinner would be below, in the cell, before another fire, warm, domestic, an atmosphere Teddy was enjoying for the first time in his life. I enjoyed it, too, though a strange tension had begun to develop that I didn't understand. I remember Chris's voice once when we were planning the next Sunday. We had, of course, talked about our experiences in southern society and alluded to our "dates."

"Bring them next Sunday, won't you?" she said suddenly.

Neither Teddy nor I answered, and Michael was nursing a drink.

"Oh, *please* bring them," Chris pleaded in such a fervent voice that the quality of the conversation changed abruptly.

"All right," I said, after a moment. "If they can come."

Chris, realizing that her sudden display of emotion had created a break in the mood of the moment, turned away. I felt Teddy's eyes on me, and I looked at him. There was a rage in them that I had never seen. Even Michael, emerging from his alcoholic mood, recognized that something had happened.

When we left Teddy skidded the monster onto the dirt road with such violence that we almost landed in a cotton field.

"Why did you *do* that?" he demanded fiercely.

"What?"

"Invite those silly cunts out."

"I didn't invite them. Chris did."

"But you agreed to it."

"She was extending an invitation. As hostess."

"Oh, shit," he said viciously, "they'll ruin the place."

"Teddy . . ." I began, not really knowing where I intended to go. But he wasn't listening.

They didn't effect any physical damage to the cabin on the lake, but the moment they stepped in the door and met Chris, they became nervous, animated, more strident than usual. Two young women whose most passionate display of carnality had been a frigid kiss at the door of their fathers' mansions now became oppressively attentive, running their hands through our hair, grabbing our arms, and laughing shrilly in unison as though they had learned methodology from the same text and were applying it lesson after lesson. It was a destructively dull evening, and Chris's charm as hostess was smothered under frivolity. But I thought I saw her retiring from what had become a struggle, retiring toward Michael with a hint of regret but also freedom.

Teddy spent the evening in a surly, scarcely concealed, homicidal rage.

When Michael came over to me in the briefing room the following week he handed me an envelope with the addressees "Lt. and Mrs. Michael Henderson," and an elaborately embossed return address.

"What is it?"

"Open it."

It was an invitation to Michael and Chris for dinner at the home of one of our aristocratic friends for the following Saturday.

"Do you know them?" he asked.

"Yes." Both Teddy and I had received the invitation several days before.

"I don't understand why they invited us."

"You must have made a big hit with the girls Sunday. It's a very closely knit society. Everybody knows everybody else." Which was true. "Are you going?"

"I guess so, though Chris wasn't very keen on it. She said she had nothing to wear."

My own explanation didn't satisfy me. I was convinced there was another hand manipulating the guest list, perhaps even with a threat. The girls, I was certain, would have preferred never to see Chris again, and I began to suspect some sort of elaborate revenge was being exacted for a spoiled Sunday. I mentioned it to Teddy that evening, but he merely grunted and opened another pint of bourbon.

It was buffet this time with about twenty-five people, just as posh as ever, with a splendid bar and a long table loaded with extravagance. The war didn't seem to be having a serious effect on these hospitable southerners.

Teddy's date was subdued as she followed him around from one room to another in his quick survey of the house after our arrival. My guess on the origin of the invitation to Michael and Chris was fully confirmed when they appeared. Teddy, with his date, had been talking, or rather listening, to a small group, his glass in hand. When he saw the Hendersons enter I was watching him. He slid away, followed tenaciously by his date, to meet Chris and Michael just as they were being welcomed by the hostess.

As usual Chris was stunning. Surrounded by frills, long colored scarves, frocks in lace and prints, she was wearing a simple dark green, woolen dress with a colored belt and a high neck, discreetly embroidered in a Navajo design. She was still without makeup, but her skin had the healthy glow of sun and the country.

An invalid quartet, they moved into the room for other introductions, and the eyes of every woman they met covered Chris quickly, registering what seemed to be some surprise and something like resentment. She caught my attention and smiled wistfully. Then I lost them.

After many drinks, a delicious assortment of rare foods, wine, coffee, and cognac, those interested in literature were invited to listen to a young southern poet read from his works. I have never been comfortable with poetry, but with several others, including, of course, Michael, I gave it a try. The poet was apparently deeply immersed in his art, but he read in such an affected, wispy voice that I didn't understand two consecutive lines of his long poem that had, I gather, something to do with the migration of a mythical tribe of nomads. All I understood was that they were having a bad time of it. I stuck it out, however, as did several others, but I left at the end of the reading when Michael began a rather incoherent commentary on the work.

Recorded music was coming from one of the rooms I passed, alone— my date as well as Teddy's had remained with the literary-minded. The song was very popular at the time, and I suddenly identified it as a melody that Teddy sang, or tried to sing—he had absolutely no sense of key—in the shower. I had never been able to

memorize the lyrics, probably because Teddy had made such a hash ⌐
of the song, but it concerned two people dancing in darkness, search- |
ing for light and love.

I, too, looked, and the room was indeed quite dark. A couple was
dancing slowly, or moving to the music without much other pretense
at dancing. They were alone, in one another's arms, and I wasn't very
surprised when I recognized them.

I don't think they saw me.

8

THERE'S A GREAT DEAL that I didn't know. I didn't know what was
going on in the cabin on the lake when we weren't there, and I
couldn't get a clear impression of what was happening to Teddy,
though I had strong convictions. Once or twice I tried to bring the
subject up discreetly, but he turned away from it, refused even to
recognize it. What I did know was that night flying schedules, which
kept scheduled instructors at the main or nearby auxiliary field until
midnight, seemed to pair Michael and me for the same nights, while
Teddy would be free. And I knew that we had almost become house
guests at the cabin, sometimes spending as many as three nights a
week there. In fact in December we became paying guests.

When Teddy first brought the idea up, *before* the Hendersons were
introduced to local society, I resisted, but as usual his logic had all the
plausibility of simple, innocent facts, laced with what seemed to be a
generous impulse.

"The rent is pretty high, and I think Michael just manages. If we
each paid him a hundred bucks a month it would help him, and we'd
be paying our way."

"But you're out of your mind, Teddy. It's . . . it's monstrous.
We'd be moving in on a family, a newly married couple. It's an
outrageous intrusion."

"We're already there every week as it is. This would just help him
meet expenses."

"He'd never take it."

"I think he would if you asked him the right way."

"*I* ask him? *You* ask him. It's your idea."

"I think he'd take it better from you. You know him better than I do."

"Just what the hell do you have in mind, Teddy?"

"What do you mean?" He looked at me with such bland ingenuousness that I began to doubt the evidence I thought I had been collecting. But it was *before* the episode of two people dancing in the dark, and by then we were locked in. If I had suddenly declared that I was breaking the contract it would have been a melodramatic gesture that would probably have caused the crisis I was hoping to avoid. And candidly I was surprised when Michael agreed. I didn't know what had gone on in the cabin, how Chris had reacted, or whether she had argued against it.

But in December we became paying guests.

To begin with it was a careful arrangement according to which we would signal our intention to arrive at the cabin by an ingenious method. There was no telephone, but the landlord had left a rather old, quite sensitive radio. On the day of the party for the French, one of the officers, who had been a radio technician, informed us that with a small part and a minor adjustment, he could build into the old set the capability of receiving transmission on the frequency we used in our airplanes. He appeared later with the part—we never asked him where it came from—and performed the operation. With a flick of a switch we could hear all the aerial conversations in the immediate area, though not from the base, which was too far away for intelligible reception.

It was convenient for Michael. If he was late, he flew one circle over the cabin, the signal he was ready to transmit, and Chris would flip the switch. And it was convenient for us, particularly, I was finally convinced, for Teddy. Once or twice when I was in my airplane several miles from the cabin, I heard a deep voice coming through the afternoon air in garbled passion.

But in spite of a subtle increase in tension, those December evenings were no less pleasant, perhaps because of the flood of bourbon Teddy provided. We would have dinner in the cave before the fire, one of us would help Chris with the dishes, usually Teddy, and we would retire to the other fireplace in the upper room for another round of drinks. Chris drank almost nothing, but Michael may have been more sensitive than I realized then. At least his drinking increased,

and by nine-thirty he was virtually inarticulate; he would stagger off
to bed not fifteen feet from where we were sitting before the fire.
Sensing that I was not making much of a contribution, I would usually
go down to the lower bedroom an hour or so later to fall asleep hearing
the low vibrations of Teddy's voice above me.

I found Michael's blindness difficult to understand. But then it
occurred to me that he might well be quite aware of what was
happening, but was unable to come to a decision about what to do.
Teddy had an occult power of overcoming suspicion, of confronting
critics of his methods, both social and military, with benign indulgence, a declaration of amnesty usually charged with wit. Before a
complaint could be registered, he forgave your ill will, your presumption at finding fault. Gently, evasively he disarmed, castrated
his critics and they found themselves contrite before they had dared
criticism. During those evenings Michael seemed to be erecting a
barrier of alcohol to deaden his awareness. In the day, on the flight
line, away from the cabin, he was alert, responsive to his duties, and
an excellent flight instructor. At night, in our presence at least, he
took deep dives into bourbon.

And Chris. I saw the turbulence behind those almond eyes that
managed to smile when we arrived. But it seemed to me that she was
suffering not only from the fatigue of providing for three men, but
trying to make a decision that was becoming an agony.

We were planning a Christmas dinner, and Teddy was to provide
the turkey. He had an apparently infinite variety of resources for
locating exotic food and drink. Since, as instructors, we were en-
couraged to fly navigational missions to develop and retain our skills,
one weekend Teddy checked out an airplane, flew it to New York,
and returned with the baggage compartment and rear seat laden with
wines, liquors, caviar, and pâtés. When we had run out of red points,
and his source had dried up temporarily, he would go to the most
expensive restaurant in town, order four steak dinners, stipulating
that he wanted the steaks raw, and when they were placed before him,
he would wrap them in the napkins, pay the bill, and deliver them to
the cabin on the lake.

The turkey had already been delivered and other rare items selected
when Chris suddenly exploded our plans. Michael told me on the
flight line. She had decided that she wanted to spend Christmas with
her family in New York. He had put her on the train the night before.

Michael cooked the turkey, and he and I ate it. Teddy refused to come. I think he spent the evening with a grateful pedicurist in town. That evening I tried to think of some way of talking to Michael, of bringing up the subject of Teddy and Chris, delicately, and he would have been able to listen since he drank very little, nothing after dinner. But it was not in my social repertory to explain to a man that his wife was about to sleep, or was already sleeping, with another man.

Chris was gone three weeks, and for three weeks Teddy spoke scarcely a word when we were alone. To Michael on the flight line he was as polite and considerate as ever, but in the evenings he started on his bourbon and Cokes and deliberately shut himself away in a morose retreat—or he entertained the pedicurist.

When my delicate WASP sense of decency had been strained to the fracture, I finally opened up on him. "For God's sake, Teddy, why don't you play it fair?"

He looked at me, his eyes hard.

"Tell the man you love his wife. Since, I suppose, she has some ideas on the subject, she should have a chance to make a decision. Or is that why she went away? To decide?"

"We're just good friends," he said finally.

"You're lying, Teddy. You love the woman."

For the first time in the many years I had known him I had him pinned. He took a drink of his bourbon and looked away. "Yes," he said.

"Does she love you?"

"I think so. But she doesn't know yet."

"That doesn't sound like Chris to me."

"Michael is the only man she's ever . . . known. It's hard for her to decide."

"Anyway, I think you ought to tell him. It's the only decent thing to do." I was very strong on decency in those days.

He picked up his drink and walked over to the window that gave onto the company street. "Okay," he said finally.

"Tell him tomorrow."

"He's off duty tomorrow."

"Well, go out to the lake."

"All right," he growled and took a drink.

"And first fly over and tell him you're coming."

"All *right*."

I knew I had pushed him further than I had ever seen him pushed, and he wasn't familiar with it.

I had just landed with a student the following afternoon when I saw Teddy strap on a parachute and climb into his airplane, alone. A few minutes later he lifted off the field, his gear came up, and he left the pattern, turning south at about two thousand feet. Ostensibly he could have been going down to one of the auxiliary fields to check on a stage.

I was in the BOQ when he came up from the flight line about six o'clock and mixed himself a drink. He sat down without a word and drank off half the bourbon and Coke. "Come with me," he said after a moment.

"Why?"

"I need you."

I had never heard him make such an admission in his life. "I'd rather not. It seems to me to be a rather private affair."

"I need you," he repeated, and finished his drink.

For years after that moment I wondered what would have happened if I hadn't gone with him. I wondered whether he had cast me in a role necessary to a scene he had worked out, or with some cunning, instinctual perception he was simply accepting the cards he had been dealt and playing them with all the force available to him, one element of that force at the moment being me.

He suggested we eat before going down since there would probably be very little in the cabin. We had a couple more drinks and went to the Club. "What time did you say you'd be there?" I asked at dinner.

"I didn't say."

We drew up before the cabin around nine and parked behind the La Salle. Following our habit we went down by the side of the house, past a very diminished woodpile to the back and entered the kitchen.

A light was on in the cave and some dirty dishes had been left on the table, but there was no sign of Michael.

"Maybe he's gone to bed," I said, starting for the porch to go upstairs.

"Wait," Teddy said.

We waited for some time, drinking the cognac that Teddy had provided.

"I'm going to wake him," I said, rising, "before you change your mind."

"Wait," he said. "Wait until morning."

"Are you going to stay over?"

"We might as well. It's late."

There was no problem, of course. We had everything we needed, and a little after eleven-thirty we were in our beds in the lower bedroom. I must have fallen asleep almost immediately, but some time later I was awakened by a tug on my arm.

"What . . . ?"

His hand covered my mouth.

Then I heard what he intended me to hear, the squeak of bedsprings just over our heads, and the shuffle of feet moving stealthily across the floor. Other sounds followed, confused and inadvertent, then a voice said, "Oh, Michael . . ."

It was a woman's voice.

Some time later the front door opened and closed softly, and the La Salle started. When the sound of the tires died away Teddy returned to his bed.

A few minutes later he was snoring raggedly.

9

THE AT-6 CIRCLED SLOWLY in the twilight sky above the cabin and Chris dashed from the terrace where she, Michael, and I were standing looking out over the lake. A blast of static crackled from the radio inside, but there were only distant transmissions, not that bass growl we all expected. After a slow circle the airplane went out toward the west and began to descend, flying back toward the lake. It came down so low that it slipped out of sight and then burst into view again just above the tops of the pines on the other side, the howl of its wide-open engine growing louder each second. It slid down to the level of the water, coming directly at us, the propeller almost slicing the surface of the lake, leaving a trail of turbulence behind. I thought he had misjudged and was too low to pull up, but at the moment we could clearly distinguish the white oval of his face behind the windshield, he snapped up over the cabin, hammering us with a blast of sound and concussion, whipping the tops of the trees down toward the cabin roof.

Expressed through that contrivance of aluminum, steel, and fire that was now climbing into the eastern sky were rage, revenge, celebration, and decision.

"My *God*," Michael gasped, "he's going to kill himself."

"*No*," Chris cried out in anguish.

I saw Michael turn slowly to look at her, and I saw Chris avoid his eyes and walk to the edge of the terrace.

The La Salle had been suffering from a mysterious ailment, so I had driven Michael to the station in the Ford to pick Chris up. She had bought a brown gabardine suit in New York, tailored austerely to the lines of her slender body. The effect was urban sophistication that I had not associated with her. Before she smiled on the platform her eyes searched Michael's face, looking for something: a confirmation, a request, an answer. But on the drive to the lake conversation turned to domestic matters, the status of New York, of her family, and the condition of the household on the lake. Michael had spent the good part of a night cleaning, washing, and, I assumed, scouring away any traces of alien presence, a fugitive hairpin under the bed, or a stain of red on a cover or towel. And he had bought dinner supplies for the three of us. Teddy and Teddy's absence were not discussed.

Although they both urged me to stay over, almost as though they were terrified of being alone together, I returned to the base after dinner. Teddy was sitting on his bed with a glass in hand, staring at the opposite wall. I stood before him for a moment, but he didn't register my presence. "Well, you're a picture of fun," I said finally.

He took a drink, ignoring me.

"A couple of feet lower and we would all have been a bloody goulash."

"I thought of it," he said.

"If you have it in mind, would you choose a time when I'm not there?"

He didn't bother to answer, and I began undressing for bed. But Teddy always timed his questions. I was almost asleep when he said, "Did she ask about me?"

"No." I felt that I had the privilege of some small revenge, so I left it at that for several minutes. "But they wondered if we'd be there for dinner on Sunday."

"They? Both of them?"

"That was the way it came out. I'm not going."

"But you've *got* to go."

"Why?" I said, rolling over to look at him.

"I can't go alone."

"Why not? I'm not involved in this shoddy business." But I was, I realized.

"Just this time. Afterward maybe we can work it out."

I went, and nothing was worked out. The three of them continued to live through a period of passionate indecision that extended for weeks, with my presence demanded. It was like being chained to a seat in the Grand Guignol.

Chris and I were alone one afternoon, and that was unusual. With spring arriving Teddy had bought a metal speedboat in which we explored the lake and the other side on the days when the sun began to warm Alabama again. Michael knew something about motors and was adjusting the engine while Teddy watched, a Chesterfield hanging from his lips.

"Chris," I began, as we sat on the terrace in sunlight, "why don't you . . . ?"

But she shook her head in torture to interrupt me. "Don't, *don't*," she wailed.

"But I can't come out any longer. It's . . ."

"Oh, *please*, Matt. It won't be the same without you. We *need* you."

Teddy needed me, Chris needed me. I didn't ask if Michael needed me. I knew I was being used, that without me the triangular balance that I was witness to would be destroyed. They *had* to have a witness. I had the sense that all three of them were waiting for an incident that would finally explode and destroy that precarious balance. They were all suffering. Michael was retreating into an alcoholic stupor every evening, and Chris was losing her lovely grace and spontaneity. Her eyes were clouded with a fatigue that had nothing to do with the physical exertion the cabin demanded. The atmosphere had become much too heavy, too thick for survival.

Chris rose suddenly and looked down at the speedboat. "What are they *doing*?"

I glanced down. Teddy had removed his tunic, shoes, and socks, and rolled his regulation pinks up to his knees. He was wading in the shallow water behind the boat, pushing something that I recognized.

The man who had sold the boat had thrown in an aquaplane—I don't think water skis existed at the time—and Teddy was attaching the line to the stern and playing it out.

"He's not going to . . . ?" Chris began and started down the path. I followed. The engine was going, and Michael had cast off when we arrived at the water's edge. Teddy was clinging to the sling at the end of the line, trying to balance himself on the aquaplane.

"Teddy!" Chris called. "Don't . . ."

But the engine began to increase RPMs and the boat maneuvered out slowly, taking up slack in the line.

"At least wear a life jacket!" Chris called out.

But if they heard her they ignored her. They were engaged in a jagged complicity, a grotesque challenge that made no sense.

Teddy Arnheim was the most unathletic man I have ever known. I had never seen him play baseball, handball, volleyball, tennis, golf, ride a horse, or ski. The world of sports bored him utterly. But there was some amazing, nervous agility in that slender body that, *a priori*, defied experience. When the tension on the line tightened he was almost sitting on the board in an absurd preparation for physical forces that he could have known only by reason. The aquaplane picked up speed, and I started stripping off my uniform to go after him when he fell, but in some remarkable display of balance, a ludicrous, clownish figure, he clung to the sling in a grotesque squat, already moving beyond my ability to reach him in time if he fell.

At the wheel of the boat Michael did not look back as he gunned the motor, steering for the center of the lake where he began turning, leisurely at first, and then in sharper, more vicious angles, crossing his own wake, never glancing toward the stern or at the man he was whipping across the water with a vengeance he perhaps did not understand. Clinging like a demented monkey, Teddy certainly knew that if he spilled, Michael would neither have stopped nor tried to rescue him. It was a homicidal display, as though Michael were trying to shake himself free of an immense weight pursuing him.

Chris grabbed my arm and buried her face in my shoulder, but suddenly she pushed me away and screamed at the lake, "That's *enough,* Michael!"

He couldn't have heard her, but he knew from the straining motor that Teddy was still there, performing outrageous feats of balance and recovery. He throttled back and turned in toward the pier, gunning the motor once more as he whipped past, to swing in a ferocious arc toward the banks, and as Teddy released the sling and fell backward into the water, the boat turned out once more toward the open lake, throttle opened to the stop.

Chris and I ran down together to rescue him, still in water over his head, but with that astonishing capacity for survival in elements that were totally foreign to him, he had managed to capture the aquaplane, and, paddling awkwardly, he floated into shallow water. We pulled him up the slippery bank to one of the boulders where he fell into sunlight, panting from exhaustion and trembling in uncontrollable spasms. But as he looked at Chris kneeling before him and clutching one of his hands, I saw a synthesis in eyes and mouth that I had never seen before. It had been an adolescent display, an acceptance of a challenge, or perhaps a voluntary expedition into peril, but he was proud of what he had accomplished for her, as though he had slaughtered the dragon and was saluting her with a bloody lance.

"You're absolutely *crazy*," Chris repeated, crying and laughing while the whine of the motorboat receded. "That was the maddest thing I've ever seen."

I turned away. I didn't want to see it. I saw Michael, far out on the lake, the boat cutting a furrow through the placid water.

When I looked back at Teddy and Chris, he was standing, extracting damp wads of currency from his pockets and laying them on the boulder to dry: tens, fifties, hundreds, in sodden rolls, the thousand or two thousand dollars he normally carried with him. He tried to flatten them out, but gave up.

Chris took him by the arm. "Come up and strip those clothes off, you dreadful man, before you die of pneumonia." And I was left with a couple of thousand dollars drying ineffectually in the sun and the defeated husband raging wildly up and down the lake.

It was oppressively clear later that what had happened could not be dismissed as clean fun. We all knew it as we sat before the upper fireplace, Teddy draped in a heavy bathrobe belonging to Michael, his filthy uniform drying, all of us drinking with a purpose, even Chris, who was taking gulps of scotch on the rocks as though she had just discovered the delights of alcohol. Some early attempts at humor about Teddy's aquatic skills had failed, and Chris's scolding both Teddy and Michael had become grotesque. She gave up and left the room to go down to the kitchen. "I'll start dinner."

We stayed before the fire, the three of us, sipping our drinks while I tried to think of something that could serve as the subject of a casual conversation, but nothing came. Neither Teddy nor Michael tried, and the silence threatened to destroy what little coherence was left to the day. Finally Teddy rose, felt his trousers and shirt, and carried them downstairs to dress. I had forgotten to return to him the wad of bills that I had retrieved from the boulder. With Teddy gone Michael roused himself enough to stir the fire with the poker, and to reach over to the wood basket, but he came up with a single, slender log.

I don't know why I volunteered to go out for more, unless it was a reaction to the profound silence from the lower floor, the total absence of kitchen noises.

"No, no," Michael said, picking up the basket. "I'll get it." And he went out the front door.

For some time I heard nothing, either from the woodpile outside or from the kitchen. Then sounds of logs being dropped heavily into the basket came from the side of the house, and a few moments later Michael opened the front door carrying the full basket. His face was blank. He stared at me as though he had forgotten what his load was for. Then he carried it to the fireplace, set it down, and studied the dying flames for a moment, apparently trying to bring the two concepts, fire and fuel, together. Reaching down, he picked up a log, seemed to weigh it, and dropped it on the fire. He performed the same deliberate actions with two more logs and turned suddenly, considerably soberer, to walk to the stairs.

What he had seen through the kitchen window I never knew, but his determination as he started down the stairs seemed threatening. *"Michael,"* I said, but he didn't stop. I rose quickly and followed him.

I wish I hadn't. I wish I had left them, the three of them, to settle their wretched problems without me. I don't like scenes.

The scene I came onto was not the violence I had feared. Michael could scarcely have caught them in what lawyers call the blazing crime, or *flagrante delicto*. After he had seen whatever he had seen through the window they must have known he was there from the sounds in the woodpile, and it was impossible to come down the stairs stealthily.

They performed a perfect triangle. Chris with her back to the sink, Teddy, his back to the bedroom, and Michael in the middle of the kitchen, saying, ". . . and if not, I don't know what you think I am, to be cajoled and cuckolded, cuckolded and cajoled. By Christ, you might have had better taste, at least. I kept thinking you'd have better taste." He was looking at Chris, but I'm not sure whom he was addressing. "And after three years, your timing is superb. There must be an amazing liberation in marriage, a convention I never believed in anyway. And you knew that. So, as I said, I think you should come to some decision, make up your mind."

There were tears on Chris's cheeks, but she was controlling herself. Teddy's face was mysterious, grieved, no doubt, but expressing relief as well.

"I've made up my mind," Chris said firmly.

"Well, are we permitted to hear what your made-up mind is?"

"I'll go with Teddy," she said, still speaking firmly, though clearly she was close to breaking.

"Well, I suppose that choice offers certain dividends."

"*Michael.*"

Teddy said nothing.

"But you needn't go anywhere because I'll save you that trouble." He walked out of the kitchen and climbed the stairs, and we heard him in the bedroom above moving about, rattling hangers.

Teddy went over to Chris and stood before her, not touching her, and she began to cry, really to cry, turning away to bend over the sink as though she were going to be sick.

Above, Michael left the bedroom, went out the front door, and after several trials managed to start the La Salle. I thought at the time how awkward it would have been if the La Salle had refused to start. Some comedy in a melodrama.

When the La Salle left the driveway I went upstairs again. The logs Michael had added were smouldering but not burning. With the poker I manipulated them until they caught.

In any army that I know about it is considered bad form to meddle with a fellow officer's wife. In the past it has led to courts martial, duels, and justified homicide. It was considered bad form during World War II also, but the results were not so openly dramatic. One result in the case of Michael and Chris was divorce, rapid and uncomplicated since Alabama divorce laws were very liberal. Another result was Michael's being transferred out into a bomber squadron. I'll never know whether he used his personal problems as persuasion, but I suspect he did, perhaps, but not certainly, naming the correspondent. He was out in two weeks and that was phenomenal since the Training Command did not like to lose experienced instructors, particularly experienced instructors who spoke French. But Michael went into B-24s, was shipped to England, and, I found out much later, was killed over France with his entire crew on his third mission.

The final result was that Teddy was also transferred out, but not until after he took a week's leave to follow Chris to New York. I didn't know what happened in New York, but he returned grim, silent, and, I decided, nearly suicidal. He left in the monster two days later for training in P-38s at Lashkam Field, and I didn't see him again until . . .

The P-38, east of the field now, climbed, still inverted, and slowly rolled over to a normal flying attitude. Gaining airspeed, it swept south, and rose into the brilliance of the western sky.

10

WHEN THE WAR ENDED I was still in the Training Command, although not in the Frog Squadron, which had been permitted to languish as the supply of French dwindled, but as an instructor in twin-engined bombers in Texas. Before then, however, I became squadron commander of the Frog Squadron and a captain, living alone in the BOQ. I had no consistent source of information on Teddy's career since he never wrote letters, but almost a year after he left the local paper carried an article reporting that he had been shot down over Europe. They treated him as a local hero, describing him as that admirable young Major Arnheim who had so delighted the town's society, and whose death would be grieved by all. I confess the news shocked me, but the assumption that he was dead seemed to me rather premature. I could not believe he was dead. He had too much instinctual competence. Since I was no longer seeing my date, I didn't know how profound the grief was, but if I had spent many hours trying to find an adjective to describe Teddy I don't think I would have ever come up with "admirable."

Just before I left for Texas I received a letter from New York, written by a Princeton classmate who was in one of the federal agencies, containing more information. Teddy *had* been shot down, but after hiding in the French countryside for a month, he had been picked up by an advance armored column. It was, the classmate added, some reassurance to the financial community, which had audibly hiccuped at the news of his death.

Then the war ended in Europe, and later, in the Pacific, and I left the service as soon as I could get out and caught a train to New York. I was almost five years older, my mother had died, and my two sisters had followed their husbands to various parts of the country. I was quite alone. After an intensive search I found an apartment on upper Lexington Avenue and decided I had better take some refresher courses in the law. I registered at NYU.

It was a common experience to seem much older than the glut of students who threatened to swamp American campuses after the war. And the law seemed to have changed. While taking my degree at Columbia before the war I had been inclined to go into trial law, but now the young men and women I associated with impressed me as much stronger and more aggressive than I remembered myself as being, and I decided on something more sedate: corporate law.

Quite apparently something more than the effects of five additional years had had a decisive impact on me. The tranquil world I had been reared in had been shattered, or perhaps more accurately, that tranquil world had been an illusion, had never really existed, and I was thrust out into a reality that I had never been prepared for. I had not, as example, really even been aware of the great disaster of 1929 until I read about it in college. At the time the only change that had registered on my insulated brain was the loss of a summer friend, Ronald, the son of our gardener, Walter, at Watermill. Always respectful though never servile, Ronald had given me some exposure to the other version of American life of the thirties.

Tired of the beach or of sailing my sloop, I sometimes tagged after Ronald and his father as they tended the gardens, mowed, clipped, transplanted, and fed various flowers and shrubs. Ronald was two years older than I chronologically, many years older in experience and awareness, and I considered him a genius. I still suspect that with education he could have become a successful engineer, or even a physicist since he was not only intelligent in practical problems but very creative as well. If a large limb had to be removed without destroying the garden below, Ronald arranged an intricate web of ropes that swung the limb out and caught it before it plunged to the destruction of hyacinths. If a whole tree had to come down, he would notch it, and with some bravado, plant a stake in the ground a certain distance from the tree, wait until the breeze satisfied him before he started sawing, and when the tree fell it would drive his stake into the ground. Ronald's skills extended to almost any emergency: electrical, plumbing, carpentry. When I was twelve he built me a small automobile from an old lawn mower motor, lumber, and some discarded cart wheels. It actually ran, very well. Until my mother objected to the noise.

Sometimes while he worked Ronald talked about his life. He was never lurid, but I sensed restraint. It was a strange and meager life to my ears. His father was forced to follow the seasons: summers with us and winters in the South, picking up whatever he could find. It was only much later that the question occurred to me: what would Ronald have accomplished if he had had my opportunities?

Then one summer, it must have been around 1934, he wasn't there, and when I asked Walter what had happened, he said, "He joined the army, Master Matthew."

I saw Ronald once more.

When I volunteered for the Air Corps, such a rich and unprecedented flow of manpower was made available to the military that they were totally unable to cope with it. In specialized services like the Air Corps particularly, a six months' wait was not unusual. When my orders finally arrived they directed me to report to Fort Dix, that vast maw that swallowed up draftees, volunteers, and a few regular army enlisted men who had put in for special training.

I arrived in a Brooks Brothers' jacket, blue button-down shirt, gray flannels, and loafers. I often wondered how Teddy arrived. Probably in a limousine driven by a chauffeur.

In the general confusion no uniforms were available to us immediately, and what was designated as a platoon, of which I was a bewildered member, spent the day picking up cigarette butts on the company street, to the amusement of the veterans of one week in uniform. After this soldiering we retired to cots in a vast barn of a barracks, and at five o'clock the next morning, before the recorded bugle of reveille had died away, the door burst open and a great, not entirely sober sergeant entered and bellowed, "All right, youse assholes, drop your cocks and pick up your socks."

Later that morning we were herded to a quartermaster warehouse, told to strip and form a line. I followed an interminable column of white buttocks past desks where PFCs and corporals were taking information and checking ledgers. In the remote distance men were drawing on uniforms to become soldiers.

Behind me a door opened, and apparently someone of authority began walking down the line of desks since the clerks in uniform suddenly betrayed signs of military training. Just as the corporal behind the desk in front of me barked out, "Name!" the sleeve of a master sergeant appeared at his shoulder. I was about to answer when a shocked voice exclaimed, "Why, Master *Matthew*!"

Naked, blanched, shriveling, deprived of rank, class, caste, I was standing before a furiously blushing Ronald.

Certainly my military episode inflicted no traumas on me. Though exposed to certain hazards from long hours in the air, I had still seen no blood, no fighting, had experienced none of that despair of men flying missions over France and Germany, knowing that if they made it back to the base once more, the next mission was already scheduled.

But the world I returned to was foreign, slightly archaic. My social life was vastly reduced. The friends I had had before the war impressed me as vaguely fossilized, clinging to traditions that had disappeared. I made a few new friends, some women, none of them very interesting but endowed with other attributes that in my deliberate way I required. And eventually I found a position in an old and conservative firm. The fact that my name was Matthew Howard did not make it more difficult to find a job. With extreme prudence I could have lived without a job, and the salary I started with did not alter my economic status perceptibly.

I heard nothing from Teddy and expected to hear nothing.

I had been in the firm for six months when in my morning mail I received a plain white envelope without a return address, mailed in the city. After reading the important mail, I almost dropped it in the basket, but opened it to discover a clipping from the society section of the *New York Times* announcing the marriage of the former Christine Henderson to an assistant professor of sociology at Columbia University. There was no other information. It was a mystery. The only person who could have sent it was Chris herself, and such a gesture was totally unlike her. If she knew my address and wanted to see me, why hadn't she enclosed a note or called?

I did nothing about it for several days, but every time I opened the drawer of my desk it was there. Finally I asked the secretary to call Columbia for her husband's home address and number. It was on the Upper West Side on Riverside Drive.

For several days again I did nothing. But one afternoon when I opened the drawer and saw the number attached to the clipping I picked up the telephone and dialed. Chris came on after the third ring.

"Chris, it's Matt. Matt Howard."

"Oh, *Matt*. How dear of you to call. How did you get my number?"

"From the clipping you sent."

"What clipping?"

"About your marriage."

She hesitated. "I didn't send you the clipping. But, Matt, I'd love to see you. Can you come to dinner?"

"I'd like to. When?"

"Uh, let's see. Friday?"

"Fine."

"Would you like to bring someone? Are you married?"

"No, to both questions."

"Lovely. And could you come a little early? Around five-thirty?"

"I'll try."

"Wonderful. You have the address?"

"Yes."

"I'm *so* glad you called, Matt. I'll see you Friday."

I hung up. There was only one other person who could have sent the clipping. I had the sense I was being manipulated again.

It was another autumn when I left the subway at 110th Street and walked west to Riverside Drive to turn uptown a couple of blocks. The trees in Riverside Park were brilliant in golds and reds, and the usual wind was blowing off the Hudson. The building was one of those beautiful old town houses that had been converted into apartments, and Chris was on the fourth floor. When she opened the door and stood for a moment looking at me I thought, my God, I really love this woman. I've always loved her. Even with all the mess we lived through I've always loved her in my way.

She threw herself into my arms and kissed me on the cheek. "Matt, it's *so* good to see you. I really *wanted* to see you." She moved back and looked at me again. "Do you realize this is the first time I've seen you out of uniform? You look very prosperous and proper.''

"Always proper, never prosperous.''

She had regained that early radiance that I associated with her. Her hairstyle had not changed. She was wearing a short jacket of green velour with a high neck, and tan slacks molded to her body, casually alluring. Her eyes were the eyes of a happy young woman.

She took my arm and led me down a short hall into a room with windows overlooking the Hudson, not a very large room, but furnished comfortably with rather worn furniture. Two of the walls were lined with books. She stepped back to look at me again.

"Did I ever tell you that you are a very handsome man, Matt?''

"No, you never told me that.''

"You are. And you look just fine. You really belong in New York. You never belonged in Alabama.''

"Did any of us?''

"No, I suppose not. I always felt like a stranger. Sit down. I'll get you a drink. What would you like? I'm afraid I don't have any Cokes.'' There was some pathos in her smile.

"If I live to the age of ninety-three I don't believe I will ever drink another Coke. Scotch?''

"Water or soda?''

"Soda, please.''

She went down the hall to the right where she began to make sounds with ice cubes.

It was a pleasant room—piano, a potted plant with broad fronds, a photograph of a young man, blond, with horn-rimmed glasses, a piece of sculpture in clay, an elongated torse that looked a little like a Giacometti. And hundreds of books.

She came back with a tray, my scotch, and a bottle of sherry, and sat on the large ottoman before my Morris chair. "Cheers.''

"Cheers. Did you do the torse?''

She turned to look at it. "Yes. I've started again. I'm taking a class at Columbia.''

"It's good. I didn't know you sculpted.''

"There wasn't much chance during the war.''

I decided I was going to be perfectly candid. "Chris, I was very sorry to hear about Michael.''

She nodded and looked down. "Yes. Poor baby. I just hope it went fast. That he didn't suffer.'' She looked up at me again. "It wasn't easy for me. For a long time. I felt . . .''

"I understand. We don't have to talk about it. I just wanted to say it. And in no conceivable way can you feel responsible."

"It's generous of you, Matt, but . . . if you put it in its simplest terms you have to admit that if this hadn't happened, that wouldn't have happened, and if that had happened this wouldn't have happened."

"But you're simply describing life. If you put it like that, I can remember a moment in the briefing room when Michael asked me to dinner for the first time, and I. . . . Can you talk about everything?"

"Of course. That's why I wanted you to come early before Tony finishes his class. What did you say when Michael asked you to dinner?"

"I suggested he invite Teddy, too. Outrageous. But I was involved, too."

"Yes, he told me. But that was understandable. You were roommates, and probably it would have happened anyway."

"I'm not sure of that." I took another drink of the scotch. "Tell me, Chris, did you know I was in New York now?"

"Of course. I saw you in the phone book. You live on Lex."

"Then why didn't you call? Or . . . that's a silly question. You probably didn't want to call."

"Oh, I *did*," she said, her eyes flashing suddenly. "I wanted very much to call, but I thought that you might not have wanted to see me."

"In the name of God, why *not*?"

She looked directly into my eyes. "Because of what happened."

"But Chris, I'm not a prig . . . or, perhaps I was then."

"And you know who sent you the clipping?"

"I have a pretty good idea now. He hasn't . . .?"

"No." She looked at me again in that singularly direct manner that had so charmed me in Alabama. "You don't know what happened, do you?"

"No. I haven't talked to Teddy since he returned to Elmore Field from New York, and he wasn't precisely in a talking mood."

"Do you *want* to know?"

"Oh, yes." She sipped at her sherry. "You've met his father and mother, haven't you?"

"Yes."

"And you know the place in Collincourt?"

"Yes, I've been there several times."

"Then I don't have to describe it to you. I don't think I could, anyway. I was invited to spend the weekend."

"When was this?"

"When I left Alabama, after the divorce. I stayed in a hotel here in town. I didn't feel like seeing my family, and Teddy made reservations for me at the Roosevelt. He apologized because it wasn't the Carlyle or the Waldorf. I realized that he didn't want to be seen. We had a lovely week together, but he told me we'd have to go out to Collincourt for the weekend, and I agreed. It was perfectly normal, I thought, to meet his parents. You know, the prospective bride and all those Old World courtesies that you were brought up with." Holding her glass in both hands she swiveled on the ottoman and looked at the sunlight streaming through the windows. Her face was golden. "But in the week we were in the city I had a strange sense that someone was watching us, following us."

"Who?"

"I didn't know. Someone. At first I thought it might be the vice squad preparing to break down the door in the middle of the night. I didn't mention it to Teddy because I was sure he'd think I was a hysterical female. As it turned out, someone was following us. Or me."

"*Who?*"

She turned back to look at me, a tentative smile on her lips. "I have to tell you something that will surprise you probably. When I was in Alabama I was a member of the Communist Party."

"My God!" I set my glass on the table.

"Oh, I've shocked you, haven't I, Matt?"

"Uh . . . yes, a little. I had no idea that you were involved in any kind of politics."

"Involved is a little strong. Do you remember that story I told, about asking the poor old Negro directions?"

She had been driving along a cotton patch, according to her story then, and had stopped to ask a black cotton picker the way to an antique shop she had heard about. He not only did not reply, but he started walking rapidly, almost running away from her.

"Yes."

"What an innocent I was. Or what an idiot. I was trying to find an organizer who was working with the sharecroppers. I had been given his name."

"But how did you ever get mixed up in all that?"

Her smile was benevolent, as though she was talking to a slightly retarded child. "In college I joined the YCL, the Young Communists' League. It was during the final years of the Spanish War, Hitler, Mussolini, and all that rottenness."

"Did Michael know?"

"Certainly."

"And did you tell Teddy?"

"Of course. He thought it was funny." She looked at me, the smile arch now. "He even offered to join himself if I insisted."

"Teddy?" I must have almost shouted since she doubled over in laughter, clutching her glass in her lap.

"Oh, Matt, what an innocent you are. You surely realize that it wasn't out of any profound political convictions."

"But you're not . . . still . . . ?"

"Oh, no," she said rising to pour another glass of sherry. "I'm no longer even political. But can you guess now who was following me? Because somebody *was* following me." She returned to the ottoman.

"I think I understand. The Old Man had you researched."

"Exactly. He was collecting his ammunition. And by the time I arrived at Collincourt he had all his guns cocked. He knew that his son was living in sin with a vile traitor, or traitress." She sipped from her glass and glanced at her watch. "Well, we drove out to Collincourt, and of course I was staggered. I expected something big and luxurious, but I wasn't prepared. I don't have to tell you. The size of the place, all those poor little maids and the butlers and servants, even at the height of the war. I think the maid who unpacked my bag was appalled. I didn't really have the right clothes. I was alone for the first two hours while Teddy must have been taking the first round from his father. And something very funny happened. I finally went downstairs and out into one of the gardens. I was admiring the flowers—I remember some enormous dahlias—when a pathetic, fat little old lady came up to me, and I thought it was one of the staff, from the kitchen probably."

"His mother."

"She looked at me for a moment, said something in German, took me in her arms and kissed me. That poor, sweet, old lady." Chris looked down at her glass and shook her head. "What a horrible, horrible life. I really don't know how she has survived. Then at seven I was dressed in the only thing I had and summoned to the . . . I guess it was a drawing room, for sherry. There he was, that vile, monstrous old man, and Teddy's mother beaming with a kind of suffering, cowlike, maternal affection. And Teddy, whom I hadn't seen since we arrived, looking frightened. I had never seen him so miserable. He came over and took me by the arm to lead me to his parents, and it was like the last mile. His mother first, and she kissed me again and spoke in German. Then his father. I have never had such an instantaneous detestation for another human being in my life. Those beady little eyes raked at me with hate. He didn't offer his hand and he didn't say anything. He bowed. Like Eric von Stroheim. Then the butler served sherry on a tray. My God! I never needed a real drink so badly in my life. I could have sloshed down a pint of bourbon and Coke. But we were offered sherry, and only sherry, one tiny glass.'' She rose again to go to the sideboard where the sherry bottle sat.

When she came back she started to take my empty glass. ''I'll wait,'' I said.

When she was sitting before me once more she said, ''His mother tried to talk to me, but her English was so weak Teddy had to help. His father said nothing. He simply stared. Half an hour for one glass of sherry, and we went into the dining room. You've seen it?''

I nodded. I remembered it as immense.

''We sat at that table ten miles long, his father at one end, glaring at me, his mother at the other, Teddy opposite me. Then his father began asking questions. It was absolutely incredible! An inquisition. He started asking me where I lived, who my parents were, and where I had gone to college. He said nothing about Michael, but he was quite openly appraising me, my pedigree, like a prize bitch. And, of course, I didn't realize then that he knew everything. *Everything*. He knew my father was a doctor, my mother came from Maine, and that I had a sister. He probably even knew what my grades in college were. And, of course, he knew all about my political past. My God, I needed help, but Teddy didn't give me any help. He sat there like a punished child, his eyes down, his face white, while that . . . orangutan tortured me. Something happened to me during that dinner, something unfair. By the time we had finished I had made up my mind that Teddy had to be rescued. But I was also trying to decide how I could get away after dinner. We were supposed to leave after lunch on Sunday, but I knew that if I stayed I would do something dreadful.'' She glanced at her watch again.

"Does your husband know all this?"

"Of course. Oh, you thought I asked you to come early so I could tell you all this in secret. Oh, Matt, you're still thinking of me in Alabama terms."

"No, I don't think of you like that, but . . . I'm sorry, Chris, I think I *would* like another drink."

She took my glass and disappeared down the hall, and I went over to the windows. The sun was a few inches from the western horizon, composing a world of bronze buffeted by the Hudson wind that shook the old windows in their casements. There were whitecaps on the surface of the ebbing river. I didn't want to hear the rest of Chris's story, but I knew I would.

She came up behind me with my glass. "I like your apartment," I said.

"We were lucky, but it took months to find. University housing is limited, mainly for professors and associate professors. Tony doesn't have tenure yet."

I went back to the old Morris chair. "Did you get away?"

"No, of course not." She sat before me again. "After dinner we had coffee and cognac in the living room before the fire, but as soon as I could I escaped to my room. I kept hoping Teddy would come to me later, but I was almost certain he wouldn't. I was sure that every maid in the house was a spy.

"The next morning I went down and wandered around that enormous house until one of the maids directed me to a smaller dining room where breakfast was waiting. No one was there, but it was like walking into one of those old English films, the sideboard covered with eggs, bacon, ham, muffins, and so on, and a small table with two places set. As soon as I sat down a maid appeared with coffee. About twenty minutes later Teddy came down, looking as though he hadn't even been to bed. He kissed me, but he was withdrawn, nervous, and terribly apologetic."

"*Apologetic*? I've never heard him apologize in his life."

"He *was*. He tried to excuse his father with some explanation I don't remember, but I told him I wanted to leave. He said it was impossible until after lunch. I threatened to pack my bag and hitchhike back, but he pleaded with me to stay, and finally, because he was suffering . . . and I loved him, I did.

"I have only one pleasant memory of that weekend, and that's mixed with pathos and comedy. After breakfast Teddy took me out to show me the grounds. My God! I don't know how many acres there were.''

"About a hundred and eighty, I think.''

"And the stable! Have you seen the stable?''

"A long time ago.''

"I've done a lot of riding. In fact I used to teach riding in Maine. There was an absolutely magnificent chestnut gelding, a five-year-old, that I was mad to ride. Teddy found some jodphurs and boots for me, and when he came back he was in boots and breeches . . .''

"Teddy?"

"Wait, The groom wasn't happy about letting me on the gelding since he hadn't been exercised for some time. While I was reassuring him Teddy arrived, and I saw the man's eyes open and then his mouth. He forgot about me and just stood there gaping at Teddy. I suppose I should have understood, but I couldn't imagine having a stable of eight or ten horses and not riding them. Teddy spoke to him quietly, and I heard the groom say, "But, Master Theodore," but Teddy spoke again, and the groom went into the stable. The stable boy was holding the gelding while I checked my saddle. When I looked around the groom was leading out a monstrous, maternal, black mare. I was too busy with the gelding to see Teddy mount. He, the gelding that is, was frisky, and he tried to throw me. It took me a few minutes to convince him he couldn't, and by then we were both ready to go. I glanced around at Teddy mounted on that great black mare and asked him if he was ready, and he nodded like a marionette. I held the gelding to a walk first, and then let him trot before letting him out. *God,* he was a magnificent animal. He went across the meadow in a dead run, and I could sense his ecstasy. I let him run until he got rid of some of his juice and pulled him in to a walk. Then I looked back. Oh, God, Matt, you should have seen him.'' Clutching her glass, she bent over the ottoman laughing hysterically. When she raised her head, tears were running down her cheeks. "I have never seen anything so funny, so ridiculous, so . . . noble and brave and foolish in my life. Not since the aquaplane. That lovely old mare was giving it the main chance. She was *calumping* across the meadow like a monstrous black phantom, and *Teddy,''* she screeched, "Teddy was just as game. He had one hand firmly under the pommel and the other under the cantle. He had lost the reins and stirrups, and his legs were flying about like an eggbeater. But he *stuck*. It was pure will, tenacity, strength, but he *stuck*. I was terrified, but I couldn't help laughing.

"When he was fifty feet or so away I took the gelding back into a trot so the mare wouldn't stop suddenly and throw Teddy over her head. They came up to us, and I shouldered the gelding into the mare to stop her. The poor old dear was heaving and lathering, and Teddy was ashen. I couldn't resist putting my arm around him and kissing him.

"All the rest was torture. That *luncheon*. I finally exploded. When the old beast started on me again I tried to control myself, but finally I exploded. I think I did it with some dignity. At least Teddy told me I did. I put my fork down quietly and said that though I was his guest I was not accustomed to being treated like a criminal under interrogation. He leapt on the word 'criminal.' I don't remember the exact words, but to the effect that that was exactly what I was. A criminal, trying to destroy the country, trying to seduce his son, to . . . oh, God, I don't know what else. And, of course, I finally realized that he had had me thoroughly investigated, and I accused him of it. He started shouting that it was his patriotic duty to unmask the country's enemies. He rose from his chair, his face crimson, Mrs. Arnheim was sobbing, Teddy was pallid, and I was trembling with rage. And *then* he accused me of luring Teddy because of the money. Teddy tried to object, but the old man stabbed at him with a hideous, gnarled finger, shouting that if he married me he would be a pauper, or beggar, I think he said. I was sure he was going to have apoplexy. He bundled his napkin up, threw it on his plate, and stalked out."

She rose and wandered listlessly around the room with her glass of sherry, stopping to feel the earth of the potted plant. "It was all downhill after that. Teddy took me back to the city, but returned to Collincourt that evening." She looked back at me. "He was . . . abject, Matt. I told him very simply that I wouldn't marry him unless he cut himself away. It was a monstrous thing to ask, I know. He was with me almost every night, and he struggled for hours. He never came out and said what I think he had in mind: 'The Old Man will die soon, and I'll be the boss.' He never said it, but I'm sure he was thinking it, and it frightened me, enraged me, sickened me. He had to leave on Sunday to get back to Alabama, and we fought it out Saturday evening. Fought isn't really the right word. We suffered. I told him over and over I would not marry him if he didn't declare his independence from his father. He wept, *cried*, Matt.''

I shook my head. I wasn't able to imagine it. If it hadn't been Chris I wouldn't have believed it.

''But some time after midnight on Saturday he picked up his bag and went to the door. He . . .''

Sounds of a key in the apartment door came from the hall, and then an opening and shutting. ''Chris?''

She put her glass on the table and ran down the hall. A moment later she led in her husband, rather small, about Teddy's height, with straight blond hair and horn-rimmed glasses. Agile, nervous, smiling.

I liked him. He was intelligent, sensitive, and obviously he loved Chris. And the dinner was good.

I invited them to dinner the following week. We saw one another quite often.

11

ON A BLEAK FEBRUARY MORNING two years later the *Times* carried the news of the death of Theodore Arnheim of Arnheim Industries, aged eighty-six. The obit was guarded but reverent. Arnheim Industries had made a major contribution during the war, but, the sketch implied, had also benefited substantially. It was the traditional Horatio Alger legend: a fragment of Europe tossed onto American shores where hard work, sacrifice, acumen (read cunning), and energy had led to spectacular success. The sole survivors were the widow and the son, Theodore Arnheim II. Funeral private. I hesitated over it long enough to speculate on what would happen now. Would Teddy take over or sell? It was a world I knew something about professionally, but in reality I was remote from it.

Almost exactly a month later the secretary buzzed me, and when I responded a very professional secretarial voice said, ''Mr. Howard?''

''Yes.''

''Mr. Arnheim calling.''

After a moment of circuitry Teddy came on. ''Howard?''

"How are you, Teddy? Sorry to hear . . ."

"Howard, I'd like to see you. Can you come over on Friday?"

"Yes, I guess so. How . . . ?"

"Bring some shit for a weekend. I'll have a car pick you up at five."

"All right."

Click.

Then I remembered I had a date Saturday, and started to call back, but the Arnheim current had begun to surge again. I called the date instead.

When I thought about it during the week I assumed that he had not recovered from Chris and intended to enlist my help in reentering her life. I made a resolution that I would not be a party to any such subversion. Another thought came that had brighter possibilities. He might have business that my firm could share with the Arnheim legal department, an opportunity that would presumably do me no harm. But a weekend at the Collincourt I had known did not promise much indulgence, though this would be a new Collincourt, and a new host. In a prewar habit when I packed my bag Friday morning to take it to the office I automatically included a dinner jacket.

The car that picked me up was a black Cadillac about forty feet long that ran down the West Side Highway to the Holland Tunnel and crossed under that tax shelter, the Hudson River, since Arnheim Industries was in Newark. I had never seen Arnheim Industries before. It was in a shabby part of Newark, and the building was old, unprepossessing, though very large. We went through a guarded gate, and stopped before a door, where the chauffeur informed me that Mr. Arnheim would be down presently and disappeared.

Ten minutes later a figure that I at first didn't recognize appeared in the shadowed light: a pin-striped suit that was Jacques Bellini or something just as rich, a stiff-collared white shirt with a modest tie, a Homburg, carrying a chesterfield coat and briefcase. The chauffeur opened the door, and Teddy sat beside me, offering his hand. But the handshake was just as perfunctory as ever.

"How are you, Howard?" he said casually, as though we had just come from the flight line.

"Fine. You?"

He took off the Homburg, and I turned to look at him. He had filled out. His cheeks had lost their hollows, were, in fact, a bit puffed. His hair was longer, ordered as I had never seen it ordered, but even in the first moments I could detect that angularity of spirit, a nervous energy almost disguised by the deliberately casual rhythm.

We had just gone through the gate when he snapped on the light behind him and opened the thin briefcase. "Make yourself a drink," he said, indicating the bar imbedded in the back of the front seat. "I need five minutes."

I pressed a lever to release the bar that contained an ice compartment, glasses, a wide assortment of liquor and six bottles of Coke. After mixing a scotch and soda I settled back in the luxury of the huge machine while Teddy glanced rapidly at a document. We were leaving Newark pointed toward the country.

"Read that," he said a moment later, pointing at a paragraph. I noticed that his fingers still had that nervous tremble. The page shook slightly.

It was a standard agreement of purchase, of what, I didn't know since it was the second page. "Looks all right," I said.

"No, Howard. There's a trick in it."

"Where?"

"I'll show you later." He slipped the document back in the case, reached for a glass that he half filled with bourbon, added ice, and topped off with Coke. Leaning back in his seat he said, "Do you like your firm?"

"It's all right. Not very exciting."

"Do you want to work for me?"

"Doing what?"

"Whatever you like. Legal."

"But you must have a large legal staff."

"I sacked half of them. I'll pay you five times your salary now. How much do they pay you?"

In the social and professional life I was accustomed to, people didn't ask questions like that, but it seemed natural to answer, "Ten thousand," for my position and experience, a fairly standard salary at the time.

"I'll pay you fifty thousand."

"Why? You can buy any legal talent you want."

"I need you."

The alarm that sounded in my brain was subdued by the static of the years that had intervened since I had last heard him say *I need you* in a subversive engagement of the heart.

I said, "I don't understand."

"I need someone I can trust. I don't trust the Old Man's team. They all suck."

"You've taken over then, I gather."

"Yeah. It's something to do. Will you come in?"

"Do you have to know right now?"

"No. Tomorrow. You can start Monday, in the legal department."

"Monday?"

"Why not?"

"It's a little precipitous."

"You can clear your shit out Monday morning and come over after lunch. I put Kellogg in as head of the legals. You can work under him, but don't trust him. Yet. Are you a good lawyer?"

"I think so."

He fished out the document and handed it to me. "Look this over tomorrow and let me know what you think of it."

A test.

I folded it into my jacket pocket, and took a large swallow of scotch. I don't consider myself an avaricious man, but fifty thousand dollars a year at that time was eloquent persuasion. On the other hand, working for Teddy involved certain risks, personal risks. I doubted that he would destroy Arnheim Industries since, unless he had fired them all, there were too many wise heads who had grown up with the company to permit him to make serious mistakes. The personal risk was that of being totally absorbed by Teddy, swallowed up by his ego in that singleness of purpose in which the purpose was never entirely clear. I didn't see myself spending the rest of my life fetching Cokes from the machine on the BOQ porch.

He had lighted a Chesterfield and he was looking out the window at the rolling hills where the green of willows had begun to announce that spring was promised. Apparently he didn't want to talk about the years that had passed since he had left Elmore Field, his experiences in the war in Europe, or about anyone he hadn't seen since his departure from New York to return to Elmore Field. Beneath the expensive purr of the Cadillac, however, I heard his deep voice humming imperfectly a melody about two people in darkness.

Collincourt had undergone a spectacular change since I had last seen it. Entering the estate through a high, wrought-iron gate and following the drive up to that monumental and extremely well-executed replica of a French chateau had always been depressing, perhaps because it always led to that brute force, Theodore Arnheim the First, but also because at night it presented a sepulchral silhouette with a single light burning under the portico. With Theodore the Second, as soon as the Cadillac turned onto the drive a dramatic transformation became apparent. The Louis XIV structure, gleaming with light from every window in an extravagant blaze, emanated a glow of gentility, luxury, and, it seemed to me as we drew up before the front entrance, seduction or threat.

The great paneled front door opened, and Ebson, the head butler, after greeting us, took my bag from the chauffeur and handed it to a waiting maid.

"Well, Ebson," I said, "it's good to see you again."

"A great pleasure, Mr. Howard."

"Have you been well?"

"Very well, thank you, sir. And you?"

"Fine, Ebson."

Teddy was already moving across the marble foyer, but he turned back. "Howard, the Old Lady would like to see you."

"All right . . . oh, Teddy," I caught him just before he disappeared, "do we dress for dinner?"

"No, Howard. Not now."

My room was in the east wing, remote from the center of the house, but as I followed the maid down the corridor there were sounds of voices from one or two of the rooms I passed, too low even to determine sex. Somehow I was not prepared for a dinner party, but I congratulated myself on my adaptability in packing a dark suit as well as the dinner jacket.

After showering and dressing I followed a maid's directions, and with a few false turns found the fourth door on the right in the west wing and knocked.

"Herein," Teddy's mother said.

I opened the door and found her sitting at a table before a fire, eating dinner. "Ah, Mattew," ("th" had always been beyond her lingual skills) she said, beaming at me with a fork in hand. "Come in, come in."

"I'm terribly sorry, Mrs. Arnheim. I'm interrupting your dinner."

"Nein, nein, nein," she said in an authentic explosion of hospitality. "Come, Mattew."

I went over to her and bent to receive the rather greasy kiss (she was eating pork chops) she smeared on my cheek. Grasping my hand, she pressed it to her own cheek. Talking with Mrs. Arnheim was always a challenge since I have very limited German, and she was never conscious of which language she was speaking, her girlhood German, or, since she had lived in the United States for fifty years, her surprisingly inadequate English. She was in her late seventies, had always been a drab, fat, little lady with iron-gray hair pulled back austerely in correct *bürger* fashion, and to my knowledge, she had never advanced an opinion on anything in her husband's presence. But along with Collincourt she had undergone a miraculous metamorphosis: her hair was bright yellow, hanging almost to her shoulders, she was wearing scarlet lipstick, at the moment confused with pork grease, and her dressing gown was an indiscreet collision of reds, greens, and yellows.

"*Setze dich, setze dich,*" she said, releasing my hand, and when I was in the chair across from her little table, smiling at me warmly. "*So ein hübscher Kerl, du Mattew.* So handsome. You are *schon* married?"

"No, Mrs. Arnheim. Not yet."

"*Ach Gott,* no one marry no more. Not my Teddy neither. You seen Teddy?"

"Yes, I drove out with him."

"Changed, *net*? Much better now. *Ein fescher Kerl* now. Some meat on his body."

"Mrs. Arnheim, I was very sorry to hear of Mr. Arnheim's death."

"Yes?" she smiled. I didn't believe she had understood me, but she went on, "Yes, he was dying. He worked always. *Immer hat er gearbeitet.* But now he have some peace. Me too. You like the hair?"

"It's very becoming."

"*Sag mir,* Mattew, does our Teddy have a woman now?"

"I couldn't say, Mrs. Arnheim. I haven't seen him in over five years."

"*Er hat geliebt,*" she said quietly, lifting a small glass of clear liquid that looked too thick for water and sipping from it. "*Er hat geliebt.* I hope he love again. I want some *Enkeln,* some little children."

I rose from my chair. "I'm keeping you from your dinner, Mrs. Arnheim."

"Nein, nein. Bleib' doch."

I took one of her hands and kissed it. "No, I should leave."

"You come back to see me again, Mattew."

"Certainly, Mrs. Arnheim. Good night."

"Gute Nacht, Mattew, *Schlaf wohl."*

I knew the first floor of Collincourt quite well, and voices led me to the great salon where a fire was burning and other guests had assembled, without Teddy.

There were seven, a number I found rather Byzantine unless Teddy had another body stashed away someplace, since with him and me, we would be nine at table, a number that would satisfy mystics but awkward for a dinner party: two couples standing near the bar, and three young women arranged symmetrically on two lounges before the fire. I didn't know any of them, but I made the rounds introducing myself, to the couples first, one middle-aged, the woman rather attractive, the middle-aged man scholarly, with rimless glasses, and the other, younger couple blond and athletic but running to jowls. Their names meant nothing to me. Then in my courtly manner to the lounges and the three young women drinking vermouth or something equally innocuous. They could have been supplied by central casting: a blonde, a brunette, and a redhead.

They were extraordinary. Flawless. Hair, skin, makeup, jewelry and gowns, models of the assiduous care, casual, polite, languorously seductive. They bore names: Catherine Somebody, Nancy Somebody, and Maude Somebody. Quite properly they did not offer their hands, but as I made the rounds they responded with the charm that only long study or having been to the manner born could have produced. They were subtly but profoundly sexual in their appeal, and I wondered if mates would arrive to claim them, or whether they were purely decorative.

I returned to the bar where the bartender I didn't recall from the reign of Theodore the First mixed me a very good martini.

"You're with Arnheim Industries, Mr. Howard?" the scholarly gentleman, whose name was Henry Cummings, asked.

"No." I was aware that they, the four of them, were examining me carefully, the wives as well as the men, as though a prospective combatant, enemy even, had suddenly been produced and they were preparing a battle plan. I decided such candor invited candor in return. "Are you?"

"Yes. John here is in the Lausanne office and I'm in London."

"Oh. Home on vacation?"

"Not exactly. Mr. Arnheim called."

Teddy called London and Lausanne to invite them to dinner? I understood the nervous tension. A new face, a possible challenge.

"I didn't realize the company had offices in London and Lausanne," I said to reassure them.

"The Lausanne office was opened a month ago. I've been in London for six years."

They were reassured and I left them to adore the three Graces on the divans, where I sat by the blond Catherine Somebody. She was a rather small, shimmering young woman with astonishingly blue eyes, large and clear, and flawless skin flushed with youth, a Day-Glo girl. She was wearing a simple black dinner dress with a gold chain around her throat, her corn-blond hair falling to her shoulders. Something about my presence was amusing her and finally, opening her bag and extracting a tissue, she leaned toward me. "You look as though you were going into battle, Mr. Howard." She scrubbed at my cheek and withdrew a very red tissue.

"Oh, thanks. Mrs. Arnheim's welcome."

"You've known Teddy a long time?" Nancy, the brunette across from us, asked.

"Yes. We met first in knee pants. He had bony knees and mine were chubby."

"I didn't know schoolboys still wore knee pants," redheaded Maude said.

"At that time in that place they did. But I always felt conspicuous, and knees could get cold."

"Does anybody know if Teddy's even here?" Nancy asked.

Lausanne and London looked blank.

"Yes," I said, "he's here. I rode out with him." My prestige line rose sharply, and the three Graces began questioning me simultaneously when Teddy walked into the room. He had changed to another Bellini creation, a soft cashmere blazer, smart gray flannels, and loafers. The Graces rose in unison to go to him, almost a steeplechase, each kissing him in turn while the European representatives and wives hovered in attendance. After being kissed he shook hands and moved to the bar where a bourbon and Coke appeared. He was never quite untouched by the Graces, two of whom were always at his side, mainly Nancy and Maude, while Catherine seemed to hold back.

With the advantage of more light I examined him again. The additional weight gave him more authority in appearance, even more facial conformity. The nose was less craggy, but the eyes were unchanged, of if changed, even more analytical, almost clinical in their penetration of whoever happened to be speaking. The hint of gray in the carefully brushed hair over his ears was a recent development.

"John," he said, after tasting his bourbon and Coke, "does the office in Ouchy have room for expansion?"

"Oh, yes, sir," John said enthusiastically.

"And the lease would let us close it down if necessary?"

"Well . . . yes. That is, I think so." The enthusiasm had been drained away.

"And the Walowsky woman is working out?"

"Yes, she's very good. Where . . . ?"

"But her security clearance hasn't come through yet. Why not?"

As a performance it was superb. Both John Stevens, Lausanne, and Henry Cummings, London, were impressed, on the verge of being stunned. A performance, but it was also a curious economy. He flew them and their wives from London and Lausanne, but he wouldn't spend time in the office stunning them.

"I put a tracer on it before leaving," Stevens said.

"Maybe Howard will go over next week to take a look at the office," Teddy said and drank some more bourbon and Coke, Maude clinging to one arm, and Nancy the other.

"Howard, sir?"

"You didn't meet Matt Howard here?" he designated me with a movement of his glass.

Both Stevens and Cummings turned to look at me vindictively, trying to disguise the indignation at what they obviously considered my deception.

Teddy's mouth smiled at me.

I didn't feel that a correction was called for.

"He'll certainly be welcome, Mr. Arnheim," Stevens managed to get out.

"Henry," Teddy continued, "did you see that factory in Manchester?"

"Yes, sir. Just before I left."

"What do you think?"

"It's run down. Antiquated methods. Close to a million dollars to modernize it."

"Good. What are the net quick assets?"

"Not more than three thousand pounds."

"All right. Come into the office on Monday."

"Yes, sir."

With Nancy and Maude, Teddy moved away from the bar toward the fire, followed by the Cummingses and Stevenses. Catherine seemed to have found her station in my vicinity, and I began to wonder about apportionment.

"When are you going to visit us, Mr. Arnheim?" Mrs. Cummings asked.

"Without warning," Teddy said.

Lausanne and London laughed without conviction.

"Teddy," Maude said, running her knuckles down his cheek, "it's boring to talk about things we don't understand."

"Then we'll talk about things you do understand. Do you think that Howard there is a handsome man?"

They turned to look at me. Catherine was at my side.

"Oh, yes," Maude and Nancy said, not quite in unison.

"Do you think he has character?"

They both studied me for a moment.

"Not too much," Maude said.

"Yes, too much," Nancy said.

"I don't know," Catherine said, looking at me.

"You're *all* right," Teddy said. "Howard is my conscience."

Stevens laughed. Cummings didn't.

"If that's so," I said, "I'm feeling very bad."

Teddy snorted quietly. Catherine laughed, and then Maude and Nancy. And when it seemed safe, so did the others.

"But Teddy," Catherine at my side said, "isn't a conscience terribly expensive?"

"Yes," Teddy said, his eyes on me, "it comes high. It's like a tax."

"Well," I said, "this tax needs another drink. Catherine?"

"No, thanks."

I went to the bar. He had changed, not surprisingly, but I wasn't able to decide in which direction, or which of the events in his life had most effected the change. He impressed me as more metallic, even more resistant to the unruly vagaries of the heart. I wanted more exposure to the new Teddy before I made the decision to grow prosperous with Arnheim Industries.

The conversation was more conventional when I returned to the arrangement before the fire, Teddy seated with Maude and Nancy, one on each side, both touching, London and Lausanne on the other divan, Catherine in an outer chair, smoking a cigarette. It was conventional in the sense that Teddy was listening rather than talking, listening to Cummings's description of the privations they had suffered in England during the war. He was trying, rather desperately, to impress Teddy with his heroic service to Arnheim Industries which, owing to its small but important contribution, had kept an office open in London throughout. With a cigarette dangling from his lips, Teddy listened, his face impassive, his eyes alert. But even skilled conversationalists eventually despaired in Teddy's presence. His conversation was like a bullet in a fencing match. He handed his glass to Maude who rose to go to the bar.

Stevens, apparently deciding to profit by London's growing desperation, seized on hesitation. "Mr. Arnheim, you had some exciting experiences in the war, didn't you?"

"Me?" Teddy said. "No. I learned not to split an S with a Kraut on my tail. Then I drank a lot of wine."

"What does that mean?" Nancy asked.

"Ask Howard. He knows all about those things."

They looked at me. "It's a maneuver in an airplane. You roll over and pull down. Providing you're high enough. Drinking wine is easier."

"Mr. Howard said he knew you in knee pants," Maude said, drawing up her legs. "I'm sure you were adorable."

"Yes," Teddy said. "Everybody adored me. Isn't that right, Howard?"

"Absolutely. He was so adorable they didn't want to let him out of the fourth form." Was he playing the straight man or was I?

"Is that an original, that Goya?" Catherine asked, looking at a painting of a bullfight.

"Yes," Teddy said without turning. "Someone sold it to the Old Man. The person who sold it thought it was a fake, but the Old Man called in an expért. The person who sold it shot himself.''

"He had unerring instincts," Cummings said, referring presumably to Mr. Arnheim and not the incompetent art dealer.

Catherine rose to go to the picture, and I followed her. I had never heard the story before though I had admired the Goya for many years.

"He was brutal," Catherine said as we stood before the painting.

"He had a political conscience.'' The others had resumed a faltering conversation.

"Like you.'' She turned to me. "What did Teddy mean? Are you really his conscience?''

"It's the first I've heard of it.''

"I didn't know you worked for him.''

"I don't, but I may. Would you?''

"Oh, *yes.*''

Ebson came in to announce dinner and we retired to the immense dining room with the long table. Teddy placed Maude and Nancy on either side of him, then me, and then Catherine. The others were strung out on the other side with Mrs. Cummings at the foot of the table. She was obviously pleased to occupy the position of hostess, but the arrangement was awkward.

After a soup Ebson sliced an enormous roast of beef while two maids served. A sommelier poured the best Margaux I had ever tasted, and everything was delicious. After dessert Ebson poured Moët, and Cummings said nice things about the champagne and the Margaux.

"The Old Man's cellar," Teddy said. "He spent a lot of years stocking it, but he never drank any of it. I'm drinking it.''

Lausanne and London were quite evidently shocked by Teddy's casual desecration of a god. Mrs. Cummings winced and looked down at her plate, and Mr. Cummings smiled painfully. Teddy was aware of it, and I suspect it gave him a certain pleasure. Cummings had, of course, been his father's man, and he could not disregard the fact that the son was looking him over.

After dinner we retired to the great salon again for coffee, cognac, and cigars. All the men but me took a cigar, and inevitably Maude and Nancy insisted on trying Teddy's, and both coughed. Catherine didn't try, but she was a heavy cigarette smoker.

Conversation after dinner was no more brilliant than it had been before, and I could see that familiar mask of boredom settling over

Teddy's face. Only Maude and Nancy were able to stir him from the lethargy that Lausanne and London were imposing on him with increasing desperation. He drank three or four cognacs while the white hands of Nancy and Maude fluttered over him like little birds, but finally he rose and threw the butt of his cigar into the fire, his two Graces at his side. "If anyone's interested in horses in the morning, don't wait for me." I had never seen a less horsey collection of people in my life. "And the tennis courts will probably be dry. See you in the morning, Howard." He turned and left, encumbered by the embracing arms of Nancy and Maude.

There was such an informal decisiveness about the departure that no one said, "Good night," but in the profound silence that settled over the room as the three of them disappeared, Mrs. Cummings looked away as though trying to deny the existence of original sin, and Mrs. Stevens clutched convulsively at her husband's sleeve. Catherine watched the exit of Teddy with his Graces, and turned slowly toward me, a light smile on her face.

"Well," Cummings said after a very heavy moment, "I guess I'll . . ." He looked at his watch. "It's . . . shall we go to bed, dear?"

Mrs. Cummings did not speak, but she rose, prepared to follow her protector, her eyes refusing to make contact.

"Good night," Cummings said.

We answered in a chorus, in relief, and the Stevenses rose to follow, leaving Catherine and me before the dying fire. She looked up at me through long lashes. "Are they real?"

"No, they're robots that Teddy had built and shipped over." I was by no means sure that I understood the protocol of the moment. I poured myself another cognac. "You?"

"No, thanks. I don't think I understood what you said about working for Teddy."

"I'm one of those people who work for a living, and he offered me a job."

"A good job?"

"I don't know about the job, but the salary is good."

"How much?" she asked simply.

"You're impertinent, little Catherine."

"How much?" she repeated.

"Five times as much as I currently earn."

"Take it."

"Just like that?"

"Certainly. Money is the most important thing in life."

"I was taught that was a vulgar attitude."

"You were taught wrong. Did you inherit a lot of money?"

"Not a lot."

"Then take it."

"Where did you come by this wisdom, little Catherine?"

"On the island of Manhattan."

"And before the island of Manhattan?"

"Wisconsin. They believe the same thing in Wisconsin, but they don't say it."

I was tempted to ask her if she was gainfully employed, but decided that it would be indiscreet. I think she may have suspected since she smiled at me rather mysteriously and stabbed out her cigarette. "When do you have to decide?"

"Tomorrow."

"And you'll spend the night struggling with the decision?"

"I hope not."

"It's simple, Mr. Howard. If Teddy needs a conscience, and he'll pay you for supplying it, everyone will be happy." She unfolded her silken legs and rose. "I'm ready for bed."

We left the salon and crossed the foyer to mount the great staircase together. Still together we went down the corridor to my room where I stopped, my hand on the knob, wondering. She took a further step and turned to look at me. "I'm there," she said, indicating the bedroom next to mine.

"Good night, Catherine."

"Don't struggle too hard, conscience," she said and walked to her door.

When I was in my room I drew the sales agreement from my pocket, removed my jacket and shoes and turned on the reading lamp above my bed. It was for a copper mine in Montana, and the price was eight million dollars.

I had never dealt in such heady figures, alone at least, and the document fascinated me. It was a preliminary agreement indicating good will on the part of vendor and purchaser to enter into contract for purchase of the mine. I saw no flaws in it until I came to the paragraph on the second page that Teddy had asked me to read in the limousine.

I immediately wondered if I would have caught it if he hadn't drawn my attention to it, and that worried me. There was a secondary "which" "whereas" clause enclosed in commas that should have been a "'that" clause without commas. Theoretically the whole clause could have been removed without altering the meaning of the sentence, but such a removal would change the nature of the agreement. Had Teddy caught it, or had someone in his legal department pointed it out to him?

I had tossed the pages on the bureau and started to undress when a light tap sounded on the door. "Come in," I said quietly.

It was Catherine in a translucent negligee gathered loosely by a cord at her waist. With her hands behind her she closed the door softly. "I've run out of cigarettes."

"I'm sorry, I don't smoke, little Catherine."

"I know," she said, coming toward me slowly.

"But I can find some for you."

"Oh, don't bother," she said, her face just below mine. "If we don't waste time perhaps I can help you wrestle with your problem."

12

I WOKE TO THE intoxicating scents of the departed Catherine and wished she had not departed. But morning was unmistakably there, and Catherine was not, a brilliant morning even at seven-thirty in mid-March. I dressed in slacks, a woolen shirt, and tweed jacket, and slipped down through the quiet mansion, out onto the brick terrace and then onto the main court and across, past the stables where Wilson, the groom, was sitting in the early morning sun, smoking his pipe. He recognized me, but I don't think he remembered my name. I quickly relieved him of any obligations toward professional services: I can stay on most horses, even horses that insist on jumping, but it has never been a passion with me. The beasts are unpredictable.

After exchanging some average banalities with Wilson I went on down the path under oaks with leaf buds just beginning to swell, and passed the immense lawn on the left where a gaggle of Canada geese were waddling and finding something to eat. I recalled the pleasures I had always experienced on leaving the vicinity of the house under the rule of Theodore the First and escaping into the magnificent acres of Collincourt, of swimming in the artificial lake that had been created by a dam when Teddy was a child. Wisps of steam were rising from the surface, and at first I thought it was a snag or a log that I saw out in the middle, but as the air cleared it became a small skiff with a figure hunched over the stern holding a short rod. The head was covered with a hat, and I took him for one of the staff of gardeners and handymen until he lighted a cigarette with a characteristic gesture, flicking the match away with two fingers. He had been given probably hundreds of gold and silver lighters that he never used.

He was totally absorbed, motionless, but suddenly he jerked on the rod and began reeling in. At the end of his line an arcing, twisting flash of silver broke out of the water into the morning sun. He removed the hook, cracked the fish over the gunwales, and dropped it in the skiff. Leaning back, he looked out over the surface of the lake and around toward the shore. When he saw me on the small dock he placed the rod in the bottom of the skiff and picked up two small oars and began to row in facing the bow.

"Hi," he said as the skiff nosed into the dock.

"Good morning." I caught the painter and tied it to the cleat.

He was dressed in old corduroys, a stained green shirt, and filthy sneakers. The felt hat had a hole in the crown.

"Is this a recent development?" I asked, lifting the basket he handed me.

"Yeah. The Old Man stocked it but wouldn't let anybody fish it." He stepped up onto the dock.

I looked into the basket. There were several good-sized lake trout. "How long did it take you to catch these?"

"Half an hour. They're dumb." He took the basket and we started up the path. From somewhere a peacock screamed, answered by another. The geese were still feeding on the lawn.

"Did you have time to look at the agreement?"

I glanced at him to see if the question was sly, but he didn't look up. "Yes. The commas and the 'which' clause on the second page."

"That's right, Howard. You just earned fifty thousand a year. Are you going to take it?"

"Tell me what you want of me first."

"I want somebody I can trust. You can work with Kellogg but when I need you I'll call you. Can you speak Italian?"

"No."

"Learn it. I don't trust interpreters. I can do French and German, but I don't know Italian."

"There will be travel?"

"Yeah, quite a lot."

We were approaching the stable where Wilson was still sitting in the sun. He rose as we approached, and Teddy handed him the basket of fish.

"All right," I said when we came to the court. "But Monday is pressing it a bit."

"I think you ought to come over Monday."

"In that case I'll have to go back to the city today, after lunch. I have a lot to do."

"Okay. They'll have a car for you. You can drive it over Monday." We entered through the French doors and he left me.

The breakfast room was set for nine, but there was no one there. Bottles of champagne in ice buckets were on the first table, and Ebson, who appeared miraculously, said, "Good morning, Mr. Howard. Some wine?"

"No, thanks, Ebson. Just coffee." At the sideboard I took two eggs and some sausage from the chafing dish and a maid appeared with coffee. I enjoy breakfast, and I refilled my plate and read the *Times*. Before I had finished the Stevenses arrived.

They seemed to have recovered from the shock of witnessing the prelude to Teddy's sexual exploits, but they were still rather nervous. On Ebson's invitation they both drank two glasses of champagne before serving themselves.

I was prompted by my still extant sense of decency to say, "I think I ought to tell you that when I said last night I didn't work for Arnheim Industries, I didn't. Now I do."

Stevens's fork skidded an egg onto the table cloth. "Pardon me?"

"I hired on this morning."

Mrs. Stevens occupied herself with restoring her mate's egg to its proper place.

"Why . . . that's splendid," Stevens managed to get out. "Will you really be coming to Switzerland?"

"I don't know, but I suppose it's a possibility."

"We'd certainly be pleased to welcome you if you do," Mrs. Stevens said with immense heroism.

"Thank you."

"May I ask which department?" Stevens said.

"Legal, I guess. I'm a lawyer."

That seemed to assuage him, and he returned to his errant egg.

Apparently no one else was inclined to breakfast, not Catherine nor the other Graces, so I excused myself and went to my room. After brushing my teeth I packed my bag and went out to the hall again. I was strongly tempted by urgings of the flesh to rap on Catherine's door, but there was no sound of waking life so I left again and went out for a walk. It had turned into a warm spring day, and I walked for several miles in brilliant sunlight, wondering if I had made the right decision. I was certain I could handle the legal responsibilities, but I wondered what other duties Teddy might have in mind. My decision had been made the night before, and it was still sensually entangled with the sweet young body of little Catherine.

When I returned to the house everyone but Teddy was sitting in the sunlight of the brick terrace having a drink before lunch. The Graces, including Catherine, were in sheer slacks, sloppy sweaters and gold bangles, and the Cummingses at a discreet distance, half turned from them, were trying to ignore the sensual world. At the portable bar, the bartender made me a martini, and I sat by Catherine.

"I went looking for you," she said, "but I was afraid I'd get lost. I have absolutely no sense of direction. And an enormous goose attacked me."

"Are you sure it wasn't a swan?" I asked.

Maude laughed.

"I don't understand," Catherine said.

"Zeus, father of the gods," Maude explained, "took the shape of a swan to make love to . . . I can't remember her name."

"Leda," Mrs. Stevens supplied.

Mrs. Cummings turned even farther away. Clearly, if their security, livelihood, very existence had not depended on Teddy they would have fled.

Teddy finally appeared in slacks and a tweed jacket, stopping at the bar for his bourbon and Coke. Nancy went over to him quickly. "Where have you been all morning, Teddy?"

He turned to look at her as though she were an impertinence. "Telephone," he said.

"All *morning*?"

Possessiveness had always annoyed Teddy, and it seemed to me that he was now no longer prepared to give or even lend himself to anyone for a period exceeding a tumble in the bed. I alone knew that he had loved, but I wondered if the capacity for love had been irretrievably shattered. Though there was patience, even tolerance, in the smile formed by his mouth, the eyes were bleak. Thrusting an arm under his, Nancy guided him to the garden settee where Maude was waiting, but Maude with more wit than Nancy refrained from touching him. He sat back and drank heavily of the evil concoction that Alabama had imprinted on him, through what confusion of images and memories I could only guess.

"Howard," he said, "do you have Delaporte's address?"

Delaporte was the French lawyer who had been my student at Elmore Field. "I have his mother's address. Delaporte was killed. His mother wrote me when she found one of my letters."

"How?"

"She was never able to get the facts. He was flying P-47s during the last weeks of the war. He was out on reconnaissance and disappeared. They found the wreckage later."

"How terrible," Mrs. Stevens said. "Was he a close friend?"

"I knew him pretty well in Alabama." Which led to questions about our mission with the French. Teddy listened while I described it, but offered nothing, though I suspect he was remembering the parts that I left out. I wondered if Michael ever weighed on him.

He rose from the settee to go to the bar for another drink which he carried to the edge of the terrace to look out over the fresh green of Collincourt. Nancy started to go after him, but Maude laid a hand on her arm, and Catherine looked at me with a question in her blue eyes. It was an awkward moment while we all stared at his back.

But for Teddy the subject had been exhausted; when he turned around he was almost jovial. "I caught eight fish this morning, for lunch."

"But Teddy," Nancy said, "there are . . ." she counted with an index finger, "nine of us."

"I never eat fish," Teddy said.

"You catch them, but you don't eat them?"

"Yes."

"I consider that very generous," Cummings said, apparently deciding they were becoming dangerously isolated.

"Oh," Mrs. Cummings took the cue, "Mr. Arnheim is the very soul of generosity. Just like his dear papa."

Teddy looked at her as though she were an extinct species. "The Old Man wasn't generous. He never spent a dollar that wouldn't bring two dollars in return."

"Oh, Mr. Arnheim," Mrs. Cummings said, "I just can't believe that. He never forgot young Henry's birthday."

"That was his secretary. He had a good secretary."

"Is she still with you?" Stevens asked.

"No. I fired her."

Ebson announced lunch, and we trooped into the smaller dining room to eat the fish Teddy had caught and drink a Meursault. I would have liked to see the cellar that Theodore the First had been collecting for years but refusing to share. I had learned more about the Old Man's personal habits in one day than in the many years I had known Teddy.

Lunch was a bit livelier than dinner the night before, or at least there was more conversation. The Stevenses and the Cummingses decided that even in Babylon it was necessary to survive, and on our side of the table the Graces seemed to be under the impression that Teddy was responsible not only for catching the fish but for imparting its singular flavor as well. Teddy ate a hamburger.

After coffee on the terrace Stevens permitted himself, "Tennis anyone, about three o'clock?"

There were no takers, and he turned to me. "You, Mr. Howard?"

"Sorry, I can't. I'm going back to the city in a few minutes."

Catherine turned to me. "Really?"

"Yes. My new boss expects me to appear Monday. I'm not quite sure why."

"I'm like the Old Man," Teddy said. "I want to get my money's worth."

"At any rate I have a lot to take care of and some explaining to do." I rose and shook hands all around, finally with my host. "Thanks, Teddy. I'll see you Monday. Do I have a car?"

"Yeah. Do you remember how to drive?"

"I think it will come back to me."

My bag was by the front door, but before leaving I went up to say goodbye to Mrs. Arnheim. Just as I was about to knock, I heard thunderous snoring within. I went downstairs again.

Under the portico was an MG sports car, gleaming from a recent polish, and the chauffeur was standing at the open door. "Would you like the top down, sir?"

"Yes, I think that would be . . ."

"*Matt*," Catherine called, emerging from the house, "could I go back with you?"

"Certainly, if Teddy doesn't mind." Why was I beginning to worry about Teddy's sensibilities?

"He doesn't. I'll be down in five minutes."

Five minutes extended to fifteen, and the chauffeur had the top neatly folded down and strapped when Catherine reappeared carrying her bag, which I stowed behind the seats. "Oh," she said, looking at the topless little car, "My *hair*."

"What?"

"I can't go like that. It would destroy my hair."

The chauffeur and I exchanged glances and patiently he began raising the top again while Catherine settled herself in her seat. Once we had passed through the wrought-iron gate, opened in some mysterious fashion, Catherine slipped her arm under mine, but showed no inclination to talk. Finally my social consciousness overcame my reluctance to break into her revery. "Teddy wasn't insulted?"

"What?" She was staring straight over the bonnet.

"By your sudden decision to leave?"

"Oh." She laughed lightly, withdrew her arm and turned to look at me. "No, not at all." Leaning toward me suddenly she propped her chin on my shoulder. "You're nice, Matt. I like you, but you're just . . . a bit innocent."

Yes, I had been innocent. I saw that, but having seen it I decided to recover with casual grace. "How long have you known him?"

She removed her chin and turned away. "About a year."

"And what do you think of him?"

"What do you mean?"

"As a man. A human being."

"He's . . . fascinating."

That impressed me as equivocal. "His mind, you mean?"

"I don't see much of his mind. His . . . presence. Is that the word?"

"Yes, that could be the word."

"He's mysterious, forceful, decisive."

I thought for a moment and decided that though I probably wouldn't have chosen those adjectives, they all applied. But then I wondered if Catherine and I would agree on the meaning of those words. Under what circumstances would he be mysterious, forceful, and decisive with her? The answer I supplied for myself was lurid.

We went several more miles toward the Lincoln Tunnel in silence while after my display of worldliness I tried to recover from the assault on my wounded male vanity. But my characteristic need for candor overcame my worldliness. "You wouldn't have come last night if . . ."

"Oh, Matt, don't talk like that. Say something nice."

"Well, I enjoyed last night."

"So did I," she said simply.

"And I'd like to . . ."

"Matt, baby," she said, thrusting her arm under mine again, "I said I liked you. Let it go at that."

"But . . ."

"But nothing. You still don't understand."

"Yes, I understand, but . . ." I stopped at the tollbooth and searched in a pocket for fifty cents, but the pocket was empty, and I reached for my wallet. "Oh, God, I left my wallet at Collincourt. Do you have fifty cents?"

"Yes," she giggled and opened her bag to pull out a dollar bill. The collector snatched it from my fingers peremptorily and palmed me a fifty-cent piece. I threw the MG in gear and we descended into the tiled maw of the Lincoln Tunnel where the noise level made conversation in the sports car impossible. Catherine tapped my arm and held out her small hand. I dropped the coin into it and squeezed it closed.

Halfway under the Hudson River some imbecility stopped traffic, and we sat there in the oppressive odors of carbon monoxide, an immense truck looming before us. As usual I tried to stop breathing, but Catherine turned to me suddenly and grabbed my arm. "I'm scared," she shouted into my ear.

"Why?"

"I have claustrophobia! Can't you *do* something?"

I turned her bewitching little face to me and kissed her heavily, passionately, and continued to kiss her while the huge truck in front of us went into gear, enveloping us in a foul cloud of diesel exhaust, and the car behind delivered a raucous statement.

She lived in a brownstone on East 70th Street, three blocks from my apartment. I carried her bag up to the door, and she turned to me in the shadows of early spring. "Thanks, Matt."
"I'll carry it up for you."
"No, don't bother. Remember, you owe me fifty cents."
"I'll send you a check tomorrow."

After lunch on Monday, I drove the MG to the Newark plant and began working for Arnheim Industries.

13

SINCE LIVING outside of Manhattan is not an option to be considered seriously, I moved downtown to a brownstone on 10th Street, just off lower Fifth Avenue, to be close to the Hudson Tubes. It was larger and more elegant than the one uptown, and without the five-fold increase in spending power it would have strained me seriously; however, it provided me with enough space to retrieve a lot of furniture and pictures that had been in storage for several years.

I did not see Teddy on the Monday following the weekend at Collincourt. In fact I didn't see him for several weeks, but I was expected when I drove the MG into the plant. I was issued a temporary I.D. card, met by an attendant who took over the car, and led inside by a young man who introduced himself as Herbert Falcon. The building was labyrinthine and antiquated; on the top floor, the third, Falcon rapped on a door that read "R. Kellogg," who turned out to be a genial, redheaded man in his early fifties, with very pink skin. He was justifiably nervous. I arrived with the prestige of being an old friend of the boss, during an agonizing period of reform, and, as I learned later, Kellogg half suspected I was there to take over his job.

When he had me seated before his desk he returned to his swivel chair across from me and promptly disappeared, his chair rocketing toward the window behind him.

"Are you all right?" I asked, rising.

His head appeared, then he pushed himself up. "Goddamn those castors. I'm gonna have the bastards sawed off. That chair avoids me like the plague." He kicked it toward the desk and managed to settle himself without further injury to his dignity or spine.

We talked for half an hour about nothing important: law school, my former firm, my years of acquaintance with Teddy, whom Kellogg referred to reverently as "Mr. Arnheim," and my future method of transportation from Manhattan. It was the standard probing, softening, calculating. The office was quite large but a bit shabby, walls lined with law books, the furniture worn, and the paint on the ceiling curling in places.

"I can't tell you yet what your job will be like," he said finally, "but I'd like to have you meet the rest of the staff." He pressed a button on his desk, and a moment later a secretary entered. "Would you show them in please, Maureen?"

Eight of them trooped in ranging in age from about thirty to about sixty, deferential, polite, ill at ease, almost servile as they lined up to shake hands while Kellogg introduced us. I had a much stronger sense that they considered me as a potential threat, and I tried to relieve them. I don't think I succeeded. When they left Kellogg took me down the hall to the office next to his, as large as his, a subtle signal in the legal, business, and industrial world. It was being redecorated.

"It should be done in a couple of days," he explained, "but I've had a table set aside for you in the library, and if you don't have anything better to do for the rest of the afternoon, you might start on history and background."

Piled on the library table was a collection of documents, the first being a history of Arnheim Industries, innocuous, worthless, a pious myth venerating the heroic achievements of Theodore the First, prepared by some anonymous flunky, perhaps from dictation. After that I graduated to annual reports, and before the week was out, seated in my gleaming, newly furnished office, I began to receive hand-delivered documents marked in military terminology: "Confidential" and "Secret." Gradually I began to understand the Arnheim Industries of the past, and the revolutionary changes that had been instituted when Theodore the Second took over. I had arrived at the early stages.

Teddy was buying. My first impression was that he was buying recklessly, extravagantly. The small mine in Montana was an example: the negotiations to purchase it were completed during my first few weeks at Arnheim Industries, which paid eight million dollars for it, money that, of course, was borrowed on very favorable terms, owing to the solid reputation of the company. The mine was located in the vicinity of the extensive Anaconda holdings, and when, later, the information became public that Arnheim Industries was moving into copper, Anaconda bid for purchase. The selling price was fifteen million dollars.

And there were others in mineral-related enterprises strung around the world. The most interesting aspect of the transactions was the timing. They were clustered as closely together as time would allow, and I learned that agents of Arnheim Industries were scuttling about the world as rapidly as the rather crude air transportation of the day would permit. Teddy himself, I gathered through various channels almost inadvertently, was away for weeks at a time.

I recognized the method. Essentially it was the same he had used in Le Cave, except instead of extracting an enormous roll of bills to smash the game, he used the enormous reputation of Arnheim Industries to frighten, in some cases to terrify a potential competitor into buying him out, at a profit of anywhere from twenty-five to fifty percent. But timing was important. The various negotiations were conducted as secretly and as quickly as possible, but eventually the pattern began to emerge, and he stopped buying.

He had used the Old Man and the reputation the Old Man had built up over the years as a formidable power. It was not unethical, but in a way he was forcing the Old Man, or the image of the Old Man, to serve his purposes.

For the first few months I was kept busy absorbing the rather complex structure of the company, though not really earning my money. I even brought my Italian grammar to the office. When Kellogg realized that I was benign, he began sending more important matters through my hands—contracts, purchase agreements, and other papers for me to look over. I made a few contributions, certainly nothing startling, but I continued to wonder when that great trust Teddy claimed he had in my moral being would surface. It came in the usual, casual manner.

Kellogg informed me one morning that there was an additional document he wanted, i.e., Teddy wanted, me to look at, but it was held in security in the library. He escorted me there and spoke to the librarian, who opened a small wall safe and handed me a thick, bound document marked "Top Secret," and informed me that I would have to read it there under his scrutiny, and that I could take no notes.

Wondering what prodigious disclosure I was about to be introduced to, I opened it and began reading. It was what was later called a "scenario" of a federal antitrust case against Arnheim Industries, carefully, meticulously presented, written, I soon understood, by the legal staff of Arnheim Industries. It was an appalling indictment of the methods the company had used to corner and control the market in precious metals. I understood why it was top secret.

The second half was the defense projected by the same legal department. It didn't convince me. According to my understanding of the federal antitrust laws, Arnheim Industries was sitting on a time bomb.

One morning in early June my door opened without a preliminary knock, and Teddy strolled in and dropped in a chair. "Hi," he said casually, and lighted a Chesterfield. He was in shirtsleeves rolled up to his elbows, without a tie.

"Hi, Teddy, how are you?"

"Okay. Did you get all the reading done?"

"Yes. Fascinating."

"You were in politics for a while, weren't you, Howard?"

"Yes, I ran for the state legislature right after the war."

"How did you make out?"

"Badly. I couldn't raise enough money."

"You know some people in politics?"

"Yes, quite a few. Why?"

"Do you think I ought to run for governor?"

"Of which state? Alabama?"

"New Jersey."

"Frankly, no. I think you'd make a lousy politician, and being president of Arnheim Industries is not an ideal political base. I suppose you're a Republican." It was typical of our relationship that I didn't know.

"No, Democrat."

"Well, that's surprising."

"The Old Man was a Republican. Do you know Warren?"

"I've met him a couple of times."

"Go down to Trenton and talk to him about it."

I had determined that my relations with Teddy would not change even though he was my boss. "Why don't you go?"

"I don't want to talk to him directly, and I don't want to be seen in the State House. You go. I'll arrange it."

He did arrange it, and I went to Trenton the next week to see Warren, who happened to be governor of the state of New Jersey. The clout I came with gave me half an hour with the amiable Democratic professional, who was in his last term since he couldn't succeed himself. When I brought up the idea he was appalled. "My God, no. Is he *serious*?"

"He seems to be."

"But why?"

"I suppose he feels some responsibility to the state that has been his and his father's home for many years."

"Mr. Howard, I don't know Teddy Arnheim personally, but I can't help being slightly skeptical about such a magnanimous gesture. His father was no friend of the Democratic party."

"Theodore the Second should not be judged on the record of Theodore the First."

"He wouldn't have the support of a single ward leader, and I couldn't sell him even if I wanted to. If he wants to do something for the party, ask him to support Jim Blaines, but not publicly. Do I make myself clear?"

"Perfectly. I'll tell him."

When I told him he wasn't surprised. "Okay," he said, his mouth curving into a smile. "Tell him it's a disappointment to me, but I'll support Blaines. You can take the support down next week."

Before I was driven to Trenton the following week, I was called to Teddy's office on the ground floor, set back in a wing that had been built off the main corridor of the building. His father had had his offices on the third floor.

"Be sure to tell him how disappointed I am, Howard, but I'm prepared to sacrifice my personal ambitions for the good of the party."

It was one of the longest sentences I had ever heard him deliver. "I'll tell him."

"And, Howard, don't forget the support." He reached behind his desk and lifted the shabby brown satchel that years before had occupied a corner of our quarters in the BOQ. "Bring it back, will you, after they've emptied the support?"

When I was ushered into the office in Trenton Blaines was with the governor. I had never met Blaines, but we had a few friends in common, and I knew something about him. He addressed me by my first name as a long-lost friend, and clapped me on the back with a solid arm. He was in his late forties, an elegant, extremely handsome man, over six feet, with an extraordinarily persuasive smile that bared splendid white teeth, and brown, curly hair that was graying at the temples to distinguished effect. A rumor had it that several years earlier he had turned down an offered contract in Hollywood to devote himself to politics. He was thought to be the rising star in the national Democratic party.

"And how *is* Teddy?" he said as I sat down, placing the support at my feet. The question seemed to carry resentment against a malignant universe that had separated born brothers.

"Very well," I said. "He wanted me to tell you that his personal disappointment would not prevent him from helping any way he can."

"Just what I told you, Jim," the governor said. "I'm sure we can count on him."

"That's the message he wanted me to convey."

"I'm very grateful," Blaines said, his eyes flicking at the brown satchel. "The first chance I get I want to thank him in person."

"I'm sure he'll appreciate it."

"On November fifth, Jim," the governor said.

"Yes, of course," Blaines laughed. "On November fifth."

"Gentlemen," I said, rising, "I won't take any more of your time. If you could . . ." I indicated the satchel. "That bag has fetichist powers for Teddy."

"Certainly, certainly," Blaines said, reaching for it.

"Uh . . . in there, Jim." The governor pointed to a door.

Blaines disappeared with the support.

"Mr. Arnheim has been widening his interests, I hear," the governor said.

"Cautiously. The company was becoming a little . . . incestuous."

"I understand. In this period some variety is probably wise. It's difficult to predict what might happen down there." He pointed in the general direction of the South, taking in Pennsylvania, Delaware, and that chunk of land on the Potomac between Virginia and Maryland.

"Yes, always unpredictable."

Blaines returned carrying a much lighter satchel. The smile on his face was transfigured with new significance. He handed me the satchel and put out his hand. "Please tell Teddy that I'm very, *very* grateful." His voice was charged with reverence.

On the way back I had the driver detour through Princeton where I ate luncheon at the Princeton Inn, and afterward walked around an almost deserted campus for a while. It was in the process of change: new buildings were going up in violation of the original architectural spirit. The postwar world was uglier than those years of relative innocence when Teddy had had lodgings just off Nassau Street from which I had engineered his entry into the dining room and the society behind the still imposing facade of the Ivy Club. I strolled by it without any temptation to enter as an old boy.

As we started north again I examined the worn, old leather bag. It was anonymous, without initials, the corners scuffed and the surface of the leather scarred with much travel and negligence. It was lined in faded red silk, and bore the almost obliterated name of a store in London that I couldn't make out. I had not had the slightest impulse to open it on the way down, and I wasn't curious about how much wealth it had carried. But I did wonder when Teddy's conscience would begin to stir.

14

I MADE TWO MORE TRIPS to Trenton, not to the governor's office, but to various back rooms in campaign headquarters. I kept reminding myself that there was nothing illegal, and therefore unethical, about the transactions, but I felt furtive.

In November Blaines won handily. He had saturated the state with images of his handsome face, with radio and television spots, and with his dynamic personal appearances. He had wide support among women, labor, and most minority groups, to all of whom he had promised special consideration. And I think he meant it.

In spite of vigorous support from conservative money and various industries, his Republican opponent seemed stunned by the magnitude of Blaines's campaign, and on one or two occasions was recorded as profanely demanding of the universe at large the source of the Democratic candidate's strength.

I don't know if Blaines ever paid that personal visit to thank Teddy on November 5 since I was out of the country, but much later, after his inauguration, it was known that the new governor spent occasional weekends at Collincourt. I assumed they were more decorous than mine. And Blaines, of course, had a splendid wife with social prestige.

I still didn't have a wife. I met a good many women, some of them very attractive, some of them very intelligent, some of them very intimate, but none I decided I could live with indefinitely. I didn't have hermitic instincts, but about the third or fourth time I was with a woman I discovered some little streak of insensitivity, vulgarity, or idiocy that shattered the beautiful image I had been enjoying. It did not take a psychoanalyst to persuade me that I was creating the image of each of these women, and when they refused to conform to the image I had created I felt betrayed. I suppose that's why I never understood woman. Finally I decided such a person should not marry, and I would remain an active bachelor—at least until my declining years.

My missions to Europe were less furtive than those to Trenton. We needed a European headquarters in a country that had an attractive tax structure, comparative political and economic stability, and relatively few restrictions on import and export licenses. England was eliminated because of the heavy tax burden of the postwar years, and France and Italy were still politically turbulent. I went to Lausanne where I was welcomed effusively by Mr. and Mrs. Stevens. John, relieved of the presence of the boss, was congenial and much more intelligent than he had given the impression of being at Collincourt. The nature of my mission was scarcely a secret, therefore it was not surprising that he had assembled most of the information I required to evaluate Switzerland as a foreign headquarters. I found it rather strange that though he could read French, his conversational skills were minimal, and he required the services of an interpreter in any serious exchange of ideas in other than English. His interpreter and secretary was Maja Walowsky who was fluent in English, French, and German, and, I learned later, her native language, Polish.

I did not accept the Stevens's earnest invitation to stay with them in their very comfortable apartment in Ouchy, only a few minutes' walk from the modest little office where Arnheim Industries had its Swiss headquarters, but took a room at the Beau-Rivage on the lakefront. When I appeared in the office I was, of course, expected, and Maja Walowsky rose from her desk before I had well entered.

"Mr. Howard?" she said a little nervously.

"Yes."

"Welcome to Lausanne."

"Thank you."

Maja Walowsky was a good-looking blond woman in her late twenties, dressed in the conservative European secretary's slightly masculine suit. Her hair was short in a bob, and her blue eyes when she removed her glasses impressed me as brittle, intense. She took me directly to John Stevens.

A few nights later when I had had too much to drink and eat at a party Stevens had produced in my honor, I walked along the lake for half an hour and then before going up to my room, succumbed to the temptation of a final *fine* at the outdoor café before the hotel. It was early summer and everything was in that tinselled nostalgia of old Europe: warm June air, casual conversations in five or six languages on all sides, some attractive women, and a moon descending over the mountains of the French Haute Savoie across the lake, spreading an hourglass of brilliance pointing at me.

I had almost finished my *fine* and was trying to dissuade myself from another when Maja Walowsky, with a very proper young man, came into the terrace of the café, and while searching for a table, her eyes crossed me, and she smiled. I returned the smile, perhaps too graciously, for she came over to me, leading her young man, who didn't seem too enthusiastic.

I rose as she planted herself before me, and conceding to the obvious, invited them to join me.

"Oh, thank you," Maja said. "This is François Fournier, Mr. Howard. I'm afraid he doesn't speak English," she said, seating herself.

"I can struggle along in French."

"Oh?" Her eyes narrowed briefly.

Fournier, who was a professor of chemistry at the University of Lausanne, listened politely while Maja offered the initial banalities about Lausanne, Arnheim Industries, the virtues of her boss, and her distant admiration for the boss of bosses back in Newark. However, he found it increasingly difficult to disguise his yawning and eventually said something I didn't catch.

"Oh, chéri," Maja said, "would you mind terribly if I stayed? There are some things I want to discuss with Mr. Howard."

"No," he said, slightly surprised I thought, and signaled the waiter.

"It's mine," I said.

Maja watched him as he stepped out onto the sidewalk. "He's sweet, but chemists are so single-minded," she said, returning to English and taking a sip of her Coke.

I wondered what exclusive interests dominated Fournier since he hadn't said more than ten words.

"You're an old friend of Mr. Arnheim's, aren't you?"

"Yes, I guess that's a fair description."

"He mentioned you several times."

"Mentioned me? I don't understand. When?"

"I was right. He never told you. Teddy wouldn't tell."

I was thoroughly confused.

"May I ask you a confidential question, Mr. Howard?"

"Certainly, though I'm not sure I'll answer it."

"Why didn't he marry Chris after the war?"

"How do you know all this?"

"You won't tell Mr. Stevens?"

"No."

She took another drink of her Coke and turned the glass slowly on the table. "I met Teddy when I was very young. Eighteen. My father was an engineer in Warsaw. In 1937 he was invited to France to work on a hydroelectric project in the Charente. When the Nazis went into Austria he sent for my mother and me because he was sure Czechoslovakia and Poland would be next. He was a very intelligent man. We stayed and applied for papers. When the Germans occupied all of France they deported my father to Germany to work in a munitions factory. He was discovered in sabotage and shot.

I ordered a second *fine*. She refused a second Coke.

"When Teddy . . . don't be alarmed, Mr. Howard. I never refer to him as Teddy in public. When he was shot down my mother and I found him and hid him. He was hurt, delirious for almost a week, and he talked. A lot. Later, when he was better I tried to get more information from him because I was jealous. I had fallen in love with him, you see, and I was very innocent. But he wouldn't talk." In repose, the eyes no longer guarded, her face had assumed that rather flat Slavic beauty. "He was the first American I had ever met." She pushed the Coke away. "The baby died. It was a little boy."

"I'm sorry. You never told Teddy?"

"No. It was long after he had left, of course. And he didn't love me. He couldn't. He was grateful to me and my mother, but he couldn't love me. As soon as the war was over we received a check for ten thousand dollars. It saved us. Really saved us because we had nothing. I didn't even know he was rich.

"But that was only the beginning. A little later I was offered a job as interpreter for the Americans. I didn't even ask for it. They came to me. I perfected my English and learned typing and stenography. When Mr. Arnheim died, and the firm opened an office in Lausanne I was hired, without an interview."

Other corridors of Teddy's character opening up.

"My mother still lives in the Charente. Every month she receives a check for a thousand dollars. She thinks it's for reparations, but I did some research on it, and it's not. It comes from a bank in Paris with a vice-president's signature." She looked up at me. "Did you know this side of Teddy?"

"No."

"Why *didn't* he marry Chris?"

"She married someone else."

"That's too bad. Doesn't he ever talk about it?"

"No. He never talks about his personal life."

She shook her head and reached for her Coke. "Do you think Lausanne will be headquarters?"

"I don't make the decisions. *I* would choose it, but I have to look at Amsterdam next week."

"Well, I hope it's here," she said, rising.

"I'm glad you told me about the other side."

"Thanks for the drinks, Mr. Howard. I'll see you tomorrow."

I don't know if my favorable report had any influence on the decision that was made, but Lausanne was selected, or to put it in its proper, active voice, Teddy chose Lausanne. Not without going over first to look at it himself. My modestly romantic side would have liked to be there when he walked in. I got Maja's version of it much later. He entered the office, shook her hand, complimented her on her appearance, and passed into John Stevens's office.

John Stevens agonized over his destiny in the new order, hoping that if Lausanne became the European shrine he would be chosen as manager. He wasn't. Robert Terrill from Newark went over, and Stevens became his assistant.

In Newark in the meantime, beneath the casual routine of the office, I sensed a new turbulence. Theodore the First had been satisfied with the relatively narrow but exclusive enterprise that during World War II, like most American industries, had doubled or tripled its wealth. Theodore the Second had no intention, apparently, of releasing that grip on the market—outside of the top secret brief prepared by the legal staff, the word "monopoly" was blasphemous. But there was evidence that Theodore the Second was developing other interests as well. The legal staff was told to prepare briefs, hypothetical cases of purchase of other types of industries ranging from frozen foods to radio and television stations, to pharmaceuticals, and to test them against existing antitrust laws. The reasons became obvious, though at the time such "broadening of interests" was unknown on a large scale; the antitrust people began to pout if an industry moved horizontally or vertically into the same or closely related enterprises. This reality of industrial life emerged during the period when Teddy was buying up other companies, holding them for the necessary six months to qualify as long-term capital gains, and selling at extraordinary profits. But he was also the sire, or one of the sires of conglomerates.

Either by chance or design, I got only a partial version of what was happening: I saw some of the purchase contracts, but not all of them. Kellogg probably saw all of them, and was able to estimate how much money was being spent collecting new interests, and how much of the new interests were in turn producing. But Kellogg never talked in generalities. I suspected that the only person in the company who had all the figures in his head was Teddy himself, and Teddy didn't talk. Or not often.

I saw him seldom. Sometimes I didn't even know where he was. He had bought a house in Miami and apparently was looking for property in Canada. But he was in Europe quite often as well. Occasionally he would walk into my office in shirtsleeves, drop into a chair and light a cigarette and talk, usually on some matter concerning a new acquisition, but occasionally just to talk. Sometimes he would send me off, south, west, or to Europe to look at something that interested him. On some of these missions he would go himself and invite me to accompany him.

Originally our transportation was the commercial airlines, but with the arrival of the functional jet age Teddy began collecting his own airline, starting with an early Lear jet, then a 707, and several smaller craft that were used for short hops in the states. He had three pilots and two flight stewards in his employ, but he usually took over the controls himself for takeoff and landing, a practice that understandably produced a nervous tic in his pilot's eyes. Once in the air he would relinquish the controls to Jacobs, his chief pilot, for the tedious hours of monitoring the autopilot.

In the 707 Teddy, with three members of the staff, me, his valet, Forster, and a secretary took off from Newark airport one spring evening for Paris. We were told to bring clothes for two weeks for formal to informal occasions. As soon as the airplane had climbed to altitude he returned to the cabin from which most of the seats had been removed to form an airborne salon. The steward handed him a bourbon and Coke and then took orders from the rest of us.

From a briefcase Teddy removed four packets of documents and handed one to each of us. It was like receiving sealed orders. "Take a look at this," he said and drank from his glass.

Jim Downing, a squat, bald-headed little man who was knowledgeable in finance and economics, and who had been with Arnheim Industries for many years though only recently promoted by Teddy to the number two position in the company, whistled softly when he saw it. It was a confidential report on the holdings, operations, and financial status of McGruder and Sons, reputedly the largest and wealthiest of the private gold-mining concerns in South Africa. A family business for three generations, it was now presided over by James McGruder, an eccentric Scotsman in his seventy-sixth year who was, like his father and grandfather, a citizen of South Africa.

There were biographies of him and of his two sons, James Junior and Junius, neither of whom, it was clearly hinted, was much interested in carrying on, or competent to carry on the family enterprise. James Junior had been married three times and spent as much of his year in London and Antibes as his father would permit. His brother Junius was working his way up through the company, but seemed to have hit a plateau far below the peak his father occupied.

The assets were reliably reported to be over a half a billion dollars and low operating costs permitted a net income of something in the nature of fifty million dollars a year. McGruder was known as one of the richest men in the world, but his lifestyle was simple to the point of unimaginative austerity. He lived in a modest house in a suburb and took public transportation to the company offices in downtown Johannesburg. Where the money went was a mystery since no stockholders shared in the fifty million dollars.

Donald Fairleigh, a Harvard Business School graduate and relatively recent addition to Arnheim Industries, looked up first. "Are you thinking of buying, Mr. Arnheim?"

"The thought crossed my mind," Teddy said.

"Is there any indication that he'd be willing to sell? The company has been in the family a long time." Perhaps it was his youth or his Harvard credentials that made Fairleigh brasher than the general run of Arnheim people.

"He's old, and he's been sick. The sons don't seem to give a shit about the business." Although his tailoring had improved immeasurably, Teddy's language had never changed.

"How are you going to ship gold out of South Africa?" I asked, indicating a reproduced abstract of the export laws that clearly stated limitations on noncitizens.

"Yeah, that's a question you'll have to look into, Howard," Teddy conceded casually.

"And if we figure out a way, and he's willing to sell, how do you intend to raise half a billion dollars?" Downing asked.

"Oh, I think you can find a way, Jim," Teddy said. "We can put up pretty good collateral."

"Mr. Arnheim," said Louis Tayler, an economist, the fourth member of the staff, "the future of South Africa could be troublesome. Apartheid isn't going to work forever. There could be strikes, riots, bloodshed."

"Yeah, that's a possibility," Teddy said. "But I think the mines will be worked, one way or another."

There was a chilling indifference in the remark that I found rather shocking. World opinion on apartheid had not yet found the voice of indignation that was to become articulate a few years later, but for anyone interested, information on the slave status of the blacks in the country and in Rhodesia was available. I felt Teddy's conscience stirring.

"Politically it's unattractive," I said.

"But I'm not in politics," he answered with smiling mouth.

I had never entirely understood the Trenton episode. Blaines, now in his second term, had become a close friend. Teddy was mentioned occasionally as an advisor on industrial matters, but aside from suppressing any radical attempts at instituting a state income tax, there did not seem to be anything of major importance a Democratic governor could do for Arnheim Industries. What influence he had in Washington under a Republican administration was not clear to me since I had lost almost all interest in politics. I was convinced that there was a subtle, more cunning plot that I had not yet discovered. The few times I had alluded to it Teddy had shrugged. "Just to help the party."

We had dinner high above the Atlantic and continued an analysis of the purchase of McGruder and Sons. As always, Teddy was a talented listener. He invited irreverent questions, quite obviously because they assaulted his own opinions and tested his own convictions, ultimately strengthening them. We looked at it from every possible angle, even though it was quite apparent that he had already made up his mind.

After the first shock the reasons for secrecy made very good sense. It was a battle plan. On Tuesday morning I was to walk into the Paris office of McGruder and Sons and make the offer of purchase. At precisely the same moment the other three were to do the same thing in London, Amsterdam, and Lausanne. Teddy would be in Johannesburg where, two hours later, he would walk into McGruder's office. We were to speak in terms of a negotiable purchase price, but only vaguely of the assets of Arnheim Industries. On the following Friday we would meet again in Paris.

After dinner we sat in the airborne salon for a while sipping cognac and asking more questions, until one by one his staff went to bed. I was about to follow when Teddy said, "Stick around, Howard," and I dropped back into my seat.

"You think it's a good idea?" he asked idly.

"No."

"Why not?"

"It's Jonah swallowing the whale. Indigestion."

He smiled askew. "Not quite that bad."

"Remember the old saw, 'Never bet the whole company.' ''

"Oh, we'll keep a little bit of it to play with."

"I don't see how you're going to put up that much capital. Just how much are you worth now, Teddy?" I suspect I was the only one in the company who would have asked the big question.

"I dunno exactly."

"The water-cooler sages run it into a hundred million."

He shrugged. "Someplace around there, I guess."

"Are you going to mortgage everything for some mines eight thousand miles away when you can't even take the gold out of the country?"

"My credit's pretty good, and we'll think of a way to ship out the product."

"Tell me, Teddy," I said suddenly, "why do you do it?"

"What?"

"Why do you continue to amass such enormous wealth? You'll never have to apply for Social Security to keep you in bourbon and Coke."

He swiveled his chair slowly and looked out into the dark night. "It's something to do."

"There are lots of things to do."

"No, not many, Howard."

"Not many worth the effort, you mean."

He grunted.

"I'm trying to remember the list Swanson made up in Eco 101 of why men make great fortunes. It started with ambition, a will to power, I think."

He nodded and sipped his cognac.

"I don't see you as an ambitious man in the usual sense of the word." I hadn't been this personal in years, but something in his attitude seemed to invite a degree of intimacy. "The next, if I remember correctly, was creativity. The creative impulse. Some men write books, some build bridges, and some build great fortunes." I studied the profile for a moment, the nose slightly askew, straight forehead, thin lips, and small, jutting chin. His teeth had been capped some time ago, and it changed the familiar expression. "Is that you?"

He didn't answer. He continued to look out at the dark Atlantic sky.

"I can't remember what came next. Oh, of course, the obvious—greed, profits."

He nodded, almost imperceptibly.

"I find it difficult to believe that you're not satisfied with the profits of Arnheim Industries, Colandra Orange Juice, Cranmer's Tools, Phillips Machine, Tyler Chemical, and so on. So it's not profit in the vulgar sense of the word."

"The profits are all right," he said in a flat voice.

"All right, I've remembered three of them. What was the last one on the list?"

"Speculation."

"That may be it. Speculation. Poker. Playing your wits against others. Does that take care of it?"

"Maybe. I don't know. Does it make any difference?"

"Probably not to the industrial world, but it's interesting psychologically."

"I've never believed much in psychology."

Psychology. I was very tempted to speculate aloud on other forces that might explain this extraordinary will to power. Repeated victories over the Old Man? By this time he had more than tripled what the Old Man had left, and that should have satisfied any young Oedipus. A vast emptiness left by a shattered love? Without even having tried, I knew any mention of Elmore Field, of Chris, was taboo; only once in a while when we were alone, and that was seldom, I could make out a hummed corruption of a song about dancing and darkness.

"I read a piece somewhere," I began again, "that suggested the world's richest men considered themselves a kind of exclusive fraternity. They're a club to themselves, and the initiation fees are so staggering that it's a very small, select fraternity. Getty, Hunt, the Rockefellers, Ludwig, Kennedy, and some Arabs and Greeks."

"I've never met any of them," he said. "I don't belong to clubs." He sipped his cognac.

We were speeding toward a dawn where a roseate flush was begining to brighten the darkness of the eastern sky.

"Kennedy," he said after a moment of silence. "Do you know the senator?"

"Jack? I knew him at Harvard when I was in my first year of law school. Not really intimately. Why?"

"I was just wondering about your club."

"Kennedy? He's not in my club. Upstart Irish. His father would never have received an invitation to dine at my mother's table."

He smiled. "Some club."

I wondered if he was recalling an invitation to join a club many years earlier. Since then, apparently, he had returned in spirit to his lodgings off Nassau Street, though those lodgings now consisted of a mansion in Collincourt, another in Miami, and another being built on a lake in Canada, not to speak of the duplex apartment the company owned on Fifth Avenue.

I decided to take a further plunge into intimacy. "How is your mother?"

"Okay. Getting old."

"On that weekend long ago when you offered me a job in Arnheim Industries I went up to see her."

"Yeah. I don't know why, but she thinks you're a gentleman."

"She asked me if you were going to marry."

"Yeah, that's her favorite subject."

"Are you?"

He swiveled slowly to look at me. "Are you?"

"Probably some day, if I can find a woman I can stand living with."

"Same with me. A lot of silly cunts around."

With the exception of a few weekends at Collincourt over the years, I had seldom seen Teddy socially. At Collincourt there was the usual gaggle of stunning young women who fluttered around him, but it was quite apparent that they were decorative and functional and would never appear on a list of prospective Mrs. Arnheims. I had no idea who would appear on such a list. His name had begun to appear occasionally in the papers as present at certain social functions devoted to fund-raising for various charitable organizations and for political purposes, but what his private life was like I didn't know.

I wasn't getting very far into that private life, but since he seemed in what was for him a loquacious mood, I decided to try him on something else.

"I suppose I should be able to figure it out, but can you tell me why you started supporting a Democratic candidate for governor in New Jersey several years ago? In your line of business the Republicans would seem more congenial."

"Yeah, I think you ought to figure it out, but since you're a dumb lawyer I'll help you." He held out his empty snifter, and the steward who had been hovering attentively at the bar came to us with a bottle and poured for both of us. "I think we'll have a Democratic administration after Eisenhower. Maybe not right away, but sometime."

"Who will it be?"

"I dunno. Younger and a better politician than Stevenson. I can ride with the Republicans without a fall, but . . ." He lifted his glass.

"I understand. As long as there's a Republican in the White House Arnheim Industries probably won't be asked embarrassing questions about just how firmly it's in control of the pricing of certain commodities. To use the ugly word, just how monopolistic its practices are. But under a Democratic president . . ."

"You're getting smarter, Howard."

"A Democratic administration that had been generously supported might be persuaded to resist the inevitable investigations that the party would normally be expected to conduct."

"I've got a smart lawyer."

"There's one hitch. You're assuming that the prospective candidate will take."

Staring into the glass of amber in his hand, he moved it gently to release some of the bouquet. "Oh, everybody takes, Howard."

15

TEDDY STAYED in the airplane at Orly while they refueled and cleaned it, and he and the crew slept before the long hop to the tip of Africa. The others caught planes to their several destinations. I went into Paris.

There are worse assignments than being driven to the Ritz in a waiting car, in May, in Paris, and spending three days alone wandering about the city. It was before the skyline had been raped by the Montparnasse high-rises and la Défense, before Malraux decided to remove the amiable grime from public buildings, even before they turned the banks of the Seine into a racetrack for automobiles. I had luncheon at Maxim's and in the afternoon I wandered across to the Left Bank where I had spent some time before the war. But Paris was changing, not for the better.

I ate dinner in the small restaurant that Michael and I had known in common, where the daughter of the *patronne* was now the *patronne* and a good many pounds heavier. On the second day I met Amanda.

It was in the Louvre.

Although I have never tried to paint I have long had a moderately well-informed passion for art, and a Cézanne exhibition had opened a week before, I was looking at some extraordinary gouaches in a rather crowded room in the south wing when a woman's voice said in imperfect and heavily American-accented French, ''Oh, *please* leave me *alone*,'' and there was a brief displacement of bodies on my left. A young woman emerged wrathfully, followed by a young man with concupiscence burning in his eyes. I couldn't really blame him. She was stunning.

I'm not at all the cavalier type, but she was flushed with distress and he was smaller than I. As she started to pass, the young Frenchman in tandem, I delivered a haughty, ''Monsieur, your attentions to my fiancée are annoying her. Please cease.''

For a moment I didn't think it would work because she had already passed, but when she heard me she turned back.

''Your fiancée, monsieur?''

''Yes, monsieur. Our appointment was for eleven. By the gouaches,'' I added for verisimilitude.

''I beg your pardon, monsieur.'' A Gallic twist. He begged my pardon, but not hers.

She stayed at my side as he slouched off with frustrated libido. ''Merci, monsieur,'' she said finally.

''You're welcome,'' I said in English.

''You're American?''

''Yes.''

''Is my French *that* accented?''

''Oh, mine is too.''

"I didn't notice."

She had astonishingly blue eyes, olive skin, and blue-black hair at shoulder length, a Ghibelline face that I had seen in some canvas of the Florentine school. Her accent was Manhattan. "I don't think you ever lose it unless you start very young."

"Do you mind if I stay with you for a while? He's been after me for an hour. A leech."

"I'd de delighted."

We returned to the gouaches and in the next room saw those brilliant studies of Mt. Sainte-Victoire that so fascinated the man from Aix-en-Provence. With the closing at noon we walked out together onto the gravel paths and in the warmth of the sunlight she removed the cardigan she had been wearing over a light blue blouse that she filled out splendidly.

"You may have exchanged a French leech for an American leech, but if you have nothing better to do I'll take you to lunch."

"My God, what a perverse invitation. But I'd love it."

"Let's see. Are you a good walker?"

"Excellent."

"There's a restaurant on Saint Louis that used to be pretty good." We started for the Seine.

"Do you live here?" she asked.

"No. Business trip. I'm a lawyer for an industry." We turned left toward Notre Dame. "I'm Matthew Howard."

"Amanda Bonn." She offered her hand. "I'm on business too. I work for a publisher. My first time in Paris."

There was a kind of flawless beauty about her that made my perineum twitch, and remarkably, she didn't seem to be aware of the sensation she created as she passed, or if aware, she was so habituated that she accepted it as just another of the hazards of being beautiful. She talked easily about herself: she had graduated from NYU with a degree in English, found an underpaid job in one publishing house working on paperback contracts, moved up to a junior editorship, and then to another house as editor.

The omelette, a specialty of the house, green salads, and bottle of white wine were served to us at the sidewalk table of the restaurant with a view of the upper channel of the Seine. "What industry do you work for?"

"Arnheim."

"Really? That's *very* interesting. We had a manuscript in the office two months ago about Arnheim Industries, or rather, about the postwar very rich and how they got that way. A chapter was devoted to Arnheim."

"That *is* interesting. Who wrote it?"

"Somebody by the name of . . . damn. I've forgotten."

"Did you accept it?"

"No. It was turned down at the top. Everybody who read it was surprised because it was well done, and the author—I remember now, Maxwell—had come up with some fascinating information. Do you know him? Mr. Arnheim, I mean?"

"Yes."

"Is he such a beast?"

"No, not at all. He's quiet, rather unorthodox, but certainly not a beast. What bestial qualities were attributed to him?"

"Not to his personality, but to his methods. Maxwell didn't have much to say about him personally since Mr. Arnheim refused to be interviewed. He mentions rumors without specifying, I suppose for fear of libel."

"What rumors?"

"Oh, that he has Roman orgies at his place in . . . where is it?"

"Collincourt."

"But the methods he describes! And the monopolistic control of the market. Like a conquistador . . . oh." She set her glass of wine down and raised her brilliant eyes, her cheeks slightly flushed. "I'm sorry."

"For what?"

"You must be in on it."

"On the bestiality?" I laughed heartily, difficult for me. "No. My role is strictly legal. But you certainly understand that big business and industry are not altruistic ventures."

"Of course," she said in relief. "But the Arnheim methods are Darwinian."

"He has bought and sold, like everyone else."

"But according to Maxwell he sets up traps. People don't even know what's happening to them until he pulls the trigger."

"You're confusing traps and guns."

"I shouldn't drink wine for lunch." Suddenly she looked at her watch. "Oh, my God, I'll be late."

"Where do you have to be and when?"

"Two o'clock, just off the Place de l'Opéra."

"No problem. We'll find a cab."

As we walked down the rue St. Louis, looking for a cab, she took my arm in a perfectly casual gesture. "I hope I make sense. I'm a little zonked."

"What's the occasion?"

"Conference with a French publisher that wants one of our books. I'm not the negotiater. A French agent will handle it for the author, but I'm supposed to look out for our interests. It was pure luck that they sent me. The man who usually does it was sick, and I begged for it. Fortunately I *do* know a lot about contracts, and in spite of my atrocious accent I read French as easily as I do English."

We caught a cab just before we reached the bridge. "My leech instincts coming out again, but can you have dinner with me?"

"Oh, I'm sorry, I can't. The French agent has asked me."

French agents suddenly became objects of loathing. "Tomorrow?" I was surprised at my own persistence.

"I can't tell yet. I have two more appointments, one at five, and I don't know what will happen."

"I'll call. Where are you staying?"

She opened her bag. "I think I have a card. Yes, here." It was off the rue de Rivoli. "You'd better make it after seven."

I paid the cabby when we arrived since I had no further use for him, and Amanda turned to me bright-eyed. "Thanks, Mr. Howard. I really enjoyed it."

"So did I. I'll call tomorrow."

She put out her hand, but I leaned over gallantly and kissed her on both cheeks. "The privilege of being in France."

She smiled. "I like it." Turning, she walked with determination into the entrance of the building.

I spent a lonely afternoon, remembering her, and wondering why. She was probably at least ten years younger than I, and I didn't even know if she was married, it occurred to me. She talked like a single woman, and I didn't remember a wedding ring though that is no longer an infallible method of determining the marital state. I decided I was suffering from an attack of banality—an undoubtedly beautiful

and charming young woman, but seen through the prism of a Parisian
May.

I walked down the Champs Elysées to the Petit Palais where there
was another exhibition.

But the next day, Monday, after another six hours of wandering
and looking I was in my room with the telephone in hand at seven-
fifteen. I asked for her, and the phone rang several times. I was about
to hang up when she came on, rather breathlessly.

"Oh, Mr. Howard. I just got in. I heard the phone from the hall."

"Are you free?"

"Yes. Can you give me a half an hour?"

"Certainly. More if you like."

"Eight?"

"Fine."

I walked slowly from the Place Vendôme down to the rue de Rivoli
and was in the lobby of her hotel when she came down, wearing a dark
dinner dress and a kind of bolero of spun gold. Her hair was gleaming
ebony.

"Am I late?"

"No. I'm not far away. I walked from the Ritz."

"My God, Arnheim Industries is lavish."

"It comes off the top line. I made reservations at the restaurant."

"At the Ritz?"

"Yes."

"Oh, *God*," she said softly.

"What's the matter? It's an excellent restaurant, and it's Monday.
Half the restaurants in the city are closed."

"Oh," she said in some kind of relief.

"Oh, I understand. You thought I was going to feed you and then
drag you off to my room to ravish you."

She laughed. "To put it melodramatically."

We caught a cab for the five-minute ride. "I suppose you have to
beat the beasts away regularly."

"It's usually not as difficult as with that lout in the Louvre."

"How was your meeting?"

"It went all right, I think. I didn't understand everything because
they talk so fast."

"And dinner with the agent?"

"Absolutely charming. He has an apartment near the Bois de Boulogne, and his wife cooked a feast. It's no myth about French cooking."

I wondered what the hell was happening to me that I was so relieved to hear the agent had a wife.

"You're not married?"

"Divorced. And you?"

"Neither divorced nor married."

"That's unusual. How have you escaped?"

"Prudence, I think, though I'm not sure."

The Ritz et Espadon restaurant is inclined to the gaudy, but the food and wine are good and the service excellent. Amanda blinked when she looked at the menu. "I'm not used to such largesse. Would you order for me?"

I ordered fois gras and suggested lobster.

"Oh, no," she said quickly.

"Chateaubriand? Ris de veau?"

"Ris de veau will be fine."

I took a fling with a Chambertin at a thousand francs a bottle, old francs that is. "How long have you been divorced?" The question was intended to stimulate intimacy.

"Almost two years."

"And you were married how long?"

"Again almost two years."

"Is Bonn your maiden name?"

"Yes. I wanted to wipe the slate clean."

"A bad experience?"

"No, not really. Painful for a while, and a little sloppy, but no real trauma."

Just below her left eye she had a tiny scar.

"The name is rather unusual. Are you French? You could pass for French or Spanish."

"No. I'm a Russian Jew. The name probably had a series of unpronounceable z's and k's that my father lopped off when we arrived, though he denies it."

I saw the attentive waiter wince almost imperceptibly as she spread some of the foie gras on a piece of bread. I understood her spontaneous refusal of the lobster. "Are you *practiquante*?"

"Religious? No, not at all."

"But you don't eat shellfish?"

"It's just a habit I grew up with. My parents aren't really religious either, though they go to temple on holy days as a social event. But they kept a kosher diet. I eat almost everything but shellfish. What Protestant heresy do you belong to?"

"I don't practice anything. My parents were Episcopalian."

She smiled.

"What's the joke?"

"You couldn't be anything but Episcopalian."

"How do you arrive at that conclusion?"

We were served the ris de veau.

"Because you *ooze* class."

"I do? Is it offensive?"

"Not at all, but your speech, your clothes, your looks, your manners are all very Episcopalian. I'll bet you went to Princeton."

"You're right."

"And before that Groton or St. Paul's."

"St. Paul's. Where does this extraordinary insight come from?"

"From coming from one class and marrying into a different class."

"Are you talking about class or race?"

"Class. But race has a lot to do in determining class. My father has made quite a lot of money—in the garment district. He's not wealthy, but he's comfortable, and he's not the stereotypical Jew. But he has no gentile friends, I mean real friends. Associates, acquaintances, yes, but his real friends are Jews. When I married a gentile he shook his head sadly and muttered something in Yiddish that sounded like a promise of the end."

"What happened to the marriage? If I'm not being indiscreet."

"It simply didn't work. Paul assumed naturally that I would quit my job and become hostess to his friends. Paul was Groton, Princeton."

"What's . . . ? No, don't tell me. Is that all that happened?"

"No. He wanted a child immediately. I didn't. And, oh, there were a lot of other things too . . . silly to talk about. This veal is awfully good."

The change of subjects was portentous.

She took several small pieces of cheese, but when the spectacular dessert cart, a Roman chariot laden with cakes, tarts, cream-filled rolls, Napoléons, petit fours, and flans, was wheeled to her, she said, *"Oh, non, merci."*

"Take something. Their pâtisserie is famous."

Reluctantly she selected a small petit four, and I took a modest flan.

"My God, that's good. Do they *always* have dessert after cheese?"

"Always. A dinner without dessert for the French is like . . . Antony without Cleopatra."

She laughed slyly. "Your simile is an outrageous mixture of cuisine and sex."

"It's precise. I once knew a Frenchwoman who insisted that any man who was not a good cook would be a disaster in bed."

She thought about it for a moment. "She may have been right."

"Paul wasn't a good cook?"

"A disaster," she said emphatically.

I was relieved that she didn't want to go to a *boite*, but we took a cab across the river to St. Germain des Prés to wander along the Boulevard St. Germain and have coffee. There was the usual street entertainment, mimes, small combos, dance groups, singers, and amiable weirdos, all of which delighted her.

"I'm so glad I met you," she said enthusiastically as we were having coffee and a *fine* at one of the sidewalk cafés.

"Curiously, the same thought was lurking in my mind."

"I would never have seen all this alone," she added, modifying the pleasure she had given me.

"You haven't really explained what you meant about marrying into a different class. We're supposed to live in a classless society."

"There's no such thing, as you well know."

"I agree, but at least we give lip service to the idea. What does Paul do, or is he idle rich?"

"No, no. Investment banking. That's all I know about it. He always gave the impression that I was too dumb to understand it."

"It's not very complicated."

"It doesn't interest me in the least. But it was class, the class of people who were his friends that made me homicidal. Boring, boring, *boring*. With the exception of financial reports I don't think one of them had read a book in ten years. And their wives were worse. I was Paul's little prize monkey from a different zoo, but when the monkey began to swing from a strange trapeze it was punished and told to restrain its simian indiscretions.''

"I like the image of you on a trapeze. But he didn't attribute such indiscretions to class or race.''

"My God, no. He's much too much of a gentleman for that. But it was clear what he meant, and he grieved endlessly that I didn't like his friends. But I'm really tired of talking about Paul. Tell me about you.''

"Another boring subject.''

"How long have you worked for Mr. Arnheim?''

"Since his father died a few years after the war.''

"You were in the war?''

"Not really. I was a flying instructor. So was Teddy, but he escaped and got into the war. Shot down over Europe.''

"That's when you met him?''

"Oh, no. I've known him since we were children. We were at St. Paul's together.''

"*Arnheim*? At St. Paul's? Impossible. He's a Jew.''

"You have some very rigid ideas about St. Paul's, Princeton, and so on.''

"Oh, come on, now, Mr. Howard.''

"Matt.''

"Come on, now, Matt. You have to admit it's unusual.''

"I suppose it was. He was isolated certainly, but Teddy isolates himself, and it's not because one grandfather was Jewish. It's a deliberate act of severance, of avoidance.''

"Why?''

"I would suspect that I know Teddy as well as anyone knows him, perhaps better than anyone else, and still I'm not sure I can answer that question.''

A little old lady selling individual roses approached our table. I bought one and handed it to Amanda.

"Thank you. It's beautiful.'' She held it under her nostrils. "But it has no odor. Strange.''

"Maybe it's fake.''

"No, it's real, but it has no perfume.'' She laid it on the table.

"When do you go back to New York?'' I asked.

"Wednesday.''

"Too bad. Can't you stay a few days longer?''

"I wish I could. I really do. But I have one more appointment tomorrow and I leave Wednesday morning."

"If you had more time we could rent a car and drive down through the Loire. It's a good season, before the rash of Anglo-Saxons starts to appear."

"I have to be in my office Thursday morning. How long are you staying?"

"I have an appointment tomorrow morning, and then nothing until Friday when Teddy arrives."

"He's in Europe?"

"Not exactly, but he'll be here Friday."

"Another trap?"

"It might be. I don't know yet. Amanda, are you free for dinner tomorrow?"

"I'm really sorry, but I'm not." She laid a hand over mine on the table. "I wish I were. I enjoy being with you."

I turned my hand over, clasped hers briefly and released it. "I hope that extends to New York since I intend to call you if you have no objections."

"No, I have no objections. I'd like to see you. But, you know, I . . ."

"What?"

"I don't know how to say it without sounding priggish. I had my two years with Groton and Princeton."

"That's an *absurd* statement."

"I know."

"I'm not Paul. There's some variety in the product turned out, even by Princeton."

"Yes, of course. I'd like you to call."

I noticed she left the rose on the table when we left to walk back, on her suggestion, though I warned her it was a rather long walk. We plunged into the labyrinth of little streets north of the Boulevard St. Germain and emerged on the Quai Voltaire to cross the river on the Pont Royal, stopping to watch a *bateau mouche* pass beneath us. She took my arm and leaned her head against my shoulder. "Such a pleasant evening."

I put my arm around her. "We can have more."

"I hope so."

"You don't sound optimistic."

She moved away from me and walked a few steps to lean against the balustrade again. "I don't mean to sound difficult."

"Of course. There's someone in New York."

"Oh . . . yes, more or less, but that's not what I mean really."

I went to her. "I don't turn you on?"

She laughed. "Oh, yes, you *do*. It's not that."

"You don't like what I do in the world. Is that it?"

"I guess so. I'm just not happy around the very rich."

"I regret to say that I'm not very rich."

"You know what I mean. People who work for big industry, who help to amass immense fortunes at a human sacrifice that I can't even begin to estimate."

"We don't have any altars for sacrificial rites in Arnheim Industries.

"Now you sound like Paul. He always laughed at me when I talked seriously."

"I wasn't laughing."

"I'm not talking about literal sacrifice, though I suspect there's plenty of that, too. But sacrifice of effort, of lives, the devotion to a deadly routine, just to make huge sums of money. Millions and millions of people drag themselves out of bed every morning to fall into cars or the subway to report to a stultifying job they hate so that someone becomes a million dollars richer."

"Is that your job?"

"No, I love my job, even though it doesn't pay much. But since I have to work I can't imagine a more interesting way to make a living."

"Paul doesn't help?"

"I didn't ask for help. I think alimony is outrageous, barbarous."

"I know several ex-husbands who would vote for you."

"What I'm talking about is obviously banal."

"No, I don't think so."

"Somewhere in our history, probably with those wretches who started the Industrial Revolution, our values went completely askew. We work at the wrong things for the wrong reasons. We don't enjoy living unless we're drunk or stoned. Even sex has become a kind of drug. Endless books on how to get more out of the drug." She turned to examine me. "Paul was always shocked when I talked like this. I'm not shocking you, am I?"

"Once more, I'm *not* Paul."

"And you *do* understand what I mean?"

"I think so."

"The vast majority of people spend a lifetime working frantically at something they detest—in quiet desperation, to quote Thoreau. Sordid, boring. With two weeks' vacation every year that they plan on so frantically they don't enjoy it. It's a monstrous perversion of the life spirit, or at least as I understand the life spirit."

"In a capitalist society people work to earn money to buy the things they believe are necessary or desirable. You don't have anything against money, do you?"

"Not at all. I like money. I'd like to have lots of money. Money permits dignity. I'm filled with quotes tonight. That's George Bernard Shaw. But I don't want to whore to make it. And I'm not talking only about America. I've seen the same thing here."

"Yes, if it's destruction, the French are leaping to their own destruction on the American model."

She buried her head against my shoulder to stifle a yawn. "I'm sorry."

"You're tired."

"Yes. The last few days have been heady. What time is it?"

It's strange that women never know what time it is. "Twelve-twenty. We can take a cab if you like."

"No. It's not far now, is it?"

"Just across the Tuileries."

We began walking again, Amanda in a determined stride, clinging to my arm. At the entrance of her hotel she turned to me. "Thank you. It's been a long time since I've enjoyed being with someone as much as I have with you. And you've been patient. You listen to me."

"The voice of the rebellious angel. I have probably forgotten to say you're not only beautiful, but you're an intelligent woman."

She looked up at me for a moment, her eyes searching mine, then she lifted her mouth to be kissed, and I kissed her.

"Are you in the book?"

"Yes."

"Where do you live?"

"On Gay Street in the Village."

"We're practically neighbors."

"I'm glad. Good night, Matt."

"Good-bye, Amanda."

*   *   *

When the Englishman, blond, forty-five or so, with very thick glasses, heard my proposition the next morning, that Arnheim Industries should buy out McGruder and Sons, he almost lost his British equanimity. His mouth opened as though he meant to say something scurrilous, and closed again.

After an interval it opened again to say, "But, Mr. Howard, I fail to understand why you present such a preposterous proposition to me." On each alliterative "p" his lips pouted more petulantly.

"Mr. Arnheim felt that representatives of the company should be consulted."

"But I make no policy decisions. McGruder and Sons is controlled, directed, managed, and to be quite candid, manipulated by one man, and one man alone. James McGruder."

"So is Arnheim Industries."

"Mr. McGruder consults neither his sons nor his hirelings. When a change is made, a decision reached, we are informed of it as a *fait accompli.*"

"But speaking theoretically, how does the proposition strike you?"

"Utterly preposterous. Mr. McGruder would never give it a moment's consideration. We are, of course, quite aware of the strength of Arnheim Industries, but I believe there has been a misunderstanding somewhere. Frankly, compared to McGruder and Sons, it's a ten-shilling affair. Do not permit yourself to be deluded by the roles of Johnson Matthey, Rothschild, and Mocatta and Goldschmidt. Our voice can reasonably be said to control the London fixings of gold."

"Arnheim Industries alone sets the price of platinum."

"Ah, yes, but are the world's reserves in gold or in platinum? No, Mr. Howard, it's a misguided maneuver, quite futile." And he began to lecture me on American presumptuousness and on the sacred traditions of McGruder and Sons that had been handed down from father to son for three generations. He was warming to his subject when the buzzer on his desk sounded. He picked up the phone. "I believe I told you that I didn't want . . . Who? Oh. Put him on." He turned to me. "Please excuse me, Mr. Howard."

"Certainly."

"Is that you, Desmond? Yes." He swiveled his back to me, listening intently, but after a few moments he turned slowly, still listening, to stare at me with increasing malevolence. "I see. Yes.

Yes. No, I'll call him. Yes, certainly. Right away.'' He put the phone down, his eyes still fixed on me in a mixture of malice and astonishment. ''If you will excuse me, Mr. Howard, I have a rather important call to make.''

''Certainly.'' I rose. ''Thank you for your time.''

He started to conduct me to the door, but the buzzer sounded again, and he leapt on the phone.

After Amanda left, I wandered about Paris, saw some other expositions, went to the theater twice, ate several good meals, and waited for Friday. At my salary, which had increased comfortably over the years, I was not being used efficiently.

Friday came. I arrived at the Tour d'Argent, where I had never been because of the outrageous prices, at the same time as Jim Downing, and we quickly exchanged accounts of our attempts to buy McGruder and Sons. Fairleigh and Tayler were already at a reserved table where champagne was being poured, and we compared reactions. There was, not surprisingly, a distinct similarity, though Tayler reported that he had almost been thrown out of the London office. In Amsterdam, London, Lausanne, and Paris the tempered outrage had had the same ring: Arnheim Industries, though a respectable little enterprise, was simply not in the same league as McGruder and Sons, and the offer of purchase had been treated as an absurd gesture.

We drank more champagne and waited, rather nervously, for Teddy to arrive.

''Are you sure we have the right day?'' Fairleigh asked suddenly.

''The table was reserved,'' Tayler said, ''and the champagne is flowing. He's only a half-hour late.''

''Oh, he'll be here,'' Downing said. ''It's part of the Arnheim method to . . .''

Escorted by the obsequious maître d', Teddy came through the restaurant and sat down. ''Hi,'' he said casually. He was in a pinstriped suit, white shirt with an Oxford collar, and a rich Cardin tie. He looked a little tired, but the eyes suggested accomplishment. The waiter poured champagne for him, and he lit a Chesterfield, the old, unfiltered version that he clung to resolutely.

''I heard you threw a scare into some people,'' he said to his assembled audience. Of course he would know, just how, I wasn't certain.

"More like a challenge," Downing said.

"More like an insult," Tayler said.

"Yeah, so I heard. Well, let's eat. I'm hungry."

"Come on, Teddy," I said. "Are we going to hear what happened in Johannesburg."

His mouth smiled. "Later." He signaled the waiter and began to order.

I took some more foie gras, a lobster, and a salad, well worth the stupendous price.

Teddy ate a steak.

As he chewed he listened while we described our various encounters with McGruder and Sons, but he said nothing about his own experiences with the eminence in South Africa. However, it was perfectly clear that he was satisfied with the results of his journey, and I wondered how he had managed to persuade a notoriously rigid Scotsman to dispose of an inherited empire.

"How was the weather down there?" I asked, "if that's not top secret, too."

"Good. Fall beginning. It's a nice town."

"Did you buy any slaves when you were down there?"

"No. I have enough already."

Fairleigh, who had been gulping champagne incontinently, snorted damply and smothered his hilarity with a large linen napkin. Tayler and Downing looked at me covertly.

"What was the state of Mr. McGruder's health?" I continued in order to put some conversation on the table.

"He has hemorrhoids, a weak heart, maybe a little cirrhosis, and ingrown toenails."

"You must have really hit it off for him to admit all that."

"I knew all that before I went down."

Something began to take shape, but I needed more pieces.

We finished with cheeses and another chariot of pâtisserie, followed by more champagne. Fairleigh was becoming a little sloppy. Reaching for his glass he upset it, spreading a yellow stain of Moët across the tablecloth that the waiter immediately covered with a napkin.

"We're merged," Teddy said without warning.

"I beg your pardon," Downing said.

"McGruder and Sons and Arnheim Industries have merged, or will merge in a month or so if the papers look right."

A profound silence descended over the table, interrupted only by a thunderous hiccup from Fairleigh.

"Why?" I asked.

"It's time for expansion, and expansion is easier as a multinational. When they float gold it will triple in price. Maybe more."

"May I ask who bought whom?" Tayler said in an unsubstantial voice.

"Arnheim Industries is buying forty-nine percent of McGruder and Sons."

"Does it mean a change in company identity?" Downing asked.

"No. No change."

"You had this all set up when we came over?" I asked.

"Yeah."

"Why the masquerade?"

"I needed some shock troops. If you had known you wouldn't have been as convincing as you were."

Fairleigh hiccuped again.

"We'll take a hop to London on Monday," Teddy said, dropping his napkin. "Let's go see some skin."

It was a typical Parisian *boite* for tourists on the Right Bank, and there was no entrance fee, but the champagne that began to arrive cost one hundred dollars a bottle. It was crowded, dark, and obscured by a smokescreen. The nude floor show was suggestive rather than indecent; no explicit acts of copulation were performed on the floor, and the male dancers wore sequined jock straps. It was strictly heterosexual but curiously lacking in erotic artistry, probably because the French don't believe that foreigners understand the subtlety of the erotic. But there was plenty of flesh, and the girls were quite beautiful.

Fairleigh quickly became a nuisance and tried to join the show. Tayler went after him and dragged him back to the table.

"Wanta dance," Fairleigh said.

"Not now, Donald." Tayler glanced at Teddy. "We'll be going back to the hotel, Mr. Arnheim."

Teddy nodded and poured more champagne in his glass.

"I'll go along," Downing said. "Good night."

I stayed, partly out of curiosity and partly because it seemed poor manners to leave our host alone for the rest of the evening. Teddy was sitting on my left, slightly closer to the table, and I was able to examine him without staring into his eyes. He was losing that lean irregularity of countenance; in fact he was becoming portly. In profile, with his head down, a double chin had begun to descend over his collar. The hair, carefully brushed, was quite gray at the temples. He seemed to me to be growing into the model that had been formed to accept him many years earlier. The hands remained the same: small, delicate, still shaking slightly with that nervous energy that a heavier body had finally succeeded in disguising.

"Are you pissed, Howard?" he asked me in a break between the shows, without looking at me.

"No. But I feel as though I had been used."

"You were. But well."

"You had the merger papers in your pocket when we came over?"

"Yeah."

"Who prepared them? Kellogg?"

"Yeah. I didn't want you in on the writing so I could use you here. Kellogg's too clumsy. Stop by tomorrow and I'll give you a copy."

"When McGruder dies what happens?"

"Depends on the sons."

All the pieces were in place. McGruder, aging and ill, one son bored by the company, and the other without managerial talents, while Arnheim Industries would be waiting in the wings.

A flute began to wail in Oriental half-tones, joined by a drum, and the lights went out. A spot suddenly stabbed into the darkness, illuminating a young woman with straight black hair, a heavy, sensual face with stylized makeup, a bra, and a skirt of ribbons. Slowly she began to manipulate her abdomen in a *danse du ventre*, a belly dance.

It was extraordinary. Erotic, certainly, but controlled by an austerity of movement within a long classical tradition. The expression on her face never changed, but I had never witnessed such an articulate belly. It quivered, rolled, expanded, and contracted in a series of consummate fleshly statements.

When the lights came on again and she withdrew to applause, Teddy signaled the waiter and spoke too low for me to understand.

"Comment, Monsieur?"

Teddy spoke again.

"Mais, Monsieur, c'est . . ."

"Demande à lui," Teddy said vigorously.

The waiter scurried off, and Teddy poured more champagne for both of us.

Several minutes later the waiter returned and bent down to speak.

"Bon," Teddy said. He pulled out a roll of francs and paid the bill. "Can I give you a ride back, Howard?"

"No, thanks. I'll walk."

I had a final glimpse of him in the vestibule, joined by a small figure in a cape. They went out the door together.

After I had breakfasted the next morning I shaved, showered, dressed, and about eleven o'clock went up to Teddy's suite, where I knocked.

"Qui est là?" a woman's voice demanded.

I turned away discreetly, but the door was wrenched open and the belly dancer, swathed in a man's dressing gown, stood before me. *"Qui es tu?"*

Arabs never seem to learn formal address. They tutoie everyone.

"Je suis copain de M. Arnheim. Est-il là?"

"Non. You American?"

"Yes."

"You come in."

"No, I won't disturb . . ."

She took my arm suddenly and yanked me into the room with the vigor of an Amazon. Closing the door behind her she stared at me with what I took to be violent intentions. *"Qui est ce con Teddee?"*

"Il n'est pas con."

"He very rich?"

"Yes."

"He married?"

"No."

"You have . . . *sérail* in America?"

"Not legally."

"He take Yoyo to *Amerique, tu crois?"*

"I don't know."

She undulated past me to a large *table roulante* that bore the remains of a breakfast of eggs, ham, croissants, brioches, coffee, and several bottles of Coke. Plastering a croissant with butter she thrust it in her mouth and began vigorous mastication. "You want one?" she asked her mouth full of croissant.

"No, thank you."

"How much he pay for Yoyo?"

"I have no idea."

"*Il m'a achetée. Combien?*"

"*Aucune idée.*"

"*Tu es copain. Tu sais.*"

"*Non, je ne sais rien.*"

"He buy me. Take with?"

"I don't know, Yoyo."

"*Il est un peu fou, tu sais.*"

"*Comment fou?*"

"*Fait des choses . . . des conneries. Fou.*" She wiped her hands on the robe and dropped it to the floor. "I dance now. Muscles need train every day."

I left her nude before the full-length mirror, her round belly beginning its eloquence.

When I returned to my room the document I had gone in search of was on the desk, and I settled down to study a draft of the merger of McGruder and Sons and Arnheim Industries. I spent the rest of the day at it. I heard nothing from Teddy, but my fellow slaves called around seven to get me to the bar. They were going out to dinner and tried to persuade me, but the mist that had settled over Paris in midafternoon had turned into a heavy, beating rain.

"I have too much homework."

"Did he show you the agreement?" Downing asked, a little aggrieved, I thought.

"It was delivered to my room. And 'show' is a bit casual. It runs to one hundred and fifty pages."

Downing whistled lightly. "Well, I suppose it will come my way sooner or later."

I returned to my homework, beginning to make notes that soon ran into a lot of yellow pad. Later I had dinner sent up and continued working. It was after midnight when I went to bed. I finished reading and making notes Sunday afternoon. Still I had heard nothing from Teddy.

After dinner Sunday the four of us had a drink at the bar.

"I wish we had a Paris office," Fairleigh said. "I'd apply for the job."

Downing, the senior slave, glanced at him. "I'd stay in Newark if I were you, Donald."

"Why?"

"It's a lot safer." It was tacit, but certainly explicit enough, though Fairleigh didn't give the impression he was concerned, and when later he asked me to describe the general nature of the merger, I didn't require the glance from Downing to avoid the question.

Though I knew Downing quite well, the four of us were not precisely intimate, and it was perfectly clear that they considered me an insider. They were guarded in their references to Teddy, apparently convinced that what was said to, or before, me would be carried to him immediately. I resented the assumption, but how to tell them that Teddy didn't invite such confidences, and that I had little inclination to act the informer?

Large American companies and industries have over many years developed a personnel policy that is ostensibly the product of democracy. In a good many instances the officers, from the president on down, encourage informality, a kind of jocular familiarity on a first-name basis.

Arnheim Industries did not participate in this mythology. So far as I knew I was the only person in the company to address Teddy by his first name before others. I had decided at the beginning that I would continue to do so since to have said "Mr. Arnheim" seemed to me fraudulent, much more dishonest than "Teddy." He, of course, never offered an opinion on the subject.

"Do you know what we're going to do in London?" Tayler asked.

Downing shrugged. "See Henry, I suppose. And Mr. Arnheim has an appointment with the ambassador on Tuesday."

"What about?"

"I don't know. He just told me to make an appointment."

"There are times," Fairleigh said recklessly, "when I think no one in the company knows what anyone else is doing."

"You're right, with one exception," Downing said, lifting his glass. "And he knows what everybody's doing."

The four of us went out to Orly at ten the next morning to board the airplane. Almost an hour later a large black Mercedes drove over the tarmac and stopped under a wing. Teddy emerged followed by Yoyo in a light blue coat.

"Who's the woman?" Fairleigh asked.

They came into the salon together, Teddy nodding and Yoyo looking rather bewildered until she saw me.

"Tu vois," she said. *"Il me prende avec. En Amerique."*

"C'est bon."

"Qui sont les autres?"

"Des copains."

"Louches," she said and began wandering around the cabin to examine the furnishings.

For once Teddy let Jacobs take the airplane off the ground while he began studying the sheaf of notes I had made. Just before we turned onto the runway he looked at Yoyo, who was still inspecting the interior of the airplane and said, *"Assieds toi."*

"Quoi, cheri?"

Teddy glanced at the steward who tackled Yoyo and forced her into a seat, buckling the seat belt as we began to roll.

She yelped in surprise.

Two black limousines met us at Gatwick and drove us to the VIP reception room for entry formalities, mere formalities until Yoyo started to pass.

"Your passport, please, miss."

"Passport? My passport in Paris."

Teddy, who was already starting toward the exit, stopped. "Oh, shit," he muttered and turned back.

"I'm sorry, Mr. Arnheim, but I can't permit this young lady to enter without papers."

Teddy looked at her as though he had made a bad investment. "Forster," he said to his valet, "take her to the airplane and tell Jacobs to fly her back to Paris."

"Yes, sir."

"And when you have her on the airplane, give her this." He extracted a wad of francs.

Then he turned, and, followed by us, went through the door.

16

FIVE WEEKS LATER Teddy, accompanied by Kellogg, secretaries, and his valet took off for South Africa.

But a few days before that Donald Fairleigh found a new job.

That was after I had called Amanda. The first two times, around nine o'clock in the evening, she wasn't in, and I began to suspect that penetrating her social life would require persistence. The third time she answered and when I said, "It's Matt," her hesitation was chilling. Then she said, "Oh, Matt. I'm so glad you called. I was wondering if you would."

Enigmatic.

"I tried before, but you weren't home."

"I took three more days and went to Fire Island."

In spite of my contempt for men who try to coordinate precisely the word and the actions of the women they are interested in, my mind began counting the days she *had* to be at her desk and the days I had been back in New York.

"Wasn't it cold?" I asked, resisting the impulse to question her on details.

"It was beautiful, warm, and peaceful."

"Do you see a dinner in the near future?"

"How near?"

"Saturday?"

"Oh, Matt . . ."

"Okay, I understand. What do you see beyond Saturday?"

"Sunday?"

Some of my disappointment dissolved. "That's fine. Seven-thirty?"

"Good. It's Thirty-seven and a half Gay. You have to go through a court."

"I'll find it."

Prudent, rational, socially conscious to the point of snobbery when I was young, or so I had been told, I began to wonder where this impulse was pushing me. Had I found someone I could stand living with? Apparently I intended to find out.

The June sun of Fire Island had deepened Amanda's olive skin to gold. In a simple, dark dress, discreetly décolleté, and wearing a pearl necklace, she looked like what I had always imagined Cleopatra as, except for the extraordinarily blue eyes, lightly accented with shadow. Cleopatra must certainly have had brown eyes.

"Matt," she said as she opened the door, "it's good to see you."

I kissed her casually on both cheeks, bringing France to the Village. "You ravish my senses." Gallantry.

"Please. I can't deal with such Old World manners."

It was a tiny apartment, the living room walls almost entirely covered with books, a Käthe Kollwitz on one wall, and a sun-splashed poster of Minorca on another. A small kitchen, bathroom, and a single bedroom made up the rest of it, almost, I felt, too small to accommodate a man. There was a huge bouquet of roses on the desk next to the window that looked out over the communal court. Even with its battered furniture, the room had a kind of diminutive enchantment.

"Have you been here since the divorce?"

"Yes. I can't find anything larger that I can afford, and I like it. You can't even hear the traffic from Sixth Avenue. I have some vodka and some scotch."

"If you have some vermouth I'll make a martini."

"Yes. And would you pour me some white wine? It's in the fridge."

I bumped my head in the kitchen, and it was so small that in order to extract the ice I had to slide out again, open the refrigerator door, and reenter for the trays.

There was a note of expectancy in her voice when she spoke. "What nefarious new plots were hatched by Arnheim Industries after I left Paris?"

I handed her her glass and sat down by her. "Nothing spectacular," I said on the edge of a lie. It wasn't prompted so much by a policy of company secrecy as by my suspicion of how she would react if she knew that Arnheim Industries had merged with a South African company.

"Well, *I* learned something spectacular," she said with a suggestion of conspiracy. "Does the name Holton mean anything to you?"

"Certainly. A chain of small papers Arnheim bought a couple of years ago."

"It's more than a chain of small papers now. It also owns two publishing houses, one of which publishes school texts, and the other, Cromwell, which I work for."

I was astonished. "Are you sure?"

"Absolutely. I'm surprised you didn't know about it."

"So am I. But not everything comes across my desk. How did you find out?"

"The Authors' Guild puts out a quarterly, and they have a section on who has moved where, on sales, purchases, and the control of publishing houses."

"When did this happen? I mean Holton buying your house?"

"About two months ago, but it wasn't public until the Guild learned of it. The people at Cromwell didn't even know about it, at least the people I work with. I learned about it when I came back from Paris."

"It's the first I've heard about it, but probably the legal business was handled by Holton's lawyers. I remember the purchase of Holton very well."

"But it makes something clear."

"You're thinking of the . . . what was his name? Maxwell. You're thinking his book was turned down at the top because of the chapter on Arnheim."

"Yes, that's what I think. In fact I'm sure of it. No reason was ever given for rejecting it. Everybody who read it made an enthusiastic report. But then it disappeared in the editor-in-chief's office and nothing more was said about it."

"Possible, I suppose."

"More than possible. Probable."

"Was it libelous?"

"What *is* libelous?"

"Malicious misrepresentation."

"Then I don't think it was libelous. Maxwell had done a careful job of research."

"Well, it's certainly possible, but I doubt that Teddy had anything to do with it. He shrugs things like that off with a smile."

"But it's still control of sorts, and I don't like it."

"So it seems we work for the same person."

"And I don't like it. How long will it be before everybody is working for him?"

We walked slowly through the warm evening toward Washington Square, still talking, almost arguing, about the role of conglomerates in American life.

"It doesn't mean that Maxwell can't get his book published if it's a good book."

"It's a good book, and it deserves publishing, but if the word has gone out that we've turned it down for certain reasons he may have problems."

"I thought that publishing was more competitive than that."

"Oh, it *is* competitive, but if one empire refuses it, and the reasons are known, another house may feel it's too risky."

The square was filled with the usual freaks, somehow more threatening than those on the Boulevard St. Germain. I took Amanda to Minetta Tavern where, because they don't accept reservations, we had another drink at the bar while waiting for a table.

"What have you decided to do?"

"I've thought of quitting."

"That would be foolish. You don't have hard evidence."

"Oh, I know you're right and I won't do anything until I know for certain. And it really hurts. I like Cromwell and the people I work with, and apparently they like me. They gave me a raise when I came back, and I think I'll be promoted to senior editor. Jobs in publishing are hard to find."

"If you like I can try to find out what happened."

"Oh, *would* you, Matt?"

"I'll try."

At dinner I tried to turn the conversation toward more personal matters, but Amanda was obsessed by the vast inequities of huge capitalist enterprise. "Tell me," I said finally, "just what shade of political radicalism are you persuaded of?"

She laughed. "Do I sound like a Communist?"

"No, not exactly."

"I guess I'm a left-wing Democrat. The first time I voted it was for Stevenson on his second attempt."

"So did I."

"*You*? My God, you've shattered the Episcopalian image. I was sure you were a Republican."

"And, by the way, Arnheim is also a Democrat."

"Oh, yes, I've seen those stories about his generous aid to the party of the people. I don't believe a word of it."

"That he's a Democrat? He is."

"No, that it's public spirit. He wants something. Maybe governor or senator."

She surprised me. There was a certain toughness about her that was quite strange to me, and I wondered if I would discover another level that coincided more nearly with her radiance. She seemed to cultivate a deliberate impersonality, perhaps for armor since it was impossible for her to walk into a room without causing a silent sensation. The thought dropped into my brain that perhaps young women had undergone a radical change that I hadn't been told about.

In a bold venture I asked, "Amanda, is there a particular man in your life?"

Worthy of a troubador.

"Oh," she looked vague, "there's someone I've known for quite a while."

"Are you . . . intimate?"

She looked at me in what I interpreted as bewildered amusement. "Do you mean do I make love with him?"

"Oh. Well, yes, I guess that's what I meant."

"Occasionally."

I wondered how often that meant. "You had dinner with him last night?"

"Yes."

"Doesn't he object to your going out with me?"

"I don't know if he objects, and I don't give a damn. I go out with whom I please."

Yes. Young women had changed, and I hadn't been told.

A man with dark curly hair, wearing jeans and an open shirt, stopped on his way to a table. "Hi, Mandy."

"Oh, hi, Sam. Thanks for the manuscript. I haven't finished it yet."

"No hurry."

"I'll call as soon as I have."

"Thanks." He caught up with his companion who was beginning to look annoyed.

"I lied," Amanda said. "I have finished it."

"Is he an author?"

"No, an agent. I didn't like the book, but I didn't want to tell him now."

"You can't make the decision on acceptance?"

"Oh, no. I write a report. If I made the decisions Maxwell's book would have been published."

"Do you want to stay in publishing?"

"Yes, I adore it. My wildest dream is to be editor-in-chief some day when I'm about sixty-five years old. To make the final decision on a book myself."

"Or own your own publishing house?"

"That isn't even in the scope of my wildest dreams."

"How much does it cost to start a new house?"

"Oh, I suppose three or four million dollars now. I don't really know. Do you want to invest three or four million dollars in me?" she asked, smiling.

"Nothing would give me greater pleasure, but unfortunately the Howards never cornered a market."

We had coffee in an Italian coffee house on McDougal Street, and afterward wandered awhile. "I lived in that building for two years while I was at NYU," she said, pointing to an old building on the corner of Sullivan Street. "Did you say you're near?"

"West Tenth."

"Oh, lovely. I'd like to see it sometime."

"Now?"

"What time is it?"

"Eleven-thirty."

"Not tonight. I have a nine-thirty appointment tomorrow."

"Where is Cromwell located?"

"Madison at Twenty-ninth. It's ideal. I walk both ways."

"Quite a walk."

"I love it, and it saves money."

"I take it that publishing does not provide vast riches."

"Not on my level."

We had turned in the direction of 8th Street. Midway down the block a wino staggered toward us, and Amanda grabbed my arm. He mumbled fifty cents, but didn't bother with the coffee.

"No," I said automatically.

"Oh," Amanda said, "give him something."

I fished out some coins and dropped them into his soiled hand.

"Thanks . . . lady," he said, leering at me malevolently.

"Why did you say no?"

"I guess it's because it embarrasses me."

"*Embarrasses* you! My *God,* that's egoistic. The poor old thing can only live if he has his drink and that embarrasses you."

"Yes. First of all I resent the fact that they always select me as the patsy. They pass up twenty people and pounce on me."

"That's because you look prosperous."

"No more than anyone else."

"Oh, yes. Wait. Stay here." She walked on a few feet and turned back to look at me. "Prosperous and . . . kind."

"Kind?"

"Yes." She came back in an animated little strut. "Kind, compassionate." She came close and looked up at me. "Are you?"

"I'm not sure I can answer that."

She continued to look at me. "How did you put it? Oh, yes. Do *you* have a particular woman in your life?"

"No."

"It's hard to believe. You're attractive, intelligent, prosperous, and kind. Why not?"

"My mother told me to beware women."

She took my arm again. "*Really,* why not?"

"I suppose because I'm . . . morbidly fastidious."

"Oh, God," she groaned.

"But I'm still not Paul."

"No, you're not. What are the other reasons that, contrary to your kind nature, you don't give?"

"I think it's because panhandlers display a jaunty disregard for the status of mankind."

"Wow!" she said. "Have you ever read Conrad's *Lord Jim?*"

"Yes, long ago."

"I think it's almost word for word."

"I thought it was original. But it expresses what I feel."

Arriving at the little gate that led into her court, she inserted a key and opened. "Thank you, Matt. I enjoyed it."

"I'll call soon."

"I hope you will." She turned her face up to me, and I kissed her much less casually than with the formality of Paris, and she was responsive. When she moved back she looked at me for a moment in the shadow of the wall and said, "Good night."

"Good night, Amanda."

I began to see her quite often. She liked the theater, and though I'm relatively indifferent to an assembly of nervous extroverts pretending that they are someone else before a larger assembly of introverts, she taught me things about the drama that increased my pleasure. On several weekends we went to museums. Eventually I invited her to my house to prove that I was a competent cook in the culinary sense of the word.

It was probably pompous to invite her since in comparison to her apartment mine was palatial, a duplex on the two top floors of the brownstone. I had had an inner staircase built between the second floor, which was my living room, dining room, and kitchen, and the top floor where there were two bedrooms, one used as a study, and a large front room where I had hung my pictures.

Amanda's reaction was spontaneous and rewarding. "How lovely," she said as she entered the living room. "Where did you find those chairs?"

"My great-grandmother found them."

Her instinct was infallible. "Is that a *real* . . . oh, who is it?" She was looking at one of my two treasures that I kept on the second floor, a small pastoral.

"Don't tell me. Bellini?"

"That's very close. It's attributed to Giorgioni, but it's never been reliably authenticated. I don't want to know."

"Where did you get it?"

"Inherited."

"And this is a real Renoir?" she said before a luminous nude.

"Yes. Also inherited."

"God, it's beautiful. You certainly chose your ancestors wisely." She walked around the room inspecting and admiring. She was wearing very tailored slacks and a sweater, her hair drawn back to a bun that reminded me of pictures of Christina Rossetti. "Are these your parents?"

"Yes."

"Handsome man. Your mother looks a bit . . . ethereal."

"She was."

I made drinks and we carried them to the third floor. "My *God.* You didn't inherit all these?"

"No. Bought over the years."

After studying one wall for a while she said, "Do you mind if I suggest something?"

"Not at all."

"I don't believe the Rothko should be next to this . . . it isn't really a Turner, is it?"

"No. One of his admirers."

"The Rothko bleeds all the color out of the . . . whoever it is."

I looked at them for a moment. "I believe you're right. But the Rothko is so violent it's hard to place."

She looked around. "How about there? In place of that collage?"

I put my glass down. "I'll try it."

When we had changed them we stood together looking at one wall and then the other. "Much better," I said finally.

She continued her inspection of the study and the bedroom. "It's really a gorgeous house. How long have you been here?"

"Years. I rented first, then I decided to buy it."

"You *own* it?"

"Yes, but prudently. The rent from the doctor's office on the first floor paid off the mortgage."

She smiled.

"Of course he could be removed," I added.

The smile disappeared.

I took her hand. "My daub is calling me."

"Yes, I hear it."

When she had tasted the daub she said, "You *are* a good cook."

Tacitly we ignored the heavy pun on cooking skills, and she began to talk about a book she was editing. "In the beginning he resisted every suggestion I made, but gradually he surrendered. It's not the same book that he wrote, but it's a better book."

"Strange sort of profession. You never see a book with title, author, and then 'edited by.' It's anonymous. Don't editors ever resent it?"

"Yes, in some cases it's almost a collaboration. Some resent it. I don't."

After I had stacked the dishes in the machine I served coffee in the living room in demitasses that my paternal grandmother had bought in China on a trip around the world in the early twentieth century.

"What did he do? Your grandfather, I mean."

"Do?" You mean his occupation?"

"Yes."

"Not much. He didn't really have to do much. He inherited."

"What?"

"Oh, a shipping company and some sawmills in New England. A classical curve. *His* father, my great-grandfather, had restored a dwindling estate after the Civil War, and my grandfather was persuaded that working was vulgar. He managed to dispose of a large part of what his father had reassembled."

She shook her head in what I took to be an expression of refusal to a question that I had not articulated. "Why not?" I asked.

"Why not what?"

"Why did you say no?"

"I don't think I said no. I was just bewildered by such familial . . . testimony. I don't even know who my paternal grandfather was. My father deliberately, severely, refuses to discuss him."

"But you shook your head with such determination that I think you also meant no."

She set the small white, gold-leaf cup back in its saucer on the table before her and stared at it a moment before looking across at me. "This conversation is becoming obscure."

"But you understand it."

"I guess so, but it's terribly . . . mannered for me."

"I'll try to be clearer. I would like to marry you."

"Oh, Matt, you know it wouldn't work."

"No, I don't know that."

"We come from such totally different traditions, classes . . . races."

"You're much more conventional than I am in some ways."

"No. But I've been through it once."

"God *damn* your presumption."

"Oh, I know. You're not Paul. But still . . ."

"I don't believe that's the reason."

She rose, came around the table, and rather surprisingly, deposited herself in my lap. "It's the main reason," she said, our lips almost touching.

"What are the others?"

"I don't want to marry again . . . so soon. I want to do it alone. I like the freedom, the sense of independence."

I had never tried to persuade someone to marry me, and I was having difficulty in recognizing myself. "I wouldn't interfere with your freedom."

"I know you wouldn't think you were, but . . . don't you understand? Just being there is a kind of threat. You would want to live here, wouldn't you?"

"Yes."

"I can understand that, but you see, it's not my house."

"You could do anything you wanted to to it, or if you insist, we could find another one."

"No, you'd resent that."

"These arguments are much too ingenious somehow. There must

be some compelling reason that you don't want to admit."

"Won't you leave it at that, Matt?" She lifted her lips to mine and kissed me with a passion that I was too distraught or angry to respond to. Pushing herself away from me she rose. "I think I'd better go."

"All right." But I wanted to hurt her. "Your lover is more exciting?"

She turned to look at me, not with the anger I had the right to expect, but with something approaching pity. "I don't have a lover. I haven't seen him in over a month."

"Why?"

"Would you get my coat?"

"Why? Why haven't you seen him?"

"Oh, *Matt,* I don't want to talk about it. Please get my coat."

It was raining lightly when we started toward Gay Street.

"You really don't have to take me home. I've walked it hundreds of times."

I pressed her arm under mine, but I was still too hurt or too confused to speak, and she didn't try again until we were at her gate. She turned her back to the wall and looked up at me. "Thank you. It was a lovely dinner, and I adore your house."

"I don't like mysteries, Amanda. You won't marry me, but you were prepared to accept me as a lover. Am I right?"

"Can't you just leave it as it is?"

"No. It's too incoherent, too inconclusive. I like logic."

"All right. Yes. I can't have relations . . . can't make love to two men at the same time. I mean . . ."

"I understand what you mean."

"I have nothing against it morally, but it doesn't work for me. And I thought . . ."

"That I was going to take you to bed."

She looked into my eyes for a moment, and nodded.

"I want to very much, but I can't escape my heritage. I want to marry you. I don't want to be your lover for six months or so and then wander off."

"Yes, I understand now. It's so very . . . foreign to me, you see."

"Will you give it some thought?"

"Yes, of course. Good night."

"Good night, Amanda."

17

I NEVER FOUND OUT precisely what had happened to Maxwell's book in the editor-in-chief's office at Cromwell, though I made some discreet inquiries. The lines of communication were complicated and the two areas of Arnheim Industries so remote that a clear explanation didn't come through. Violating the integrity of one unit in the immense network of holdings was allegedly against the Arnheim doctrine, though Teddy himself was known to reverse managerial decisions without offering a reason. On two occasions that I knew of such intrusions resulted in abrupt resignations.

But when Amanda later reported that the book had never been sold, I decided without telling her that I would go directly to the source. Not Teddy, of course. He would simply have ignored such impertinence. But to the author himself.

I learned Maxwell's first name from Cromwell and had a secretary track down his address in Westchester County. A phone call reported that the line had been disconnected, and a letter was returned "Not at this address." I was beginning to feel sorry for the guy when I wrote to the local post office and received a forwarding address: it was in San Remo, Italy. I felt less sorry for him.

I didn't tell Amanda.

Our relationship changed. Contrary to rational expectation, it was more nervous, less intimate. We seemed to be positioned on opposite sides of some obscure dividing ground, envious of the other's territory. I didn't attempt persuasion, and she avoided physical contact. The pleasure of being together was strained, and I knew that if such a fragile truce continued too long I would lose Amanda, and I didn't want to lose her.

We still saw one another regularly, and I waited for a sign that didn't come. Her friends and mine, the few that I still saw, assumed we were in training for marriage—living together. In fact we were seldom alone.

After a miserable winter, another summer came in redeeming the cruelty of an insufferable spring. The merger of Arnheim Industries and McGruder and Sons had begun to pay off handsomely, but when it seeped slowly into public awareness, Teddy's name was added to the list of public swine. He received threatening mail, and his valet was replaced by a larger man who went armed.

Amanda's reaction was predictable: she exploded, and again threatened to quit her job at Cromwell, but when she was unable to find another house with the same opportunity, promise, and pay, she delayed, uncomfortably. She was in that harrowing situation of having an ideal tested by sordid reality. She restrained herself from attacking me, with difficulty, as a member of that parent company, but the industrial merger did not assist in that other merger I had in mind.

At my desk in mid-June, a Friday, my telephone buzzed.

"Yes?"

"Mr. Arnheim calling," my secretary said.

"Yes, Teddy?"

A man's voice in a curiously resonant connection said, "Mr. Howard?"

"Yes."

"One moment please. Mr. Arnheim calling."

And Teddy came on. "Howard."

"Yes, Teddy?"

"Take a few days off and come up."

"Fine. Where's up?"

"Cantrell Lake."

That was his place in Canada. I didn't even know he was out of the building. "Okay. How do I get there?"

"I'll have them crank up an airplane for you at the lagoon tomorrow morning."

"All right."

"And Howard, bring somebody. If you know anybody." The radio-telephone connection went off with a click and a hum.

Bring somebody. No more Catherines. I had an inspiration. I called Amanda.

"But you're crazy. I wouldn't think of it."

"Wait, Amanda. This is the beast in his lair. Remember? I claimed there is no evidence of bestiality. Don't you have any curiosity?"

She obviously did have some curiosity because her voice had changed when she said, "But . . . where is it?"

"The place in Canada I told you about."

"It's for the weekend?"

"Longer maybe. I don't know."

"Matt, I can't just tootle off for an unknown period."

"Don't you think that under the circumstances if it goes on into next week it could be arranged?"

"Oh . . . yes, I suppose so. But what's it like? What should I bring?"

"I don't know the answer to the first question. I've never been there. To the second, slacks, sweaters, a dinner dress, maybe a bathing suit, though I don't know if the ice has melted."

I picked her up at eight-thirty the next morning in a cab that took us across the Hudson to the tidewater lagoon north of Newark airport where some of Teddy's airline was moored in a brilliant, cloudless day that I found reassuring. A young man was waiting by a four-seater Cessna, a sleek, single-engined little airplane floating in the water by a low pier. Stripes of blue and red, the colors adopted by the company some time ago, curved down from the nose to the fuselage where in modest lettering "Arnheim Industries" was printed below the pilot's window.

The young man stowed the baggage in a compartment behind the rear seats. "You'll find charts, course, and weather prepared," he said, "and I'll call for a clearance as soon as you're ready to go."

"We're ready now. Are you the pilot?"

"Oh, *no,* sir. Mr. Arnheim said you would fly it."

"The son of a *bitch,*" I muttered.

"Sir?"

"Can't you fly it?" Amanda asked, her voice registering sudden terror.

Instructing in the Air Corps had removed any glamor that might originally have been associated with the wild blue yonder, and with the exception of a few rentals to Martha's Vineyard and Southampton, I had not seriously engaged in flying an airplane in fifteen years. "That's a good question."

"*Matt,* I won't *go.*"

"*Calme toi.* It's like riding a bicycle. You never really forget. But I'm going to shoot a couple of landings alone first."

"*What?*"

"Take it off and land it a couple of times. Stay here. I'll be back for you."

My habitual prudence is multiplied many times over when it comes to flying an airplane; I studied controls and instruments for some time before starting the engine and signaling the young man to cast me off. I had never flown a seaplane, though I thought I understood the theory of getting it off the water. After taxiing around a while to get the feel of it, I went downwind, turned around, and opened the throttle. It came off the surface of the lagoon easily, and I climbed around to the left to make a few turns before throttling back for a landing.

A lot of water went flying in a far from expert landing, but I took off again for another trial. The second landing was better, but nothing I would have congratulated a student on. However, it was almost ten-thirty, so I taxied in to the pier and cut the engine.

When the young man opened the door for Amanda he said, "There are sandwiches and coffee in the compartment there. Shall I call for a clearance?"

"Yes, thanks."

"Are you sure you can do this?" Amanda asked.

"Flying the airplane is simple. Locating Cantrell Lake may be more complicated, but they've laid out a good course, and we have lots of navigational aids." The lake was almost due north in the province of Quebec, north of Montreal and slightly to the west of some place called Jerome, but there were hundreds of lakes scattered about. On a sheet with the charts and weather report, the frequency and call letters, ARN, of a small directional transmitter were described, having a power radius of about fifty miles, and I assumed with all the other aids I could get that close.

The young man came back and rapped on the door. "You're cleared at six thousand feet. Late weather reports indicate clear sailing all the way."

"Okay, thanks." I snapped Amanda's belt and started the engine.

"I hope you know what you're doing," she said.

"So do I."

"Don't *say* that."

"Just hold that chart and relax. I don't have suicidal tendencies."

At six thousand feet I leveled off in crisp, calm air above the industrial haze of the metropolitan area, cold enough to turn on the cabin heater. After leaving Newark control I checked in with Albany and we followed the Hudson River though the brilliant sky of June with the green fields of the valley unfurling below us. When she lost her nervousness Amanda began to enjoy the sensation of flight in a small airplane, and I taught her how to crank in the various frequencies on the radio compass. There was other, more sophisticated navigational equipment, but I didn't know how to work it. There were also dual controls.

"Do you want to fly it?"

"What do I do?"

"Almost nothing. It will fly itself. Hold that altitude and that course."

She put her hands on the wheel and her feet on the rudder pedals as though she expected the worst, but after a few minutes she said, "This is easy."

"Turn a couple of degrees to the left. Rudder and wheel together. There. Now straighten out."

"I like this. Could you teach me to fly?"

"Certainly. You're climbing a bit. See the altimeter? Push the wheel forward, gently. There. Good."

"What time do we get there?" she asked later.

"Our ETA, estimated time of arrival, is four-fifty, but I think we'll land at Burlington and top off the tanks."

"Are we running out of gas?" she asked quickly.

"No, but we'll be about half empty at Burlington, and full tanks are comforting, particularly when looking for a small lake among a hundred other small lakes."

"This *is* fun," she said a few minutes later.

I glanced across at her. Her eyes were shining, and her lips were parted in a smile of excitement. She was ravishing.

"If you marry me," I said boldly, "we could have an airplane."

Without looking at me she said, "All right."

I wasn't sure I had understood. "Did you say all right?"

"Yes. I'll take you with the airplane. I'll take you even without the airplane."

"I'm stunned. When did you reach this decision?"

"Just now."

"You won't change your mind when we leave six thousand feet? It's difficult to stay up here without gas."

"No, I won't change my mind."

I took her hand from the wheel and kissed it. "What color airplane do you want?"

"Oh, something that will go with my hair. Fuchsia?"

"Fuchsia it will be. There's an airplane on your right."

"Where?"

"It's all right. He's below us. That's Lake Champlain ahead of us. Reduce your throttle setting a bit."

"What?"

"Pull that lever back a bit."

The engine tone changed, and we began to settle. "Now this little wheel, forward a bit. It's the trim."

"You'd better take it."

"You're doing all right."

"No, you take it."

I landed, rather more expertly, in the seaplane area marked on the chart, taxied in toward the service facilities where a man on the pier caught the wing and swung us around. After the tanks were filled I taxied out into the small bay and cut the engine again. "We'll drift and eat lunch, but first a chaste kiss on the ruby lips of my bride."

"You almost make me change my mind."

I kissed her for some time, not very chastely.

After opening both doors I extracted our lunch consisting of caviar on toast, shrimp salad, ham and cheese sandwiches, fruit, chocolate, and a thermos of coffee.

"My God," she said, "if this is lunch what will dinner be like?"

"It's usually good, but I don't know if he flies his chef up from Collincourt or has local talent."

"What does he do up there?"

"Fishes, I imagine. He likes to sit in a boat with a rod and a case of Coke and bourbon."

"Ech. Does he really?"

"Yes, really. When will you marry me?"

"Whenever you like. But not a religious ceremony."

"My God, no. Next week?"

"If you like. But you have to take a Wasserman first."

"I think I can pass it. When did this resolution mature?"

"Up there. Really. But I've been thinking about it. Matt, I have to add a line from about fifty nineteenth-century novels. I don't know if I love you. But I'm very fond of you, I admire you, and I find you physically attractive. Can that contract work?"

"I think it can work. I'm not an authority on love, but I think that's what I feel for you."

"I can't remember which of Henry James's heroines I remind myself of."

"None, I hope. I could never understand what they were thinking or saying. Will we live in my house?"

"Of course. And you don't even have to evict the doctor."

"We may want to later."

"I intend to stay on the pill, Matt."

"As long as you like."

Suddenly she began to laugh.

"A good joke?"

"Probably the most passionate engagement of the twentieth century."

"It's the first time for me. How do others do it?"

"A lot of heavy breathing, clutching, and kissing. Some tears maybe."

"You supply the tears, and as soon as I get this ham and cheese swallowed, I'll do the kissing."

I kissed her lightly, and we drank our coffee while a sailboat floated by.

The St. Lawrence River had long muddy slivers stabbing into the blue when we passed Montreal off our left wing. Amanda was on the controls again, and she had learned to hold course and altitude remarkably fast. I cranked in a station in Jerome, and a few minutes later the needle turned to five degress.

"Correct to zero."

"That's . . . to the right, isn't it?"

"Yes. There. You're doing very well, Amanda."

"I love it. Could you really teach me?"

"Of course. You could solo in six or seven hours."

"Oh, God. The thought of it scares me already."

"It's really very simple unless you run into weather or some kind of emergency like losing an engine."

"What do you do then, take the A train?"

"You land in the best field you can find. With pontoons and all this water it would be simple."

Half an hour later a town appeared below us, and the needle swung. "Now pick up a course of two hundred and eighty degrees."

"To . . . the left?"

"Right. I mean yes. It should be about eighteen minutes from here."

We turned into the brilliant western sky to fly over a magnificent wilderness of forests, lakes, and streams.

"How are we going to find the right lake?"

I cranked the ARN frequency into the compass. "It looks like a snake, or a lizard on the chart, and when we get closer the radio compass should pick up his signal. We're doing all right. That lake just ahead is here on the chart, and that crescent-shaped one over on the right is where it should be. We're doing pilotage and dead reckoning."

"I don't like the sound of that last one."

"It comes from deductive, not dead."

A few minutes later the needle began to swing irregularly and then settled unsteadily on three hundred and fifty-eight degrees. "We're close . . . yes, I think that's it just off to the left. Hold that course for a moment longer." I shifted the headset down over my ears and waited. Static at first, and then ARN came in in Morse. The needle started to drop slowly, and as we came abreast of the lake, about three miles long, it shifted down to one hundred ninety degrees. "That's it, down there. Fly over it and circle."

She turned slowly and stayed in a shallow turn. Just as we started a second circle, below us a flare went up into the golden afternoon sky, dividing into the Arnheim colors of blue and red.

"Okay, throttle back and trim."

We began a slow, circular descent toward the azure surface and a structure almost hidden by pines gradually showed itself. When we went through three thousand feet, turning east again, I had a curious sensation similar to, but not quite, a *déja vu*. The house, or cabin, was large, but its position on the eastern side of the lake, and what I could make out of its architecture were familiar. And then even the lake came through to me. A log cabin, immense though it was, built on the eastern shore of a long, relatively narrow lake, had been modeled on another cabin on another lake. In our slow turn I even caught sight of a long porch behind a large terrace where some people were sitting.

"Won't you take it?" Amanda said.

"What? Oh, I'm sorry." I took over the controls.

"What were you thinking of?"

"Another cabin and another lake. I'll tell you some time."

Out in the middle, north of the house, was a small boat with a solitary figure hunched over the stern. Under a hat, the white of his face became visible as he looked up at us. "That's Theodore Arnheim the Second down there."

There was a wind sock indicating a gentle southerly breeze, and tied up near the shore were two other airplanes, one quite large. Losing altitude I went north and turned to make my approach, almost over Teddy in his boat. The surface was so calm I misjudged slightly and sent a lot of water flying.

"Lousy landing," I said, turning back toward the house. A power-boat left the dock and started toward us spreading white plumes of foam and turning to lead us in. Fifty feet from the pier, modeled on another pier, he turned and ran his finger across his throat. I cut the engine and he came up, put a line through an eye in one pontoon and towed us to a buoy where he tied the airplane up. Circling back he reversed to the left side of the fuselage. "Good trip, sir?" he asked, opening the baggage compartment.

"Excellent."

When he had our luggage stowed he moved up to the door, and we climbed in. At the pier he lifted our bags out and led us up a path hidden from the terrace, but permitting a view of the right side of the house. Whoever had done the architecture had produced a miracle: the layout, style, even the contours were precise replicas of that other log cabin, magnified some twenty times. The bedrooms that lay off the top floor were discreetly hidden in the hillside to suggest that the door leading from the living room, at the side of the immense fireplace, provided access to a single room, whereas it opened on a hall with a dozen or so doors beyond. The architect must have suspected Teddy's sanity since he had imposed a rigid model to which the size of the house conformed with difficulty.

A maid showed us to adjoining rooms, and when she left I opened Amanda's door. She was examining the ponderous pine furniture and rich rusticity of the paneling. "It's really gorgeous," she said, "but I don't understand why he had them built to look out the back and not on the lake." From the two windows a dense forest of pine and oak ran up the hillside, almost obscuring a second structure. The lake was invisible.

"He had a model and he stuck to it." I opened a door onto a

bathroom. "He did make certain concessions. The model had a single, antiquated bathroom on the first floor."

"What was the model?"

Briefly I described the house in Alabama, mentioning only that we had been paying guests.

"He must have been mad about it to reconstruct it in the Canadian wilderness."

"Apparently he was. Do you want to go down?"

"Should I dress now?"

"No. You're very taut in those slacks. Take a jacket. It might be cool."

I led her expertly through the fifty-foot living room to the stairs I knew would be at the end, down to the immense cave of a dining room which, like its model, was not walled off from the kitchen, through the long porch onto the terrace where drinks were being served.

It was typical Arnheim hospitality: his guests were there, including, inevitably, two nymphs, and four other people I didn't know, two couples, but the host was out fishing alone on the lake. We introduced ourselves and ordered a drink at the bar. The conversation was burdened by repeated and slightly awed appreciation of the Canadian wilderness which was very wild and very remote. Silence lay over us like a threat that voices tried to push back only to be overwhelmed by the immensity of sky, forests, and water.

The nymphs were standard models, almost indistinguishable from others I remembered from Collincourt. Seated on a large swinging chaise lounge, they were whispering to one another in deference to the vast solitude.

The couples, in tweed jackets, turtlenecked sweaters, men as well as women, looked very sportif, and I wondered why they weren't out on the lake for late afternoon fishing.

"Have you been here long?" I asked.

"No," said one of the men, blondish, with a ruddy complexion. "We arrived about four o'clock. We haven't seen Mr. Arnheim yet." He spoke with some Scandinavian accent, and I wondered what new areas in the north of Europe Teddy was planning to conquer. His wife, also blond, middle-aged, with rosy cheeks, wore her hair in two Nordic braids. "We are from Norway," he continued, "but Mr. and Mrs. McClellan are from Scotland. We fish together, sometimes in

Norway, sometimes in Scotland. Mr. Arnheim is so kind to invite us here for the fishing. Do you fish?''

"No.''

"And you, Mrs.?'' he said to Amanda.

"No, I don't either. I've never had the time. It takes a lot of time, doesn't it?''

"Yes, a bit of time,'' McClellan said, "but very enjoyable and very challenging. You put your mind against instinct. Angling is a pensive sport. You are with Arnheim Industries, sir?''

"Yes. Are you?''

"Shipbuilding. Pederson here, and I have a small yard in Norway. Mr. Arnheim was good enough to look in on us last year.''

Shipbuilding. Another Arnheim venture? I knew nothing about it. I didn't even know that Teddy had been in Norway.

"Very pleasant place he has here. Promises good fishing. A shame you don't go in for it.''

Inversely something of the same train of thought was going through my mind. If Teddy was going to buy out McClellan and Pederson, he certainly didn't need my presence, or if he did it would be back in Newark to look over the purchase agreement.

Amanda and I walked to the edge of the terrace to look out over the lake. "I couldn't stand this very long,'' she said. "Too much nothing.''

"Trees, water, sky.''

"I'm a city girl. I need some noise and the assurance that there's someone next door. I don't want polar bears for neighbors.''

"A little far south for polar bears.''

"But I'll bet there are some mean things hidden out there.''

Teddy, in his boat, appeared, rowing awkwardly toward the shore. "Here comes one of them now.''

We studied the erratic course of the boat toward the pier, and Amanda took a sip of her white wine. "I'm going to meet my boss. I wonder if he knows he's my boss.''

"If you mention Cromwell he'll know. He had an uncanny ability of knowing everything that Arnheim Industries is engaged in.''

"Who are the two dolls?''

"Uh . . . Teddy likes crowds.''

She turned to look at me. "They don't actually constitute a crowd, or . . . oh.'' She laughed. "He's an *à trois* person.''

"Apparently, though it's simply the evidence of mathematics. I haven't presided over such mysteries. Does it shock you?"

"Oh, no, it's a popular sport."

I had an impulse to ask her if it was one of her sports.

Teddy had reached the pier where the boatman tied the painter and took the basket handed to him. The way he handled and carried it following Teddy up toward the terrace suggested weight. When Teddy appeared at the far end of the terrace the nymphs, the McClellans, and Pedersons gathered to meet him and admire the contents of the basket that the boatman opened. There were expressions of wonder and little cries of disgust from the nymphs.

"Well," I said, "shall we say hello to our host?"

"Wait a minute," she said, putting a hand on my arm. "I'm a little nervous."

"He's not dangerous."

"I know, but he's my boss, and I'm not prepared to like him."

Teddy, in an old corduroy jacket and stained hat decorated with flies, had lighted a cigarette and with his back to us was answering questions as the boatman held up one fish after the other.

"What a beauty!" McClellan said as a particularly large trout appeared. "A battler, I'll wager."

Teddy's answer was inaudible, but our separation was becoming awkward. I took Amanda's arm, but a few feet from Teddy's back she freed herself. He turned to me as I came up to his side. "Hi, Howard. That was a lousy landing."

"I'm surprised there were any survivors. Amanda, this is Teddy. Amanda Bonn."

He turned his head to look at her where she was still hesitating to join us, and said, "Hi."

"Hello, Mr. Arnheim."

He examined her for a moment, and I was looking at her, too, while the others continued to exclaim over the marvels he had drawn out of the lake. She was wearing a short black jacket over the white sweater, and the tight slacks clung to her thighs. A wisp of her shining black hair caressed her cheek in a breath of early evening, and she brushed it away. The blue of her eyes had deepened in the late light.

"Howard didn't get you lost on the way up?" Teddy asked finally.

"No." She smiled. "I loved it."

"She was on the controls most of the time."

"Do you like to fish?" he asked, still looking at her.

"No, I'm afraid I don't."

I couldn't say why there seemed to be something mysterious and hidden in the question and the answer, some exchange of symbolic language that I had not been taught. The nymphs also seemed to think there was too much attention being given to another woman, or perhaps they had tired of looking at fish. They joined Teddy, one on each side.

"Are we going to eat those horrible things?" one asked.

"You are. I'm not."

She screeched in mock horror to suggest the delicacy of her psyche. She didn't look over nineteen or twenty, a slender, full-breasted girl with streaked blond hair. Her name was Mary O'Shaughnessy. In what amounted almost to a challenge she turned to Amanda. "Do *you* like them?"

"Oh, yes. They may seem more familiar to you cooked."

"I wish I had never seen the horrible things raw."

"Have another drink," Teddy said. "I'll be back in a little while." He started for the porch. It was totally uncharacteristic of him to explain his movements or to promise a reappearance.

"What do you think?" I asked Amanda as we went back to the bar.

"Very strange. Certainly nothing like what I expected. There's a kind of gentleness or maybe it's boredom or . . . patience."

"Some of each. But he seems contented here. Unusual."

"He's certainly no Adonis. Even slightly repulsive." She accepted another glass of white wine, and I took another vodka martini. "I'm tempted to tell him I work for Cromwell just to see his reaction."

"His reactions are always controlled. In the many years I've known him I think I've seen him react emotionally just once."

"A woman?"

"Yes."

The Pedersons came to the bar and ordered a strange, ominous drink, some kind of schnapps that had obviously been laid in for them, and the McClellans took Chivas Regal.

"We are planning an early fishing trip tomorrow morning," Pederson said. "You would not like to join us?"

"Oh, thank you, no," I said. "I'd be in your way."

"Oh, not at all. Please don't think of that. We would be most pleased."

I didn't understand his persistence. "No, I won't come, but thank you."

When he had moved away Amanda said, "There's something slightly demented about this obsession with fishing."

"It must be associated with childhood. You drop your hook into the water and wonder what kind of present will be attached to it."

"A fish is a fertility symbol."

"Maybe that explains it. None of them looks excessively fertile."

The nymphs complained of the evening chill and wandered off, and the fishing foursome strolled over to look at the equipment the boatman had assembled for them.

"Why does he always call you Howard?"

"Early school days. It was considered bad form to use first names."

"You're really close to him, aren't you?"

"No one is close to Teddy. I'm probably as close as they come."

"It's hard to believe that such an insignificant little person controls so much. I expected him to be domineering, a brigand."

"He dominates subtly. He's never angry, passionate, or violent. But he's always in control."

She turned to look out at the lake again. "Somehow I think it was a mistake for me to come."

"Why?"

"I don't know. I wanted to be angry with him, but I'm not. I feel sorry for him."

"That's a wasted emotion. He doesn't need it."

"I think you're wrong. I think he does need it."

"Be careful, Amanda." I wasn't sure what I meant.

She turned to look at me with what impressed me as a sudden hostility, and I began to believe she was right. Perhaps I shouldn't have brought her.

We went up to shower and change, and when we entered the vast living room there was a fire burning, and the others were already there, having more drinks, McClellan and Pederson standing before the fire, and Teddy seated, surrounded by the four women, a bourbon and Coke in his hand. He must have been quite witty since everyone was laughing, Mrs. McClellan almost in hysterics. He rose when we entered, and I had not seen such serenity in his eyes since another time long ago in another cabin.

"But he didn't actually *eat* it?" Mrs. McClellan gasped.

"Yeah, but I guess it didn't taste very good because he said something in Japanese and passed out." He smiled, almost a genuine smile, at Amanda and me. "Do you know how to row, Howard?"

"Your memory is failing you. I crewed at Princeton, if you'll recall."

"Yeah, but I always thought that little guy in the stern had a motor."

"Why don't *you* use a motor?"

"They never start when you need them, and they scare the fish. I'll let you row for me tomorrow morning."

"That's very decent of you. Don't you have any other galley slaves?"

"Yeah, but they don't like to get up that early."

"How early is that?"

"Five o'clock."

"That's a good hour. Can I punch a time clock for overtime?"

"Yeah. I'll have them put it in your envelope next week."

The bartender took our order, or rather mine. Amanda took nothing.

"Mr. Arnheim," she said in what seemed like a sudden decision, "Matt and I were discussing this fascination for fishing. Can you explain it?"

"It's something to do," he said, looking at her almost shyly.

"But is that all?"

"I guess it's because they're so dumb they make me feel smart."

"Oh, Mr. Arnheim," McClellan said, "I must differ. Fish are very cunning."

"Maybe Scotch salmon are, but Canadian trout are dumb. They never learn. You drop a worm in front of their noses, and they take it every time."

"But you must know where to drop it and at what depth."

"I think it's terribly cruel," the nymph Peggy said.

"But, miss," Pederson said, "do you not eat meat?"

"Oh, yes, but I don't see the cow before I eat it."

It became clear that she ate meat later when we went down to the dining room where another fire was blazing and where from the distance of the kitchen meat smells came from a flaming grill. Teddy's seating arrangements always baffled me: the result of a whim or some deeply contrived symmetry. He placed Amanda at the head of the table, scattered McClellans, Pedersons, and me along the sides, and at the foot surrounded himself with nymphs. The service started with bowls of iced Beluga, sustained a high level with excellent *truite meuniere* served with a chilled Moselle, and came into flower with three-inch filets of beef from *bleu* to well done, served on a platter by an oversized French Canadian in a red-checked lumber jacket who spoke only French and addressed Teddy as *mon commandant*. The wine was a Bordeaux that I had never heard of, but it was very good, deriving, I learned later, from a vineyard belonging to Arnheim Industries. There was some obscure, hard Canadian cheese, and great bowls of plebeian ice cream with chocolate sauce, followed by a flow of Moët.

In a carnivorous frenzy the nymph Peggy consumed two very rare filets and hesitated over a third when the Canadian giant came in with a fresh platter. "No, I shouldn't," she said reluctantly. "No, no more. I'm positively stuffed."

"Superb," McClellan said, accepting another steak. "Do you fly everything in?"

"Yeah," Teddy said. "From Jerome."

"What is the source of your electrical power, sir?" Pederson asked.

"Generator buried out there in the woods."

"How very American," McClellan permitted himself.

"But it must get terribly cold in the winter," The nymph Mary said.

"Probably. I don't know. I've never been here in the winter."

"You don't have any neighbors on the lake?" Mrs. McClellan asked.

"No. I bought the lake."

"Really stupendous," McClellan said. "Simply couldn't happen in England or Europe."

"There are several dukes in England who own ten times this much property," Teddy said. "In France, too."

"Ah, but that's a vestige of feudalism. Money and class handed down from as far back as the Normans or at least Henry the Heretic. In

America it's possible for a man with intelligence to succeed handsomely by his own efforts."

"I inherited Arnheim Industries," Teddy said patiently. "If I hadn't I would probably have been a bookmaker."

"What is bookmaker?" Mrs. Pederson asked at large.

Her husband spoke to her in Norwegian, and turning to Teddy said, "Oh, I cannot believe that, sir. Your knowledge is known across the world, and knowledge is power."

"No," Teddy said flatly. "Real knowledge doesn't make money, and money is power."

"But surely, Mr. Arnheim, your father was a man of great knowledge," Mr. McClellan insisted.

"No," Teddy said flatly again. "The Old Man was ignorant, but he was sly and afraid. As a child he was hungry, and he decided he would make enough money so that he wouldn't ever be hungry again."

Amanda, silent until that moment, looking at Teddy with speculative eyes, asked suddenly, "But what do you mean by knowledge, Mr. Arnheim?"

"I mean all the baggage you're expected to claim on the way. It gets too heavy to carry."

"Cultural baggage?"

"Yeah." He smiled generously. "That would be a way of saying it."

"If I understand you," she continued, "too much learning, too much knowledge produces indecision, a conscience?"

"Yeah. I pay my conscience."

I didn't respond. Over the years the joke had worn thin.

"And that frees you to . . . carry on your father's work?"

"Yeah. To keep me from being hungry."

"But that's ridiculous, Teddy," Peggy said. "You've never been hungry."

"Yeah, once. I was hungry for a while."

It was too unlikely, too mysterious, for a reply, though I knew he was not talking about the naive hunger of the belly.

Other bottles of Moët appeared and were consumed. The nymphs fondled his shoulders automatically, and Mrs. Pederson became quite giddy, speaking lyrically in a language that was not quite English. The others were learning what Teddy's guests always learned, that conversation with him was a series of beginnings. The ball crossed the net perhaps twice and was smashed. Amanda, after drawing him into a brief volley, returned to watchful silence.

We returned to the living room for coffee and cognac before the renourished fire where Teddy offered immense cigars accepted by Pederson and McClellan.

"Some bridge, Mr. Arnheim?" McClellan asked, nourishing the ash of his indiscreet cigar.

"I don't play bridge. Poker?"

"I warn you," I said, "against playing poker with him because he will win, and you will lose."

Peggy curled up on the sofa next to Teddy, her eyes half closed, and Mary wandered through the depths of the great-timbered room away from the fire where anglers' tales were contrived by Pederson and McClellan while Teddy listened. Amanda, withdrawn, in half light, listened, her eyes on Teddy, a cinquecento profile.

Suddenly, from the depths of the room the sounds of a big band of later thirties vintage burst out with Cole Porter and everyone turned to look at Mary before the console of a complex hi-fi. "I just touched a button, and it started," she explained apologetically.

Waves of what were, for Teddy and me at least, nostalgia swept over us with "Night and Day," "Begin the Beguine," "I've Got You Under My Skin," and then on to "Smoke Gets in Your Eyes," and inevitably "Dancing in the Dark," while Mary began to dance alone in the darkness of the long room. She was good, had obviously had training, and there was not the slightest trace of self-consciousness as she emerged from darkness. Before Teddy and Peggy she turned languidly, swaying to the music and held out her arms.

"Dance with me," she said.

"I can't dance," Teddy said.

"Someone dance with me," she pleaded.

Pederson started to rise from the sofa, but his wife laid a restraining hand on his arm.

"Oh, don't be a bitch," Mary said clearly.

"What she say?" Mrs. Pederson asked her husband.

He spoke to her in Norwegian and remarkably she smiled and released him, unfortunately for Mary since he was not steady and he moved with her in his arms like an ill-trained bear. The McClellans rose to join them stiffly, and I glanced at Amanda, without enthusiasm since two people moving aimlessly about the floor clutched in one another's arms has always impressed me as foreplay performed in public. She gave no evidence of wanting to join, but smiled, a little wanly.

"Are you tired?" I asked above the music.

She nodded.

"We can leave."

She glanced at Teddy and Peggy. "Let's."

When he understood our intentions, Teddy actually rose to his feet encumbered by Peggy's embracing arms. "I'll have them wake you, Howard."

"That's very generous of you. Good night."

We left them standing before the fire, not dancing, while the music looked for the light of a new love to brighten up the dark.

And I left Amanda before her door.

Fishing with Teddy was a singularly placid experience. It was just turning light when I paddled him out onto the tranquil surface of the lake the next morning to the clamor of birds. A flock of ducks was feeding in the shallows, and overhead a late formation of geese flew a compass course north. I had never seen so many fish break the surface of the water, and casting with a fly, Teddy soon started pulling them aboard in an abundance that threatened to swamp us.

The sun was on the western shore when the other fishing party went aboard the power boat to head toward the southern tip of the lake where bass were said to feed. Some time later one of the nymphs and Amanda appeared at a table on the terrace for breakfast served by the giant Canadian in his red-checked shirt. Amanda waved and I waved back. The nymph also waved, but Teddy was concentrating on his fly which just then was taken by a large fish arcing into the sunlight.

"Is the brute in the red shirt a local?" I asked, the first human voice in the clatter of nature.

"Pelletier's brother," he said, reeling in the trout.

Pelletier. He had been one of the instructors in the Frog Squadron, who had been killed in a freak taxiing accident while ferrying an airplane to a field in Florida. I even remembered that he had come from an impoverished, fatherless family in Montreal, and his death had removed the wage earner. I wondered how many other former squadron mates, acquaintances, and Polish refugees were on the payroll.

Since fishing has never interested me I didn't bother with the other rod in the boat, but when the sun became warm I took off my shirt and relaxed in the bow, picking up the oars occasionally to move to a different location on Teddy's directions. It was perfectly clear that he didn't need or want conversation, but I sensed that my presence was somehow rewarding to him. Hunched over the stern of the boat he fly-cast until the sun was too high, and then began to fish shadowed pools with a worm, reaching into a styrofoam cooler every once in a while for a Coke. There was no bourbon aboard.

Later the nymphs appeared fringed at the edge of the water, hazily nude, bathing in gasps at the shock of the lake's temperature. Amanda disappeared and reappeared on the terrace with a book. The Scottish-Norwegian fishing expedition was invisible around a bend in the shoreline.

In the second exchange of the morning I said, "I don't think the roof over the porch slanted that steeply."

Teddy did not turn to look. "You're wrong, Howard. I had the angle measured."

Someone had been dispatched to an artificial lake in Alabama to take measurements.

The fish were beginning to observe that caution—or maybe it's indolence—that comes with the approach of midday when Teddy slowly reeled his line in and laid the rod against the gunwales. Tilting his hat up, he lighted another cigarette and said, "Where did you meet her?"

"Amanda?"

"Yeah."

"On company business in Paris when we went over to raid McGruder and Sons."

"Are you going to marry her?"

"That's my intention providing she doesn't change her mind."

"Someone you can stand living with?"

"I think so. You haven't found one yet?"

"No. A lot of silly cunts around. But the Old Lady is getting worried."

"How is she?"

"Okay, but she's almost ninety. Wants a grandchild before she dies."

"Well," I said, picking up the oars, "that's not asking too much. You know how to do it."

"Yeah." Changing the subject abruptly, he said, "I want you to go down to Washington on Wednesday. Kennedy's having some people in for a talk."

"Why don't you go?"

"I think it would be better if you went. He's in your club, and I think he'd appreciate it if I didn't show right away."

I guessed I understood. "How much did Kennedy cost you?"

"Oh, a few bucks. But I'm not sure he remembers. He's got an eager brother. If you get the right chance you might remind him."

"Are there signals?"

"Not yet, but it's early. I think something may be cooking in antitrust. It's worth the trip."

"All right. Anything special you want me to say if I get the chance?"

"Just a reminder that West Virginia was important to him."

Obviously some things had been going on that I didn't know about, and I wondered who had carried the brown satchel, or if more sophisticated means had been discovered.

I rowed slowly past a float with a small catamaran tied up, and into the pier where a ten- or twelve-year-old boy was waiting to receive us. "How many did you catch, *mon commandant*?" he asked in the curious language that passes for French in Canada.

"Enough for your lunch, Thierry," Teddy answered in the language that he passed for French. "How many did you catch?"

"Enough for your dinner, *mon commandant*." He lifted the basket onto the pier.

"A member of the family?" I asked.

"Pelletier's son. His mother does the housework. Bright kid."

I could not remember ever having heard Teddy address a child, but Thierry obviously adored him and trailed us up to the house, lugging the heavy basket and questioning Teddy on his catch. They disappeared together into the kitchen, and I went in search of Amanda.

The Norwegian-Scots party was dining on the water, the nymphs, Amanda, and I had a buffet lunch on the terrace, and Teddy disappeared into his bedroom which, following the model, lay off the kitchen. The word was passed that he would be on the radio-telephone for most of the afternoon.

On the terrace there was a lobster salad, grilled trout, hot rolls, and white wine, with strawberries for dessert.

"I've gained three pounds already," Peggy said, pouring cream over strawberries, "but I can't stop eating. There's something unhealthy about all this air."

"Swim it off this afternoon," Mary suggested.

"Too cold."

"I'd like to go in this afternoon. Is it really too cold?" Amanda asked.

"Not on the surface, but if you go lower than about a foot it's icy."

"Shall we try it?" Amanda asked me.

"I'm willing."

"It's for brass monkeys," Peggy said, scooping up strawberries. "I'm going to collapse in the sun."

"Do you work for Teddy?" Mary asked me a moment later.

"Yes."

"You, too, Amanda?"

She hesitated, and I could see she intended to lie. "No."

"Why did he ask those weird foreigners?" Peggy asked.

"Paying a social debt, I gather. Apparently they were his hosts last year."

"Real zombies. I nearly cracked when you were dancing with that Swede last night, Mary."

"The bastard nearly broke my back."

"I thought his wife was going to break something else." She poured coffee and lighted a cigarette. "A real swinging party. I really wonder what the hell fun there is in sitting in a boat and pulling in those dumb fish. Even Teddy says they're dumb."

"Nobody's making you do it, love," Mary said, rising. "I'm going to take a nap."

"Wait," Peggy said. "I'm coming too."

Amanda watched them cross the terrace and disappear in the house. "He certainly doesn't select his playmates for their wit."

"I assume they have other talents."

"Matt, how does it happen he's never been married?"

"Under that moral . . . indifference there's a very conservative man. It's a classical division between—excuse the word—cunts and the idealized concept of womanhood."

"His mother?"

"Oh, no. His mother is a good-hearted, simple, *Kinder, Kirche, Küche* specimen."

"I really don't understand it. He's worth millions of dollars, he flies all over the world, he's obviously intelligent, and in a queer sort of way, attractive."

"You've changed your mind about him."

"Yes, I think I have. It's the old banality. The attractions of the ugly. He has a kind of quiet charm, an impatience with pretense."

"You understand the man better than most. Even those who work for him consider him a man without character."

"I still wish I didn't work for him."

In swimsuits and robes later we walked down to the pier. Holding my arm Amanda stuck one foot into the water. "Oh, God, it's liquid ice."

I dropped my robe. "I'm the sudden death kind. If I do it in degrees I lose the faith." I poised at the edge of the pier and dove. It was annihilating, a bath of snow, and I came to the surface in an involuntary howl. *"Jeezus."* But Mary was right. The top twelve or fifteen inches were possible.

"How is it?"

"Stay on top."

She took off her robe, unwrapping a gorgeous body in a white bikini, with sleek long legs, and full breasts, her skin light gold. She started down the ladder. "Oh, my God!" She hesitated, almost changed her mind, and suddenly pushed out into the water.

We swam furiously for the float some fifty feet away and pulled up onto the canvased surface warmed by the sun. "Madness," she panted. "I've never been in water that cold. It wouldn't melt an ice cube."

"I have some between my toes."

She lay on her stomach, shivering. "How are we going to get back? I don't have the will to do that again."

"I think I can manage that catamaran. I'll take you in." I rolled over in the warmth of the sun, my body tingling deliciously. "But it's almost worth it now."

"I'm not a masochist." Her arm brushed mine and I took her hand.

When we had recovered I said, "Where would you like to go on our honeymoon? I believe that it's a custom still observed."

"Yes, I want to go on a honeymoon. France? Remember I've never been outside Paris."

"Provence perhaps. Down around Aix."

"That would be lovely."

"Where did you go the first time?"

"Minorca. But it was August and terribly crowded."

"We should try for June. We still have a couple of weeks."

"I'm not sure I can get away that soon. I'll have to ask a couple of weeks in advance."

"I should think that under the circumstances it could be arranged."

She raised her head from the canvas. "I'm not going to use a casual weekend as the guest of the boss to manipulate my career at Cromwell. In fact I don't want him to know I work for Cromwell. Don't tell him."

"All right." I leaned over and kissed her on the cheek. "I have no intention of corrupting you. We'll try for July."

She rested her chin on her hands. "Isn't it possible to be married by a justice of the peace in Connecticut or New Jersey?"

"I think so, but I'm not a specialist in matrimony. Why?"

"I don't want to be married in the city again. I'd like to stand before some paternal justice of the peace in Connecticut who has a maternal wife."

"Immediately upon returning to the city I will begin research on paternal justices of the peace in Connecticut."

She rolled over onto her back. "I don't want my family to know until it's done."

I sat up to look at her. "You really are convinced that there's a racial, religious threat."

"Not convinced, but I don't want to take the chance. I don't want my father to pronounce some ancient anathema again."

"Just as you like." I lay back in the warmth of the sun and closed my eyes. It was a strange sort of caution, but I was certain I could relieve her of such anxieties once we had settled into the house on 10th Street, and she discovered that I would not interfere with her professional life or try to modify her relations with her family.

I believe in reason.

I slept for a while, and Amanda must have, too. A cold blanket had covered my feet and lower legs when I became aware of her chin on my chest.

"You're turning red. Do you burn?"

"Not seriously." I put my arm around her and brought her lips to mine lightly. "Do you?"

"No, but I turn several shades darker until I'm almost aboriginal."

"I have always wanted an aborigine for a wife."

"We're going to be in total shade in a few minutes."

"Okay. I'll see what I can do with the catamaran."

It was sloop-rigged, the sails dropped. After a couple of trials I managed to get the small mainsail up and the boom swung in the faint breeze. "All right, climb aboard and cast us off."

She stepped onto a pontoon and worked at the painter.

"Would you like to take a turn around the lake?"

"No, thanks. Too cold. But you go ahead."

Though I had never sailed a catamaran I reached the pier without tacking, rather surprised at how fast the little boat moved. "I'll be back in half an hour. Give me a push, will you?"

I caught the breeze and turned around, with some difficulty, since the catamaran seemed reluctant to come about. Heading for the opposite shore I crossed the lake from sunlight into shadows, but when I tried to turn the catamaran went into stays. Releasing the tiller I raised the small jib and tried again, drifting closer to the shore. On the third try, within a few feet of some great boulders, it finally came about and I turned south. Even in the faint breeze it moved with astonishing speed.

Some huge beast I took for a moose was drinking in the shadow of the western shore, but when he saw me he turned, snorting, and plunged up the bank into the forest with a splintering crash. Ducks and other birds I couldn't recognize rose at my approach to fly a few hundred feet and land again. For a few minutes I was beyond sight of the cabin, alone in the immense wilderness, but rounding a small thrust of trees I came upon the boat containing the Pedersons and McClellans, moving slowly up the lake, trolling.

I came about again heading for the eastern shore, and for the first time caught sight of a gigantic, anvil-topped thunderhead in the eastern sky moving above a squall line with ominous signs of violence in an ochre base.

Rounding another small, tree-covered jut of rocky shoreline, I came back in sight of the house blazing in the last rays of the sun. On the terrace were two figures, alone, motionless, solitary statuary, too distant to recognize.

By the time I had tied up to the pier, the house was in shadow, and the figures had disappeared.

The thunderhead was closer.

18

I'M NOT SURE that at the time I understood what happened that evening. Perhaps what I've always considered a natural prudence is really naiveté, or an inability to escape from my own convictions about the nature of experience.

First of all I met Jacobs, Teddy's chief pilot, in a dinghy coming around the other side of the pier.

"Hello, Jacobs. How have you been?"

"Okay, Mr. Howard. How did the Cessna behave on the way up?"

"Fine. What are you up to?"

"We're in for a blow, and I want to check the airplanes to be sure the windows are closed, controls locked, and the moorings sound."

"Can I help?"

"No, thanks. I have time. Toss me the painter and I'll take the catamaran back to the float."

"I haven't lashed the sails yet."

"I'll do it."

"Thanks. Let me know if you need help."

"I will."

Next I went up to my room and showered. When I was dressed I knocked on Amanda's door.

"Matt?"

"Yes."

"Just a minute . . . all right."

She was sitting before the dressing table in her robe, staring at herself and then raising her eyes to my reflected self, her face covered lightly with some kind of cream. I came up behind her and put my hands on her shoulders. "My skin was dried out from the sun." Her eyes on my reflected eyes were very large.

"Whatever you do, keep doing it. I like the results."

I couldn't tell whether her smile, under the masquerade of the cream, expressed appreciation or pathos. She laid a hand on one of mine on her shoulder, and the movement slipped the robe from her left breast. She covered it quickly.

"Matt," she said quietly, "I'd like to leave."

"Leave where?"

"Here. Go back to New York."

"*Now?*"

"Yes."

"But, my darling, that's not possible."

"Why not?" She swiveled suddenly on the little bench to look up at my true self. "Can't we fly by night?"

"Yes, but it's more complicated, and there's a storm coming up."

"I wish we could go."

"But why?"

"I can't explain it. I just want to get away."

"What's happened?"

"Oh . . . nothing. Can we leave tomorrow morning then?"

"If the weather's right. I'll have to speak to Teddy."

"For God's sake," she said venomously, "don't you ever make a decision without consulting him?"

For a moment there was a shattered charge between us, and then she reached for my hands. "I'm sorry, Matt. I think I had too much sun or too much ice."

"He *is* our host, after all, and . . ."

"Your, our, boss."

"That's less important at the moment than the conventions of hospitality."

She looked up into my eyes as though searching for the answer to some obscure question, then she turned back to the mirror and began to remove the cream with a tissue.

"But," I added, "if the weather permits we can leave tomorrow."

She nodded and stood, pulling the dressing gown around her. "Would you . . . ?"

"What?"

"I want to dress."

"Oh . . . yes." I turned to leave.

"I'll be ready in ten minutes."

When we entered the living room, the house, the lake, the great forest beyond lay in that ominous vacuum that invites turbulence, a painting in lurid yellow by a color-blind artist. The effect was strange enough to have drawn everyone to the windows.

"Your man Fallon was right," McClellan was saying. "We wanted to stay out longer, but he said a storm was coming in and it could get nasty."

"Yeah," Teddy said, bourbon and Coke in hand, "they get heavy up here in the summer."

At his side Mary shuddered. "Spooky. Is it supposed to look like that?"

"Yeah," Teddy said.

Below us on the lake, Jacobs was rowing in rapidly. At the pier he hauled the dinghy up, inverted it, and lashed it down securely. Before starting up he turned to survey the fleet of airplanes once more.

A distant statement of thunder came from the east and a slight gust of wind disturbed the tops of the tallest trees on the other side of the lake.

"It approaches now," Pederson said. "I think it will be strong."

Teddy turned to Amanda and me, his eyes illuminated by the flat, yellow light coming through the windows. He looked at Amanda before he said, "I hear the water's pretty cold, Howard."

"Yes, why don't you heat it?"

"I thought of it, but the fish wouldn't like it."

"Mr. Howard," Pederson said predictably, "you missed a fine day's fishing. We caught almost fifty bass and trout, some very large."

"I hope we're not going to eat fifty fish for dinner," Mary said.

"No, no. Mr. Fallon is having them cleaned and frozen. We will take them with us. I desire especially to show some of them to friends in Norway. I believe they will be surprised."

A heavier shock of thunder hit the house.

Mary turned her back to the windows. "Thunder scares me. Can I play the hi-fi, Teddy?"

Teddy shrugged.

She went over to the console and the tape of Cole Porter started again. "Don't you have anything else?"

"No," Teddy said.

" 'Like the beat, beat, beat of the tom-tom,' " Mary began to sing, but suddenly yelped as the room filled with light and a heavy blast of thunder shook the house.

"Very close," McClellan said.

Abruptly the trees were ravaged by violence and the rain hit in a wall of water from behind the house, descending heavily across the terrace and down to the lake. Before they were suddenly hidden from view, the airplanes turned into the wind together obeying a violent command.

Amanda, standing between Teddy and me, said, "Wonderful! I love it." Her eyes were flashing in excitement.

Teddy turned to look at her, and I had an irrational impulse to move between them, to take her from his presence. I drank more of my martini, assuring myself that even with his millions of dollars, his power, confidence, undeniable intelligence, he could scarcely be considered a threat. He had added more weight in the last years, was approaching obesity, his face was still asymmetrical, his ears still protruded in crude geometry from his skull, and so far as I had been able to observe, he had disposed of that wayward charm that had once seemed irresistible to southern ladies. The women he surrounded himself with now were on contract, a hired harem of accessible flesh.

The first assault of the storm subsided, and the lake came back into view, but only briefly. Another blast of rain hit us and a jagged blade of cold, blue light struck at the trees directly across the lake, shaking the house with violent threat.

Amanda winced and clutched at my arm. "That one frightened me. It's like being bombed by the gods. I've never really understood lightning."

"Electrical charge separation," Teddy said. "A positive seeking a negative."

"Or a negative seeking a positive," I offered.

"Can't we have an agreement?" Amanda asked.

"As the gods decide," Teddy said.

I was beginning to wonder if I was mistaken. He was becoming positively lyrical.

We joined the others before the fire that was swirling madly from the wild currents of air passing over the house. "No fishing tomorrow," McClellan said. "Lake will be a mud pond. Bad luck."

"Oh, I've had enough with today," his wife said. "I'll be happy with a book on the terrace."

The house was battered by the shock of another bolt of lightning, and Mary, who was still listening to Cole Porter, squeaked from the other end of the room and came running to Teddy, hiding her face in his chest. "Make it stop!" she wailed.

"Stop," Teddy said.

And a great lull spread over the lake while the first wave of the storm rumbled away to the west.

He waited in nervous expectation and finally McClellan cleared his throat, and Mary lifted her face to look up at Teddy.

"Oh, I *say*," McClellan said, and Peggy on the sofa began to giggle.

"Did you merge with them, too?" I asked.

"Yeah," Teddy said, "but I had to sign in blood."

Amanda's hand tightened on my arm.

"Mr. Arnheim is a troll," Mrs. Pederson announced ambiguously.

"Stop it, Teddy," Mary said with a note of hysteria in her voice. "You're scaring me."

"Start," Teddy said.

Two or three heavy seconds passed and lightning cracked sharply behind the house. The rain began to fall ponderously once more.

"I'll let them take over again," Teddy said walking toward the bar.

Whether it was the result of Teddy's necromancy or the continued violence of the storm, something compelled us to repeated trips to the bar: for years I had permitted myself no more than three martinis. I had five. The Pedersons finished a bottle of white lightning between them, the McClellans' scotch took on a darker hue as they cautioned the bartender against excessive soda, and whatever the nymphs were drinking, Dubonnet, Campari, or sherry, seemed to disappear remarkably fast. Even for Amanda I carried three glasses of white wine, and as usual it was impossible to tabulate Teddy's bourbons and Coke. In addition, owing to storm-related difficulties in the kitchen, the happy hour stretched interminably. It was almost nine before we assembled in the dining room to taste a venison stew which, Teddy explained, Pelletier insisted on producing at least once on every visit and grumbled deeply if there was resistance.

It was probably very good: venison, carrots, potatoes, heavy in onions and mysterious herbs, but I'm not sure we appreciated it. The liquor consumed before dinner, the wine, and the repeated waves of violence that swept over the house distracted us from Pelletier's cuisine, though he pressed it on us.

In a brief relief from the assaults of lightning Mary raised wide eyes from her plate to ask, "How did you really do that, Teddy?"

"What?"

"Stop and start the storm."

"I have a contract."

She looked at him for a moment and then turned to see what impression his answer had on the others. "I don't understand."

"A contract with his majesty Satan," I suggested.

"Don't," she said. "I *believe* in the devil."

"There isn't anything else *left* to believe in," I said wittily.

"Ah, old chap," McClellan said, "you've forgotten the other party."

"No," Teddy said, "the other party's forgotten us."

Arnheim and theology?

Amanda at the head of the table was silent, watching, listening.

"I don't think it's funny," Mary said emotionally, looking down at her plate again. She was curiously stunned, drugged, on a mixture of wonder, fear, and alcohol.

"It's not," Teddy said, "but the other party never had much of a sense of humor."

She raised her large, moist eyes to him. "But I'm Catholic, and I believe."

"And you must go on believing, dear," Mrs. McClellan said.

"I believe that God created the world in six days, and on the seventh . . ."

"He went fishing," McClellan offered.

"Oh," she said, "that's blasphemous, I think. I can't listen to any more of this." She rose, upsetting her wine glass and moved away from the table, staggering slightly. Mrs. Pederson followed to offer comfort though it was unlikely that she had understood the exchange.

"Do you have additional contracts with that gentleman?" Amanda asked.

Teddy smiled slowly at her. "I do his work so long as the price is not too high."

"What do you consider too high a price?"

"Boredom."

A shattering force struck so near us that the house shook in an outrageous clap of simultaneous thunder. Women screamed and except for the swirling light of the fire we were in darkness.

I found myself on my feet along with McClellan and Pederson, but at the foot of the table Teddy slowly reached for a bottle of Moët in the ice bucket and, rising, began to refill our glasses. When he came to Amanda she said, "Have you ever heard of acedia, Mr. Arnheim?"

"Yeah," he said. "I studied Latin. But it didn't help me much." He passed on in firelight.

A flashlight appeared from the kitchen, and then a lantern carried by Pelletier filled the dining room with light and shadow. He spoke to Teddy and Teddy said, *"Non, demain,"* and continued pouring Moët. "It hit the power line from the generator. We won't have electricity until tomorrow."

Pelletier began lighting candles.

"I don't think it's safe to be around you," Peggy said. "Please don't talk about God and the devil any more."

"I don't think they mind being talked about," Teddy said, and thunder rumbled across the lake. "They probably mind it when you stop talking about them." Still carrying the bottle of Moët he walked to the large divan before the fireplace where Mrs. Pederson, with an arm around her shoulders, was comforting Mary, and offered her a glass.

"No, thank you, sir." Indicating Mary, she said, "She sleeps."

Teddy looked down at the paradox of offended Catholicism for a moment and turned back to us assembled before the fire. "I didn't know she was religious."

"Only when she's scared," Peggy said.

"I say, it *is* a storm. Enough to frighten one," McClellan said. "They don't come this big in Scotland."

I sat by Amanda on the small couch to the left of the fireplace and took her hand. The storm had made me amorous. Probably the alcohol had something to do with it also. But Amanda was watching Teddy with a curious fascination, as though a rumor had turned into a fact.

Releasing her hand she took a sip of the champagne he had poured for her. "Mr. Arnheim," she said with the determination of a sudden decision, "was it the first gentleman we were talking about that led Arnheim Industries to merge with McGruder and Sons?"

Still holding the bottle of Moët, he turned to look at her, one side of his face in darkness, the other lighted by the fire, the lips curved in an interested smile. "No, he didn't have a vote in that."

"But it resembles his work."

"No, I don't agree. Unless we have the wrong word on him."

"Apartheid is certainly something he would approve of."

"But I don't think he would approve of giving jobs to thirty thousand black people who otherwise wouldn't have the money to buy food and clothes for their children."

"Under slave status," Amanda continued vigorously, "without unions, without voice, without any power to improve their status, buying in company stores at outrageous prices, working ten hours a day underground."

"They work eight hours a day now, and they're more efficient. The prices in company stores have been reduced twenty percent, and they buy more. If they want unions badly enough they'll get them."

"At what price?"

"A fight."

"A massacre, you mean."

"In a war people get killed. This will be a war."

"But why does there have to be a war?"

"Because some people have property, money, goods, and they want to keep them. Other people don't, and they want them." He was speaking slowly, patiently, but without condescension, not to a student but to an equal apparently exploring an obscure question to which he himself had discovered an answer only after long thought.

"Wouldn't it," Amanda continued after a moment, "be more humane to give them some of it to avoid the war?"

"Yes, but nobody has ever figured out how to get people to do that."

"Couldn't you?"

Teddy was obviously enjoying this, for him, marathon conversation. "No. I don't know how to persuade people to do something they don't want to do. I can force them if I have the power, but not persuade them."

"So there will always be that war."

"I think so." He started to pour more Moët, but the bottle was empty. To the crash of another bolt of lightning he walked back to the ice bucket.

McClellan, who had been listening, said, "Mr. Arnheim is too modest. He has great powers of persuasion."

"No," Teddy said, returning with a fresh bottle, "when I offer something to somebody I try to know if he wants it before I make the offer. If I don't think he wants it I don't make the offer."

McClellan turned to smile at Pederson.

"On an airplane some years ago," I entered the conversation, "you said you didn't believe in psychology."

"What is psychology?" he asked.

"The science of human behavior."

"Then I don't believe in it. I don't believe it's possible for human behavior to be described by science. I only believe in facts, and the facts about people are simple: fears and desires. If that's psychology it's a big word for simple things."

"But fears and desires are often quite irrational," Amanda said.

"I didn't say people are rational. I said they have fears and desires."

Amanda took a sip of the champagne he had poured for her and looked up at him. "Do you," she asked slowly, "have fears and desires, Mr. Arnheim?"

He smiled. "Yes. I have both." He turned and poured more Moët.

I needed to move in again, to interrupt the charge between them, as palpable as the series of charges and discharges occurring in the wild night outside. "Do you feel like describing them, Teddy?"

He finished pouring in Mrs. McClellan's glass and straightened to turn to me. "No," he said in that flat, incontestable voice that sent shudders through the slaves of Arnheim Industries.

Another bolt of lightning struck nearby, and Mary came out of her slumber with a little yelp. "Isn't it ever going to stop?"

Mrs. Pederson extended a maternal hand, but Mary twisted away. "Oh, let me alone, you old hag." She rose unsteadily and limped to Teddy. "Make it *stop*, Teddy."

The expression on his face did not change, but the eyes annihilated her from the universe, then they turned to Peggy, who rose and went to her. "Come on, Mary. I'll put you to bed."

"I don't wanta go to bed . . . without Teddy. I'm scared."

"I'll stay with you," Peggy cajoled. "Come on, baby."

"Oh, Mary, Mother of God, I'm a sinner," she began to moan, "I'm a terrible sinner and God is snapping after me." She began to weep in arhythmic sobs.

"Come on, Mary," Peggy said.

"Leave me *alone*," she screamed, pushing Peggy aside and beginning to run like a drunken gazelle to the door leading to the screened porch, and a series began so fast that it was like an accelerated movie. First a great blast of wind extinguished the candles, and Teddy and I started moving at the same time, but before we had reached the porch Mary had discovered a door to the terrace. A bolt of lightning illuminated her, already drenched, her hair whipping across her face, and she began running again into darkness. We groped through the heavy rain for her but when the next illumination lighted the terrace she had disappeared.

I started for the stairs at the left end, but Teddy said, "Get a flashlight," and I turned back to meet Pelletier with a light cutting through the curtain of water.

"Here," Teddy said from the edge. He took the light and flashed it down, searching in the bushes and boulders twenty feet below.

"*Là, mon commandant,*" Pelletier said.

Extending from under the tortured, shining leaves of a bush was one bare leg and foot with ruby toenails like a string of holly berries.

"Stay here with the light, *mon commandant,*" Pelletier said, "Come, monsieur," he said to me, producing another flashlight.

It was a wise precaution. After descending the stairs we beat our way through sodden underbrush to the point where Teddy's light directed us, and Pelletier swore in French as he knelt to examine her. I couldn't see clearly, but raising his head he said, "She's alive. Just." Then he lifted the visible leg and swore again. Her left leg was twisted at the femur into a grotesque acute angle. Handing me the light he carefully drew the broken leg down straight. "Hold it," he said and thrust his arms under her body.

As we stumbled back below the edge of the terrace I had a morbid fear that if I fell I would be holding a great, bleeding stump in my arms which somehow I would have to dispose of before entering the house.

When we finally had her on the divan before the fire, Pelletier held the lantern over her and shook his head, pointing to a ragged wound already swelling on the left side of her forehead.

"The hospital in Jerome," Teddy said in French.

"*Oui, mon commandant,* but how?"

"I'll take her."

"Wake Jacobs," I said.

"No. I'll take her."

"You're crazy. Wake Jacobs."

"No."

"Wait, *mon commandant,*" Pelletier said and left the room.

"Listen, Teddy, you've been drinking, and it's a wild night. Call Jacobs."

Amanda, covering the maimed body with a counterpane, looked up at us.

"No."

"Well, you're crazy, but I'll come along."

"No. You stay here. I'll take Pelletier."

Pelletier returned with leg splints and bands, and set to work expertly immobilizing the shattered leg. She was still unconscious, and nothing we did brought her around.

Loading her aboard the eight-passenger, twin-jet Beechcraft required all the skill and strength of Fallon, Pelletier, and what I was able to offer. Fallon took the boat in close, but even after Pelletier opened the door and pulled himself up into the airplane, the wild surges of water and wind made it almost impossible to lift Mary up to him without shattering a pontoon or ramming the fuselage. Finally Pelletier leaned out and with one arm scooped her body up.

"Teddy," I yelled as he was preparing to climb up, "does the radio-telephone work?"

"Yeah. Goes onto batteries automatically."

"Call as soon as you get there."

"Okay. Go up to my office." He put a hand on the ladder and Pelletier pulled him in.

We had to cut the line when Teddy had the engines started, and he let the airplane drift out with landing lights on, nose into the violent gusts of wind to avoid being turned over.

Fallon and I were tying up again when a spectral, roaring blot of light began to move down the lake and disappeared into the turbulent night.

It was almost three o'clock when the telephone on his desk rang.

Peggy was asleep in the large adjoining bedroom, and after a feverish but fragmented analysis, the others had gone to bed. I had left Amanda with a candle before her door, and in my room stripped off my rain-soaked clothes and put on a dressing gown.

"Hello?"

"Howard. She died ten minutes ago."

"Oh, Christ. Do you need me?"

"No, but there will be an inquest. You'd better prepare a statement and ask everybody to sign it."

"Yes. There's nothing I can do there?"

"No."

"All right. Teddy, Amanda wants to go back today."

There was a moment's hesitation, then he said, "Okay. Don't forget Washington on Wednesday."

"No."

He hung up.

It was a brilliant, thoroughly scoured morning, and the flight back to Newark was uneventful, though there wasn't much conversation.

When we were just east of Montreal again Amanda said, "That was very courageous of him, wasn't it?"

"Taking her to Jerome?"

"Yes."

"Courageous or foolish. Risking three lives to save one, and in the end it was futile."

"Futile, but brave."

I let it go at that.

In a cab I dropped her off at Gay Street and said I'd call as soon as I returned from Washington on Wednesday.

19

WE WERE KEPT WAITING, but not for long, the twenty or so of us, steel, petroleum, coal, automobiles, aluminum among those I recognized and several others I didn't. Everybody else recognized everybody else, but nobody recognized me. When I identified myself there were polite acknowledgements and some well-disguised curiosity. Quite clearly none of them knew Teddy personally, but just as clearly there was restrained respect.

When the president walked in, apologizing for the five minutes he had kept us waiting, those who were sitting rose, but we were not precisely representative of an American citizenry who would burst into unbridled enthusiasm over a young, energetic, Democratic president.

I had not seen John F. Kennedy in the flesh for over twenty years, though television and photography had prepared me, not quite accurately. At Harvard he had been slender to the verge of gauntness and though he had put on weight, his face was not as full as television gave him. But as I watched him coming down the irregular line a signal came through. Although he had that serene accomplishment of the master politician of listening, concentrating on the person at hand, as though there was no one else in the room, and then shifting skillfully to the next person, when he listened, his face immobile beneath the courteous mask, there was pain, in the eyes mainly, and I wondered if he was seriously ill.

He shifted from steel on my right, and his eyes locked onto mine. *"Matt,"* he said, thrusting out his hand, "what the hell are *you* doing here?" It was both flattering and astonishing.

"Representing Arnheim Industries, Mr. President."

"Is that so? I didn't know you worked for Arnheim. How long?"

"A good many years."

"He wasn't able to make it?"

"He's a very shy man, Mr. President."

He looked at me for a moment speculatively, and then a roguish smile smothered that brief flash of pain. "Oh, yes, I've heard about that shyness. If he gets any shyer we may have to pay him rent for this place."

I smiled, cordially I hoped. "Real estate isn't really his line."

"You wanted to talk about something, I imagine."

"If you have a moment, sir."

"Wait until I've read the lesson." He passed on to petroleum.

It was a consummate performance, without notes, easy, informal, calculated to appeal to his small audience seated in a semicircle before him while he stood casually, speaking in that Bostonian accent and gesturing with his right hand. He was charming and witty, his mind filled with information.

Essentially it was a discourse divided into two parts, the first to assure us that though a liberal Democrat, he had no intention of dismantling the capitalist system and economy of the country built upon the solid principles of competitive enterprise. The nation had been founded and had become mighty on such an economic philosophy, and his administration was dedicated to the continuing prosperity and progress generated by those principles.

His smile at the general applause was charming, and vestiges of that good humor remained as he moved into the second phase of his brief talk, almost as though he wanted to share a joke with us. He expected the industrial community to assist him by avoiding any precipitous and unwarranted increase in prices. It was not ominous, not even explicitly a warning, but the intention was quite clear.

He finished at five-thirty with, ''Well, let's have a drink,'' to very modest applause, and I got the impression they were applauding the drink rather than the message.

I watched him working his way through small groups, any one of which represented the weight of a good many billions of dollars, bringing the glass of sherry to his lips rarely, and eventually moving obliquely in my direction.

He laid a hand on my shoulder—no one else had been honored with such intimacy—and moved me a few feet away from the others. ''How have you been, Matt?''

''Very well, Mr. President.''

''Do you have a family?''

''Not yet, but soon, I think.''

Somewhat closer to my ear. ''Does he want something?''

''He has no political ambitions, but he was wondering . . .''

''. . . if I've forgotten.''

''He has implicit faith in the presidential memory.''

''I understand. The antitrust goons.''

''Yes.''

''Matt, you'd better see Bobby about that.''

''Wouldn't it be more effective if you spoke to him?''

''That's not easy. You know Bobby. He might hang one on me.'' He smiled and removed his hand. ''But I'll look into it.''

''I hope you're in good health, Mr. President.''

''Is it that obvious? Well, it's something I can live with. My damned back. In every sense of the word it's a pain in the ass.'' He put out his hand again. ''Good to see you, Matt. Come back sometime.''

And he turned to another billion-dollar clutch.

For a couple of days the incident at Cantrell Lake threatened to have nasty consequences. A local Canadian paper carried a story on the death of Mary O'Shaughnessy resulting from a lurid episode at the fishing lodge of the American multimillionaire, Theodore Arnheim, and U.P. picked it up. Ignoring general advice Teddy had always refused to set up a public relations office, and when the

Newark office was besieged by reporters on Thursday morning I had
to take over since Teddy had apparently remained in Canada. Before
admitting them I tried to reach him, but the radio-telephone had either
been turned off or was not working.

Finally I gave the word to open the door to the dozen or so members
of the press and they trouped into my office with photographers and
began firing questions. Kellogg insisted on being present.

"If you'll permit me I'll read a statement first," I said. It was a
copy of the statement I had made for the inquest and it had seven
signatures: the Pedersons', McClellans', Peggy's, Amanda's, and
mine. I had made the initial longhand copy—the only typewriter in
Teddy's office at Cantrell Lake was electric—in the early hours of the
morning after Teddy's call, and before leaving the next morning, in a
moment of inspiration, I had copied it and asked everyone to sign
both copies. One I left for Teddy, and the other I had taken with me. It
was a clear and careful account of Mary's fear of electrical storms,
her sudden hysteria, dash across the terrace, and fall.

They listened, but I could see they weren't satisfied, even when I
distributed photocopies I had had run off before letting them in.

"Who are all these people?" one of them asked.

"Houseguests." I identified the Pedersons and McClellans.

"And Margaret Porter?"

"Houseguest. I had never met her before."

"Amanda Bonn?"

"My fiancée."

"Was this Mary O'Shaughnessy bombed?"

"No."

One large, aggressive lout from a tabloid looked up with a lubri-
cious smirk. "I count three couples, then the two girls and Arnheim.
How come?"

"How come what?"

"Two to one?"

"Houseguests. I believe the two girls were friends, though I don't
know."

"Was he laying both of those broads?"

"That's an impertinent question which I won't dignify with an
answer."

"Where can we reach Margaret Porter?" another asked.

"I don't know."

"Mr. Howard," another said, "did you know that Mary O'Shaughnessy's father has a small grocery store in Philadelphia?"

"No. I had never met her before."

"Doesn't sound like the kind of man whose daughter would be a houseguest of Mr. Arnheim's."

"Mr. Arnheim is a man of profound democratic convictions," I said stiffly.

Somebody said, "Right on," and somebody else asked, "Do those convictions extend to democracy in South Africa?"

"We're speaking of an unfortunate accident on a lake in Canada," I said even more stiffly.

"Why can't we see Mr. Arnheim?"

"He's not here."

"Do you know where he is?"

"I would assume he's in Canada, though I'm not certain. He is not a man to run away from an inquest."

Eventually they trouped out again, in a surly mood.

Kellogg was looking down at his hands. His pink skin was fiery red. He was blushing.

I called Amanda that evening but she was out. I hadn't seen her since Monday after our flight back from Canada.

On Friday morning my phone rang a little after ten. It was Teddy. "You did a good job with the papers, Howard."

"How did you know?"

"Kellogg came up last night. He'll stay for the inquest."

"Are there any problems?"

"No. How did it go with Kennedy?"

"Smoothly, and he said he'd look into it, speak to the attorney general."

"Okay. Howard, something has come up in Lausanne. I want you to go over."

"Oh . . . all right. When?"

"Now. As soon as you can get on a flight."

"All right. When are you coming back?"

"I dunno. The fishing is pretty good up here. I'll see you next week probably." He hung up.

Even on a couple of hours notice a single first-class reservation is not difficult to arrange, and my secretary offered me a two o'clock directly to Geneva, or a four o'clock to Paris with an hour's layover and arrival in Geneva at seven Saturday morning. The Lausanne office would be open until noon. I took the four o'clock and asked her to have a company car ready at one. Then I called Cromwell and asked for Amanda, but she was out of the office and they didn't know what time she would be back.

The car waited on 10th Street while I packed and then took me to Idlewild where after checking in I called Cromwell again, but Amanda was still out. I started to write her a note, but decided I'd call her from Lausanne.

At Geneva I rented a car and drove to Lausanne where Maja welcomed me once more. Indispensable now, she had been assigned as Terrill's private secretary and head of the secretarial staff. "It's good to see you again, Mr. Howard. How is . . . Mr. Arnheim?"

"Fine. And you?"

"Booming," she said with a smile. She must have meant blooming. "I married Professor Fournier. You remember him?"

"Yes. Congratulations."

She moved to the door, knocked and opened. "Mr. Howard, Mr. Terrill."

"Hi, Matt." Terrill was a big man with straight blond hair and a rather heavy, boyish face, in his early fifties, whom Teddy had raided from U.S. Steel.

"Hello, Bob. How have you been?"

"Okay. You?"

"Fine."

"How's the boss?"

"He's put on another ten pounds, but he seems to be all right. What's the problem?" I asked, sitting in the chair he offered.

"It isn't really a problem. And that's what surprises me. I called him last week, and in passing I mentioned that James Junior had stopped by on his way to Gstaad, and I took him to dinner. Have you met him?"

"No."

"A real slob. He belted down a good many drinks and talked a lot. He told me that Old Man McGruder had some kind of attack, heart maybe, but he refuses to go into a hospital. He's running the shop from his bedroom. Mr. Arnheim seemed interested."

I thought about it for a moment. "I suppose that could be important, but I don't understand why I came to Lausanne because McGruder has a stomachache.''

Terrill shrugged. "I don't either. If he dies I'd think Mr. Arnheim would head for Johannesburg himself. What the hell's he doing in Canada?''

"Fishing.''

He looked at me blankly. "Is he really?''

"Yes. He has a lake and he goes out in a rowboat and fishes. Didn't you know?''

"No. But I don't know him very well.''

"Have you called McKenzie?'' McKenzie was our representative in the Johannesburg office.

"No. I thought Mr. Arnheim would call, and when he said you were coming over I decided to wait.''

"When did he tell you I was coming over?''

"Yesterday afternoon sometime.''

"Do you remember the exact time?''

"No, wait, I'll ask Maja.'' He picked up the phone. "Three-thirty,'' he said, replacing the phone.

"That would be . . . eight-thirty in the morning our time.'' He had called me at ten. "And when did you report on Junior's conversation?''

"It was . . . last week. Thursday.''

"Did you call him at Newark or Canada?''

"Newark. Why?''

"Oh,'' I said, looking out the window at Lac Leman, "I was just trying to put something together.'' On Thursday of last week he had learned about McGruder's illness. On Friday or Thursday afternoon he had gone to Cantrell Lake, suggesting that he had not been precisely panicked by the information. On the same day, or Friday, he had invited me to go up. In other words he had known of McGruder's illness the whole weekened. On Sunday, or rather Monday morning, Mary O'Shaughnessy had died, and Amanda and I had returned to New York. Wednesday I had been in Washington. Thursday I met the press, and Kellogg had gone to Cantrell Lake. Friday, yesterday, he had called to instruct me to go to Lausanne.

There was a poker game going on, but I couldn't see the cards I had been dealt.

We weren't able to reach McKenzie in Johannesburg, and I

doubted that it would have been worth the call anyway. I turned Terrill down for lunch: he was a bit All-American for me, and I was sleepy. At the Beau-Rivage, where Maja had made a reservation for me, I slept for a while and after lunch on the terrace, walked along the lakefront for a couple of hours, trying to put the various pieces of the game together. I was certain I was being used again in some master plan maturing in the recesses of the Arnheim skull, but I couldn't find the pattern.

At five I returned to the hotel and called Amanda at her home number, hoping to catch her before she left for the office. After ten rings I gave up. It worried me that I hadn't been able to explain my sudden disappearance.

Since the Terrills had whipped up a guest list of some ten people with miraculous speed for dinner that evening I couldn't very well refuse the invitation. It was a large house up behind Lausanne near Chexbres, overlooking the lake, not easy to find, and I was forty-five minutes late. Myra Terrill, a very athletic, small blond woman was polite, but clearly annoyed as she introduced me to the other guests, mainly English and American with one French and one Swiss couple. Representatives of various English and American businesses, they were all members of the English country club, and all fiercely dedicated to golf, a game I had always found prodigiously banal. But they were lyrical about the afternoon's chip shots, forty-foot putts, and slices on the perilous sixteenth fairway. It was not until we went in to dinner that I realized a languorous, dark-haired woman in her early thirties was my partner for the evening. The only name I caught when she was introduced was Soad. She had startlingly green eyes behind lashes so long I was sure they were accessories, very dramatic makeup and long, deliberately unruly bundles of black hair. With the exception of the eyes her face was slightly closer to Middle Eastern than European, an exotic blend. She was quite tall, and her gown, a Pucci or Cardin or some other such frivolity, was an astonishing engineering feat: all in black, even fringed in black lace, and caught up on one side for an exposure of dazzling white flesh. She spoke perfect English with an English accent, Parisian French and, I learned later, Arabic, Italian, and German, or rather Austrian.

We were seated together, and when released from a conversation on her right she turned to me and asked, "How is Mr. Arnheim?"

"Very well. Are you a friend?"

"Yes."

"I'm sorry, I didn't catch your name."

"Soad. My last name wouldn't mean much to you."

"I guess . . . Egyptian."

"Clever of you. My father was Egyptian, my mother's Irish."

"How do you happen to know Mr. Arnheim?"

And another chapter in Teddy's life came out over veal cooked in wine: her father, a relative of King Farouk and a high official in the royal government, had been stripped of everything but his life when Nasser came to power. He had gone into exile in Italy with his wife and nineteen-year-old daughter, where, after Farouk's refusal to help him, he had committed suicide, gamely, with a pistol. Her mother, a nurse in the English army who had stayed in Egypt after the war and converted to Islam for the marriage, had returned to Ireland, but Soad had stayed in Rome studying photography and then spent two years in Vienna as an apprentice. On her own finally, she had moved to Lausanne and opened a small studio.

"But what brought your father and Mr. Arnheim together?"

"I never knew. Egyptian fathers did not invite such questions from their daughters. It was some kind of concession my father was helping him with for, I suppose, a considerable sum. But Mr. Arnheim was our guest twice, once in Cairo and once in Alexandria. I was madly in love with him."

"With *Teddy*?"

"Yes. He was the most charming man I had ever met."

"Are we talking about the same person? Theodore Arnheim the Second, of Arnheim Industries?"

"The same person. And he was not only charming but generous. My first year was marginal, on the low side of the margin. But when I learned that Arnheim Industries had opened an office here, I wrote him to ask if I could do a portrait of him the next time he was in Lausanne. He refused."

"Generous."

"*But* the letter contained a check for ten thousand dollars for a studio and equipment. And within a month I began to receive calls for portraits. Important people. And now my appointment calendar is a month long." She took a spoonful of sherbet.

How many lifelines were manipulated by the Arnheim fingers, I wondered again.

Coffee and cognac were served on the candle-lighted porch above a forest of pines and the lake glistening in moonlight. Soad stayed at my side on a low wicker footstool. "I'd still like to do a portrait of Mr. Arnheim, but he won't sit. Will you let me do one of you?"

"I don't think I'd stimulate your business."

"It doesn't need any further stimulation, but I'd like to do you anyway. You have an interesting face. There are two sides to it."

"With the exception of some Picassos, there are on most faces, aren't there?"

She had a low, almost raucous laugh. "The problem would be which one to exploit. I like facial problems."

"I'm enough of an egoist to want to know what the two sides are."

"The gentleman, conservative, perhaps a bit timid, but disguising timidity under manners."

"Stop," I said, trying to laugh. "I don't want to know the other side."

"The other side has poetry and the capacity for love. Are you married?"

"No. You?"

"Not now."

"You two are really indecently intimate," Myra Terrill said, coming between us. "Spread some of that charm among the others."

I ended up talking to a vice-president or manager of Nestlés, and Soad joined the women's convention in the living room. The Nestlés man was very interested in Teddy. "Astonishing person," he said. "Everything he touches prospers. A finger of gold."

As I was preparing to leave, Soad came to me. "Tomorrow? Will you come?"

"Have you decided which side to exploit?"

"Yes." She drew a card from her evening bag, but took it back. "That's the studio. Here. Come to the apartment around eleven, and after I've exploited you I'll give you lunch."

I tried calling Amanda once more when I returned to the hotel, six-thirty New York time. It bothered me that I had not been able to reach her before leaving, and I wondered if she had gone to Fire Island. She had a sixth of a rental for occasional weekends.

Soad's apartment was not large, but it was a penthouse in a new, shining building in Ouchy with a glorious view of the lake and the mountains of Haute Savoie on the other side. When she came to the door she was exotic again in slacks and a light jacket richly embroidered with Egyptian iconography, her heavy hair in two braids.

There was a bookcase filled with her various languages and a discreet wall of paintings, most of which I couldn't identify. One small watercolor seemed familiar, a nude man and woman, Neo-Expressionist.

"Is this a Schiele?"

She looked at me with some surprise. "Yes."

"Wherever did you find it?"

"In a shoddy little shop on the Kärntnerstrasse in Vienna. They didn't know what it was."

"The kind of luck everybody dreams of. Who's this?"

"A Swiss painter from Berne. Klökli."

"Very good."

"Yes, and the poor dear is almost eighty now and has never received the attention he deserves."

On two other walls were examples of her own work, the first a blowup of an immense, round, smiling man's face on a hairless head, with a wart on the end of his nose. It epitomized satisfaction with self, contentment, success, and it was impossible to look at it without smiling.

"Wonderful."

"I did several others of him that made him look more mysterious, masterful, but he chose this one. He's just what the picture says, a very successful businessman here in Lausanne. He adores it."

There were others, not all portraits, dramatic, with bold lighting, and some interesting chiaroscuro effects: a female torso that looked like a Roman sculpture in shade, a nude male dancer descending from a *grand jeté,* his limp phallus aloft, and some gauzy female nudes. But what interested her most was obviously portraiture, and her lighting and texture were very good.

"Some Man Ray?" I asked.

Again she looked at me with surprise. "Yes. I went through a Man Ray period, and I guess some of it stuck."

"Who's the subject of this one? Looks like Lenin."

"He was a cobbler in Vienna. When I told him he looked like Lenin, he said, 'Who's Lenin?' Would you sit over there, please?"

I sat in the straight-backed chair in sunlight.

"Would you mind taking off your jacket and tie? I'm going to exploit the poetic side."

She picked up one of several cameras and began to move around in

front of me, sighting. "Would you turn just a bit more to the right?
There." She began snapping from various angles and then knelt
before me. "Look up." She snapped again several times and stood.
"You don't like to have your picture taken?"

"No."

"Why not?"

"I think because one carries an image of himself around and the
camera violates that image. It's like being asked to assume responsibility for an act that you'd rather forget."

She lowered the camera and looked at me. "Your Protestant ethic
is showing."

"It's a reflex rather than an ethic."

She came up close to me and rumpled my hair purposefully, and I
was very conscious of full breasts a few inches from my nose.
Moving back she began snapping again. "I just shattered the Protestant reflex."

"Yes, I can feel it leaving."

"Okay," she said, putting down the camera. "I'll develop later.
Let's have a drink. What would you like? It was vodka martinis last
night, wasn't it?"

"Yes, but I try to avoid such heady indulgences before six o'clock.
A Kir?"

"Two Kirs." She went to the kitchen and came back with ice. At
the small bar she poured drops of ruby cassis and filled the glasses
with white wine. "Let's go out."

There were some big pots with shrubs and small trees, and others
with geraniums, petunias, and pansies. The sun was hot on the tiled
terrace.

"Did you say you are a lawyer?"

"I don't remember saying it, but I am."

"Probably Myra told me."

A distant phone rang, and she said something Arabic that sounded
irregular, and put her glass down on the wall. "Excuse me." Inside
she began speaking French, but so softly that all I could understand
was a string of negatives. Finally the phone went back on its cradle
with vigor, and she reappeared.

"I hope I'm not throwing a . . . spanner into the works."

"No, not at all." She picked up her glass. "It wasn't important. I
turned the phone off. Do you come to Lausanne often?"

"Four or five times a year, irregularly."

"You'll have to make it more often than that if I'm to become your official photographer . . . *there* now, that's a different expression, a smile I haven't seen. Can you do it again?''

"I doubt it unless you have a repertory of such charming phrases.''

She took our glasses. "I'll check in my phrase book.''

We had luncheon in a corner of the terrace under a large, varicolored parasol while sailboats tacked slowly across Lac Leman, scarcely moving in the midday calm, birds retired from the heat of noon, and a sensuous indolence fell across the part of Lausanne we occupied. She rolled out a *table roulante* with a *pâté,* two large *salades niçoises,* rolls, and an ice bucket with Fendant.

"A good salad.''

"Thank you, but I had them sent up. I'm a very limited European cook. My mother tried to teach me to make an Irish stew, but I couldn't resist spices and it turned into an explosive Arab dish. I cook pretty well in Arabic, but it doesn't travel.''

"You knew Farouk?''

"Ugh, yes. He's my third cousin. A beastly man.''

"You were married in Egypt?''

"To my second cousin when I was sixteen. I was a princess in the king's Egypt.''

"I can well believe it.''

She looked across at me with an inquisitive smile. "You're very gallant for an American.''

"That is what is called a putdown in America today. What happened to your husband?''

"He stayed in Egypt after Nasser took over. To the astonishment of my father and everyone else, he had been a member of the very militant Free Officers' Corps, Anglophobic. Today he's quite an important person in Egypt. But my family was caught in a crossfire, under two curses. Nasser distrusted my father because he had married an English, or Irish woman, and after the abdication, Farouk detested him because his son-in-law had been a member of the Officers' Corps. My husband made some points by divorcing me, and we landed in Rome frightfully broke.''

"Farouk is where?''

"Monaco mainly, but he has a lease on the top floor of your . . . of the Beau-Rivage. I shouldn't think he'll last long with his appetite for food, drink, and girls. He's positively porcine.''

"He doesn't drink Cokes, does he?''

          "Coca-Cola? My God, no. Nothing but champagne."

After coffee we left the shade of the parasol and stretched out on mats in the great light of the June sun. "I'm an Egyptian cat," Soad said. "I slumber after lunch." She rolled over onto her stomach, her hands under her chin. The eyelashes, I had decided, were not accessories. Through preposterously long fringes she studied me. "Why don't you take your shirt off, you great morsel of America, and absorb some Swiss sun?"

I sat up and removed my shirt, and her eyes covered me quickly. "A hairless Greek chest. I hate men with huge mats of black hair on their chests, like Onassis. The Greeks must have changed a lot since the Periclean age. I've never known a modern Greek who could have modelled the Belvedere Apollo. You could."

          "Are you sure the sun isn't affecting your vision?"

          "Yes, I'm sure. I see very clearly."

          "The Belvedere Apollo is Roman, incidentally."

          "But a copy of a Greek original. Is practicing law interesting?"

          "Not very."

          "Why do you do it, then?"

          "I developed a lamentable habit of taking solid and liquid sustenance every day."

          "Does Mr. Arnheim pay well?"

          "That's a question that seems to intrigue everyone, and it's impertinent."

          "I know, but I like impertinence."

          "The answer is yes, he pays me well."

          "You've known him a long time?"

          "Yes."

          "Do you understand him?"

          "Not entirely."

          "I do."

          "Good. Explain Theodore Arnheim the Second to me."

          "He's maimed because he loved once. I don't know who it was or when or where. And he's been trying to find someone he could love again. Without love all his energy goes into creating an empire, and in creating an empire he destroys other empires."

          "Destroy is a little strong. Absorbs."

          "It amounts to the same thing. He absorbs other identities. He likes to break things and rebuild out of the rubble."

"I don't find that very illuminating. It's what the psychologists call substitutive achievement or something pompous like that. Why can't he find someone he can love?"

("I don't know. There's some element missing for him."

"Where does all this information about Teddy come from?"

"Oh . . . I know quite a lot about him."

The Swiss sun, jet lag, and the wine were leading me away from the mystery of Theodore Arnheim the Second. I closed my eyes. Just before I fell asleep I heard Soad change her position.

Some time later a fly insisted on landing on my chest and returning with demonic regularity when I brushed it away. I opened my eyes and sat up. Soad, lying on her back, had removed her jacket, and there was nothing under it but flesh. Even on her back she had prominent breasts with erect, red nipples.

"Do you mind?" she asked without opening her eyes.

"No, not at all. You look a little like a Modigliani, the Golden Nude."

She smiled without disturbing those extraordinary eyelashes to open her eyes, and searched for my hand. "Don't you think," she said languidly, "it would be a good idea for us to make love?"

I believe that essentially I'm a monogamist, but I had not yet received the privileges that would permit monogamy. "Yes," I said, "I think it would be a good idea, but I suspect that among the many laws regulating morals in Switzerland there is one that prohibits making love on a terrace in daylight."

"I believe that I have a solution to that," she said, still holding my hand and rising slowly.

She led me to the bedroom where she turned to look at me. "Do you think the Swiss will still object?"

"Probably, but they consider foreigners hopelessly immoral anyway."

She came to me and pressed her breasts against my chest, looking up with her green eyes through those absurdly long lashes, and I kissed her.

Her every movement was languid, calculated, but the calculation was profoundly erotic. For Soad making love was an art of leisurely control up to the moment of orgasm, but in orgasm she responded with a ferocity that resembled a detonation.

With a bottle of champagne on the candlestand near the bed we spent a good part of the afternoon detonating. Later, after I had taken a shower, we went to dinner in a restaurant that specialized in Viennese cooking: *Wiener Schnitzel, Knödel,* a chilled Moselle, and a dessert of *Schlagsahne* with chunks of chocolate, while a surprisingly good Salvation Army quartet of two men and two women sang old Swiss songs in French and German.

"Tomorrow night I'll take *you* to dinner in Amphion," Soad said over a demitasse.

"Where's that?"

"Across the lake in France. Actually it's up in the mountains above Amphion."

"Splendid, if Theodore Arnheim the Second doesn't suddenly order me to go to Lhasa."

"Oh . . . if he does, tell him I haven't finished your portrait yet."

Back in the hotel I had my hand on the telephone to call Amanda at six o'clock New York time, but with the musky perfume of Soad's body still clinging to me, it impressed me as a bit crass.

Although Terrill found things for me to do, we were both confused about my continuing presence in Lausanne. We had lunch together, and at four o'clock, a decent morning hour in Newark, I called and asked the operator for Teddy. He wasn't in the building, and she didn't know, or wouldn't say where he was. I asked for Downing.

"Jim, do you know where Teddy is?"

"Still in Canada."

"Is there a problem with the O'Shaughnessy girl?"

"Not now. He called to have us send a check to her father. A quarter of a million."

"Christ! I wonder how he decided on that figure. Do you know what the hell I'm supposed to be doing here?"

"No, he didn't mention it."

"Well, I guess I'll call him."

"He's not accepting calls. He calls, but then he turns that thing off."

"Do you think he's hiding out until the O'Shaughnessy thing blows over?"

"That's not characteristic of him."

"Well, if . . ." Terrill appeared at the door of my improvised office making telephone motions and pointing to his office, mouthing Arnheim silently.

"Jim, he's calling on the other line. I'll see you later." I hung up and went into Terrill's office to pick up the phone. "Yes, Teddy?"

"Howard, there are some chemical people in Rome who may want to sell. Go down and take a look at it. Here's the name and address." He read some Italian that sounded like Fifth Form Latin.

"All right, but what to you want me to do afterward?"

"Give me a call when you've seen them. I'm going back to Newark tomorrow."

"But should I stay in Europe?"

"Call me." He hung up.

I wasn't enthusiastic. I knew nothing about the chemical industry, and the night classes in Italian I had taken at NYU years before had not left me fluent. I hoped they would have some interpreters.

As arranged, Soad appeared before my hotel at six in a Lancia sports car with the top down, her hair covered with a scarf. She was undeniably dramatic in a raffish yellow jacket and slacks, and long jade earrings.

"Did he call?" she asked as we climbed up toward the autoroute.

"Yes. I have to go to Rome tomorrow."

"Oh, lovely. I'll go with you."

"Can you?"

"How long will you stay?"

"A day or two, I suppose." I already had some misgivings about her driving, clearly the aggressive European style.

"Oh, easily. I'll cancel two days. Do you speak Italian?"

"Scarcely."

"I'll interpret for you."

We had reached the autoroute to Geneva, and within seconds we were traveling at a hundred and sixty kilometers an hour which is around a hundred miles per hour. "My God, Soad, the restaurant isn't going to burn down before we arrive."

"What?"

"Slow down a little."

"Don't you like to drive fast?"

"No."

She reduced her speed to about a hundred and forty. "That's the other side of the face, the side I didn't exploit. Genteel, law-abiding."

"No. Just the sentimental habit of living."

"What's the trip about?"

"Some chemical industry he's interested in, apparently."

"Absorbing another identity?"

"Perhaps. I don't know. He just said they're interested in selling. There must be something wrong with it if they want to sell."

"Do you just go in and buy a company like that?"

"*I* don't. But there's a lot of preliminary handshaking and investigating, looking at the physical plant and the reports. If it seems promising a specialist in whatever the line is looks it over, and contracts to purchase are drawn up."

"It sounds boring."

"Most of it is. If there are competitors it can be more interesting."

For a few minutes she devoted herself to aggression on the autoroute, apparently offended by anything ahead of her. "If you were offered the Lausanne office, would you take it?"

For a flashing moment I had a *déja vu* that I was unable to grasp before it faded into those mysterious recesses of unrealized memory. "No, I don't think so."

"Why not?"

"Cultural shock. I've always lived in Manhattan when the choice was mine."

"I could help you over the cultural shock."

We were well up to a hundred and sixty again, and to avoid the perils that a fertile imagination can provide I turned away from the road to look at her. There was a slight smile on her lips, generated either from the *frisson* that speed offers some people or from some perverse, secret source of pleasure. She began to impress me as threatening, and though she handled the little sports car very well, she drove through Geneva and the old city at a speed that amounted to public outrage.

The restaurant two thousand feet above Lac Leman was splendid. We had drinks and afterward dinner, on the terrace directly across from Lausanne, luminous in the early evening, under a perfect cross of pink jet-trails. The blanquette de veau was the best I had ever tasted, and the patron, apparently an old friend of Soad's, was charming.

"What time is our flight tomorrow?"

"Ten."

"I'll call my agent."

"Don't bother. I'll have the secretary book for you. I don't think there will be any problems, and she's good at solving problems."

"Maja?"

"You know her?"

"Slightly. I'll bring the pictures. I think you'll like them."

That led to a discussion of photography, Soad describing it as the art of the potential moment in which there must be a *punctum*, a governing point, that drew the eye into expectation. "Good photography is all expectation, the stimulus to move beyond the moment captured by the lens."

"Even still-life photography?"

"Even still life. The first photograph ever made, in eighteen twenty-two by Niepce, is a still life of a set table. It's expectant, *attendant*."

"I know very little about photography, but I don't think I agree with you. I want completion in art, the moment after, rather than the moment to come."

"I think," she said slowly, "that reflects your character. It's a moral and not an aesthetic preference. The most obvious, the most banal example is the distinction between the pornographic and the erotic. The pornographic is static, finished. The erotic is expectant. You'll see what I mean when I show the pictures."

"My God. You mean the distinction between pornography and eroticism is made clear in photos of *me*?"

She laughed boisterously and nodded.

"Well, that's interesting and rather surprising."

"You weren't aware of expectancy?"

"I don't recall."

"I have met men with more skill at flattery."

"I'm sure you've had enough flattery to sustain you."

She interrupted the application of brie to a piece of bread to look at me calmly, appraisingly, for a moment. "Lausanne doesn't hold any temptations for you then?"

"Oh, yes, it does, but I'd miss the beastliness of Manhattan eventually."

"We can produce some beastly fogs and rain in Lausanne."

"It's the beastliness of the inhabitants I'd miss. You've never been in New York?"

"No. Somehow I haven't caught the fever that has swept across Europe. But I was thinking of London when Mr. Arnheim more or less settled me here."

"Destiny's hand. Moving people about like chess."

"What do you mean?" she said, startled, almost angry, it seemed to me.

"Nothing serious. But he does enter lives rather mysteriously at times. Yours, for example."

I couldn't quite decide what had come over her. She seemed suddenly nervous, defensive, and only a few minutes later she said, "We should probably go back. I'll have to pack and call my appointment agent to cancel." She signaled for the check and signed it, ignoring my objections.

At the Lancia I took her arm and seated her in the right bucket seat. "What . . .?"

"I'll drive."

"Macho," she said as I settled behind the wheel.

"No. Survival." I started the car and began to negotiate the winding descent toward the lake, Soad huddled resolutely in her bucket, leaning away from me. I was too busy with hundred and eighty degree turns to look at her, but it was not until we had crossed into Switzerland again and had reached the autoroute that she moved and spoke.

"I'm sorry, Matt," she said suddenly, and leaned her head on my shoulder.

"I can't forgive something I don't understand. What happened?"

"Oh, I don't know. I thought . . ."

"What?"

"It's nothing." She lifted her head and kissed me on the cheek. "I'm a little neurotic. I imagine things."

I could not imagine what things she had imagined, and she had nothing further to say on the subject. In that curious maneuver of European women, her hand began to caress the nape of my neck, an endearment that I'm told is intended as erotic, but which has never captured me. When I drove up before my hotel, she said, "Aren't you going to invite me in?"

"Yes, certainly."

"You're not very enthusiastic."

"My Protestant reflex."

There was an envelope, hotel stationery, in the box when I asked for my key, but I didn't bother with it until Soad was prowling around the absurdly large suite, commenting on its appointments. The note informed me that a Mr. Downing had called and requested me to return the call, at his home if after six o'clock Newark time.

"Excuse me," I said to Soad who was returning from an inspection of the bedroom. "I have to make a call."

"Do you want me to close the door?"

"No, don't bother. There's a bar over there if you want something."

"Do you?"

"Pour me a cognac, please." I lifted the phone.

It took the operator some time to get through, and there was a lot of overtalk on the line. Downing's wife came on after Soad had handed me a glass and disappeared into the bedroom. "This is Matt Howard, Mrs. Downing. Is Jim there?"

"Yes, he just walked in."

"Matt?" Jim said in a curiously fuzzy voice.

"Yes, what's up?"

"McGruder . . ." His voice trailed away.

"I didn't get it, Jim."

"McGruder died yesterday . . . down to Johannesburg."

"McGruder died? I didn't get the rest of it."

"Mr. Arnheim left for Johannesburg. He wants . . ."

"Again, Jim."

"He wants you to join him."

"In Johannesburg?"

". . . join him there."

"The Italian chemical thing is out?"

". . . don't know . . . to Johannesburg."

"Is he going to pick me up in Geneva?"

"No . . . directly."

"All right. I guess I understand. Thanks, Jim." I hung up and finished the cognac. The idea didn't intrigue me, and I realized I had begun to look forward to Rome with Soad.

I crossed to the door of the bedroom. Soad's yellow slacks and shirt were flung across a chair, and she was in bed under a sheet drawn up tightly to her chin, her glossy bundles of hair tossed across the pillow. When I was standing above her I could see tear lines running down her cheeks from under long, closed lashes.

"Why are you crying, for God's sake?"

She shook her head. "I don't know. You're not going to Rome?" She opened her eyes.

"No. How did you know?"

"I heard you mention Johannesburg."

"And?"

"I know that Mr. Arnheim has some interests there."

"What else do you know?"

"What do you mean?"

"You seem to know quite a lot about Arnheim Industries."

"What I know is common knowledge." Reaching for my hand, she pulled me down to the bed and pressed her tearstained cheek to mine, kissing me in a kind of despair.

It was well after two o'clock when I turned out the light on the night table. The extension phone was a gaudy red. It was early morning in Gay Street.

Lightly Soad began to weep again in my arms.

20

SIX DAYS LATER I landed at Idlewild exhausted and a bit feverish from some mysterious germ I had picked up along the circuitous route from Lausanne to Johannesburg.

That route had begun the following morning when Soad insisted on driving me to Geneva, leaving my rented car to be returned by the office. Standing by the Lancia at the Geneva airport, she looked up at me, her green eyes moist. "You'll come back soon, won't you, Matt?"

"Yes. I still haven't seen the pictures."

"Damn. I hate to cry," she said, lifting her lips to kiss me. "Matt, I love you . . . no, don't say anything. Whatever happens, remember I love you." She turned and dropped abruptly into the Lancia. With a scream of tires the little car hurtled down the cement, arousing stolid Swiss indignation that then settled on me as a residual culprit.

On the leg to Marseilles I pondered over what she could have meant by "whatever happens," and I continued to ponder at Marignane airport waiting two hours for the flight to Casablanca. Maja had offered me a flight to London with an overnight layover and a direct flight to Johannesburg with two stops. Unwisely I chose the Marseilles, Casablanca, Brazzaville, Johannesburg route with a layover of two hours in Casablanca, three in Brazzaville, and the last leg ventured by a very fatigued DC-4 that lost an engine somewhere over Angola and landed in Johannesburg at six o'clock in the morning.

At the Johannesburg Hilton I slept until ten and then called Teddy's suite where his valet-bodyguard informed me he was not in. Johannesburg depressed me from the beginning, and although autumn should have been well settled in, the weather was stifling. The offices of McGruder and Sons were shabby, something out of Dickens, and it took a call to some mysterious presence to admit me to a waiting room with a male secretary and a massive, unadorned iron door. The secretary, who spoke English with a heavy Afrikaner accent, could not seem to get me through the iron door, so I waited for almost an hour, fighting a ponderous need for sleep.

Finally the door opened with a very Dickensian squeal, and Teddy emerged followed by Kellogg carrying a heavy dispatch case, Lloyd Gray, our chief accountant, also burdened, McKenzie, our man in Johannesburg, two elderly men dressed in severe black suits with stiff collars, and a young man with closely cropped blond hair and thick glasses. The male secretary immediately stood at attention.

"Hi, Howard," Teddy said casually and introduced me to the three McGruder men, the two elder being the head of the company legal staff and McGruder's manager, and the younger, Junius McGruder, who looked uncomfortable, stricken, perhaps, by his father's death.

With introductions completed, Teddy, with the two McGruder representatives, started for the door. "See you later, Howard." Junius was following them when the manager spoke to him. He stopped, blushed, and disappeared in the hall.

We left McKenzie in his shabby little office and caught a cab. "What's he up to?" I asked as soon as we were seated. Kellogg put his finger to his lips, glancing at the driver.

At the hotel, Gray, Kellogg, and I settled at a large table in Kellogg's room before a prodigious stack of documents that they drew from their briefcases.

"Let's have it," I said finally. "What's he up to?"

"If everything works out, he's going to take over."

"Buy the boys out?"

"That's the plan. Fifty-one percent now, with option to buy the rest gradually. Junius is totally incompetent, close to imbecilic. All he wants is a guarantee of his job, and a $975,000 raise in his salary."

"Pretty imbecilic."

"Dembke, the manager, tells me that everything he does has to be checked and usually done over."

"What about James Junior?"

"That's still a sticky wicket. We finally located him in London yesterday, but even Mr. Arnheim couldn't pin him down. He seemed ready to come to an agreement, but then he said he'd have to think it over. He was not entirely sober, I gather. But one thing is certain. He wants nothing to do with running the company. He won't even come down for his father's funeral. Mr. Arnheim will probably go up to London when we finish here."

"How can we finish here without Junior's agreement?"

"I think I'll go to my room," Gray said suddenly, gathering up his documents and calculator. "I can't concentrate while you're talking."

"Okay," Kellogg said, "but don't leave without letting us know."

"How the hell could I leave? It's going to take at least three days to go over these figures."

When we were alone Kellogg said, "To answer your question, we'll set it up with a blank for Junior's demands. He'll probably come pretty high, but a few million down and a share of receipts should satisfy him."

"How does Teddy plan to get around the exporting problem as a noncitizen? We'll have to file, won't we?"

"That's not certain, but if we do there's a lot of protection. It will still be McGruder and Sons if we file."

"You mean there will be two agreements? One for filing and one for us?"

"That's the way it's done here apparently."

"And if they find out?"

"Mr. Arnehim seems to think there will be a solution."

"Mr. Arnheim is beginning to skate on pretty thin legal ice."

"He expected that might be your reaction."

"It doesn't bother you?"

"I wouldn't touch it in the States."

I didn't see Teddy again in Johannesburg.

But I talked to him on the telephone for about five seconds. He spent the days in a helicopter going from one mining location to another with Prescott, his chief mining engineer, whom he had brought with him from Newark. Apparently he had a good deal of modernization in mind.

While Kellogg and I were working late in the afternoon of the second day Teddy called and talked to Kellogg and then asked for me.

"Howard, how would you like to be manager in Johannesburg?"

"I wouldn't like it at all."

He paused, then he said, "Okay. How much more work do you have?"

"Another day or so."

"Okay. When you're finished you can go back to Newark. Tell the others to wait for me." He hung up.

"He offered you the management here?" Kellogg asked casually, turning away from me.

"Yes, but I can't imagine why. I don't have any experience running a gold mine. He ought to give it to McKenzie. He's an engineer, and he knows what's going on."

Kellogg was easily embarrassed, but I could not understand what had come over him suddenly. "What's the matter, Roger?"

"What?" He turned back to me, his face flushed. "Oh, nothing. Let's get back to work."

It was three o'clock of a steaming July Wednesday when I caught a cab at Idlewild. I had never reached Amanda by phone. The lines from Johannesburg to New York were still apparently primitive, and the one time I made contact with Cromwell she was out of the office. Finally I had sent a long cable explaining my absence, mentioning that I had tried to reach her countless times. Her repeated, mysterious absences from the office had begun to bother me, and I wondered if in some sudden burst of integrity after Cantrell Lake, she had decided to quit one of Arnheim Industries' small relatives.

As soon as the air conditioning was working on West 10th street, I dialed Cromwell and asked for her. I was shunted onto a line, and to my surprise a woman's voice said, "Miss Bonn's office."

"May I speak to her, please?"

"May I know who's calling?"

"Matthew Howard."

"One moment, please."

There was a delay, and finally Amanda came on in a small voice. "Hello, Matt."

"I'm terribly sorry, Amanda. I tried to reach you at least ten times from Europe and Johannesburg."

"Oh . . . that's all right. How was the trip?"

"Very tiring. Did you get my cable?"

"Yes. When did you get back?"

"I just arrived. What time will you be home?"

"About six-thirty."

"I'll pick you up at seven for dinner."

"Oh, Matt, I don't want to go out. I'm exhausted. I'll buy something on the way home and make dinner."

"Come here, then. I have plenty of time to shop."

"No," she said firmly. "I'll do it."

"If you're too tired I can control myself until tomorrow."

"No, but come around seven-thirty."

"All right. What's this bit about 'Miss Bonn's office?' "

"I'll tell you."

I put the phone down. For a moment a small, anonymous anxiety disturbed me. I attributed it to my "infidelity" in Lausanne, and obeying a moral code that must have been a vocation in my family for some centuries, I decided that if it became too oppressive I would tell Amanda.

I went through the small court on Gay Street where some nasturtiums and pansies had been ravished by the sun, and met Amanda at the door. She did look tired. There were shadows under her eyes that I had never seen before. I kissed her but her lips slipped away from mine, and she turned to enter the small dining room–living room with such a languid twist of her body that I was slightly alarmed.

"Are you ill?" I asked following her.

"No, just tired." She dropped into one of the aged overstuffed chairs and reached for a glass on the small table. "Get yourself a drink, Matt, and sit down. I have something to tell you."

"That sounds ominous. *Cela paraît néfaste*," I repeated in French for some reason. "What are you drinking?"

"Vodka and tonic."

I had never seen her with a drink upon my arrival; in fact I had never before seen her drinking hard liquor. I maneuvered the kitchen and refrigerator doors and made a vodka and tonic for myself. Something was cooking on the small stove. It smelled like a spaghetti sauce.

I came back with my drink and sat in the other overstuffed chair. A vagrant spring exerted unequal pressure on my buttocks.

"Matt," she said immediately, looking directly into my eyes, "I'm editor-in-chief at Cromwell."

My glass was halfway to my mouth. It stopped there for two or three seconds, then continued to my lips, and I drank. Between the impulse to drink and the satisfaction of that impulse, I suspected my life had been altered. "I see," I said.

"You see?"

"Yes. Congratulations." I put my glass down and started to rise.

"Please don't go, Matt."

"I think it might be better if I did." I stood before her, for the first time in my life tempted to do violence to a woman. She looked so fragile, so evil now, so compellingly beautiful I wanted to shatter a symmetry that threatened my profoundest convictions, but that inherited vocation for restraint, for acceptable conduct prevented me.

"Please don't go. I have to explain what happened."

By then I was overcome by the, for me, unprecedented banality of the scene. It had been played out before me years before, but I had not been involved, or only remotely involved. I had been an observer then, marking every movement in an awkward dance of seduction and betrayal. The dancer now, I had lumbered about in monstrous innocence from Cantrell Lake, to Newark, to Lausanne, to Johannesburg, a display of naiveté that I suddenly found beyond belief. My tender soul had accumulated guilt even over my absence and a couple of tender encounters with Soad.

"I think I can supply the details for myself," I said evenly.

She looked up at me, her face registering a question that was not yet ready to be formulated. "But won't you let me explain, Matt?"

"You went back to Cantrell Lake?"

"Yes. He called me, and I went back with Mr. Kellogg. You see," she said, with what promised to be a smile, "somehow he knew I worked for Cromwell all the time."

The scenario had finally become quite clear. Kellogg's embarrassment in Johannesburg. Teddy's, "The fishing's good up here."

(Or had he said ''up her?'') I had been needed suddenly in Lausanne because McGruder had had a stomachache the week before, which, however, had turned out to be a heart attack.

"And I suppose you stayed the whole . . . what was it? A week?''

There seemed to me to be a singular indifference in the way she said, "Yes, almost.''

I should have left then. It would have been much neater. Even while my sadism began to stir I was partly aware I was playing second villain in a melodrama, and a very substantial cliché became clear to me: when we're injured we like to injure. I wonder why. Revenge? Pity for oneself? Or simply the unreasoning effects of outrageous anger?

Already finding myself contemptible while I began to speak, and remembering an almost identical statement, in a kitchen in Alabama many years earlier, I said, "A very profitable weekend.''

She looked at me for a moment, her glass in hand, her eyes widening, and then she set the glass down and rose from her chair to stand before me. I was appalled at my own coarseness, but that spontaneous energy of the wounded continued to throb. "Did you learn to enjoy fishing?''

I saw the brief flash of anger in her eyes, but before she spoke it had turned to contempt, even pity perhaps. "Thank you for saying that,'' she said calmly, "it makes a lot of things clearer for me. You wouldn't wait for me to explain, would you?''

Already beginning to relent, I continued to assuage my tender ego. "I don't believe an explanation would have helped.''

"Oh, my poor Matt. You're a book I've already read.'' She turned and retrieved her drink. "Is Teddy back in the States?''

The ''Teddy,'' that oblique confession of intimacy, reinforced my maimed intentions. "I don't know. Hasn't he been calling you?''

"No. I told him not to. But now I'll call him.'' She took a long drink as though she had completed some violent physical exercise and set the glass down again. "Listen to me, you . . . you Wasp virgin. There were no strings attached . . . no clauses in my becoming editor-in-chief. In your bloody, *bloody* Wasp terminology, I didn't pay for it. He asked me to marry him, and I said I couldn't. I said I was going to marry you. *Then* he asked me if I would like to be editor-in-chief. I said I would if I could publish any book I wanted to publish, including Maxwell's. He agreed without a moment's hesitation.''

"And now?" I asked.

"Now, I think I will marry him, if the offer holds."

"Do you love him, if that word applies?"

"No, I don't think so. But he's a book I haven't read."

"All the world's a book," I said with admirable equivocation.

A strong smell of burning onions, garlic, and tomato sauce had begun to fill the room.

"Oh, my God," Amanda said hurrying toward the kitchen, "it's ruined. I'll have to . . ."

I didn't hear the rest of it. I closed the door behind me, passed by the blasted garden, and walked into the heavy heat of Gay Street.

In comparison to the disasters that were being prepared for America mine was a small matter, but for a while it threatened to capsize me. I stayed home for the rest of the week, dropped into bed by a combination of my disaster and the germ I had picked up, running a fever and suffering from diarrhea. Finally I dragged myself to a doctor who gave me some antibiotics and told me to stop drinking, for a while at least. Teddy, I learned from Downing, who did not even know that I had returned, was in England persuading James Junior, successfully it turned out, to sell McGruder and Sons.

I had nothing to do in Newark until he returned. My resignation would be a personal confrontation, not a letter.

On Monday I called Downing again and asked if Teddy had returned.

"Yes, but he's not in the office."

"Do you know where he is?"

"He said . . . he was going to spend a few days in New York." The hesitation suggested he knew something.

"Would you have someone call me when he's back? I want about half an hour with him."

"Is it something I can help you with?"

"No."

"All right, I'll let you know."

I tried to dismiss Amanda from my life, unsuccessfully, of course. In the somewhat less than three weeks since our engagement at six thousand feet so much had happened that I had not really prepared myself for marriage, and it occurred to me now that I had never really believed in it. I tried to convince myself that the collapse of ideals and rebellion in the face of wealth and power had diminished her to

insignificance, but my argument wasn't persuasive and didn't relieve
me. She was neither a fool, a hypocrite, nor a coward. *I* had played
the buffoon manipulated by Arnehim cunning.

When Downing called me on Tuesday I had recovered, but I had
lost about ten pounds. He said Teddy would expect me Wednesday
afternoon. I took a large briefcase to carry a few items back to 10th
Street; the rest I would have packed and stored until I had decided
what I was going to do. I hadn't given much thought to finding a new
job, though after years at Arnehim Industries I didn't think it would
be too difficult. I even thought of opening my own firm. With my
habitual prudence I had invested nearly half of my considerable
salary over the years, and I could survive even without working,
though on a reduced scale.

He was sitting at his desk when I entered the office, and he glanced
up from some papers that probably weren't even props. He probably
had been working up to the moment his secretary announced me. He
was in shirtsleeves, an unfiltered Chesterfield dangling from his
lips.

"Hi, Howard," he said casually.

I sat in the usual chair before his desk. "As you probably suspect,
I've come to resign, and since I'm no longer an employee I will
permit myself some insubordination. I've known you for thirty
years . . ."

"Thirty-two," he corrected softly.

"All right. Thirty-two. I can't say that I've ever really understood
you, but I've always been convinced that you were decent, honest, in
human relations at least, and that you had some . . . I'm not sure I
have the right word, affection for me, assuming you're capable of
affection for a male. Now I believe I was mistaken."

"Why?" he asked simply.

"Don't play the clown with me. I don't have the patience for it."

"I just want to know why you changed your mind."

"You know goddamned well what I'm talking about."

He looked at me for some time with flat, slate eyes, and then
pushed himself heavily out of his chair. He had gained more weight.
He walked to the window behind his desk and looked out into the evil
haze of Newark. "I need her," he said.

"I've heard that before. You seem to need a lot of people."

"No. Just two."

"Well, apparently you have one. She'll have to do for both of us."

"Don't leave, Howard," he said, his back to me. "I need you, too."

"Don't you have enough puppets to play with? Isn't the world you construct obedient enough? Doesn't the power you control satisfy you?"

"You don't understand."

"I'm the first to admit it. I don't know why you do what you do."

He breathed deeply, turned back to his desk, and lighted another Chesterfield. "Do you want a drink?"

"No, thanks."

He crossed ponderously to a vast paneled wall and pressed a button, activating doors that opened to expose a bar with a refrigerator, and poured a bourbon and Coke. How does somebody else do this? I wondered. The honest way, honest to the injury, the muscles, the supine manhood of legend, of course, would be to punch him in the nose and walk out. I could not conceive of punching Teddy in the nose.

After taking a generous drink, without turning, he said, "Come here a moment, Howard."

I rose to join him staring into the mirror.

"What do you see, Howard?"

"Two men advancing into middle age."

"But there's a difference. The one on the right is tall, broad-shouldered, handsome. See the cheekbones, the strong chin, the eyes that seduce a woman without touching her. The one on the left, short, fat, a confused face, all ears and nose."

We stared at one another in the mirror for a moment before I said, "But I think the one on the left has more brains than the one on the right."

"Uses them with less scruple."

"Where are you going now, Teddy? You can't make me believe that everything you've accomplished is compensatory."

"I don't know what that word means. You asked me a question a couple of weeks ago in Canada. Do I have fears? The answer is, yes, I'm always afraid. I'm afraid that I'll always be alone, that there will be no one there to love me. It's a hard job to love me."

"There have been those who did."

"Yeah, maybe, but most of them have been silly cunts."

"Not all." I realized I was in danger of succumbing. "I'm sorry, Teddy, but the Amanda caper is too much."

"I can't apologize because I never feel guilty. It's simple. I need her. But I need you, too."

I turned away from the bar, but he stopped me. "Howard, why did you get me into the Ivy Club?"

"Because you belonged there."

"No, I didn't. At all. Was it because I was going to inherit some money?"

"No. I thought the Ivy Club needed *you*. Surely it hasn't made any difference in your life because you were a member of the Ivy Club?"

"Yes. It was the first and last club I ever belonged to. What I learned was I didn't need a club. I send them fifty thousand dollars a year for that."

"That balances out the five hundred I send them." I went back to the desk.

"Do you want more money, Howard?" he asked from behind me.

"No, for God's sake. You pay me more than I'm worth now. But why the manipulation? Why didn't you tell me, call me? Why the trap? Why don't you ever play straight poker?"

"You don't win when you play straight poker. I play to win."

"You have only one method, whether it's personal or business?"

He settled himself behind the desk again. "It's the only method I know."

"In your world you make all the rules."

"I haven't found any better ones. Mine may have faults, but at least they're consistent."

"Somebody, Montaigne or Emerson or somebody else, said, consistency was the hobgoblin of little minds."

"I can understand that because I have a little mind. It only works in one direction."

"To win?"

"Yeah."

My determination was faltering, and I rose to leave.

"Think about it, Howard. I need you."

I left him sitting at his desk.

21

As I SEE HISTORY, that tinderflash in eternity, the United States has experienced five major traumas since becoming a nation: the Civil War, the Great Depression, Joseph McCarthy, the disastrous involvement in Vietnam (which was just beginning), and another absurdity that was waiting in the wings. All, even the Depression, the result of mindless violence.

My traumas come from an incapacity for violence.

I did not resign from Arnheim Industries. Perhaps my failure to act was the result of the new dimension in Teddy's character he had exposed to me in a kind of despair I did not really understand, or perhaps it was simply inertia, a slack will. I was tied to him in a long symbiosis, and he refused to release me.

Fully aware of the strategy that was being practiced on me, I was sent back to Johannesburg a month later and stayed for six weeks assisting in the transition. I also gave serious thought to contingency plans in case Arnheim's controlling interest in McGruder and Sons was discovered. Under McGruder, shipment had been routine and simple, small consignments sent by regular air service to Brussels, London, or Antwerp. McKenzie and I explored other, illicit methods: third party transactions, shipment to Durban by rail and then by sea through the Suez, or McKenzie's favorite inspiration, smuggling it out in shipments of cereal. He was a good engineer, but he had never recovered from reading the novels of his landsman, Robert Louis Stevenson. McKenzie had a romantic streak that I did not associate with engineers. He was rather slight, blond, and very intense. When we were turning over one idea after the other, his fingers trembled slightly.

I was aware that there was another reason for my presence in South Africa. It would have been awkward to send me a wedding announcement and bad form not to send me one. So I was out of the country when Teddy and Amanda were married.

But even before I left Johannesburg some small waves of a revolutionary change began to arrive, suggesting that a new tide was coming in. In order to avoid attention the inadequate and depressing offices of McGruder and Sons had been retained unchanged, and my burrow, with its single grimy window, resembled a hastily converted broom closet. Into this squalor McKenzie led a man in his midthirties one morning whom he introduced as Tom MacIntyre from Yale, recently arrived from Newark. "Listen to him for a while, will you, Matt? I have to get out to Grootvlei."

There was just enough room for him to sit down on the other side of my desk, and he began to talk the moment he sat down. Like McKenzie, he was blond, though showing signs of premature baldness, and he had quick, lively eyes, a mustache, and small blond beard. He spoke very rapidly about "enucleated family infrastructures," and I soon understood McKenzie's urgent mission to Grootvlei.

"I'm sorry, Mr. MacIntyre, but I'm not following you. Could you start over again and tell me how I can help you?"

He looked surprised. "Didn't Mr. Downing explain?"

"Not to me."

"He wrote two weeks ago."

"I never saw the letter. Perhaps you could explain."

He did. Rapidly. He was a sociologist who had written his doctoral dissertation on sociological implications of apartheid, several chapters of which had been read with interest by various journals, and the entire work was to be published in the spring. Although he had talked only to Downing, the articles must have come to Mr. Arnheim's attention since he had been invited to Newark and offered a contract to do a study of family and working conditions in the mining fields of McGruder and Sons. The opportunity was so exciting and, I suspected, so rewarding, that he had arranged a leave of absence from Yale, with some difficulty, since the semester was about to begin, and caught the first plane to London. I thought I recognized Teddy's fine hand: McKenzie, MacIntyre. The new troops were coming in in kilts to blend with the established Scots presence.

"Mr. McKenzie thought you might show me around the mines and camps."

"No. I've never seen them, and I don't intend to see them. You should speak to Mr. Dembke."

"I already have. He said the best advice he could give me would be to take the next plane back to London."

"Well, after so much research, you must know your way around."

"But I've never been in South Africa before. It wasn't really necessary with the Yale Library and the New York Public and government publications.''

"Oh. Well, we'll find somebody to help you. I hope exposure to reality doesn't shatter some beautiful theories. I'd like to see a copy of the book when it comes out. Who's publishing it?''

"Cromwell.''

I left the early spring of Johannesburg to return to the early winter of New York and the routine of Arnheim Industries in Newark. The transition from McGruder and Sons to Arnheim Industries had gone smoothly, and there were no interruptions in the shipment of the product to various European cities.

I didn't see Teddy for several months, though he called more often than usual, mainly from New York, but also from Miami, London, and Paris on not very important issues. I had the impression he wanted to be certain that I was there, fulfilling that mysterious need. From several sources I learned that the wedding had been a private affair at Collincourt attended by a select number of people from Arnheim—Downing and Kellogg and their wives—and a few members of Amanda's family. Mrs. Arnheim, now ninety, had blessed the union with Germanic enthusiasm. The newlyweds had gone to Miami for a single week after the wedding, and when they returned a new apartment on Waverly Place was ready for Amanda, though apparently she spent weekends at Collincourt. A gossip columnist asked with some malice what multimillionaire is permitted to spend three nights a week in his wife's apartment in Manhattan, and returns the courtesy by inviting his wife to pass weekends in his thirty-five room mansion in New Jersey? Thirty-five, I believe, was slightly exaggerated, but I had never counted.

Cromwell's spring list created some interest. Among other unusual titles was Maxwell's *The Superrich*, apparently updated. The chapter on Teddy was remarkably accurate, though there was no mention of the merger and purchase in South Africa, and Teddy scarcely appeared as a living person. But it sold very well, perhaps because of the bizarre circumstances of its publication, though, as Amanda had claimed, it was well researched and well written, with just enough of the sensational to appeal. It was reviewed favorably by the *New York Times*, and Maxwell, apparently paroled from San Remo, was interviewed on television. A handsome beginning for Amanda.

Soad wrote me regularly. She mentioned Teddy's marriage once, and asked me when I would be coming back to Lausanne, but I seemed to be stuck in Newark, mainly because of something that was happening to Teddy. There was no mystery to the amount of time he spent in Manhattan, but gradually the long absences from the Newark office became the subject of quiet speculation, and my position in the company changed accordingly. I had less and less contact with the legal department and more with management. Finally, either on Teddy's orders or because it just worked out that way, I found myself number three man in the company under Downing, who consulted me on almost every decision.

One day when an important question came up and we couldn't reach Teddy, Downing and I made the decision (it concerned pricing—the Brazilians were giving us problems), or rather I made the decision and Downing concurred.

Since it had been almost six months since I had seen Teddy, I asked, "What the hell's going on, Jim?"

"I think he's bored with the business. Expanding, buying, trading interested him, but it's at optimum now, and simply running the shop doesn't have any appeal to him."

Downing had never referred to Amanda in my presence, but I assumed that Kellogg had conveyed certain information, though Kellogg was far from being a gossip. "Do you think it's his wife?"

He avoided looking at me. "Partly, yes. I think she's trying to interest him in politics." He turned back to me. "He's pretty close to the vice-president, you know."

"To *Johnson*? No, I didn't know. Since when?"

"Just the last few months. He's seen him in Washington and at least twice he's been invited to the ranch."

I was genuinely surprised. I could understand his sending me as a substitute to talk to Kennedy, but what possible affinity he could have with that affable political professional from Texas I couldn't imagine.

I thought about it later. The antitrust threat seemed to have dissipated miraculously. The idea of Teddy's actually running for office was as remote as his suddenly deciding to become a sheepherder. I had never heard him make a speech in his life, at least of more than thirty words, his physical presence, appropriate to the epoch of William Howard Taft, would certainly disqualify him, and his control of McGruder and Sons would surely become known in America eventually. I wondered what Amanda had in mind. A kind of expiation for having married one of the world's great capitalists who did business in South Africa, but whom she might lead now into the paths of righteousness?

Overingenuous probably.

The episode with Amanda left me maimed, angry, even sick for a while, but I did not choose the currently popular relief of handing my psyche over to a stranger. I chose the therapy of earlier days—escape, geographical escape. My social life had almost ceased to exist, and even a beautiful, seductive woman did not arouse the animal spirits that had never failed me before. I began having harrowing nightmares, and it came to me as a mild shock that I was impotent. I had become one of those industrial eunuchs who work too hard, drink too much, and collapse into bed after a fifteen-hour day. What Teddy had handled almost alone took three or four of us to manage.

I have no prejudice against shrinks. Some I've met have been very intelligent, but their practice has always impressed me as closer to mythology than science. My therapy was literal displacement.

Another winter had come in. I went south, to Miami first, and then to the Keys where I rented a small house for ten days to swim, read, lie in the sun, and eliminate (almost) alcohol from my diet.

When Downing walked into my office five minutes after I had arrived on Monday morning, he was as close to hysteria as I had ever seen him. "Read this," he said, thrusting a thick, plastic-bound document into my hands. It was the survey by MacIntyre, two hundred and twenty pages long. "Come to see me as soon as you've finished it."

It was extremely well done, an appalling picture, even worse than I had imagined, of miserable housing, unsanitary plumbing, squalor, and rigid restrictions that separated the mine workers from their families for months at a time, since wives and children were not permitted to live in the company camps. The men were allowed "family leave" for one week every three months, but they were not paid for this time off, and they had to find their way to and from the bush on their own initiative, some of them using almost the entire week in transit. For obvious reasons, it didn't mention apartheid (apart-hood), but the last fifty pages were devoted to corrective measures, in view of present conditions, a realistic utopia in which the shantytowns would be razed, new buildings constructed with modern, if simple, facilities, medical care, families reunited, or if that was not possible, family leaves permitted more frequently at full pay, and transportation provided.

I put it down wishing I had never read it.

When I dropped it on Downing's desk he said, "You don't know the worst yet. When I finally reached him on Thursday he told me to start getting cost estimates immediately. It's going to amount to a bundle."

"Yes, but in a good cause."

Downing was a decent person, but despite the pious claims of immense companies and corporations, decency and high profits are not normally compatible, and his mind when he arrived at Arnheim Industries every morning dwelt rigidly on profits. "This is not a charitable institution. We are in business, as I understand it, to make money. My guess is that McGruder and Sons will run a deficit for a couple of years if we go ahead with this."

"Probably, but it doesn't stop there."

"What do you mean?"

"Strictly speaking, we're in an illegitimate business in South Africa, in the sense that we're working behind a cover. For South Africa this document is the equivalent of the Communist Manifesto. How will the other industries—Anglo-American, for instance—and the government react when they hear, and they're sure as hell going to hear."

"Oh, God," he said, stricken. "I'm failing. I hadn't even thought of that."

"I have a strong suspicion that when we begin this operation we'll be investigated and our export license will be lifted."

"I'm sure of it," he said, tilting his swivel chair back. "I'll have to call him."

"Without question he's already thought of it."

"Yes, probably," he said rather curtly.

"I didn't mean it that way, Jim."

"But it's true. I just don't think in political terms. Well, I'll call him anyway. I'll let you know."

As I expected, Teddy had thought of it, but it made no difference in his decision, and cost estimates were contracted for immediately. They ran to nearly fifteen million dollars for the buildings alone, but as soon as the weather permitted temporary shelter to be erected, the old camps were razed and construction began. Since commitments to Junius and James Junior were firm, Arnheim Industries' share of income would not cover operating expenses for the year.

But that year had its own special thunder.

My Victorian therapy produced no miracles. I remained a eunuch, and the nightmares, which had faded away in the Keys, returned. They were filled with shadowed violence of a particularly malevolent kind since almost inevitably I was the inflicter of violence, of cruelty, of loathsome sadism. I couldn't imagine where all this evil came from.

The first thunder of the year came in midsummer. I had seen Teddy a few times when he came to the office unannounced to spend a few hours on matters that Downing and I had shelved for him. But in spite of his need, it seemed apparent that he was avoiding me.

One afternoon late in July I was summoned to his office to find him with Downing and Kellogg in a conference that was no surprise. McKenzie had called from Johannesburg to say that the South African government had cancelled the export license of McGruder and Sons. The "product" could no longer reach the markets that had been its European outlets for years. Downing had an aggrieved I-told-you-so expression on his face, and Kellogg was depressed.

Teddy looked up and said, "Hi, Howard."

We spent two hours going over all the contingency plans that Kellogg, McKenzie, and I had considered and dismissed as impractical, too expensive, or legally too risky. Teddy's expression did not change, but clearly he was becoming impatient, and the simple aluminum ashtray at his elbow was piled high with butts of unfiltered Chesterfields. He picked it up to empty it in the wastebasket, but before he settled it back on the desk, he seemed to weigh it in his hand.

Pressing the switch of the intercom he said to his secretary, "Would you ask Mr. Prescott to join us, please?"

While we waited, everyone silently examined the ashtray in Teddy's hand as though it held a mystery about to be revealed. "I don't know that my mind works faster than Kellogg's or Downing's, but I knew Teddy better, and I knew his capacity for approaching a problem laterally when a head-on assault failed. Before Prescott entered I thought I understood.

Prescott, who had degrees in both mining and metallurgy from the Colorado School of Mines, was a large, rather unkempt man who had joined Arnheim Industries a few years after me. He always looked a little sheepish, but he was intelligent and quick. "Mr. Arnheim," he said in greeting, and nodded to us.

Teddy handed him the ashtray. "That could be turned out in other metals, couldn't it?"

Prescott examined it, turned it over, and looked up as though waiting for the punch line. "Oh, sure," he said slowly, "anything heat-resistant."

"Gold," Teddy said.

"No problem. Heat and a simple die."

"And how much would it weigh in gold?"

"The same size and design?"

"Yeah."

"About . . . two pounds."

"And you could coat it with something that would disguise the gold and scrub easily?"

"Oh, sure." He also understood now.

"Two pounds," Teddy said. "That would be around . . . twelve thousand dollars this morning."

"Roughly, yes."

"Okay," Teddy said, retrieving the ashtray. "You're off to Johannesburg this evening. Buy the equipment you need down there, and set it up. Keep it quiet. As soon as you've produced the first ashtray call me and I'll go down. Do you need anyone else?"

"No, I don't think so. I'll have McKenzie." He turned to leave. "Oh, Mr. Arnheim, can I have the ashtray?"

"No," Teddy said. "I like this one. Buy another one at Woolworth's, but don't spend more than twenty-five cents on it."

22

IN A TRULY extraordinary achievement, before the summer ended, Prescott had his stamping mill in operation under a top-secret cover, and Teddy flew to Johannesburg to examine the prototype ashtray produced by Arnheim Industries. I never learned whether Amanda took these trips with him, but I suspected she did not. Knowing her as

I thought I knew her, I was certain she had laid down certain restrictions, and her new, exalted position at Cromwell must have kept her busy.

Kellogg went with Teddy to arrange for shipping permits. Ordinarily any flunky could have taken care of it, but it had to be a precise operation, and by October the first consignment of Piltdown ashtrays left Johannesburg in a private (disguised Arnheim) jet with a hundred items to test the run. The name was an example of Arnheim humor with a sniff of danger since the Piltdown Man had recently been discovered to be a hoax. The ashtrays were glazed thinly with something that looked like obsidian to account for the weight.

The operation went very smoothly. The plane landed in Nairobi, Kenya, the product was transferred to a regular freight run to end up in Brussels where the glaze was removed and the gold resmelted into ingots for the market.

Simplicity sometimes succeeds in a world that has manifestly become too complex.

A second load consisting of two hundred items, four hundred pounds, two million four hundred thousand dollars, went through without a hitch, and I began to wonder how much money passed under the table to various minor officials to assure such a smooth transition.

The McGruder operation of Arnheim Industries survived the first year, and a second year promised profit, not in the level that James McGruder had extracted with his slave labor, but substantial. The very precariousness of the ashtray business apparently challenged Teddy once more. He followed the shipments to Brussels with a new interest, reducing the number of flights to Nairobi, but increasing the loading so that each flight represented a greater profit but also a greater risk if caught or lost. Direction of the rest of the conglomerate was almost entirely in Downing's and my hands, and, though not through our acumen, it thrived. As closely as we could figure it, on paper Arnheim Industries had gone over the billion-dollar threshold.

There is a popular capitalist myth that a no-growth industry invites suicide. Teddy did not subscribe. After the first period of rapid expansion he bought no more new businesses. Each of the twenty-some enterprises was profitable. If it wasn't the manager was sacked. If under new management it didn't produce, it was sold.

I was remoter from Teddy than I had been in twenty-five years, and it was only through various in-house channels and the newspapers that I learned where the income from Arnheim Industries went. He paid his top people well, very well, but he spent immense sums on the personal lives of Mr. and Mrs. Arnheim. He bought, or rather Arnheim Industries bought, a yacht in defiance of the rumor that the day of the yacht as status symbol was over. Being one hundred and thirty-eight feet long, the *Amanda* did not belong to the class of the really legendary vessels, one hundred and fifty feet being the minimum length for that exotic category, but a large sum was spent on improvements and modernization since the *Amanda* had been built in Holland in 1951. A helicopter and pad were added; the swimming pool enlarged, and a lot of gadgets were installed. Watertight doors on the port side, when opened, permitted a seaborne Cadillac and a jeep to move down a ramp to the astonishment of whoever happened to be on whatever wharf they were tied up to.

I, of course, was never aboard for those weekend or week's cruises. I saw the *Amanda* once as she was leaving Port Newark. She was sleek and white.

There were other purchases. To Collincourt, the cabin in Canada, the house in Miami, the apartments in New York, were added a house on Grosvenor Square in London, opposite the American Embassy (several paragraphs of a column in the *New York Post* were devoted to this coincidence), and a large apartment on the Avenue Wagram in Paris. Since occupying all of these lodgings even briefly in one calendar year would have strained the most energetic of travelers, they were lent for periods to various people, who were, if not friends, at least influential, mainly in Washington.

The thunder of that year cracked again late in November. It was preceded by a death. Mrs. Arnheim the First died in her ninety-third year just before a birth and another death. On the morning of November 22, Mrs. Arnheim the Second gave birth to a daughter in Doctors' Hospital in Manhattan. In the afternoon John F. Kennedy died in a hospital in Dallas. For a while everything stopped.

I had not been one of his idolaters, but I felt I had lost not only a president but a distant friend. I never believed in the conspiracy theory. I believe it was another example of that mindless violence that is the despair of civilized man and that will not end until the light goes out.

*   *   *

In the new year, almost as though to console me, Teddy began to appear again, even dropping into my new office to smoke a cigarette. I had not been inclined to send whatever you send at the birth of the child, but I asked after its health.

"Okay," he said. "I wish it was a boy."

"You can probably do it again," I said crudely.

"Yeah. You liked Kennedy, didn't you?" he asked in a characteristic flanking maneuver which alerted me.

"Yes. He was witty, intelligent, attractive. I think he might have become a major president. I was never really close to him."

"He remembered your name."

"He worked at those things, and he was a superb politician."

"How would you like to meet the new one?"

"Johnson? Why?"

"I thought it might interest you."

"What the hell are you putting together this time, Teddy?"

"Nothing. Think it over," he said rising. "I'll probably be going down to see him soon."

Since we were already in the countdown of an election year, I thought I understood everything but his desire to have me go with him. Why I would make any contribution to an Arnheim venture with the new president I could not fathom, but I stumbled onto other information quite by accident.

At one of the very infrequent cocktail parties I attended, I met a woman in her early forties, a journalist accredited to the White House. Physically Patty was one of the most unattractive women I had ever met: tall, emaciated, prognathous, and craggy. She was also one of the brightest and wittiest. She bore a high Boston family name, and she had known the Kennedys for years.

"We weren't related, of course, God scourge the day, but he [she was talking about JFK] always said we were, and always kissed me at the White House. In press conferences when he called on me he always said, 'Don't throw me a curved ball, Cuz.' God, I loved the guy. I went on a three-day drunk when that obscene little shit killed him."

She was a little drunk at the moment, the first woman I had met in twenty years who drank martinis—*gin* martinis, without the rocks.

"Do you know the brothers?"

"Bobby. He's different. Something of a fanatic. Teddy's still a blob, an amoeba. But Jack had everything. I never met a woman who could resist him. I would have hurtled myself into the sheets if he'd asked me. Of course," she brayed, "he never did."

I liked her. In spite of her alleged sexual alacrity, she was totally asexual. So was I. After we had both made the rounds again, separately, I asked her, "Can I take you to dinner?"

"Oh, God, yes."

When we were on Sixty-seventh Street she said, "Let's go to the Chink's on Sixty-sixth." I'm not a passionate admirer of Chinese food, but it was good Szechuan.

"What do you do, Matt?" she asked after the third or fourth course.

"Lawyer."

"Dynamic trial?"

"No. Counsel for industry."

"Which one?"

"Uh . . ." I realized I had become defensive. "Arnheim."

She dropped her chopsticks and leaned back. "Oh, my God. The Fat Man!" It was just below a yell.

"That is not the way he is known in the company."

"Theodore Arnheim?"

"Yes."

"My God. I took you at least for a surgeon or a professor of Old Low Franconian. Which one does he want?"

"Which what?"

"Which embassy?"

"I don't know that he wants any."

"Don't tergiversate with me."

"Don't *what*?"

"He's after something, and when Lyndon is elected on his own in two months Fat Man's going to be down there pounding on a door."

"Where do you get this information?"

"Never mind. It's off the record, but it's accurate. He makes regular visits to a large white structure on Pennsylvania Avenue carrying a little brown bag, and comes out half an hour later with the same bag, and you can bet your ballocks it wasn't filled with Wheaties."

I shrugged, not very convincingly. "The American system. Do you still have the White House card?"

"Oh, sure, but what a difference. They've changed the air. For the bad."

"He hasn't had a chance to do much yet. He's trying to win an election."

"He'll win it all right, but oh, God, its depressing. Completely new turf. Mucho hombresville. I was invited to a shindig for the press a couple of weeks ago. He's trying to win Kennedy people to his side, and it was really laid on. I decided to do a piece on it and I had been taking notes for two hours when he noticed and came over to ask me to dance. But first he took the notes and held them up to that great nose and said, 'Smells like spyin'.' Then he tucked them into his jacket pocket. After we galloped through the Perdinales Parade, he kissed my hand and walked off with my notes. What the hell could I do? With two hours' work pitty-patting against the Executive heart. If I had gone over to reach for them I would have been a colander in two seconds."

"Did he give them back?"

"Oh, gallantly. He has an uncanny awareness of what's going on around him. Just before he left he came over to me, pulled them out of his pocket and stuffed them into my bosom and said, 'Make it good, Patty.' "

"Do you think there's a chance at an embassy?"

"Who knows? Lyndon will probably make a lot of silly mistakes."

"You would consider it a mistake?"

"Does Fat Man have any qualifications?"

"He's bright."

"Like a shark."

"He can be very persuasive."

"Persuading illiterate black men to dig gold is not the same as persuading Her Majesty's foreign secretary to free the Irish."

South Africa was known.

"Which reminds me of another story, an accurate story, told by somebody who was there. Your boss flew down to the ranch for a nice homey barbecue. He was flying the plane himself, some big, fat-assed jet, and apparently he had some problems, or at any rate a lot of smoke came off the tires when he landed on Lyndon's private strip. After he parked the plane Lyndon met him in a jeep and yelled up at him, 'Not long enough for ya, Teddy?' Fat Man apparently said no. 'How many more feet do ya need, Teddy?' Fat Man said something, and Lyndon yelled at some guy sitting on a bulldozer, 'Hey, George! Another two hundred feet!' "

*   *   *

I saw Patty several times after the Johnson landslide. When she came up from Washington she called, and I took her to dinner, and a couple of times when I was in Washington I called her, and she took me to dinner. She couldn't cook. It was always a relaxed, loud, but easy evening, and she always had some new Lyndon stories, most of them scatalogical. She was in the presence when the scars were bared and when hounds were lifted by their ears, and although she admitted that he had an idea about racial equality, she predicted he was going to plunge the nation deeper and deeper into disaster in Southeast Asia. "He's demented on the subject of dominoes."

The last time I saw her, in Washington, she was big with anecdote and couldn't wait to relieve herself. Over the first martini she said in that booming voice that carried to every corner of the bar, "Well, he's got more brains than I would have given him."

"Who?"

"Lyndon. Fat Man came down for his reward, and in words that should be chiseled into the cement at State, Lyndon said, 'Aw, Teddy, I love ya, son, but I cain't send ya off to London or Paris or I'll have a flock a niggers after my tail.' "

23

THE STORY, or some version of it, must have been accurate since, so far as I could determine, Teddy lost all interest in politics. He disappeared for longer periods and no one seemed to know where he was. I wondered what was happening between Amanda and him, whether he was escaping not only from the tedium of an immense enterprise that ran smoothly without him, producing huge profits every year, but also from a marriage that was not running so smoothly. Cromwell was also flourishing, turning out a select list of books of intriguing variety every year, some trade, but also some offbeat studies that were generally very well received.

I was approaching the ambiguous age, permanently neutered it seemed, a sacrifice to someone else's obscure energy, perhaps suffering from an ancient trespass that I could not identify, apparently unable to wrench myself away from a stultifying routine that made sense only when I submerged myself in a problem each day. The grotesque element in this slavery, not even to an idea, but to inertia,

was that I no longer really needed to work. My prudent lifestyle had
produced solid security, and I was told that my collection of paintings
would probably go for over a million dollars.

Trying, as usual, to avoid direct eye contact with myself in the
mirror while shaving, one morning I surrendered to an impulse for
confrontation. I was graying at the temples, and my eyes had a hollow
look, but there was something left.

I made a decision: I would quit Arnheim Industries on my fiftieth
birthday. That gave me a few more prudent years. But the wind of
circumstance had begun to blow, and I could not feel it.

On a June evening I had showered and was beginning to dress for
dinner at the apartment of some of the few friends I still had, a lawyer
and his wife, when the phone rang.

"Howard."

"Yes, Teddy?"

"Yeah."

I was astonished. He had never called me at home.

"I'll be over in twenty minutes."

"But I have a dinner . . ."

"It'll have to wait." He hung up.

I wasn't even sure he knew where I lived, but almost exactly
twenty minutes later the bell rang and I admitted him. He heaved
himself up the stairs, entered the living room without a glance at
pictures or furniture and settled heavily on one of my great-
grandmother's fragile chairs. He was wearing a lightweight, dark,
pin-stripped suit, but he was sweating from the brief exertion of
climbing the stairs. I hadn't the remotest idea of what was coming.

"Do you want a drink?"

"No. Machade called from Nairobi. The last shipment never
arrived."

"What happened?"

"I dunno. It left three days ago, but disappeared after calling in at
Dodoma."

"Where's that?"

"In what used to be Tanganyika. It's Tanzania now."

"Have they sent out a search?"

"No. I told them not to."

"Why not?"

"Because we'll do the search."

I looked at him for a moment, rose, and went to the bar to make myself a drink. "No," I said, turning back to him.

"Six people," he continued, ignoring my impertinence, "know about those ashtrays, not counting the receiving end in Brussels. You and I, Downing and Kellogg, McKenzie and Prescott, and three black workers who run the mill. Not even the pilot and copilot know what they're hauling."

"The three blacks aren't people?"

"They're well paid."

"No," I said again.

"The ashtrays are packed in small wooden boxes," he continued, "and they're not opened until they reach Brussels."

"Do you want a drink?"

"No."

"How many ashtrays were on the flight?"

"Twelve hundred and fifty. Two thousand five hundred pounds. The biggest shipment to date."

"And that's worth how much today?"

"Over nineteen million dollars."

I restrained myself from whistling. "Teddy, I have a dinner date. I'm already late."

"Call them." "He looked at me steadily, his eyes flat.

"You know I could quit right now."

"Yeah, but you won't. I need you. Call them."

We looked at one another for a few moments, I took a drink, and rose to go to the phone. Before I dialed I said, "This doesn't mean I agree."

When I returned, having, I suspected, placed a heavy strain on one of my remaining friendships, I said, "The idea of two middle-aged men, one of them fat, floundering around in central Africa is absurd."

"I've rented an airplane in Nairobi. We'll fly a search pattern. When we find it we'll land and offload the cargo."

"Why don't you send in a team of experienced people?"

"Anybody who finds the cargo will know the story. If the airplane is wrecked some of the glaze will have cracked off."

"You can take a nineteen-million-dollar loss for once."

"Yeah, but if it's found it will close down the operation, probably mean seizure of the mines, and fines of more than nineteen million."

"Well, I advise you to find a stalwart deaf-mute to join you on this one."

"The car's waiting below, and Jacobs is waiting in Newark. All you need is a toothbrush. We'll have clothes in Nairobi."

"Sounds like the squadron commander talking."

"Not an order. A request."

"It's crazy."

"It's easy."

I didn't really give a damn if he lost his nineteen million dollars, but my decision was one of those spontaneous acts that you're not even conscious of performing. Perhaps it was the chance of breaking out of the sterilizing routine I was locked into.

"All right," I said finally. "I'll go. If they catch us they'll boil you first. I wouldn't even make a decent entrée."

"If it's where I think it is, it's Masai country. They eat beef."

Nairobi is over a mile in the air. The center of the city is modern. I never saw the center.

Jacobs landed us at the airport in the afternoon, two days later, and after some delay while we got parking instructions from the tower, taxied over to the most ancient C-47 I had ever seen, the wings drooping in despondent fatigue, and the rudder cross-stitched with innumerable patches. A black guard with a rifle was asleep in the shade of the left wing. Jacobs didn't ask questions, but after one glance at the C-47 I saw his eyes on Teddy, appraising the state of his sanity. His orders were to remain with the 707 and to monitor our frequency every day between five and six. We would return to Nairobi in the evening to eat and sleep in the 707. Teddy didn't invite him aboard for our inspection of the C-47.

Machade, the Arnheim agent in Nairobi, had been very efficient: there were bush clothes and boots, two rifles and two pistols with ammo, a large assortment of tinned food, water, various tools, medical supplies, sleeping bags, field glasses, a case of bourbon, and five cases of Pepsi. My tastes had not been consulted.

We spent the rest of the afternoon in the air-conditioning of the 707, going over charts of the area to the south. On paper it seemed perfectly rational. We drew a course from Dodoma to Nairobi, the line followed by the ashtray express, approximately three hundred and eighty miles long. Then we blocked out rectangular search patterns in sectors one hundred miles long and twenty-five miles on each side of the course line. We would fly back and forth in five-mile swathes, crossing the course line until we had covered the entire five thousand square miles of the sector, and then we would go on to the next. It seemed simple enough though not ideal since there would be very few checkpoints once we had crossed the mountains into the Serengeti Plateau, and the search legs would be defined roughly by timing.

"If it's down in those mountains, even if we find it we won't be able to land."

"Yeah, but we'll know where it is."

We had drinks and dinner, served by the steward. Jacobs, the copilot and radio operator–navigator, had gone into town. Teddy was not in a garrulous mood, and I was pondering the depths of our folly. A diesel generator, supplying our power, rattled noisily under our right wing, and at lengthy intervals an airplane, usually propeller-driven, took off or landed.

"Does Tanzania have an air force?" I asked later.

"I dunno."

"I hope they won't object to our intrusion into their airspace. We could start a nice little war in Central Africa."

"We have a week's geological clearance."

"If you're running true to form we'll probably find the ashtrays in a pool of oil."

We took off right after daybreak the next morning. As Teddy settled himself in the left seat and began to study instruments and controls, I said, "Have you ever flown one of these things?"

"No, but it has two wings and two fans. It ought to fly."

It flew, but in such an agony of squeaks, rattles, and groans that I felt certain basic aerodynamic laws were being violated as the old beast staggered up to ten thousand feet, five thousand above the ground where we leveled off on a southerly course. The scenery that was cranked by us was dazzling. Snow-covered Mt. Kilimanjaro, nineteen thousand six hundred and fifty feet, off to the left in the southeast, and just visible in the west, the shore of Lake Victoria.

We had charted our first search sector to begin thirty miles south of Nairobi, assuming that if anything had crashed closer than that word would have reached the city. Nothing had been reported.

The best altitude for a search is between three and five thousand feet over the ground. Higher you can't see clearly, and lower, the extent of the scan is too limited. With Teddy at the controls I went back to the open hatch in the waist carrying the field glasses and searched as he flew the slow, tedious pattern fifty miles to the east and fifty miles to the west, half an hour on each leg, over the desertlike surface to the mountains in the east and back to the mountains in the west. Glasses are of no help unless you think you see something. Twice I thought I saw something which, with the glasses, turned out to be cans or tinfoil strung on lines.

After two hours I went forward and handed him the glasses. "I'll take it. You go back," I said settling into the right seat. He was not used to receiving even quasi-orders, but he heaved himself out of the seat and disappeared. The chart was marked with every leg covered, and I made my additions, flying the old thing with its stiff controls, like an overlarge automobile without power steering.

We completed the first sector by eleven o'clock, and I turned back toward Nairobi. When Teddy appeared I tapped the fuel gauges. We had used up three-quarters of our supply.

As we approached the airport I took my hands and feet off the controls. "It's all yours."

"Go ahead, land it."

The airplane, inherently unstable, had begun a slow turn to the left. "I don't want to land it."

He lighted a Chesterfield. "You know how it's done."

"I've never flown one of these things."

"Neither have I."

The airplane was continuing its turn and beginning to lose altitude. I let it turn.

"Well," he said, "I guess one of us has to land it. I'll flip you for it." He extracted a nickel from his pocket. "Heads you land it, tails I land it."

"Okay."

He flipped, heads of course. "May I see that nickel?" He handed it to me. "Okay." I reduced the throttle settings. "You might give the tower a call." He called and we were cleared for landing. "Give me some flaps," I said.

"How much?"

"Oh, whatever strikes your fancy."

He gave me ten degrees, and I turned toward the runway. "Now, if it's not too much to ask, would you put the gear down?"

A great rumbling occurred and the old C-47 shuddered. "Full flaps, and for God's sake, put out that cigarette."

"Oh, you won't spill us, Howard." He gave me full flaps.

There was a lot of hot-air turbulence, and I had to fight to keep the wings level. We hit the runway in a violent encounter of rubber with asphalt, bounced ten feet, and settled heavily.

"Lousy landing," he said while I struggled to keep it straight.

"I can hardly wait to see how you make out this afternoon."

While they serviced the airplane we ate sandwiches and drank coffee in our seats. Within forty-five minutes we were airborne again, headed for our second sector, which took us over the Tanzania border above the plateau of a vast flat grassland with occasional lakes and scattered clumps of trees. My knowledge of the geography of central Africa is limited to some early films in which a blond heroine was usually pursued by howling natives for what were assumed to be beastly purposes; a few books including one by Hemingway in which he shot and killed everything that moved; and newspaper stories on the Mau-Mau who only ten years earlier had been performing atrociously in Kenya. I saw very few animals, a herd of zebras once, and something big and reddish that may have been a rhinoceros, but it was half hidden by the grass around a lake. Teddy had been right about the beef. In the greener areas there were herds of what, with the glasses, turned out to be long-horned, hump-backed cattle tended by men with a staff or spear, wearing something draped from one shoulder.

We had not finished the second sector when Teddy at the controls turned back toward Nairobi. He was talking to Jacobs when I dropped into the right seat.

"A story came in about an explosion," he said.

"Where?"

"We didn't talk about it on the air. Machade has been circulating in the native quarters, and it came through the grapevine. He called Jacobs."

Teddy made a wheel landing and let the tail drop slowly as we lost speed. It was very smooth. I didn't bother to congratulate him.

As soon as he had bathed in the aluminum tub in his quarters he dressed and went into Nairobi. He didn't invite me, and I wouldn't have gone if he had. After a remarkably good steak dinner catered by

one of the Nairobi restaurants I read until ten-thirty and went to bed. I
heard the door of his quarters close a couple of hours later.

He didn't talk until we were in the air the next morning and then
only when I asked him. "They say a god struck the earth, and as far as
Machade could make out it was somewhere in there." He pointed to
the chart. A circle had been pencilled in in North Tanzania, north of
Arusha and west of Kilimanjaro. It was just outside our second
sector.

"We covered that yesterday."

"Not quite. We'll have another look."

It was relatively easy to chart the search legs with the great presence of Kilimanjaro towering above us. Below the snow line forests
began, and then orchards that even with glasses I couldn't identify.
On the westward legs the elevation fell away to the familiar grass-
lands. We crossed a north-south road with a truck throwing up plumes
of dust.

In the flatlands, toward the end of a westward leg, I saw a circular
dark patch that I took to be a clump of trees, but when I put the glasses
on it it resembled a large black hole. I had seen other such depressions, and dropped the glasses again. But with the naked eye there
was something strange about the symmetry of the circle. I put the
glasses on it again. It was a burn in the grass that had apparently been
stopped by rain, and in the middle something that looked like a
charred tree flashed in the sunlight.

I went forward quickly and tapped Teddy on the shoulder. "Look
down there to your left." I handed him the glasses and took the
wheel. He rose heavily from the seat to get a better view, and I started
a slow circle to the left.

When he sat down again he nodded. "That's it. We'll go down and
take a look."

"We're running short of juice," I said, tapping the gauges.

"It's better than being loaded when we put a ton of gold aboard,"
he said, reducing the throttle settings and beginning the letdown. He
was right, of course, but I get nervous when the gauge hits the quarter
mark.

He went down to five hundred feet and started a slow circle around
the burned patch while with the glasses I studied the remains of an

airplane that had hit the ground almost vertically. It was totally demolished, a shambles, with only fragments of the fuselage pointing in a grotesque angle toward the sky.

"What's the melting temperature of gold?" I asked.

"One thousand sixty-four degrees centigrade."

"And what's that in American?"

"About two thousand degrees. An open gasoline fire won't touch it."

I was wondering about the melting temperature of the human body.

We circled twice, going down to a hundred feet, and there was no question that we had found the ashtray express, but there were mysteries. What remained of the fuselage was less scorched at the upper end, but there was no tail section, and in the accumulation of debris spread around the wreck, nothing resembling a tail section was visible. Some large, ponderous birds spread out and became airborne below us.

Teddy pulled up again to begin a survey of the immediate area.

"We know where it is now," I said. "We'd better go back to Nairobi and get a truck."

"That would take at least three days. It's been there a week already. Somebody's going to take a look at it, if they haven't already."

"At least let's go back and put some fuel in this thing."

"Oh, we'll have enough. If necessary we can find some around here someplace."

I glanced around at miles of grass and scrub. "Have you discovered a friendly Esso station in the neighborhood?"

"That looks pretty good," he said, dropping down to a flat stretch of grass a mile or so from the wreck. "Let's take a look at it." He went down to about twenty feet to drag the area. "That ought to do it," he said pulling up again. "Wind's from the north. We'll make our runway when we land."

I tightened my harness. "I'll say once more I think it's a mistake to land."

"Well, Howard, everybody has a few mistakes to make. Give me ten degrees."

I put the flaps down as we flew a parallel course to the south at two hundred feet.

"Now the gear."

The C-47 shuddered again as the gear went down on the crosswind leg.

He turned on final approach. "Full flaps." The tail rose and the nose cocked down from the lift of the flaps.

He laid it down gently, skillfully, just above a stall, and the gear started to rumble while the propellers chopped through the higher grass. We bounded along over rough terrain, both of us standing on the brakes. One heavy shock threatened to wipe out the gear, but finally we slowed down to about twenty miles an hour. My hand was already reaching for the harness release.

24

I THINK they're called wadis, natural ditches that fill with water in the rainy season and then dry up.

We didn't see it, of course. There was too much grass.

We were skidding, brakes locked, when we hit, and the wheels dropped into a chasm, the nose buried into grass, the propellers chewed into earth, sending a storm of rocks and earth against the fuselage, and then snubbed down to an abrupt demise.

We had both snapped forward against the safety harness, and then back against the seats.

The impulse to leave a wrecked airplane is both instinctive and rational; it's something that has failed you—or you've failed it—and it has a habit of going up in sudden flames.

But it was an uphill climb since the tail was cocked skyward at about thirty-five degrees. We smashed through the fragile door together, scrambled over our supplies that had miraculously remained lashed to the deck, up to the hatch which I unlocked and kicked open to drop fifteen feet to the grass the landing gear had crushed flat. As I rose, slightly jarred, I heard the impact of Teddy's body as he hit and a sound I had never heard coming from him: a smothered moan that ended more characteristically. *"Shit."*

I turned back but he was crashing through the grass on hands and knees like some great beached walrus.

"Are you all right?" I shouted.

"Yeah," he puffed, still on hands and knees.

We finally stopped perhaps fifty feet away, Teddy coming in a poor second, and looked back at the C-47. It was silent, motionless, a weary but valiant assemblage of ancient aluminum thrust against the sky in an angle of reproach. It had completed its service. It would never fly again. But even in death it was true to service: It didn't explode and go up in flames.

We looked at it for fully five minutes, Teddy sitting, recovering from the adrenalin that had sent at least my heart pounding. "Well," I said finally, "we have our supplies, and perhaps a radio, though I doubt it."

Teddy leaned forward, with difficulty because of his paunch, to work at the laces of his right boot.

"What's the matter?" I asked.

"I broke something. Ankle I think."

"*Damn!*" I dropped to my knees at his foot to untie the laces and remove the boot and sock. Upon that slight skeletal structure had been imposed the burden of a weight it had not been genetically designed to carry. The drop from the airplane had exceeded the design. The foot was grotesque, swelling and flushed, the toes sticking out like small pork sausages.

"Does it hurt?" I asked inanely.

"Yeah."

The heat of the midday was bludgeoning us, and the wings of the airplane flat on the ground provided no shelter. I stood up to look around for the small grove of trees I had seen on our approach. "We'll have to get you into shade. I'll pull you up. Put your arm over my shoulder."

Pulling him up was not simple since he couldn't help much and I had to balance him at the same time to keep the injured foot off the ground. The grove was about two hundred feet away, but it was the most exhausting two hundred feet I've covered. He hopped and between hops the greater part of his weight bore down on my shoulders. We had to stop several times to breathe, sweat soaking our clothes. When we finally reached the meager shade we both collapsed, drawing in huge gulps of air.

When I had recovered I rolled over onto my back to look up through the gauze of stunted leaves and twigs, and my fatigue began to fill me with unreasonable resentment. "Well," I said, when I had caught my breath, "you've made one of your goddamned mistakes."

"Yeah."

"You don't have to make any more for the rest of your life."

He didn't answer.

I turned to look at him. He was lying on his back, his great belly laboring for breath.

"Are you all right?"

"Yeah."

"Loosen your belt."

His delicate, pudgy fingers struggled with the buckle, but gave up. I rolled over to him and released the buckle, and he opened his eyes. The Arnheim half-smile cracked his lips. His face was very red.

"Are you thirsty?"

"Yeah."

I pushed myself wearily to my feet. "I'll start hauling up our supplies. Don't wander off."

His stomach quivered in a laugh that wasn't quite audible.

Hauling up our supplies presented a tactical problem I was not prepared for. I couldn't reach the open hatch to swing in, and the aluminum ladder we used was stowed inside. The door at the pilot's station had no outside handle. I wandered around studying the problem. I never wear a hat, but the sun of one o'clock was beginning to penetrate my skull. I walked into the only shade available, cast by the fuselage. I was sweating heavily and had developed a ravening thirst.

I had never been separated from civilization before, and I realized I was totally inept, without wilderness skills. The idea of my being a Boy Scout would have been abhorrent to my mother, and the one year she decided to remove me from the summer temptations to pubescence in Southampton by sending me to the perils of camp, I howled so horribly she quickly abandoned the idea. I knew gentlemanly sports—crewing, fencing, tennis, skiing, sailing—but I had never fought a grizzly with a bowie knife.

I went out into the blast of the sun again to look at the old aluminum torso. The antenna was strung from a post over the pilots' station back to another post directly over the hatch. Climbing onto the right wing presented no difficulty, and I mounted the fuselage clinging to the first post. Crawling on my belly over the heated aluminum, I reached the second post and trusting to its solidity let my legs down onto the bottom edge of the hatch, but I remained an arc glued to the skin of the airplane unwilling to release my hold on the post. If sweat and fatigue had not made the decision I might have remained there like a barnacle adhering to the skin of a whale, but I slid heavily onto my buttocks, striking my head against the upper edge of the hatch. I was shaken, but I was in.

It took another half hour to position the ladder at an odd angle and make several descents to five feet above the ground depositing what I thought we needed immediately: one of the twenty-liter plastic jerry cans of water, food, medical and survival kits, and after some deliberation a rifle and the two pistols. I don't like guns, and the only experience I'd had with them was an unsatisfactory encounter in training in the Air Corps. The rifle I took was a Springfield with a bore large enough for my middle finger. The other one said it was a .375 H. and H. Magnum, and I think it could have knocked over a tank. I left it.

On the first trip back to the grove I carried water and one of the survival kits. Teddy had pushed himself up to a tree for a backrest.

"Did you go all the way to Nairobi?"

"Yes. They're looking for a gold smuggler."

"What was the floor show?"

"A belly dancer named Yoyo."

He looked almost happy. "A good lay."

I poured tepid water from the jerry can into the aluminum cup from the survival kit and handed it to him.

"Where's the bourbon?"

"In the airplane. Do you want to get it?"

"I can wait for the next trip."

"Does it hurt?"

"Yeah."

"There's probably morphine in the kit. Do you want a shot?"

"No, I'll wait for the bourbon." He handed me the empty cup. I refilled it and drank, and then I examined his foot again. It looked like a large red cantaloupe, and there was a nasty scratch across the distended flesh where the ankle bone should have been. "How did you get that?"

He leaned over to look. "I dunno."

"It's not the best geography to have a scratch." I opened the medical kit which was remarkably well supplied and packed. After pouring alcohol over the scratch I found three bottles of some antibiotic with a simple posology of three capsules a day against infection. "Take two of these." I filled the cup again.

On my third trip to the airplane I climbed in through the hatch, extracted two bottles of bourbon and four bottles of Coke, except that it was Pepsi, and not Coca-Cola. When I returned I planted them at his side.

"You forgot the ice."

"Gristede's was closed."

He opened the bourbon, poured it into his cup, and added a dash of Pepsi. "You want a drink, Howard?"

"No, thanks. I don't know how you can go on drinking that vile brew."

"I like it."

"That's very apparent. You've been drinking it for . . . what, twenty-three years now." I opened two small cans of corned beef and handed him one with a spoon. "You're not going to be very mobile with that foot, and even if I knew how to set it, it wouldn't help much."

"No," he said, and took a drink.

"And even if I could turn out some crutches I don't think you'd get very far."

He took another drink of his bourbon and Pepsi.

"So," I continued, after swallowing some corned beef, "if the radio doesn't work, I'll have to start out for help. That road should be twenty-five miles or so."

"Did you try the radio?"

"No. I'll wait until Jacobs is monitoring at five. I don't want to use up the batteries. No way to recharge them."

He took a couple of spoonfuls of corned beef and set the can down. "When are you going to take a look at the ashtrays?"

"Oh, to hell with your fucking ashtrays." Vocally I was becoming very virile, but I knew what was bothering me. I dreaded a trip to the wreck because I knew what I would find. Vultures don't gather for gold, at least not flying vultures. "If we get ourselves out of here we'll worry about the ashtrays later." Flies had begun to swarm over his uneaten corned beef. "Are you going to finish that?"

"No." He poured more bourbon in the cup.

I threw both cans far into the grass and using a little water washed the spoons. The gentle breeze, only tipping the tops of the grass, did not relieve the massive heat of the afternoon. "I'm going to sleep for a while."

He didn't comment.

I lay on the short grass under the trees and using the survival kit as a pillow tried to sleep. In spite of flies and things that crawled, I did, for almost an hour. A nightmare woke me. I was performing some gross bestiality on a woman whom I did not recognize. She whimpered, "Oh, stop, oh, stop," and since I don't dream in color I didn't see the blood, but my hands felt sticky. They were sticky with sweat when I woke up. It was five minutes after four. Teddy had not changed his position. The cup was still in his hand. He looked a little like a Buddha.

"How's the foot?"

"Better with the bourbon. You snored."

"Everybody snores." I rose with an effort. Some muscles had been used for the first time in years, and they didn't like it. "I'll go down and see if the thing works. Do you need anything?"

"No. More bourbon."

The airplane was superheated, and I opened both windows. Then I took off my shirt and before throwing the switch examined the batteries, the cables, and the set itself. I couldn't see any damage, but the batteries, cocked at an angle, were seeping acid, so I loosened the frames and propped them level.

When I threw the switch at five o'clock the light came on, and the headset clattered with static. My God, I was grateful to the old thing for being so decent even though I heard only irregular transmission, so garbled I couldn't understand a word. Adjusting the receiver dial slightly, both left and right, produced no improvement. More important was transmission, but without reception I wouldn't be able to tell if I was transmitting.

With a sweaty thumb I pressed the mike button. "Jacobs, this is Matt Howard. Do you read me?" I released the button and listened. Nothing intelligible. I depressed the button again. "Jacobs, I'll count to ten." I counted and listened. Nothing. "Jacobs, we're down, airplane washed out, Mr. Arnheim with a broken ankle. Our position is . . ." and using the chart I described it as accurately as I could. "I have to conserve batteries. I'm now cutting transmission, but I'll come on again in exactly ten minutes." I threw the switch. I wasn't optimistic. Our position located us at the outer edge of the set's limits airborne, and we were down behind some mountains.

While waiting I searched in the cargo area for another piece of equipment, an automatic, battery-powered transmitter that would send a signal for twenty-four hours. It wasn't there. Machade hadn't thought of everything, but I did find a flare pistol with five flares which I tossed out onto the grass.

Ten minutes later I repeated our location, but the reception was still so garbled I couldn't even identify the language.

Returning to Teddy I carried the other survival kit, the sleeping bags, and another bottle of bourbon. The one he had been working on was half empty. He looked at me questioningly.

"It works, but I can't tell if I'm transmitting."

"Did you receive?"

"Static, garbled voices. It's probably too far."

"Yeah."

I sat down and drank some water.

After taking another drink he said, "Are you going to look at the ashtrays?"

"*Yes,* for God's sake. I'll look at your fucking ashtrays!"

He lighted a Chesterfield and extinguished the match carefully. "You're doing all right, Howard."

"Don't cajole me to get what you want, Teddy. I know you too well." I reached for the half-empty Pepsi bottle, dumped it, and filled it with water. The plug I made of grass wasn't very substantial, but I strapped it upright in the survival kit after emptying everything else but the machete and the compass.

"I'm going down to take a reading from the C-47. I'll leave from there." I picked up the Springfield, a box of cartridges, dark glasses, and a safari hat.

"Don't get lost."

"If I'm not back in two hours start blowing off with the pistol every five minutes."

"Okay."

I started toward the C-47.

"Howard, bring back a couple of ashtrays."

"All right, goddamnit." I was growing petulant.

With the compass I climbed up the fuselage until I could see the ragged stump of the other wreck and took a reading. It was a course of thirty degrees. In fact I didn't really need the compass since the course was laid out in a direct line with Kilimanjaro, though in the high grass Kilimanjaro could be hidden.

It wasn't easy. I began to imagine thirty-five miles of it. At the rate I was going it would take me three or four days to reach the road if I had to make that trek. In the beginning I shouldered the rifle with the sling, and hacked grass with the machete to avoid the annoyance of the spears against my face and clothes, but within ten minutes my right arm was quivering with fatigue. Oh, those years of security, protection, physical indolence, in which the greatest exertion had been a five-block walk to the Hudson tubes in the morning, and a five-block walk back at night with the reward of the vodka bottle waiting.

I returned the machete to its sheath strapped to my belt and began thrusting the grass aside with my hands. When I came to a real tangle I went around.

Various birds that I seldom saw, and didn't recognize when I did, flew away violently at my approach, and once some great beast crashed through the grass on my right, and I raised the Springfield in a funk. I never saw it, but it sounded enormous. I visualized myself confronting a great round-eyed, red-tongued cat by the Douanier Rousseau. I thought all the larger African animals were now on reserves. But perhaps I was on a reserve. I hoped not.

I had left the C-47 at six-fifteen. At seven I had still not reached the burn. Surely I was moving faster than a mile an hour even through the grass. Someone had recently run a mile in under four minutes, but the runner and the conditions were different.

I hadn't seen Kilimanjaro for some time. Removing the compass I took a reading, and it lied wildly, informing me that I was following a course of one hundred and ninety degrees. Impossible. The lowering sun was still coming over my right shoulder. Then some small fragment of enlightenment, memory, returned to me. I dropped the Springfield and the machete and walked a few feet away. The compass swung back to reality, thirty degrees.

I heard it and smelled it a few minutes later before I saw it: hoarse cries at my approach, the heavy beating of huge wings, and the odor of a slightly rancid barbecue. I stopped, struggling to keep the corned beef down.

I had never been on the field of battle. I had never seen chopped or charred human bodies. I had led a pampered life, relatively free from danger, always spared the ominous potential of the waking nightmare.

Emerging from the grass I stepped into the scorched circle where the last two vultures were rising reluctantly on six feet of wing.

I delayed, walking around the wreck, trying to find an upwind reprieve from the formidable stench, but as I detoured around the remains of a wing a hoarse scream came from the shattered carcass followed by a repeated clubbing beat as if someone was trying to free himself. I could feel my scalp tighten. It was impossible that anyone had lived through the impact and the fire. I ran around the shattered wing and stepped into the charred shell of the crumpled fuselage, and confronted a huge, obscenely naked head, soiled, curved beak, and two giant wings beating frantically against the carbonized interior. He screamed again, and I heard myself yell in horror. He drove the murderous beak down at his right leg snared by a wire and screamed again. I stumbled back, ripped the Springfield from my shoulder, pumped a shell into the chamber, raised it, and squeezed the trigger. The hammer clicked solidly. I had pumped no shell into the chamber. I had forgotten to load it. Slowly I moved toward the ragged hatch, put one leg out, snagged the other, and fell outside on the grass.

From the interior there came a sound of violent rupture and in a whipping of wings the vulture suddenly appeared above me perched on the torn frame of the hatch. He stared at me malevolently for a moment, vile, rapacious, worse than predatory, ghoul, chewer of the dead, his head went down, and he sprang into the air, his wings almost touching my face as he sailed over me, ten feet of copper wire dangling from one leg. I turned my head onto the grass and closed my eyes, recognizing the symptoms from childhood that surged up from my stomach and chest to my throat. I wanted to howl. I couldn't.

Leaving the Springfield in the grass I pushed myself up and reentered the aluminum charnel-house, breathing through my mouth. The tangle of melted metal, festoons of wire bared by the fire, and strange clots of what must have been some consumed plastic prevented me from working all the way to the shattered flight deck, but I was close enough to look. I wish I hadn't. The nightmare awake, the horror of teeth, bones, gobbets of burnt flesh hanging in strings.

I turned back to search, but all I could find were ashes, gray, black, mauve. Behind one bulkhead that I had missed on my way forward in the dread of expectation, there was a square ash outline and inside round contours of ash which collapsed when I touched them.

I climbed out again to breathe the hot but purer air of early evening. I was totally mystified. I walked around the right wing, which had torn loose, leaving a gaping hole in the fuselage. The aluminum was crumpled, bubbled, ash gray, and fragile at the stump. In a pile of black ash beyond, I saw another square heap of cinders and ten feet farther, the unmistakable outline of a burnt box. It crumbled when I touched it, but inside there were round black forms of ash. I looked farther. Twenty feet away was a box intact, scorched but whole. Printed on the top the words "Piltdown Products" were just legible. Using the machete I pried up the seared top, uncovering rows of black ashtrays stacked three deep, the cinders of some packing material between them. One had a crack running from side to side. I picked it up, and it came apart in my hands.

I'm not a metallurgist, but I know that gold is yellow, ductile, malleable, and not brittle. Though the surface had retained its glaze the sides of the fracture were black and porous. A scenario by an unknown author began to reel through my mind.

I took the cracked one and three others still intact back to the survival kit and stowed them. Then I walked slowly around under the high after end of the fuselage where there should have been a tail section, vertical and horizontal stabilizers, a rudder and elevator, and where there was nothing but a stump of ragged aluminum. Had the impact snapped it off? Unlikely. The aluminum skin of an airplane bends, but does not crack cleanly, and though because of the height I could not be certain, the roughly torn edges seemed to be splayed outwards. If it *had* snapped off it should be somewhere beyond in the direction the airplane had been traveling laterally when it hit. I found nothing.

At seven forty-five Kilimanjaro was flushed in sunlight, but a skirt of shadow had begun the ascent up over the orchards at the base. It was time for me to start back. Shouldering the kit and carrying the Springfield I took up a reciprocal course of two hundred and ten degrees toward the C-47.

The trip back wasn't any easier, but I had at least learned not to squander energy in fighting the grass. I was more than halfway, had even caught a glimpse of the C-47's tail when Teddy fired the pistol. I loaded the Springfield and fired into the air carelessly and it almost took my shoulder off in its vicious kick. The raucous cry of birds came from all directions.

Twilight had settled over the plain by the time I reached the grove, but behind me Mt. Kilimanjaro was blazing red above purple. Teddy had not moved. The cup was in his hand, and the bottle of bourbon was empty. He watched me as I approached and laid the kit and rifle down.

"Did you find it, Howard?"

"Yes."

"Did you bring some back?"

"Yes. Do you like surprises?"

"No."

"Then you're not going to like this." I reached in the kit, extracted the three sound ashtrays and handed them to him. He examined them in the failing light, hefting them for weight.

"They seem all right. They weren't in the airplane?"

"No. But here's another one. From the same box." I handed him the two pieces of the fractured ashtray.

He took a piece in each hand, studied them, and then joined them carefully. "A good fit," he said and separated them. Holding one piece up he examined the rough edge, running a finger down its length. "Graphite, probably. The ones inside were burned?"

"Yes."

"Let me have that machete a moment." He took it, spread his legs, placed one of the intact ashtrays between them, and brought the machete down solidly, cleaving the ashtray in equal halves. He studied it for a moment, pulled out a Chesterfield, lighted it, and placed the dead match in an intact ashtray. "They make good ashtrays," he said.

I knew it was coming, but I didn't know how it would come. It started with a sudden rippling of his great belly, still silent, but working up to his chest and throat, bursting out in a prodigious clap of laughter. He throbbed, he shook, he thrashed his arms helplessly, he began coughing and stabbed the cigarette out in the ashtray, howling, the first time I had ever heard him laugh without the restraint of some remote, protective control. It was still light enough for me to see the tears streaming down his cheeks. He choked and searched blindly for a full bottle of bourbon which he opened and drank from directly, but he was seized again and blew the bourbon out in a spray, thrusting the bottle to me, more to get rid of it than inviting me to drink, but automatically I took an enormous swallow of fire.

For several minutes I stood over him watching his convulsions in the grass while he suffered in the hilarious captivity of the absurd, but then, as though something in the bourbon carried contagion, I snickered, almost a hiccup that altered into a strange giggle that I had never heard before, but watching Teddy floundering helplessly, his paunch throbbing in the agony of laughter, I began to laugh with him, either from the spectacle of that mound of heaving flesh or the enormous and ultimate absurdity of two middle-aged men who had traveled eight thousand miles to a remote plateau where their still more remote ancestors had broken one another's skulls with hammers of stone, eight thousand miles to collect ashes. I slipped to my knees and rolled over onto my back, howling.

I'm told that animals don't laugh, but we turned into two laughing animals, groveling in the grass of Africa to cries of alarm and resentment from the nonlaughing animals around us.

"Graphite," Teddy finally managed to get out. "Twenty-four hundred pounds of graphite. A lot of pencils," and he went into convulsions again.

I was so strained from the exertion of laughing I had to lie flat for a few minutes to recover. When I finally pushed myself up I reached for the cup, poured some bourbon in it and added some of the dreadful, tepid Pepsi. After drinking I said, "There's more. I think the tail was blown off."

"Why?" he said, trying to control another outburst.

"It wasn't with the wreckage, and the aluminum was bent outwards."

He reached for the cup, tasted it, and added more bourbon.

"They didn't have parachutes?" I continued.

"No."

The tail blew, the airplane went out of control into a dive, and in a matter of seconds two men had been converted into the grotesquery I had looked at. It didn't seem to bother Teddy. "Can you put it together?"

"Yeah, I think so. A truck or another airplane left after that one, probably."

"And who was in it?"

"I guess McKenzie."

"McKenzie? Impossible!" I shouted.

"He ran the operation alone with the three blacks. Two people knew the size of the load. McKenzie and I. Only McKenzie could have handled the graphite."

I took the cup from his hand, but it was too strong for me. Reaching for the other survival kit I extracted the other cup and made a weaker drink. "Yes, I get it now. He planted a bomb with a timer, knowing that a search would be run, and that would take time. Enough time for him to get away."

"I've got a smart lawyer."

"And he knew you wouldn't report it because that would blow the operation."

"Yeah."

"I wonder where he took it."

"By truck to Durban probably, with a shipping invoice prepared. By airplane anywhere."

"Did you call him after Machade called you?"

"Yeah. They said he was out on an emergency."

"An emergency he built. But it's hard to believe of McKenzie."

"Oh, everybody takes, Howard." He drank from his cup.

The sun had left the summit of Mt. Kilimanjaro, and it was turning dark. I located one of the flashlights and examined his foot. It was blue and monstrously swollen, but the scratch was not infected. I gave him another pill that he washed down with the bourbon and Pepsi, then I looked over the supply of food. There was enough for at least two weeks, canned meats, vegetables, rice, soups, caramels, and chocolate. On the small primus with a bottle of gas I heated a beef stew and some green beans which we ate out of the cans, Teddy washing it down with his bourbon and Pepsi. Night animals called, scolded, and argued. I couldn't identify any of them. It was not difficult to identify the mosquitoes. Below nature's voice I heard that cracked bass humming the song that had been with him for twenty-five years, but he never got it right.

"No," I said. "It goes 'Dancing in the dark . . .' I sang, not very expertly, but closer to the original than Teddy's version. He listened until I had finished.

"Is that the way it goes?" he asked.

"More or less."

For a while he didn't speak. Then he said, "I like my way better."

"You always have."

We were quiet again listening to other sounds in the darkness, hearing about the colossal occupation of nature around us. "I'll wait one day more," I said finally. "I'll try the radio tomorrow at five again, and if nothing happens by noon the next day I'll start for the road."

"There are some villages closer."

"Yes, but I could miss them. I've tramped through that grass and I know what it's like. I can't miss the road. Besides, I don't know how I'd talk to the villagers unless someone speaks English or French. What's the local language, Swahili?"

"Yeah."

"My Swahili is not fluent. Once on the road I'll flag somebody down, but it's going to take at least three days to get there. You think you'll be all right here?''

"Yeah."

"Does the foot hurt?"

"Less."

"Do you want a shot of morphine?"

"No."

I cleaned up and broke out the sleeping bags, mosquito bars, and insect repellants. Getting Teddy into his bag wasn't easy. He winced, but he didn't make a sound.

I had fallen asleep, but something funny woke me up. "For God's sake, are you still laughing?"

"No."

Then I heard it again. It was coming from a distance, from the direction of the wrecked airplane with its ashes.

25

I'M NOT A STRONG ADMIRER of oatmeal, but after condensed orange juice, that's all there was for breakfast. I botched the first batch. It turned into a thick, glutinous substance that was totally inedible. The second batch with powdered milk and sugar wasn't bad, and the instant coffee was actually quite good.

After a spoonful of oatmeal Teddy said, "St. Paul's."

"You're right. I was trying to remember what it reminded me of."

I washed the breakfast kit and then began to wonder if I was squandering water. The jerry can I had brought up was still three-quarters filled, but I went back to the C-47 to check my memory. There were four more, twenty liters each, enough for a week or ten days without washing or shaving. I already had a stubble.

With the chart and compass I climbed up onto the fuselage again and looked around. There was a village marked south of us about twelve miles and another to the west about fifteen miles, provided I had our position exact. But a village, if I found it, would probably mean a few huts and a language barrier. I figured the road at thirty-six miles.

When I returned to the grove Teddy was still lying with his back against the tree. "You ought to move around. If you stay like that you'll atrophy."

He looked down at his belly. "I don't think I'll atrophy."

"Not the fat. The muscle."

He shrugged.

I went through the survival kit again and found a small saw with the blade snapped into a handle.

"What are you going to do with that, Howard?"

"Make you a pair of crutches."

Locating two limbs strong enough and with the necessary crotches took me longer than sawing them, and the finished products were primitive, but I carried them back. "I'll help you up."

The help was strenuous, but he was finally onto his good foot. The crutches were too long, and I had to cut the ends off. "Now take a stroll."

It was an awkward and precarious stroll. He almost fell once, and I grabbed his arm. At the end of five minutes he was panting and streaming with sweat. He propelled himself back to the tree and sat down again. Clearly the rush of the blood to his ankle was painful, but he made no complaint. The antidote to pain was his first bourbon and Pepsi for the day.

"What are you going to do about McKenzie when we got out of here?" I asked later.

"Nothing."

"Just let him wander off with nineteen million dollars?"

"Yeah. He was smart. He deserves it."

"A small matter of the morality of the thing doesn't bother you?"

"I let you worry about that."

"Murder and embezzlement. Grand larceny?"

"I insured both of the pilots for a half a million dollars. They were killed doing a job. We're all killed doing a job. Their families will inherit the money. The embezzlement only hurts me. I can stand it."

"By God, you must be some kind of monster, Teddy."

"I'm big."

"But I've seen your sense of justice in action. You may not be aware of it, but I know about Maja Walowsky and her mother. I know about Soad. You sent the O'Shaughnessy girl's father a quarter of a million dollars. Pelletier was killed in Florida, but his brother works for you. I don't know how many others there are."

"I don't have a sense of justice because justice doesn't exist. It's an idea cooked up to let people with power do what they want to do."

"But you give."

"And I take."

"Then the important thing is that it's you who decides."

"You could put it like that."

"You don't have much confidence in your fellow man."

"No, not much."

"I wonder why that is."

"Because just before the breaking point they all take."

"And that offends your moral soul?"

"I don't have a moral soul. I don't know what a soul is."

"In Freudian terms, your superego?"

"I don't have a superego."

"Is there something you believe in, God for instance?"

"Which one?"

"Any one that appeals to you."

"No. I haven't seen any evidence of a God. If he was there I'd let him take over, but I don't think he'd do it any better than I do."

I stood up and walked out into the blistering sun of noon. Metaphysics on the Serengeti Plain.

After lunch I slept again. Teddy didn't. He sat there in the Buddha posture sipping bourbon and Pepsi and smoking Chesterfields. Both ashtrays were filled when I staggered awake at three o'clock.

"Howard," he said, "when you go down to the airplane would you bring back some more bourbon?"

"All right."

"Are there any more cigarettes down there?"

"I don't know. I'll check."

There were eight bottles of bourbon and enough Pepsi to last for a year. I carried the bourbon and five Pepsis down the ladder and then I searched for cigarettes, but Machade had not been infallible. There were none.

At five o'clock I turned the set on again and called Jacobs, repeating everything I had said the first time. I transmitted for five minutes with breaks for reception, but nothing intelligible came in. I went off power and returned ten minutes later to repeat the message and count to one hundred. I was using up a lot of battery, but I was still determined to leave the next day if nothing appeared during the morning. I thought I had enough power left to transmit if we saw anything in the sky.

When I carried the bourbon back to the grove he asked, "Any luck?"

"I'm still not receiving anything that makes sense. I transmitted." I started back to the C-47.

"Howard, were there any cigarettes down there?"

"No."

"Well, I guess I'll quit smoking."

He sat impassively through the long afternoon, sipping his atrocious drink, and after finishing the last cigarette he emptied the ashtrays carefully and leaned back against the tree again, his hands folded on his belly.

That impassivity began to annoy me, unreasonably I realized. There was nothing he could do but sit and wait until I, or somebody from the outside, succeeded in rescuing us. Perhaps it was that placid assumption that made me want to interrupt the display of oriental stoicism. It certainly was not a benevolent impulse.

"How's Amanda?" I asked.

"Okay. Pregnant."

"Is it working out? The marriage I mean?"

"I don't know. I don't know how marriages are supposed to work. Do you?"

"No."

"She says she loves me, but I don't know. It's a hard job to love me."

"We went over that before."

"Yeah."

So much for Amanda.

We ate dinner, another stew, and I said, "If nothing comes over by two o'clock tomorrow I'll start for the road."

"Okay."

"You have the flare gun and the five flares if you see anything."

"Yeah."

"We could probably get you up the ladder into the airplane to use the radio, but it's hot and you'd fry."

"No, I like the scenery here."

"I think I can make it to the road in three days. I'll flag down the first thing that comes along and phone Nairobi to have them send in a helicopter."

He was examining the Very pistol, breaking it open to try one of the flares. "Shit," he said.

"What's the matter?"

"Wrong size. It doesn't fit."

"For *God's* sake." I shined the light on it. The cartridge was oversize. "Try the others."

"They're all the same size."

I took it from him and tried, but they were all about a quarter of an inch too large. "Maybe there's another pistol or other flares. I'll go down to have a look."

I searched for half an hour and found nothing.

"Somebody goofed," I said when I was back in the grove. "That's all there is."

"If they come close enough to see two wrecked airplanes they'll send someone in."

"I suppose so, but some kind of signal from the ground would help." I was captured suddenly by one of those obscure flashes in which the mind is seized by metaphor, by the repeated similarity of experience. "It's like Lake Mason. Transmitting to the cabin but receiving nothing."

"Yeah," a voice said remotely, also perhaps captured by memory.

Was it Lake Mason I was remembering or Cantrell Lake? Two figures standing in the blaze of sundown above Lake Mason and also above Cantrell Lake. For a moment they blended together and then stood apart vividly. "Something I never understood," I began, "was why Michael let himself be caught with . . ." But almost a quarter of a century had intervened, and in that time I had seen others caught, and in fact . . . been caught myself. I began to retrieve the past under an entirely different light as though a prism had been changed.

"But you never went out to Lake Mason then?"

It was dark and I could just see the shape of a body propped against the tree, shrouded in a mosquito bar.

"I saw you take off and head south, but you never called to warn Michael that we were coming."

I saw the arm lift the cup, but the only sound was the hysteria of hyenas in the distance.

"You knew, or thought you knew what was going on, but you wanted me there as witness that he was being unfaithful to Chris. 'I need you,' you said. That was the first time you said it. 'I need you.' Oh, you have a sense of justice all right, but it's crude, vindictive, self-serving, monstrously egocentric. If Michael was being unfaithful you could move in without a scruple."

He remained silent, but the noises of night had become shrill.

"I asked you a question, Teddy. You never went out to the lake, did you?"

After a long silence he said, "No." A voice out of darkness, impersonal, belonging to the night.

"By *God*," I said, rising. "For you the whole business of living is a series of stratagems. You meant it when you said you can't play straight poker, because somebody else might win." Compelled by some energy that I could not resist, I began pacing up and down in the darkness.

"Have some bourbon, Howard."

I stopped. "Have some bourbon! Let's settle down in the BOQ and knock over a few pints of bourbon. All right, by God, I'll have some bourbon, but maybe, finally, we can clear up a few things." I found my cup and poured. I had it to my lips when the veil shrouding the past was twitched up a little further. "And you *knew* about Amanda, didn't you? You know about *all* your slaves. You call me from Cantrell Lake. 'Bring someone, if you know anyone.' You knew it would be Amanda I'd bring. But you played it like an ace-high straight. 'Where did you meet her?' you asked me. You knew about Amanda. She told me later. Someone at Cromwell mentions this bright gem of a woman that I was seeing. But you don't do it the way it's done. You invite her to Cantrell Lake through me, and once she's there you turn on the Arnheim charm surrounded by the Arnheim opulence. You knew about Amanda, *didn't* you?"

"Yeah."

"Yeah, *yeah*." I walked over to him. He was a great, shrouded bulk. "Why don't you ever say 'yes,' Teddy? You went to Princeton. You were in a club, the most exclusive club. I got you in, not without resistance. Why don't you ever say 'Yes'?"

"It's too hard to say."

"But other things aren't too hard for you!" I had begun shouting. "You can swoop down like a vulture and carry off women. And you can kill. You *killed* those two men out there, in fact. You *killed* Michael. Did you ever think about that? You took over, you usurped and sent him off to be slaughtered. *You* killed Polly Kraft. If you'd had the guts to stand up to the Old Man and marry her she wouldn't have smashed up on Route Seventeen. If you'd had the guts to stand up to the Old Man, Chris would have married you. I know all about that, you see. She told me after you sent that wedding notice. But when it came to losing the poker game, you gave her up.''

He said nothing.

The veil was suddenly torn away entirely. I saw almost a lifetime of incredible innocence. ''And *Soad*. Finally I understand something that Soad said to me at the Geneva airport. 'Whatever happens,' she said, 'I love you.' She said she loved me, even though she was playing a part you assigned her. While you have your week with Amanda at Cantrell Lake you send me off on a pretext to Lausanne. In Lausanne the Terrills invite me to dinner and Soad just *happens* to be there. And she just *happens* to want to take a picture of me. It just *happens* that we fall into bed together, as Michael fell into bed with some girl at Lake Mason. That satisfied your crude, perverse, infantile, macabre sense of justice.''

He was immobile, silent, monstrous, an amorphous, shrouded shape in the darkness. I went over to stand above him. ''I *need*. I *need*. I need you. I need her. Did you ever think that someone else might need?''

He didn't answer.

''You've been like an octopus in my life. I've never been able to free myself until this minute, but now I'm through. I'm going to leave in the morning. You've got everything you need, food, bourbon, water. I'll bring up two more jerry cans. When they come in for you, don't wait for me. I'll make my way back to Nairobi and then to New York.'' I lifted my cup to drink but I required some melodrama. I splashed it across his veiled face. ''Have some bourbon, Arnheim.''

He said nothing.

I slept in the airplane. I didn't want to be near him.

As soon as it was light I put my kit together. I found two canteens in the airplane and filled them with water. I had one of the survival kits, the Springfield, food, and my sleeping bag, which I decided to leave. It was too heavy.

The sun was flashing just above the horizon south of Mt. Kiliman-jaro when I stepped down from the ladder, and shouldering the Springfield, started on my course of thirty degrees. At the top of a small knoll I was visible for a moment from the grove.

"*Matt*," Teddy yelled.

I stopped and looked over at him. He had not moved. He was still shrouded by the mosquito bar.

"What do you want?" I yelled back.

"You think I'm a shit?"

"Yes!" I bellowed, "an unmitigated shit!"

I turned and started toward the road.

There were no vultures at the wreck when I stopped to rest an hour later. The vultures, hyenas, worms had done their work, and all that remained was shattered aluminum and ash that would soon be cov-ered by the grass of the plain. Patches of green had already begun to appear below the burn.

It was impossible to tell how much territory I was covering in an hour, but I calculated it as not more than an average of a mile since in thickets I had to cut my way through with the machete or make a considerable detour. The sun beat fiercely on my safari hat, my glasses fogged with sweat, and various insects gorged themselves on the repellant I had smeared on my face and arms.

I gave myself five minutes' rest every hour, and half an hour for lunch in another grove that provided very little protection from the sun directly overhead. I had left a little after six and had covered, roughly, six miles as I figured it. I would have to go another six miles in the afternoon, twelve miles a day to do it in three days, but I was already exhausted. I wanted desperately to stretch out on the dried grass and sleep, but with more discipline than I realized I possessed I started out again. It was a mistake.

I knew about mad dogs and Englishmen, but I tried to reassure myself that Americans had never succumbed to anything so colonial as the siesta. An hour later I knew I was succumbing. I had to clear the sweat from my dark glasses every two or three minutes, my heart was pounding, my legs trembling, and my vision was becoming distorted. I saw stitch-worked clouds that disappeared when I rubbed my eyes. I had rationed myself to a swallow of water each hour and a salt tablet every two hours, but I had an almost irresistible impulse to drain the first canteen in one long pull. The rifle and pack had become unbearably cumbersome. By two o'clock I knew I could go no farther. I would have to wait for evening. Forcing myself, I reached another clump of starved, ignoble trees off to the right of my course, and dropped.

I had not once thought of Teddy, but lying on my back, looking up through the fragile web of branches, I felt a moment's anguish that gave way to renewed anger. Because of him, his insatiable, devious egocentricity, I had been stunted, circumscribed, castrated. Because of him I was lying incongruously a few degrees south of the equator in the middle of June, with thirty miles to go in order to reach what was probably no more than a dirt road used by a few trucks a day. Because of him I had become moderately well off, but I had lost everything else, even my self-esteem.

Stung and bitten by swarms of insects, I fell asleep.

It was almost four o'clock when I woke up, stiff, aching, and nauseous, one eye swollen almost shut. I waited for half an hour, dreading the venture into sunlight again, and for the first time seriously doubting that I could reach the road in three days, or four days, or even reach it at all. Clearly I could suffer a sunstroke and die on the great expanse of grass, and what remained of me would disappear very rapidly. As I started out I glanced at the sky to see if others, the scavengers of the plain, had come to the same conclusion. I saw nothing but the brazen shell of blue.

I met no animals but continued to surprise various birds, until almost six o'clock when I heard the low song of cattle off to my left. Thrashing through the grass I broke suddenly into the open onto a herd of cows and a tall native some forty feet from me with a rifle pointed directly at my head. I stopped abruptly and stood very still.

"Do you speak English?" I called out.

He said nothing but allowed the butt of the rifle to slide down to his chin without releasing immediate firing capability.

"*Parlez vous Francais?*" I tried again.

There was no reason to think he would have Italian, but I tried with no better success. The rifle had gone down to his waist, and with the Springfield hanging from the sling over my shoulder I decided I presented no threat. I started walking slowly toward him. The barrel of the rifle did not move from my chest and his hand was on the trigger ring. Ten feet away I stopped. He was taller than I, and though he was dark, his features were not Negroid, but slender, with an almost aquiline nose and strong chin. He examined me with remote dignity, an aloofness without threat though scarcely amicable.

"English?" I tried again.

This time he shook his head slowly, suggesting that he knew it was a language, and said something I supposed was Swahili.

I was exhausted and the total inability to communicate added frustration. I tried to mime an airplane striking the earth and then pointed to the west. Without moving the rifle he looked in that direction and then back to me. His language had a lot of consonants.

I pointed to the east and tried to mime an automobile on a road, with hopelessly inadequate results. He looked to the east as though it might offer a surprise and then back at me as though I were an itinerant madman escaped from some African bedlam.

It was futile. I left him standing with his cattle, the rifle still held at readiness, watching me as I plunged into the grass once more with the shadows of twilight climbing Mt. Kilimanjaro.

That dark night remains vague in my memory. I stumbled eastward until it became too dark to see my footing in spite of the half moon that rose later, and finally I collapsed in another clump of trees. I took a drink of water, but I didn't even try to contend with the cans of food I had packed. I fell asleep with a crash.

The moon had risen twenty degrees toward the summit of Mt. Kilimanjaro when I woke to the canticles of night, birdcalls, the harsh rasp of insects, howls, and the laughter of Africa. I had read that lions cough. I don't know if it was a lion, but something not too far away seemed to have a bad cold.

I slept again.

The sound that woke me much later when dawn was already well advanced was more familiar: the whistle of jet engines low in the sky. I staggered to my feet and emerged from the trees. Caught in the rays of the rising sun, an airplane, a four-jet airplane, was moving slowly from the north in the western sky. It crossed my mind that he must have flaps and spoilers extended to move that slowly with safety. It was three or four thousand feet above the ground, and while I watched, it banked slowly into a turn to the left, in my direction, and began to circle, descending until it was almost out of sight behind the tall grass. But I saw it again, still circling over the area I had left twenty-four hours earlier.

Somebody, perhaps Jacobs, had found the wrecks. They would send help.

I looked to the east into sunlight. The road was at least twenty-five miles away across that broad stretch of plain with grass, wadis, animals, and heat. Two more days at best.

I returned for the Springfield and the pack and started back in a feeble trot.

Climbing toward the north, the airplane rose in the western distance. If they were going for a helicopter, the only rational means of returning, I would have probably three or four hours. The jet would be in Nairobi in thirty minutes easily (it was already fading from sight); it would take time to find a helicopter, unless they had one waiting; and it would take a helicopter two to three hours to make the flight back. In four hours I had to cover what had taken me an entire day.

The first time I tripped and fell the pack dug into my neck and back. I pulled it off and tossed it into the grass, keeping only the Springfield and the two canteens, one half empty. The rays of the sun became tangible weights on my head and back. I went two hours without stopping, but when I fell again I stayed down, listening to someone groaning.

I began to wonder if I had hallucinated the airplane. I would stumble back to the grove where Teddy would be lying, drinking bourbon and Pepsi, and he would say, "Fast trip, Howard." If he did I'd kill him.

I rolled over and looked up into the enameled sky. There was not a cloud in sight, nothing to soften the damaging violence of that great ball of fire, though as I turned to gather determination, a shadow crossed my face in an instant caress and was gone. I looked up. High in the sky, as though expressing reluctance, decency, but no doubt, was one of those birds whose profession it is to clean up after mortality. Indolent on immense wings, he hovered, circled, and passed on slowly in an ominous exhibition of patience. And then there was another, and a third. I had read someplace, or had been told, that vultures know more about death than the victim, who may be convinced that he has the strength and determination to survive. I took another drink of water, to my surprise emptying the canteen, and tossed it in the grass.

A long part of that day is very hazy in my memory. I walked until I was physically incapable of lifting the foot that was on the ground, and fell once more. Lying on my stomach, some time later I heard the distant, flat impact of chopper blades drawing near. I raised my head. "No!" I tried to shout, but it came out as a croak. "Not yet! Not yet!" But the sound grew louder like the slap of darkness in a nightmare. I crawled a few inches and staggered to my feet. And I saw it. Still far west of me, headed south.

I went on, falling and rising again, while the noise of the chopper grew louder, and in a final open avenue of sound the slapping hammered on my eardrums. I saw it turn, begin to circle and descend. It went down out of sight. It had landed. And there was silence.

I walked on over terrain that slid, heaved, and dropped away, where sworls of orange and red flashed before my eyes, knowing the moment would come when I would once more hear the engine and the slap of the blades in takeoff. I had arranged my own destiny. Teddy would report that I was on my way to Nairobi and then New York. "Don't wait for me," I had said in my moment of illumination. I would reach a deserted grove with perhaps some food and water left.

But again I began to suspect I had hallucinated the airplane and the chopper. Surely it had been on the ground long enough to load Teddy aboard and take off. There would be no waste of time searching for me, but I couldn't judge how much time had passed. I couldn't see my watch clearly, but I had the impression it had stopped.

And then some time later, minutes, hours perhaps, since it seemed to have grown darker, I heard the pop of an engine, still distant, a rising whine, and the beat of blades striking the air slowly at first but picking up momentum into a roar. Suddenly it was there, above the grass, straining, lifting, moving forward, turning to the left toward me. I shouted, but then unslung the Springfield and started firing into the air, knowing even as I pulled the trigger that they couldn't hear me above the roar of the motor. In a faltering rage I brought the sights of the rifle down to the pilot's station of the large craft, intending, I don't know what, to stop it, bring it down to go through the long wait with me. I didn't fire.

It was turning toward me, blasting the air, and rising. I began to dance drunkenly, waving my arms, knowing they would never see me, never look down, convinced that I was miles away, about to step onto a road to flag down a truck and find my way alone.

The inspiration must have come from expectation of crossing the burn once more. I hadn't. I pulled the watertight cylinder of matches from my pocket and struck one which fizzled because of the sweat from my fingers. The second broke. The third lighted, and when I held it to the grass a small flame appeared, smouldered, and then caught, beginning to spread rapidly, sending up a crooked spiral of smoke.

The helicopter had made its turn almost over my head and started northward, but with that characteristic jerk of flight pattern it turned to the right and circled back over me. It went around twice and began to descend upwind of the smoke, not fifty feet away. Even before the blades had made a final revolution a door opened and a small black man in the uniform of some constabulary jumped out with an immense red fire extinguisher. "Oh, sir," he yelled as he came toward me, "must not start fires. Very forbidden," and he gamboled off to pump chemicals on the blazing grass.

I saw Jacobs then. He was coming toward me weaving sinuously as though he had become insubstantial, and someone in a white jacket followed, performing the same serpentine glissade. I dropped the Springfield and fell to my knees just before they reached me. Hands under my arms pulled me up and a blond head came into my vision. A voice, very British, said, "Oh, I *say*. We'll just get this one off to the hospital."

With one on each side supporting me I reached the ladder of the helicopter and climbed with help until I could see the interior of the cabin. The pilot turned to stare at me with a sick smile that did not disguise revulsion, but otherwise the cabin was empty.

"But . . . where's Teddy?" I wheezed. "Where's Mr. Arnheim?"

"Please get in, Mr. Howard," Jacobs said.

"But . . . my God, you *couldn't* have missed him. He was in that clump of trees, just . . ."

"Sir," the medic said, "you need care. Please . . ."

I slid down the ladder. "But for Christ's sake! He's hurt. He's just over there. You can't . . ."

Jacobs took my arm. "Mr. Howard," he said. "There." He indicated an aluminum stretcher attached to the side of the fuselage where an immense white shroud was strapped.

Pushing Jacobs aside and supporting myself on the fuselage I staggered toward it and began tearing at the canvas. "He'll suffocate. Get him . . ."

The medic took my arm firmly. "I wouldn't do that if I were you, sir. Vultures, hyenas, you know."

The last thing I remembered was turning to grab him when the earth came up to hit me hard.

26

"IT WAS THE COUNT of one hundred that did it," Jacobs said, sitting by my bed. "I heard you on the earlier transmissions, but I couldn't understand a word. When the count began coming in I knew something was wrong. I called the tower and they got a direction but not a fix, of course. That's what took us so long."

The inquest took place two days later when I was released from the hospital. It was conducted by a district judge without a jury, a soft-spoken black man with an Oxonian accent and immense dignity. He asked his questions and listened patiently while Jacobs, the medic, and the constable related their versions, but I sensed some cynicism, suspicion even.

"And the prints on this," he indicated a pistol lying on a handkerchief, "matched the fingerprints of the deceased?"

"Yes, sir."

"How was it possible to take fingerprints? He had been lying exposed for over twenty hours, I believe you said, Doctor. That's a long time in Africa."

"The precise amount of time was not easily determined since an autopsy was . . . difficult under the circumstances, but the left hand was intact."

"Was Mr. Arnheim left-handed?" he asked, turning to me.

"Yes, your honor."

"Mr. Howard," he said slowly, "when you left Mr. Arnheim, was there any indication that he had such a rash action in mind?"

"Mr. Arnheim was . . . not an easy book to read. But the answer to your question is no."

He studied me for a moment. "His ankle was broken, you say, and the medical examiners concur. But otherwise he was uninjured. He had food and water and . . . whisky enough to last for many days. You believe that he understood your intention to go for help?"

"Yes, clearly."

"Then why did he take his life? He was a man of large wealth, married, a father, known, I understand, throughout the financial world for his acumen and intelligence. Why would such a man destroy himself?"

"I am unable to answer the question, your honor."

"And yet you have known him many years."

"Yes, sir."

Again he examined me without malice, but as though he were weighing me in a scale of values that had taken years to construct and that was constantly being threatened. "Mr. Howard," he continued finally, "I am satisfied that you did not murder your friend and employer. The testimony offered by the others, the hard evidence of fingerprints of the deceased on the pistol all seem to confirm that opinion. However, beyond the strictly legal evidence, I am not satisfied that you were not in some way responsible for his death. You yourself must be prosecutor, court, and defendant in that case." He turned to the cardboard box on the table, extracted the whole and the shattered ashtrays and studied them intently, turning them over and reading what was stamped on the bottom. Jacobs had told me the constable had been intrigued by them and had carried them back. "We come to these objects found in the vicinity of the deceased's body," he began again. "They appear to be ashtrays. Did Mr. Arnheim always carry such ashtrays with him?"

"He was a heavy smoker, your honor."

"That is not an answer to my question."

I had been certain the ashtrays would finally emerge, but I had not decided how I would explain them, if I would lie, or tell everything. The constable, who had gone over to examine the other wreck (explaining the amount of time between the landing and the takeoff), had not discovered the intact box.

"Yes, your honor, he always carried them."

I could feel Jacobs's eyes on me.

"Bizarre," the judge said with a French intonation, and returned them to the box. "One final question, which is, legally speaking, not a part of this inquest. Why, Mr. Howard, did you and Mr. Arnheim travel eight thousand miles and risk your lives, and lose one of those lives, to search for the wreck of the other aircraft, since I assume that is what you were engaged in."

"Mr. Arnheim was like a father to his employees. When he heard that two of them had disappeared he insisted on searching for them himself." Why was I lying for that corpulent ghost?

The black eyes that fixed on me expressed a complex mixture of responses, but all I recognized was contempt.

I was the sole passenger in the airplane for the return to Newark, but not quite. Stowed in Teddy's quarters was a sealed urn. Jacobs had talked to Downing in Newark several times, and Downing had relayed instructions from Amanda. On strong advice she had agreed on cremation in Nairobi.

I had not talked to Downing since I no longer considered myself an employee of Arnheim Industries.

We crossed Africa and the Atlantic in easy stages, stopping overnight in the Azores to give Jacobs and his crew some rest. I think he was relieved that I did not offer to take the controls. It was the third of July when we landed in Newark. I took a cab directly to Manhattan, and I had been home long enough to strip and turn the shower on when the phone rang. It was Downing. His voice was choked.

"*Matt*. When will you be over?"

"I won't. I've resigned. You'll get my letter in a couple of days."

"Matt, you can't do that to me. The place is exploding. I can't handle it by myself."

"I'm sorry, Jim, but I'm through. You'll work it out."

"But Matt, I *need* you."

"Don't *say* that."

"But I do. At least come over for a few days."

"No. If you want to see me, you come here."

"Oh, God, I've got so much . . . all right. It's three o'clock. I'll try to make it by five-thirty, and Matt, you'd better turn your phone off. The papers have been after me for three days. If they know you're in town they'll be pounding on your door."

He was right. I had just stepped into the shower when the phone rang again. I turned it off.

Downing was not a heavy drinker, but he put away several scotches while I told him the story, almost exactly as it had happened, with the omission of the final minutes and the morning I left him. When I came to McKenzie, he exploded. "Why that son of a bitch! I never did trust him. I'm going after him."

"How? It's foolproof. You'll blow the operation if you do. I don't care if you blow it, but they'll shut the mines down."

He swore under his breath. "But how could he do something like that?"

"He apparently decided the time had come to take. Do you want another drink?"

"No . . . or yes. One more."

When I brought it to him he looked at it for a moment and then at me. "Why did he do it? Mr. Arnheim, I mean."

"I don't know. But he wasn't quite the chunk of granite that most people took him for."

"I never really knew him."

"Not many people did."

"You did."

"Maybe, but not everything."

He brooded for a while, shaking his head and sipping from his drink. "I just don't get it. I've never known anyone who was less suicidal, less . . ." He breathed out and glanced at his watch. "I've got to get home. Ruth's having a pre-Fourth cookout." He finished the drink. "Matt, do me a favor and look at them, will you?" He had brought a sheaf of papers. "I'll keep you on the payroll for July."

"Oh, all right. I don't promise miracles."

"I don't expect miracles. Just some help." He started for the door. "And I'd get out of town for a while. They'll be after you."

He was right again. When I took him down to the door there were three or four men on the stoop who tried to get in. I shut and locked the door. When I went out to dinner later I had to go through the back entrance and the mews.

I rented a car and drove to Camden, Maine, where I had some friends who were very discreet. It was all right for a while, but then *Time* magazine carried its story on Teddy under the title "Mysterious Death of a Billionaire," and both Teddy's and my pictures were included, the picture of me that made me look like a poet. At a diner where they had good fried clams a man on my right was reading the story, and putting his coffee cup down, he happened to glance at me and then back at the picture.

"Say," he said with a down-east accent, "aren't you . . . ?"

"No. But there is a resemblance."

"Ayah, shore is."

When I had looked over the papers Downing left with me I called him and gave my opinion. He was very grateful. "Matt," he said after he had taken some notes, "Mrs. Arnheim is anxious to see you. She asked me to call as soon as I heard from you."

I didn't want to see her. "I'm not going back for another week or so."

"Will you call her?"

"No."

"Do you have a number where she can call you?"

"No."

Ten days later I went back to New York. There was no one waiting before the house, and I hoped they had abandoned the search. I turned the telephone on. It was another mistake. Half an hour later it rang, and a reporter from the *Daily News* asked to see me, and I gave up. I called the *Times* and the *Post* and made an appointment to see all three. A good many others arrived with photographers, and I told precisely the same story I had told the judge in Nairobi. They got very rough and hammered at me for motives for the suicide, and I repeated over and over again that I couldn't help them. Then they shifted to reasons for the search.

"Did you find anything in the wreck?" one asked.

"Two charred bodies."

"What was the purpose of the search originally?"

"We were looking for two employees. Mr. Arnheim was like a father to his employees." I thought I heard a cracked bass voice laughing.

"Did it have anything to do with Arnheim's takeover of McGruder and Sons?"

"No."

They left finally, a very surly group. The stories ranged from the lurid to the suspicious to the mysterious.

Two days later Amanda called. "Matt, I want to see you." Her voice was subdued, but there was an icy quality that I didn't recognize.

"Well, I'm going to be in town."

"Would you come over this evening?"

"No. If you want to see me, you come here."

"Oh . . . all right. What time?"

"Any time you like."

"I can't get away before six-thirty, and it will take close to an hour."

That seemed rather long to me. "Make it seven-thirty."

Since I had no white wine I went down to the liquor store on 8th Street later, and just as I was about to close the door upon returning, a long black Cadillac drew up before the house, a uniformed chauffeur moved quickly to open the door, and Amanda emerged. She was wearing a dark dress with a light jacket, and she was very pregnant. I went down to meet her.

"Hello, Matt," she said and put out her hand.

"Hello, Amanda," She was even more beautiful than I remembered her, in that strange bloom that comes to some women in pregnancy.

She studied me for a moment. "You've lost weight."

"Yes."

She turned and mounted the stoop.

In my living room she walked about slowly, looking at the furniture again and the Giorgioni. "Have you had it authenticated?"

"No. Excuse me." I took the white wine to the kitchen and put a bottle in the deep-freeze compartment. When I returned she was sitting in one of my great-grandmother's chairs. "The white wine will be chilled in a few minutes."

"Oh, thanks. I'm not drinking. But don't deprive yourself."

"I won't." I went to the bar and made a vodka martini. When I came back I sat opposite her. "Cheers."

"Cheers." Her eyes were searching, expectant.

When I set the glass down she said, "What happened?"

"He shot himself."

"I know that. It never occurred to me that you killed him. Why?"

"I don't know. Why do people kill themselves?"

"Because of despair from loss, or from self-doubt."

"He never suffered from self-doubt, but he lost nineteen million dollars."

"When he found out how he lost it I'm sure he laughed."

"Yes, as a matter of fact he did."

"Why did he do it?" She was not mourning a husband. She was ferreting out a mystery.

"People commit suicide on a whim. Maybe it was withdrawal symptoms. He had run out of cigarettes . . ."

"*Matt,*" she said in a voice charged with menace.

"He was alone. In pain. He may have decided that rescue was impossible."

"Shit," she said with a vulgarity I had never heard from her. "He never knew despair and he never doubted you. Why did he do it?"

"You're asking me something I can't answer. I wasn't there."

"You're the only one who *can* answer it, and I want an answer. Something happened before you left. What?"

"Nothing important."

She rose from my great-grandmother's chair to walk heavily across and stand above me threateningly, her round belly a few inches from my forehead. "You're not stupid, but there's something singularly obtuse about you when it comes to Teddy if you don't know what you were for him. *You* offered him kindness when he needed it. *You* were an accomplice in the most important emotional event in his life."

"I was *not* an accomplice!"

"You were honest, decent," she continued, ignoring my declaration of innocence, "the example of moral virtue that he admired but suspected. He idolized you."

"And you're crazy."

"There was only one man in the world he had respect for, love even. *You.*" Her eyes were burning in a rage I had never seen before. "You never, never understood him."

"I admit that, but obviously you didn't either. I was of very little importance to Teddy except as he could make use of me."

"What will always remain a mystery to me is how he could have been so mistaken."

"I'm tiring of this conversation, Amanda."

"If that's an invitation to leave, I'll leave when I'm ready. But not until you tell me what happened."

I was losing my temper, as she probably intended that I should. "All right, goddamnit, something did happen. The last night before I left I discovered to what extent he *had* manipulated me, and I accused him of it. He admitted it. The whole shoddy series of events, first involving a woman in Alabama.''

"Chris.''

"Involving you, and then another woman in Lausanne.''

"Soad.''

"That for thirty years I was a chess piece he moved about, manipulated, for his own purposes.''

"You were born to be manipulated by Teddy.''

"I think you'd better leave, Amanda.''

"I'll leave when I'm ready. I want the rest of it. So when this vast illumination occurred you went after him, deserted him.''

"I did *not* desert him. I was going for help.'' I rose with my glass and went to the bar.

"You know what I mean. Deserted him psychologically. Called him a manly series of names.''

"He phrased it. I agreed.''

"*Look* at me, Matt.''

I turned back.

"We can use the language that Teddy didn't believe in, laughed at. That incident in Alabama and later in New York was his life crisis, his trauma. And you were there, sharing it with him. It defined him, stunted him emotionally. He never recovered from it. He wanted love, but after that he couldn't accept it. 'It's a hard job to love me,' he kept repeating. *I* offered him love, but he couldn't believe in it, couldn't accept it. He depended on you.''

"He did *not* depend on me. Months would go by without my seeing him.''

"But he always came back because he needed your support, if not your approval, at least the knowledge that you were there. When he called you his conscience he meant it.''

"You're creating a fantasy to explain a mystery that you can't accept. I say again, I don't know *why* he shot himself.''

"Just what particularly virile string of expletives did you heap on him?''

"I did *not* heap expletives. As I was leaving the next morning he called out to me.''

"What did he say?''

"He said, 'Hey, Matt!' ''

"He called you *Matt*?"

"Yes."

Her eyes flashed in vindication. "And?"

" 'You think I'm a shit?' "

"And?"

"I said, 'Yes, an unredeemed,' or maybe 'unmitigated shit!' "

She stared at me for a moment without speaking. "How could you be so blind, or *stupid*? You should have *known* something had happened when he called you Matt. It was his way of saying goodbye. His loss was *you*. You betrayed him. You killed him."

"Nonsense."

"Oh," she said viciously, "I wish there was some way I could get at you. I wish you hadn't retired so that I could have the pleasure of sacking you." She started to leave, but at the Giorgioni she stopped and looked back. "I understand now why you don't want it authenticated."

I forgot the white wine. When I opened the freezing compartment the next day it had exploded into crystals of ice and glass.

I saw Amanda once more.

In September I received a letter from a law firm that I didn't know, requesting my presence at the reading of the will of Theodore Arnheim. There were some twenty people present when I arrived, most of them members of the staff at Collincourt, like Ebson, who had been pensioned off earlier by Teddy. Pelletier was there in a checked shirt. Amanda was sitting in the front. She was no longer pregnant. She was slender and ravishing. She turned once and saw me, and the expression in her eyes was annihilating.

The will was long and detailed, first listing generous bequests to servants who had been with the family for many years. Other benefits running from ten to fifty thousand dollars were left to people I didn't know. Tabulated roughly, these legacies ran to two million dollars. The bulk of the estate, the company, the other holdings, and the real estate were left intact to Amanda. I wondered why my presence had been requested.

When the reading had been completed the attorney said, "I come now to a document, a codicil, that may be described as irregular. It is dated June twenty-third of this year, in the bush of northern Tanzania, and it is irrefutably in the deceased's handwriting, of that there is no doubt. The question arose, however, under what circumstances it was composed, whether under coercion, sickness, or instability resulting from intolerable pain. There are no witnesses. It has, however, been accepted as authentic by the court of probate. It was discovered near the body of the deceased with instructions that it be delivered to me by hand. It was sealed with . . . a natural product. It reads, 'I, Theodore Arnheim, being alone, but in sound mind and body, leave to the only friend I ever had, Matthew Howard, of 26 West 10th Street, New York City, the sum of two million dollars.'' It is signed 'Theodore Arnheim.' ''

I rose. "I won't take it."

Amanda turned to look at me with triumph and contempt.

I took it.

Amanda now occupies the office on the ground floor of Arnheim Industries in Newark, and she lives in Collincourt with her two daughters. Immediately after assuming control of the company she sold Arnheim's interests in McGruder and Sons. According to Downing, who comes to Manhattan occasionally to have dinner with me, she is an astute, imaginative, resolute, and dynamic director of the affairs of Arnheim Industries, which continues to thrive. She has also set up a foundation for the arts, dispenses scholarships at several universities and subsidizes unpopular books through Cromwell. Her dinners at Collincourt assemble a radical heterogeneity of artists, businessmen, professors, and politicians. She is vigorously pursued by admirers of her beauty and substance, but so far she has remained single. She has recently begun to involve herself in politics.

I read a good deal, look at my pictures, and occasionally add to my collection. Two or three times a year I travel in Europe. I never go to Lausanne.

I am, as the French say, still *impuissant,* and I suspect I will remain that way for the rest of my life.

Teddy (Am = no Adonis, even slightly repulsive 213 * no
215 therapy
4 T dominates subtly. He's never angry, 216 astray
passionate or violent. But he is always in control
4 Am: I feel sorry for him (T)
5 serenity in his eyes 218 Kennedy
not believe (conspiracy
55 he answered shyly death
34 = fish = fertility symbol P. 221 222 Lost Tute
politics
57 Real knowledge doesn't make money y .225 lost cargo
power — money y lost
p236 bestiality
57 Am: too much knowledge produces indecision p242 * X
& conscience —? learning
p193 the other
side of face (genteel-
59 foreplay law-abiding
P.161 → Teddy (subj. marriage p194 = (for about
Teddy
p162 — absorbing
63 Am (for T) the attraction of the ugly another
identity?
171 → Teddy (Satan 194 she (Egyptian
threatening
173 T: In a war people get killed —
174 T. I don't believe in psychology (but p241-242
fact) people (fears and desires) = to laugh
Amanda: fears are irrational (T: I didn't say
people are rational
p245 * monster
p183 * poker game (ends together p 246 justice * *
p184 I was used (but I couldn't find the pattern)
p185 So sad =(I was madly in love with Ted (Egypt + Irish 249
strategy
p.186 Howard (two faces) gentleman, conservative, timid 249
under manners (timidity
p188 (picture) INFANTILE MACABRE ← ← p250
sense of justice
p189 you are very gallant for an American 250 I need
p190 — 190 He is maimed because he loved one
without love all his energy goes into
creating an empire and in creating an empire
he destroys other empires
-- He likes to break things and rebuild out of the rubble

26 → Marie Louise

p24 - I missed-
        injured me -

p. 27 the way a good lay
27

✳ 29 breath of circumstance

35 Teddy = clown-god
36
38 ferocity

39 Father (of Teddy

p41 - girls visited → house (Christ

(p43 song Teddy (shower) 2 people dancing in darkness
searching for light y love

46 delirium (on that day
I was very strong

66 a monstrous black phantom

71 Teddy (a melody (2 people in darkness
         humming

74 women (description

75) 3 women (the Greeks

76 Teddy (eyes)

77 Teddy = Howard is my conscience
78) Teddy impressed me as more
metallic, even more resistant to the
unruly vagaries of the heart

22
annihilating boredom

Thoreau 120

Bernard Shaw =
Money permits d

178 Teddy → shy ma

190 = there is some elem
missing for him (Teddy

✳ (good p.195. the pornographic
differ   static, finished -
          the erotic → expecta

195) A. but I m
beestliness of Ma
of the inhabiten

concupiscence = ya